WAR OF THE NETWORKS

Vicki -
Thanks for reading
and all your
support.

WAR OF THE NETWORKS

Katie Cross

Antebellum
Publishing

War of the Networks

Young Adult Fantasy

Text copyright ©2016 by Katie Cross

Cover designed by Seedlings Online at www.seedlingsonline.com
Ebook productions by E-books Done Right at www.ebooksdoneright.com
Print typesetting by Atthis Arts LLC at www.atthisarts.com

Published by Antebellum Publishing.
Visit www.antebellumpublishing.com for more information.

ISBN (paperback) 978-0-9966249-4-7
(ebook) 978-0-9966249-5-4

Visit the author at www.kcrosswriting.com

Visit The Network Series at www.missmabels.com or on
Facebook at www.facebook.com/missmabels

To Grandma.

Because I'll always be part yours.

The Letter

To the Assistant Ambassador, my friend Bianca Monroe,
Please forgive me for writing you unexpectedly, but
I must request the pleasure of your company in a
meeting. Please do not tell your father or Marten of
my request, as I ask something of a personal nature. Let me assure
you that my intent is pure; since becoming High Priest after my
grandfather's death, I've found I have few true friends, and you are
among them.

If you find this request acceptable, please come to Magnolia Castle
in the Eastern Network as soon as you are able. My Assistant will
direct you to wherever I am. No matter what I'm doing, speaking
with you will take ultimate precedence.

Your friend in the East,
High Priest Niko Aldana

White-capped waves rippled around my bare ankles, retreating
back to the green ocean with angry, unwilling hisses. I'd never been
a big fan of large bodies of water. Not knowing what moved beneath
me made me shudder. I preferred the warm, mossy arms of the forest.
But even I felt intoxicated by the power of the ocean.

A chubby, short witch named Hector, Niko's Assistant, pointed to a ship with white sails bobbing in the ocean. "His Greatness is out there," he said, drawing out his i's in the soft tones of the Eastern Network accent. "He told me to expect you."

Hector had a barrel chest with a mat of thick black curls that grew up onto the exposed flesh of his lower neck. The ends of his shirt flapped in the wind. For an Assistant to the High Priest of the Eastern Network, he had no semblance of a manicured, professional air. I liked him immensely.

"Sure," I said, digging my toes into the warm sand. "Why not be on the water? There's only a storm moving in. Massive waves don't seem dangerous at all." Frothy gray clouds darkened the horizon, moving in with a cool wind and flashes of lightning. I marveled that a storm could take up so much sky.

Hector shot me a sidelong glance. The corners of his lips twitched. "I will take you out there if you don't want to try transporting to the ship," he said, his face scrunching. He clearly didn't want to, but I had no doubt Niko would take grave offense if Hector didn't treat a visiting Assistant to the Ambassador with utmost dignity. Never mind that I didn't even bother to wear shoes.

My simple linen dress with capped sleeves and a high neckline whipped in the wind. An oblong case hung on my back, held by a single strap that crossed over my chest. Inside it hid my precious Volare, a magic carpet that could fly. Despite its strict allegiance to me, I wore it everywhere to be sure of its safety. Underneath my dress lay my sword, Viveet, tucked in the folds of my skirt and tied to my thigh with a special sheath that allowed the sword to shrink to fit. No one would notice it. I'd taken a calculated risk coming back to the East alone, but that didn't mean I'd come unprepared.

"It's not really safe to transport onto a ship you've never been on before," Hector continued, "but Niko wanted to speak to you the moment you arrived. Because of the danger, I don't want to bring him to the land. The West is attacking, you see. The East Guards on the water need his guidance."

The idea of traveling onto a ship appealed to me—I'd never actually been on one. Except for standing in the licks of water around my ankles now and nearly drowning after sharing Mabel's mind six weeks

2   *Katie Cross*

before, I hadn't spent much time in the ocean. The Central Network was the only landlocked Network in Antebellum.

"The West is attacking?" I asked.

Hector gestured with a jerk of his head. "You might not be able to see it, but there's another ship in the distance. There may be many more sailing behind it."

"A fleet from the West?"

He nodded. "They attack in numbers," he said in a droll voice, with just a hint of a smile.

"Why are you amused?"

"Because you don't know anything about the ocean or our skill in working it," he said, puffing out his chest. "There's no Network that can best us on the water. The Western Network tried six weeks ago when—" He dropped the sentence, reddening through his cheeks, and finished with a gruff, "Anyway, we won, and they haven't been back. Until now."

Six weeks ago. That's when the Eastern Network High Priestess Isobel had revealed herself as the nefarious Angelina, Mabel's mother. Who in the Eastern Network knew Isobel's secret? Did Niko? Based on Hector's hesitation, someone knew something. The Eastern Network had maintained that West Guards had murdered Diego and Isobel on the same night, leaving Niko to reign at twenty-six. I didn't blame their cover-up. Niko wouldn't want to introduce mistrust and panic in a time of war and new leadership.

"I'll just transport out there and save you the trouble of rowing out," I said. "The waves are quite high, and I don't have much time anyway."

While my transportation skills had been nothing to brag about in the past, with Merrick's careful guidance earlier this year, I'd honed them sufficiently. The more I concentrated on where I wanted to go, the more I proved able to get there. Merrick, on the other hand, could transport onto a pentacle coin he couldn't even see in the grass. He'd demonstrated it often enough, the show-off.

"It's no trouble to row you out," Hector said, but he sounded relieved. "Though transporting would be faster."

He let that thought linger, as if I needed one last argument to convince me.

"Thank you," I said. "You've been very helpful."

I transported away with the salty tang of the wind on my face. Seconds later, I landed on a wet deck amidst the raucous calls of sailors hurrying around in an organized sense of chaos. The Eastern Network jewel, Magnolia Castle, loomed in the distance, blooming like a fresh white flower on the sandy shore. As Hector had predicted, a whole fleet of Western Network ships bobbed on the ocean, moving in as if they brought the storm with them. The black scorpion of the Western Network flag waved in ominous greeting above their masts. The Eastern Network only had one ship in the fight. Prowess in the water was one thing. But taunting the enemy?

"Ay!" a voice shouted. "Woman on deck!"

My hair billowed behind me in unruly black strands. The ship rocked, sending me flying into a railing, but I caught myself before I flipped off the side. Waves crashed off the sides of the boat, sending sprays of saltwater at me. Beneath us lay a dark, troublesome ocean, and its unsteadiness weakened my stomach. A firm hand grabbed my arm. I jerked free and whirled around to meet Niko's charming smile.

"Miss Bianca Monroe," he said with a deep sigh. "I am very grateful to see you, but I did not expect you to come all the way out here." He frowned. "Hector should have come for me. It's not safe on the water right now."

"I asked to come out," I said, lest hairy little Hector get in trouble. "The water seemed difficult to row in, and I've never been on a ship. Not to mention the approach of the Western Network's fleet."

His easy grin returned. "Ah, yes. I forget. You are . . . what do you call it? Brave or . . . a free spirit?"

I smiled. "Something like that."

"Your eyes," he said, rearing back a little. "They are the color of the storm. I did not notice when we first met."

"Gray," I said. "Like my Mama's."

He smiled. "They are beautiful. Come," he said, steering me toward the middle of the ship and away from the front mast, where distrusting East Guards leered at me. "Let us talk in the safety of my cabin. This is no place for a refined lady."

I nearly snorted. Sweet Niko. He still pictured me as refined even though I'd shown up with wild, black hair around my shoulders and visible ankles.

Above us, sailors scurried up posts that led into a complicated weave of ropes. The ship groaned with each battering wave, but it sounded less like a protest and more like an invitation to war. Niko ushered me up a set of wet stairs stained with sea salt and into a beautiful cabin. Once he shut the door, the harried noises of battle preparations calmed, and I breathed a bit easier. Glass covered the entire wall to my right, but it appeared to sparkle, no doubt enchanted to remain free of stains or cracks. The spacious cabin had likely once belonged to his grandfather, Diego, who, despite all his quirks, possessed a keen eye for refinement. The white wicker furniture—all nailed to the floor—was no exception. A painted portrait of the former High Priest hung on one wall. Diego and I hadn't seen eye to eye, but I did mourn his death on Niko's behalf.

"Please." Niko gestured to a padded wicker chair. "Have a seat. I have already instructed a cabin boy to bring in some cold tea and something to eat."

If the round windows on either side of the cabin had been open, they would have allowed a current to move the thick summer air. The ship continued to rock back and forth on the tempestuous waves. I pressed a hand to my stomach.

"Don't worry," Niko said with a smile, sitting in a chair next to mine. "The tea will calm you. Witches are always sick the first time they board a ship."

"How are you doing?" I asked. "I keep up with news of your Network through our Border Guards. You haven't had it easy since Diego died."

His eyes dropped, looking like deep wells of melted chocolate against his beautiful olive skin. He grimaced, brushing a thick black curl off his forehead.

"It has been a struggle," he said, forcing a diplomatic tone. "The deaths of my grandparents are part of the reason I have asked you here today, Miss Monroe."

"Bianca."

He hesitated. "Bianca," he said, but it came out a bit choked, as if the informality caused him physical pain. "Believe me when I say that the Eastern Network is in grave trouble."

"I can see that. You have an entire fleet of West Guards moving into your port."

Niko brushed that aside with a scoff. "They are irrelevant. The problem comes from within."

"Aren't you concerned about the—" I glanced outside, counting the sails spread out on the water, "—eight ships coming in?"

Niko grinned. "You know nothing of the sea, Miss Bianca," he said. "There is more here than meets the eye, I promise. We are ready for their attack. In fact, we eagerly await it. My witches desire revenge. Mabel will soon see our strength on the water."

"Oh," I replied, leaning back against my chair again. "Well, you're certainly right in one regard. I know nothing of the ocean."

A timid knock sounded on the door. "Come in!" Niko called, and a cabin boy, who couldn't have been older than seven, brought in a tray of tea and small cakes. He exited without a word.

"My grandfather may not have appeared to pay much attention to the war," Niko said as he reached for the tray, pouring the tea himself. "But he had been preparing and training our navy since the day your High Priestess, Mildred, died."

Of course he had. For all his stubbornness, Diego had been a strong, wily kind of witch. My stomach rolled when the ship pitched, so I reached for the teacup he offered. The cold tea tasted like ginger, with just a hint of lemon and something else I couldn't identify. Niko leaned forward, his elbows on his knees. The gesture lacked his usual formality and betrayed the extent of his worry.

"The West Guards continue to attack on land. Their black flames burn villages every night. We lost a small town not far from Magnolia Castle this morning. Forty innocent witches died, ten of whom were children caught in an orphanage's flames."

"An orphanage fire?"

His jaw clenched. "The West Guards show no mercy."

I took another sip of tea, and a warm tingling sensation coated my upset stomach. My nausea disappeared. "No, Mabel will never show mercy."

"The strength of my Guardian force is diminished," he said, lacing his fingers together and pressing them to his lips. "Our real strength lies in the navy, and now that our ports are under attack, I cannot spare as many Guardians to protect the land as I must to protect our ports. That leaves our land vulnerable, and witches are dying."

Poor Niko had inherited a war, a fracturing Network, and a grieving, betrayed family. I couldn't help but feel sorry for him, even though I knew he didn't want pity.

"My grandfather loved his rules, but the time may have come to set those rules aside," he continued. "I am hesitant, you understand, to change too much." Sailors scurried back and forth above our heads. Their orders, in a language I didn't understand, filtered through the thick wooden walls. "Witches will be frightened if I veer too far from familiar traditions. But I cannot continue this way. I need help."

"You need the Central Network," I said.

Niko met my gaze. "Yes. I need your father's help, but I did not want to ask him for it if he would not give it. That is why I asked you here, as a personal favor, to learn your thoughts. Can the Central Network help us while defending her own villages? Would your father consent, even though my grandfather denied him an alliance?"

Excellent questions. Could the Central Network defend itself? With the West Guards pestering the Eastern Network, the ravaging of our villages had slowed. Our witches were also more prepared than the Eastern Network's witches, who lived lives of art and refinement, not war. With Angelina out of the way, we'd eliminated most of the violent Factios gang in Chatham City, though Mabel showed signs of influence among their remaining members. But still, the war raged on. Guardians and innocent witches perished. Fires burned within our borders.

"I don't know about what we can or can't do, but I do know that Papa isn't likely to leave you to save yourselves," I said. "We're stronger together than we are apart."

Niko drew in a great breath and let it all out in a long whoosh. "That," he said, "is relieving to hear. I do not expect you to speak on behalf of your father today—after all, I asked you here as a friend. But I appreciate you giving me hope. I did not want to present my witches with the prospect of aid without cause."

I leaned forward. "May I ask you something?"

His shoulders tightened, as if he already knew what I was going to say. "Yes," he said, bowing his head. "I owe you at least that much."

"You know, don't you?"

The question hung in the air like a glass of tea perched on the edge of a shelf. Although I hadn't been specific, I knew he understood.

You know that your grandmother lived a lie her entire life, don't you?

"Yes," he said in a haunted voice, putting a hand over his heart as if to ease the ache. "My grandmother Isobel killed my grandfather, though she didn't know I watched."

My heartbeat doubled in speed. I hadn't heard this.

"What?" I asked. "You saw him die?"

"When Grandmother left, after she'd killed him, I ran out from my hiding place to save him. But it was too late, of course. She'd done her job with precision. Grandfather took his last breath in my arms."

"Do you know who Isobel really was?"

He faced me with dull eyes. "Yes," he whispered. "I believe I do."

I reached over and put my hand over his. Niko and I lived in different worlds, but it didn't matter. Grief spoke every language and lived every life. "Mabel killed my mother in front of me," I said. "I know how it feels to lose someone, although I can't imagine the pain of Isobel's—Angelina's—betrayal."

"I'm very sorry," he said. "I would not wish pain like that on anyone."

"Does your family know?"

He shook his head. "No. Only Hector. I lied, started rumors that the West Guards came, killed Grandfather, and threw Grandmother into the ocean."

I didn't tell him that I'd watched Isobel die, that she'd been intent on murdering everyone who stood in the way of her goals. The depth of her betrayal and lies didn't matter now.

"Mabel killed Isobel," I said. "She killed her own mother."

He blinked. "I know." He glanced down at his hand, where a small gold ring glittered on his pinky finger. "At least, I assumed that's what happened. Later that night, this ring came to me. It would only have done so if Grandmother had died. I admit," he said with a hoarse laugh, "I was both relieved and deeply depressed. How do I mourn the life of a witch who lived a lie when I cannot speak of it to anyone? My Network would fall apart if they knew the truth. Some days I think I am not strong enough for this."

"You can speak to Papa and me about it whenever you need to."

"Please," he straightened, panicked, "do not allow this rumor to spread. Angelina, in the eyes of Antebellum, is by all accounts a different person than my grandmother. If my Network found out, all trust in the Aldana family would be lost. Chaos would reign. Mabel, as you say, would certainly take over the world."

"Your secret is safe with us. It has been the past six weeks."

He let out a breath. "Thank you. That is appreciated."

"Talk to Papa," I said, squeezing his hand. "He'll support you."

For the first time since we'd entered the cabin, Niko gave me a smile filled with hope. "Thank you, Miss Monro—"

"Bianca," I said. "Please, call me Bianca."

"Mees Beeanca," he said with an exaggerated accent. "You have given the Eastern Network much hope."

A powerful blast rocked the boat, throwing me off the wicker chair. The tempestuous black cloud on the horizon brought the Western Network ships ever closer. West Guards scurried around the decks, rushing to prepare for battle. Niko looked over my shoulder and smiled.

"You should be going," he said, taking my hand to help me stand. "We will have a fight on our hands soon, but don't worry. I can take care of this. Go. And we will talk more when I discuss this with your father on an official visit to the Central Network."

You Have Graduated

The hot shingles of the castle roof prickled against my bare feet the next morning, so I skittered to the top, where the view was the best, and sat on my dress.

The sweltering summer sun beat down on the roof in hot, sticky waves. Sweat dripped between my shoulder blades. My hair flopped onto my neck in a long, black braid, nicely out of my way. Summer in the Central Network brought a broiling green forest to life, so I didn't mind it, despite its wretched heat and humidity.

Below me, the Captain of New Recruits belted out commands to a group of poor, scrawny witches, gangly and fresh out of adolescence. They scrambled to obey him, bumbling over their own feet and nearly hacking off their limbs in the process.

"Where are you, Merrick?" I murmured. "This isn't any fun without you here."

One of our favorite activities—watching the new Guardian recruits practice—held little excitement without his smart-aleck quips. I hadn't heard from him in six weeks, and I missed the way the skin around his eyes crinkled when he laughed.

"Guardians!" the Captain bellowed. "Stand at arms!"

A few of them tumbled into position. I giggled. Merrick would've had some witty comment that I—

"Bianca, why are you sitting on the roof? You're eighteen now. Aren't you a little beyond this?"

The unexpected voice startled me. I jerked, lost my grip, and went sliding down the gritty, sun-warmed shingles. Clawing for balance,

I pitched off the edge of the turret roof. The flagstones in the castle bailey seven stories below rushed toward me with frightening speed. I had just managed to remember the transportation spell when my back collided with a soft carpet. The sensation of falling ceased. I stared up at the sky, my breath held, running through a mental checklist.

Still breathing. Arms intact. Hovering in the air.

The tips of my fingers brushed something soft, and I relaxed. "Oh," I whispered, recognizing the pliable fabric of the Volare. "Thanks, my friend. Fast work."

The Volare levitated me back up to the turret window where my best friend, Leda, waited with a queer expression on her face. I slipped off the rug and through the window.

"Did you see that?" I asked, landing nimbly on my feet. "The Volare is so fast! I didn't even call for it."

Leda rolled her eyes. "Why are you climbing on the roof?" she asked. "You know it's not safe. And it's not ladylike. I could see the backs of your knees."

I slipped into the Witchery, our own private turret, arching my brow as the Volare settled onto the ground next to me. Leda's white-blonde hair was pulled back in a tasteful bun, accentuating her high cheekbones. A light blue dress with a beaded bodice and rounded sleeves capped her shoulders. She looked lovely in a fragile kind of way, with her pale skin and different-colored eyes.

"You saw the backs of my knees while I was plummeting to the earth, you mean?" I asked. "Sorry. I wasn't too worried about etiquette while plunging to my death."

She sniffed. "Decorum knows no bounds, Bianca." Her brow furrowed. "Why were you up there, anyway? It's so hot outside."

"No reason," I said.

A mischievous grin played on her lips. "You were watching the new recruits, just like you used to do with Merrick, weren't you?"

"Yes," I said, sighing. "I miss him."

"No sign of his return?"

I shook my head.

"Well, I am sorry you haven't heard from him," she said, "but if you don't hurry, we're going to be late. I won't be tardy to my own personal graduation ceremony. Especially not when it's held by the Head of Education, thank you very much."

"Oh, no!" I cried. "I forgot!"

"Oh, yes!" She pushed me toward the water bowl. "Clean up a little. I won't have you looking like that. Camille, Michelle, and Priscilla are going to meet us in Miss Scarlett's office."

After scrubbing the grit from my face and hands and using a spell to clean the stains off my dress, I passed Leda's sharp inspection.

"Better," she said, her lips pressed together. "Let's go."

"You didn't mention Rupert," I said as we spiraled down the Witchery stairs. "Will he be at your graduation?"

Her back stiffened. She trailed the tips of her fingers along the wall.

"Absolutely not."

Rupert, Leda's boss and the Assistant to Council Member Jansson, had a savage crush on her. Despite being ten years older, he treaded carefully, like a puppy trying to court a lion. He must have done or said something she didn't like. Getting her to talk about him was as fruitful as planting potatoes in the winter soil, but her hunched posture told me something was off. Hopefully I could coax it out of her.

"Something wrong?" I asked.

She gazed at me from the corner of her eye. "Not wrong," she said, sounding choked. "Just . . . awkward."

"What happened?"

Leda clenched her jaw and mumbled a response.

"What? I can't understand you."

"Rupert asked me to marry him yesterday!" she cried, burying her face in her hands. I stopped in the middle of the stairwell, aghast.

"What?" I screeched.

"Oh, it was horrible," she growled. "He was so nervous he couldn't stop stammering, and by the time I realized what he was trying to do, he had a cord of engagement in his hands and—" She broke off with a huff. "It was awful."

I bit the inside of my cheek. "Really?" I asked, suppressing a giggle. "I can't believe he had the courage."

"Me either," Leda muttered, with just a hint of amusement dancing in her eyes.

"What did you say?"

"No, of course," she said, shaking her head. "Oh, Bianca. It messed up everything. Why did he have to go and fall in love with me? Everything at work is so awkward now. He started to cry!"

If she hadn't been so serious, I would have burst out laughing. Knowing she'd take great offense and stubbornly refuse to talk to me for weeks—she'd done it before—I suppressed my laughter and maintained an even tone of voice.

"I guess you're just irresistible."

She didn't refute me, but the most hesitant signs of a smile appeared on her face.

"What are you going to do?" I asked.

"Well, I'm not giving up my job," she said, folding her arms across her chest. "My family needs the currency more than ever now that my oldest brother has joined the Guardians. Rupert's just going to have to put up with seeing me every day."

I felt a moment of compassion for poor Rupert. Leda could be as stubborn as a brick wall when she wanted to be. Her courteous and professional air would torture poor Rupert, still so wildly in love.

"Well," I said, infusing merriment into my tone, "now that you've graduated and broken his heart, maybe Rupert will quit, and you can take his job. You can be a real Assistant instead of just an Assistant's Assistant."

"That would be lovely," she said with a little smile. We broke into giggles, then turned and hurried down the turret stairs before it was too late.

Miss Scarlett's office was a small, square room with a high window not much bigger than a book. A wall of bookshelves filled with titles ranging from *Education in the Networks* to *How to Teach a Child Arithmetic* took up the right side of the room, just behind a crimson divan and a chair with clawed feet. Not a single speck of dust nor an errant knickknack could be found. Just like her classroom at Miss Mabel's School for Girls, the place smelled warm, like cumin.

Camille beamed as we walked in.

"Merry meet!" she cried, reaching out to squeeze our hands. "I'm so excited for you, Leda. Do you like my sign? I just finished it this morning."

A banner hovered in the air, blinking the words, *Congratulations Leda*. Enchanted confetti rose and fell in a waterfall over the whole room. Miss Scarlett's gaze flickered to it every few seconds. If the flare of her nostrils meant anything, she didn't appreciate Camille's décor.

Leda gave Camille a tight smile. "Uh . . . it's great. Thanks."

Michelle and Priscilla stood near the back wall. Michelle tucked her large hands behind her, highlighting the small smudges of dough and flour on her apron, remnants from her job in the kitchens. Her small eyes disappeared into her face when she smiled. She'd only come around to our turret twice since marrying her beau, Nicolas, six weeks earlier.

"Merry meet, Bianca," she said with a quiet, shy smile. "It's good to see you again."

I waved to Priscilla, who wore a mint green dress with a fashionably high waist. With her green-flecked eyes, brilliant red hair, blemish-free skin, and long lashes, she resembled a porcelain doll. Pale, graceful, and feminine. My perfect antithesis.

Miss Scarlett stood behind her desk, a thin scroll in hand. A simple burgundy dress stretched across her broad shoulders, highlighting hints of red in her dark bun. She cleared her throat. "Let's begin," she said. "I have a meeting in ten minutes."

Leda stood in the middle of the room with her back to us, her spine as straight as a sword. She held her head high. Students who graduated early, like Leda, rarely received anything but their graduation scroll in the mail. Miss Scarlett, however, had agreed to a small ceremony to honor Leda's dedication and hard work. I suspected that Camille's unwavering insistence that Leda be acknowledged had something to do with it, although Camille took no credit.

"Leda," Miss Scarlett said. "You have graduated from the Network

School system through the prestigious Miss Mabel's School for Girls as of this day, the third day of the second week of the third month of summer. My compliments on your early graduation."

The thin scroll floated from Miss Scarlett's hand over to Leda, who accepted it with a perfect, unwavering curtsy.

"That's it?" Camille hissed, leaning toward me. "I did all this work for two senten—"

I slapped a hand over her mouth.

"Thank you, Miss Scarlett," Leda said, tilting her head with a regal nod, unbothered by the perfunctory service. "I'm honored to have attended the school and grateful that you took the time to give the scroll to me personally."

Miss Scarlett nodded. "Good luck in your endeavors."

Leda spun on her heels, a wide grin on her face. "I—"

The staccato blast of a high-pitched bugle cut her off. My heart dropped into my stomach. That particular tune meant that West Guards were attacking somewhere in the Network. Marten and I would need to leave immediately to investigate and help the survivors.

No, I thought. *Not again. Not now. Give Leda her moment. Just let Leda have this moment.*

But the bugle repeated itself a second time. Resigned, I dropped my chin onto my chest with a heavy sigh. This war wound its way into everything with tenacious tentacles. Leda closed her mouth. Camille sucked in a breath, her face pale. Miss Scarlett looked at me.

"Bianca?" she asked.

"I'm sorry. So sorry," I said to Leda. "I have to go. I-I'll see all of you tonight."

"Be safe," Camille whispered.

Their worried expressions faded from sight as the darkness of transportation fell over me, whisking me away.

Dansbury

The rubble of an entire village lay at my feet.
Smoke billowed out of the piles of rock that still burned with black Almorran fire. The thick, oily flames licked at what little wood remained. Almorran fire could destroy anything, even stone. It had turned the sweet thatched-roof cottages and stacked stone walls of the village to ash. Water had little effect on the black fire until it dwindled to embers. With no counter magic, we had few ways of fighting the roaring inferno. Five or six witches stared at the wreckage, their faces drawn and haunted. Nothing remained but smoke and cinders.

Dansbury was such a quiet, peaceful place, filled with rolling potato fields and quaint cottages. What could Mabel want from it?

Nothing, I thought. *Nothing except to scare us.*

"It happened so fast," Marten murmured. He stood at my side, his brow furrowed. "And in the middle of the day. The West Guards normally attack at night."

"They must be changing their strategy," I said, eyeing a piece of cloth flapping in the middle of the road. A small breeze overturned it, revealing a doll with a broken face. The wails of witches mourning in the background filled the silence. A heaviness hung in the air, typical of the aftermath of Almorran magic, as if there had been any doubt who was responsible for the destruction.

Marten sucked in a deep breath, even though the air reeked of burning tar. "Well," he said, rubbing his hands together. "Let's be grateful that we don't have to fight this time. Let's get to work."

There was nothing left, so little could be done for the survivors except to find suitable lodging. They'd be sent somewhere else, just like all the other displaced witches who had lost their homes. Unfortunately, this wasn't the first time Marten and I had been called to such devastation.

We started into the village together, surveying the damage. Marten stopped when we came across a witch, dead on the side of the road. The flesh around the witch's face had been stripped away, leaving it raw and red.

"Flesh-eating potion," Marten muttered, his jaw tight. I turned away, sickened by the sight. No matter how often I'd seen similar injuries on the Guardians who came through Chatham Castle, I could never get used to the brutality of war.

"They store the potion in bottles," Marten said, squinting. "When they throw them, the potion explodes, which means it can hit several witches or animals at the same time. They've been extremely deadly among the Guardians in the Southern Covens, but this is the first I've seen them in use against witches in the villages."

"There's no stopping the potion either," I said.

"No," he said, rummaging in his pocket, "but we can mitigate the pain. Stella gave me some of her healing oils. Let's walk around and see if anyone needs it. We're too late to help this poor soul."

A whisper of magic reached into my heart, warming my chest. I stopped. Only the magic of Letum Wood spoke to me that way.

Fire, it wailed. *Fire.*

"Marten," I said, stopping him. "I'm going over there."

I pointed west, where the towering trees of Letum Wood rose nearby. Uneven black scars and smoking dirt told me that more than just the town had felt the devastating effects of today's carnage.

He hesitated but knew me well enough to yield. I wouldn't be swayed away from the forest. "Stay within my line of sight," he said. "And be careful. West Guards could still be lingering."

The keen of Letum Wood rang ever louder in my heart as I jogged toward the trees. When I reached out and touched the trunk of the closest tree, the collective voice of the forest splintered into many, filling my head with desperation and fear.

Fire, they all cried. *Fire!*

I pulled away, unable to bear it. A few saplings and bushes had been consumed. Inky soot replaced the undergrowth. The outside bark of several towering trees had been burned, but they would live. Thankfully, the damage wasn't as extensive as I'd seen in other places. The fire had already abated, leaving the ground hot.

Using an incantation, I turned the ash on the hot earth into water, soaking the dirt. Smoke billowed up in great gray plumes but receded quickly. The frantic edge of the frightened forest ebbed as I saturated the ground.

"The fire is gone," I said, staring into the high canopy once I finished. "The embers are out now."

The magic stirred softly at first, as if searching to see if I was right. After a pause, the voices faded, leaving only one behind. *Retribution,* it whispered.

"You want retribution?" I asked.

No more fire. No more loss.

I heard footsteps behind me, heralding Marten's approach. At least an hour had passed since we'd arrived. Blood stained the front of his clothes. A warm breeze rustled through the trees, blowing the curling smoke behind me.

"Everything all right?" he asked.

"The fire destroyed some of Letum Wood."

Marten tilted his head back to study the canopy. "What does Letum Wood say when it speaks to you?"

"Well, not much. I mean . . . it's not an actual conversation. Mostly fragments."

"Has it said anything to you just now?"

"Yes. It says it wants retribution."

To my surprise, Marten's lips pursed and his brow drooped. "I have little doubt it will get what it wants," he said. "Mabel is taking this war to the whole world. I fear all of Antebellum will be driven into the fight."

The canopy of Letum Wood cast a dark shadow, with only pinpricks of light streaming through its layers to illuminate the ground. I stared at it. While Letum Wood possessed a sentient magic of its own, I doubted it could truly understand what it called retribution. I'd seen Mabel's mind; I'd shared her power. I knew exactly what she was capable of.

And how much she wanted to win.

"Are you ready to go?" Marten asked, interrupting my thoughts with a heavy hand on my shoulder. "Your father will be looking for us by now, I think. The remaining witches here in Dansbury have left to stay with family. Everything is taken care of."

"Yes," I said, grateful to leave it behind and more grateful to have a place to return to. "Let's go."

The magic of Letum Wood spoke to my heart once more before I transported away.

No more loss.

The Forgotten Children

"So the rumors are true?" I asked Papa the next morning when I flopped onto the chair across from him.

He ate breakfast at the table, wearing a worn suit of half-armor over his broad shoulders. His dark hair had grown out slightly, curling in the damp summer heat. Dirt and sweat streaked the white shirt he wore underneath his armor. I wondered what he could have been doing to get so dirty at this early hour. Then again, Papa was the most unconventional High Priest the Central Network had known—he traded fancy dinners for battles, and meetings for action. Likely, he'd been helping new Guardian recruits train or fighting West Guards in the failing Southern Covens.

The pale light of the sun had just crested the sky, highlighting the steep, gabled spires of Chatham City in the distance. A bevy of unopened messages had collected for him overnight. They lay scattered across the table, some opened, some waiting. Three twirled above his head, the word urgent marked on them in bright red ink. They'd follow him until he opened them, the annoying twits. Everything was urgent these days.

Papa lifted an eyebrow. "What rumors?"

I tossed the newsscroll at him. He caught it in one hand without looking. A new headline blinked across the top of the *Chatham Chatterer.*

SOUTHERN COVENS EXPECTED TO FALL TO SOUTH GUARDS

Despite massive resistance against the combined forces of the Southern and Western Networks, Central Network Guardians have been unable to safely retain land in the Southern Covens. Many witches anticipate High Priest Derek Black to announce a full withdrawal of Guardians within the week.

"We haven't lost them yet," he said, waving it away with a spell. "But we're well on the way if the Southern Network continues to receive support from the West Guards. Which they will."

"The South Guards can't do magic, yet we're losing a chunk of land to them?" I asked. "How is that possible?"

Papa leaned back in his chair. "Magic or not, they still have arms and legs and weapons to fight with. Not to mention the West Guards using Almorran magic to support them. You know as well as anyone that we can't stop the black fire."

"Why am I just now hearing about it?" I asked, wounded that as Assistant to the Ambassador—and daughter of the ruling High Priest—I wasn't kept appraised of new developments in the war.

"Because it's a rumor."

"A rumor with an element of truth to it."

He warily conceded my point. "True, but not one I want growing out of control, the way most rumors seem to do. The *Chatterer* shouldn't have published this, but you know how reporters are during a war. They think they're gods."

I smiled when he winked at me. A knock at the door startled both of us. Reeves, our self-appointed butler who had shown up one day and refused to leave, opened the door with a spell. Marten waited on the other side.

"Marten," Papa said. He stood, and the two of them clasped forearms when Marten strode into the room. His shirt hung off his skinny shoulders; he'd lost weight after Mildred, his sweetheart, died. The sunlight streaming into the room reflected off his bald head. Despite the bleak circumstances, he always wore a ready smile.

"Morning, High Priest. Bianca," he said. "You called for me?"

Papa's expression grew serious. He leaned his fists on the table. "Yes," he said. "I'd like your advice on a situation in the Western Covens."

I straightened up and stole a chunk of bread off Papa's plate, eager to hear more.

"What's happened?" Marten asked.

"The Western Network is attacking the dairy farms in the Western Covens," Papa said. "Over a thousand cows were slaughtered last night. Most of the meat has spoiled in the heat already. They saved what they could, but it wasn't much. I was hoping you could give me some advice on dealing with the repercussions. The Network, especially the Western Covens, will suffer from the food loss."

"Of course."

"Let's go to my office. The reports are there."

Papa snapped his fingers. All the messages collected into a pile and flew into his hand. He flicked the top of my head as he gathered up his favorite quill.

"What are you doing today, daughter?"

"Looking for the *Book of Light* in a library in Newberry and going for a run in Letum Wood. All this war business has me stressed out."

The *Book of Light*—which wasn't much more than a rumor—was a lost tome we hoped held the counter to Almorran magic. So far, my search over the last six weeks had proven futile. I'd rummaged around the whole Central Network—Niko had even let me sift through Magnolia Castle—to no avail. Despite my failure to find it, I refused to give up. It could turn the tide of the war in our favor.

"Haven't you already looked at the library in Newberry?" Marten asked.

"Yes, but I'm worried I may have missed it." My brow furrowed. "Of course, all of this may be for nothing. Mabel could have it in the Western Network. Maybe the Southern Network. But that doesn't seem likely, at any rate. I believe she'd keep it close. If she has it," I said, holding stubbornly to hope.

Papa's brows knit together. "Whatever you decide to do, be careful," he said. "I don't like you running around Letum Wood without Merrick."

"You're the one who sent Merrick away," I drawled. "Maybe you should bring him back."

"He's doing far more important work than running with a wild teenager in the forest."

"Oh?" I asked, forcing casual nonchalance. "Like what?"

Papa narrowed his eyes at me. "Mm-hmm . . . I see what you're doing, B. You won't win. I won't tell you where Merrick is or when he'll be back. And no. I'm not bringing him back just because you miss him."

I slouched in my chair. "Fine."

The amusement in Papa's face abated. "I'm serious, B. Be careful out there. Except for Dansbury, Mabel's been strangely quiet the last few days. I don't like it. She's up to something."

"I will, Papa. Marten has been training me on defensive spells, and my transportation has come along beautifully."

Papa hesitated. The last time he'd restricted me from running in Letum Wood, my powers had strengthened beyond my control. His reluctance to forbid me from running was grounded in history—my magic didn't cope well with being stuck in a castle.

"You're an adult now, Bianca," he said, sounding strangled. "The decision is yours. Just know that I'm wary of it."

"She's learned with surprising speed to use magic to block another witch from transporting her," Marten said with a wink. "I was surprised she picked it up so readily."

"Hey!"

Darkness fell down on me like cascading water, but I used silent magic to counter it. My vision went dark. The magic reached a crescendo, but I fought back. The swimming darkness faded. I faced Papa with a smirk.

"Marten is constantly testing me," I said self-righteously.

Papa laughed. "Good," he said, pushing his hand against my face. "See that you don't get into trouble, and check in with Stella when you get back."

"Yes, Papa."

"Love you, B."

"I love you, too."

Fire!

My slamming heart spurred me through northern Letum Wood that evening. Hoping to find new, more-challenging runs, I'd started transporting farther away from Chatham Castle and discovering new trails. Tonight, I sprinted through a section of the forest near the Northern Covens, speeding past bracken and through curtains of ivy. My bare feet hurdled over boulders and skimmed past dark pools of moss. The Volare banged against my back, and Viveet bounced on my right hip with every step. A wild feeling of panic pushed me, even though my lungs burned with a desperate need for air.

Run, the magic of the forest whispered. *Fire!*

"I'm . . . running . . ." I muttered.

A heavy blanket of humidity lay over Letum Wood, making it difficult to draw breath. The sun cast long, dark shadows on the ground. Hair clung to my neck and forehead, and sweat dripped from my elbows and face. The dim light left shadows on the ground below the dense canopy. I sprinted on faith, following bushes that bent back and tree limbs that moved out of the way, guided by the magic of the forest. When Letum Wood commanded, I obeyed.

Fire! cried the magic. *Run!*

I spilled out of the forest and skidded to a stop in an open meadow filled with haze. An old house sat in the middle of the field, barely visible through the fog. Fire climbed up the wood, radiating heat so strong I felt it on the backs of my hands. The flames moved quickly, speeding across the front of the house with an orange glow. Pounding drums in the distance matched my racing heart.

Drums. I knew those drums.

"West Guards?" I panted, ducking behind a nearby tree. "In the Northern Covens?"

The shrill screams of children rang out over the tops of the waving grasses. Young faces flashed in the windows of the orphanage. Two West Guards guarded the front door, and one stood at the back. My eyes narrowed. Who would they be guarding so far north? The face of a child appeared in the attic window, her eyes wide and terrified, before disappearing again.

Children. Northern Covens. Fire. West Guards. Niko's voice rang through my mind.

"Forty innocent witches died, ten of whom were children in an orphanage fire."

Why weren't the West Guards using black fire? Doesn't matter, I thought, glancing back. *Fire is fire.*

There would be no dead children on my watch. I ducked low, closed my eyes, and repeated a transportation spell. A heady darkness pressed on my face for less than a second before it disappeared, leaving me crouched on a stair landing inside the orphanage. Pandemonium reigned. Hysterical young girls clung to the dresses of older children. Two teenage boys attempted to guide smaller kids to the back of the house, where the smoke was thinnest. Miss Scarlett stood at the bottom of the stairs, barking commands.

"Miss Scarlett!" I called, running down the stairs. "Miss Scarlett! How can I help?"

Her head snapped up. "Bianca!" she cried, her eyes widening. She grabbed my arms, shaking me. "What are you doing here?"

"I'm here to help!"

"No! You must go."

"Miss Scarlett—"

"Run, Bianca!"

Her terror frightened me. "What's happening?" I asked. "What's going on?"

"Go!" she said, shoving me toward the door. "Transport to your father's presence *immediately!*"

An onslaught of darkness overtook the room, forcing me to the ground and ripping me away from Miss Scarlett's firm grip. My head hit the floor with a *crack*. The scream of a little girl pulled me back from a confused, swimming fog. A familiar face, like one peering out of the murky depths of a long-forgotten dream, appeared in the darkness. My stomach clenched.

"Ah, Bianca darling. So lovely of you to join us. You were almost too late."

My spine stiffened at the drawling, sultry voice. The smell of flowers overwhelmed me, so strong and sweet it stank. My upper lip curled over my teeth.

"Mabel," I hissed.

The darkness hiding her ebbed away, revealing a goddess of a witch, almost maniacal in her dark glory. She wore a black dress with a plunging neckline and short sleeves. Tongues of black flame undulated around her legs in smoky waves, highlighting the blonde hair cascading in ringlets past her shoulders. Perfection. Mabel was cherry-lipped, blue-eyed, cynical, stunning perfection.

This isn't going to be good, I thought.

"Mabel?" she repeated with an amused lift in her voice. "Since when do you not address me with the formal respect I deserve? I punish students who don't address me as Miss Mabel."

"I'm not your student anymore."

"A shame, isn't it? We could have been so great together."

Her cool smile sent panic through me. Mabel always had a plan, and something told me that *I* was part of her plan now. No doubt she'd schemed this dark idea herself, ambushing me at an orphanage. Miss Scarlett tried to move toward me, but Mabel sent her flying into the wall.

The orphans continued to scream in the background as the heat of the flames radiated through the walls. Out of the corner of my eye, I saw a girl's lips moving as she attempted to open the windows with magic, but they didn't budge. She slammed her palms into the panes, but it was no use. Even the Orphanage Mother pounded on the back door, but it wouldn't give way. Mabel must be suppressing their magic somehow.

"It's been too long, hasn't it?" Mabel asked, inspecting her nails.

I snarled. "Not long enough. What do you want?"

Her predatory gaze glowed as red as simmering coals. Mabel had many demons. Just seeing her again made me relive them, remembering the hellish time I'd spent locked in her mind, sharing her pain and madness.

"Isn't it obvious what I want?" Mabel asked, glancing around. "I want to finish the job I meant to do six weeks ago when Mother dearest died."

"Attacking an orphanage of innocent children?"

"No, you silly fool. Kidnapping you. They are simply the means to the end."

She took a step forward, but I unsheathed Viveet. Her bright blue flames danced high, casting a circle of light on the floor. Mabel stopped and lifted an eyebrow.

"We've done this before, Bianca," she said. "Do you remember? It wasn't too long ago that you and I fought."

"And you lost."

Her eyes tapered. "Naturally, I let you win to gain my own advantage. I was hoping that Mother dearest would kill your father while I was hiding in the dungeon, but of course she failed. She wasn't as strong as I am, you see."

A wooden beam fell from the kitchen ceiling in a spray of cinders. Miss Scarlett staggered off the floor, a trickle of blood rolling down her cheek. She put herself between Mabel and the children.

"I'm willing to make a deal," Mabel said, extending her right arm. A silver manacle dangled from her index finger. The edge of her sleeve slipped back, revealing her circlus, a round tattoo on her wrist. I had one just like it, a symbol of education.

"What deal?" I asked.

"You," she said, twirling her finger in a circle, "for all of them. Come with me willingly, and I'll spare their lives."

"Why don't you just take me?"

Mabel laughed. "Because I know you can block my transportation spell. I'm way ahead of you, Bianca darling. I've been watching you, you know."

I swore under my breath. Mabel knew I'd never allow so many innocent children to die for me, just as she must have known I'd be running through this section of the forest. Her ability to play on my weaknesses worked to her advantage yet again. I frantically tried to form a plan. Mabel would repel any curse I tried to use. Papa wasn't here. For all I knew, the Protectors were infiltrating Letum Wood to prepare for an imminent counter attack, but I couldn't bet on it. If I went with Mabel, she'd hold the biggest pawn in this game of war: me. Papa would be livid and might act rashly, which wouldn't end well for the Central Network. No matter what I chose, something bad would happen.

"You have to prove that you'll let every witch here live," I said. The ravenous fire ceased, leaving my ears ringing.

"Of course I will, see?" She held her arms out. "But only if you come willingly."

The flames roared to life, stronger than before.

"You don't have much longer to hesitate," Mabel called over the raging inferno. "Do you want to die with all these beautiful, forgotten children?"

A portion of the roof fell, crashing into the top floor. Miss Scarlett skittered backward, her arms outspread to protect the children from the flying cinders. The entire building would fall in on itself within minutes.

The sanctimonious victory in Mabel's smile turned my stomach. "Now or never!" she cried. "Which do you choose, Bianca?"

"Bianca!" Miss Scarlett yelled, "Transport away immediately!"

I held out my arm to Mabel. "You have me. Now stop the fire."

The inferno ceased the moment the manacle slid onto my wrist. My skin turned cold where it touched me, and the chill crawled up my arm like a wave of ice. Viveet fell from my hands, landing on the floor, inert. Miss Scarlett's mouth opened in horror.

My own sense of heavy dread pressed upon me when Mabel giggled.

"Tell Papa not to do anything thoughtless," I said to Miss Scarlett, dropping the Volare's oblong case on top of Viveet. "And please take my things back to Chatham Castle."

Before Miss Scarlett could respond, Mabel grabbed my arm above my elbow. The darkness of transportation pressed in on me, taking me far from my home and everyone I loved.

Precautionary

When the darkness faded, I found myself in a familiar cavern with red and yellow rock walls. Mabel's personal chamber in the Western Network. The arid air turned my mouth into cotton in moments. Floor-length drapes edged in yellow lace split the space in two, and the hint of a canopied bed peeked through their gauzy linen. A curved balcony with a waist-high railing revealed a dark sky studded with stars.

Mabel released me with a sneer.

"Welcome home, Bianca darling."

I paused to survey the room, my heart pounding. *Know where you are*, Papa had always taught me, and the memory of his voice calmed my hot panic. *Memorize everything you can.*

Books filled a mahogany shelf on the side opposite the balcony. A bright painting of fire filled the far wall, nearly blending into the rock behind it. The dry air seemed to crackle.

"I'll just be needing this."

Mabel grabbed my braid. A pair of scissors appeared in the air next to her. She clipped off a lock of my hair just before I jerked out of her grasp.

"Don't be so reactive, Bianca," she purred. "It's just a little piece of hair for the protective magic."

The lock of hair drifted to the doorframe that led into the hall and pressed itself into the wood, as if drawn there by a string. Mabel spoke under her breath, and a line of red flame zipped around the edges. A flare of heat rolled by me, so intense it stung my face. I turned away even though it disappeared in a flash.

"There," she said with a satisfied smirk. "No one—not even you— would be stupid enough to try to cross that threshold now that the magic knows you."

My stomach dropped. She was right. Papa had told me about spells like this before. If I moved too close to the doorframe, the red fire would shoot toward me in warning. If I pressed on, it would consume me until I burned to death.

Lovely, I thought.

"I'm sure I don't need to state the obvious," Mabel said, motioning around us with an outstretched hand. "But you are my prisoner. That manacle will prevent you from leaving the Arck. You may try to leave my room." Her eyes flickered to the doorway with a wry grin. "But I wouldn't recommend it."

The manacle on my right wrist glowed light blue and silver, almost obscuring my circlus. The weight, though not enough to slow me down, served as a stolid reminder that she controlled me.

"You're keeping me here?" I asked. "In your chamber?"

"Yes."

I stared at her. "You're not going to lock me up in some kind of hellhole and torture me with your all-powerful Almorran magic?"

She didn't respond to the sarcasm in my voice, but her pause led me to believe something was off-kilter.

"No," she said. "I want you where I can see you at all times."

"Because you know Papa's coming after me, don't you?"

Mabel grinned. "I'm counting on it."

She glided across the room with the same dangerous appeal she'd always had, this time magnified by her magic and the swirl of silent black flame around her legs. I'd witnessed many variations of Mabel since our first meeting, but never had she looked so unnerved.

"Aren't you afraid?" she asked, turning around to study me. "You're in the hands of the enemy. Once again, I hold your life in my hands. It's a wonderful feeling, you know. I rather enjoy the power."

I ignored her question. "Papa won't let you have me for long. You just made a dangerous enemy."

"You put a lot of faith in him. He's not so wise as you think in all matters."

"Papa doesn't have to be all-knowing to best you."

She lifted an eyebrow. "Oh really? Please, enlighten me. What does the infamous Derek Black need to beat me?"

"Motivation. He won't stop until you're dead."

A flash of something like uncertainty flickered in her gaze, then disappeared. She snorted.

"Derek can try. I hope he does. He'll never beat me. I'll prove I'm better than all of them."

I was about to ask who *all of them* were, but a rustle of movement in the corner of my eye caught my attention. A graceful, spotted cheetah strolled through two of the white curtains and stopped. My heart jumped into my throat. Why did Mabel have a cheetah?

Mabel beckoned the cat closer with a twitch of her fingers. He responded to her silent call, settling with an obedient growl at her feet. She trailed her fingertip down his nose and over his neck.

"Beautiful, isn't he? His name is Juba."

Juba meant *death* in the Almorran language.

"He's the male and very territorial," Mabel said with a little tsk in my direction. "He never leaves my room. You might as well become friends with him because he'll always be here . . . watching you."

I made a sound in my throat. Did her strange ways have no end?

"This is Juka." Mabel waved a hand toward another cheetah that strolled over from the balcony. Their chests rose and fell rapidly in the sweltering night air. "She follows me everywhere. Precautionary, of course."

"Precautionary?"

"Stay here long enough, and you'll see what I mean. I wouldn't get on their bad sides if I were you."

"Right," I muttered, warily surveying their dark amber eyes. "I wouldn't worry about that."

Juba stared at me with a sense of keen intelligence that made me wonder if he was a cheetah or a witch. There was no way of knowing by looking at him; I hadn't learned the skill of magical detection, and

I wasn't powerful enough to overcome transformative magic without practice and direction. Juba's nostrils opened and closed as he lifted his nose in my direction. He was a little bigger than Juka. They shared the same white underbelly, narrow waists, and elegant movements. A ridge of hair flowed down the backs of their necks and between their shoulder blades, giving them a wild look.

"So this is your plan?" I asked, whirling around to face Mabel as she strolled toward her bed. "You're going to keep me in your room with a cheetah until my father rescues me?"

"Yes."

"What happens if I escape?"

She smiled. "Why don't you try?"

I didn't rise to the occasion. While living with Mabel, I'd have to choose my battles. Getting myself hurt this early in the game would be unwise. Of course I would try to escape, but I wouldn't be stupid about it.

"I'll pass," I said, forcing nonchalance.

She shrugged and continued on.

"Wait," I called, following close behind her. "What about—"

Juba crossed the room in two leaps, snatched my arm in his pearly jaws, and yanked me to the floor. I fell to my knees with a cry. Pressure and pain shot through my muscles, right into my bone. The shock rendered me stunned.

"Oh," Mabel called airily over her shoulder. "Juba's protective of me. It's best that you not get too close unless I give you permission."

Juba snarled as he released me. Blood stained his white teeth and dripped down my skin, staining the rocky floor. Two crimson holes in the fleshy part of my arm dribbled blood when he slinked away. I wrapped my other hand around the puncture wounds, my breathing fast and shallow. The pain ripped through my arm in waves, catapulting my mind into panic.

Stay calm, Papa's voice directed from a memory of when I'd fallen out of a tree at age twelve and broken my arm. *Always stay calm, B. It keeps your heart rate down and mitigates the pain.*

Mabel gestured to the bare floor at the foot of her bed. "Your accommodations while you're here," she said, chuckling under her breath. "Sleep well. I have some business to take care of and won't be back until late. Don't wait up."

A chain shot out and attached to the manacle around my wrist, jerking me off my knees with a cry. It dragged me across the stone floor until only a length of chain the size of my arm allowed movement. My arm throbbed, and I held a sob in my throat. The lights vanished, plunging the cave-like room into darkness.

Juba settled on the floor near the balcony, his eyes glowing in my direction. Struggling to keep my breathing under control, I clutched the bite wound and counted slowly to one hundred. Once I regained control of my thoughts, I reached for the hem of my dress. My bloody hand left rose-colored marks on the fabric when I tore off a long piece. Using an incantation to temporarily numb the pain, I gritted my teeth and carefully wound the bandage around my arm. At least I could still do magic. The enchantments on her room didn't seem to suppress that ability.

Juba settled on the floor not far away. I lay back, ignoring him, and stared at the striations on the ceiling while the magic wore off and my arm began to hurt again. Mabel thought herself clever, no doubt, managing to steal me—and Isadora—from the Central Network. Surely the old Watcher was here as well, hidden away like the *Book of Light*. My desire to retaliate momentarily overrode my fear. How wonderful would it be to turn my kidnapping back around on Mabel? To use this opportunity to gather information, to observe the enemy.

To win.

No matter how powerful her magic, there had to be something I could do to escape. Some hole in her reasoning, a flaw in her emotional, crazed plans. I'd figure it out. And then?

I'd find Isadora and the *Book of Light*.

A pair of gleaming fangs woke me the next morning.

Juba's breath hit my face hard and fast, smelling like decay and iron. His teeth shone with dripping, hot saliva. I waited, holding my breath to keep from screaming. After what felt like an eternity, he slunk away. My heart slowed. I stared at the red rock ceiling until I gathered my composure.

I winced when I sat up. My hips ached from sleeping on the stone floor, but they didn't hurt as much as the bite on my arm, which had swollen in the night. I'd have to take care of it with magic to keep it from getting infected.

Waves of heat already permeated the air, making everything move like a mirage. The chain connecting my wrist to the bed had disappeared, so I pushed myself to my feet. Juba watched my every movement but stayed sprawled on the cool floor, panting. A small porcelain jug of water stood on a table near the head of the bed. I padded over, unwrapped the cloth, rinsed the blood from my arm into the bowl, and surveyed my throbbing wound. The two puncture marks appeared black in the morning light, surrounded by a purple and blue bruise. I cast an annoyed look at Juba, who twitched his tail as if he were amused.

"Witch," I muttered. "Definitely a witch."

A few pieces of flat, warm bread, accompanied by a small jar of thick brown paste, waited on a low table across from the bookshelf. I ate while surveying the room, eyeing the walls for hidden doorways or anything that seemed out of place, and headed to the bookshelf as soon as I finished. I sat on the floor and started pulling books off the bottom shelf. Most of them were new, with fresh pages, a fine script, and a leather binding that indicated they were handmade. I sorted them in stacks and fanned through the pages. The *Book of Light* could look like any book. Mabel could have disguised it with magic to be something simple like the tattered *Everyday Potions Volume 23*.

After sorting through each book, I used a revealing incantation, which would force any magic to undo itself, but nothing significant came of it. *Dark Potions and Everyday Use* fell apart, crumbling into little more than a pamphlet with no spine, no cover, and handwriting so illegible I didn't even try to decipher it.

Thoroughly frustrated, I lay on my back and stared at the ceiling, feeling the weight of Juba's constant stare.

"Nothing," I said. What had I expected? If Mabel possessed the counter magic, wouldn't she just destroy it?

Unless she couldn't destroy it. It stood to reason that the counter magic would be just as powerful as Almorran magic, only less evil. Maybe she couldn't destroy one without the other.

The manacle lay heavy on my wrist. I wrapped my hand around it, feeling its cool weight against my skin. With one quick movement, I tried to jerk it all the way off my arm. The cool silver metal tightened, fitting so close to my wrist I could barely spin it.

Too easy, I told myself. *If I'm going to outwit Mabel, it's got to be more complicated than just removing the manacle.*

Juba sighed, resting his head on top of his paw. My eyes narrowed on the balcony. Could I go outside? That opened a new bevy of possible escape routes.

Juba watched me with detached interest as I abandoned the mess of books and slipped onto the balcony. The sun seared my skin the moment I stepped outside. The red rock castle, despite having endured thousands of years of the unforgiving sun, felt cooler than the scorching summer air. When nothing painful prevented me from going forward, I moved into the middle of the balcony with measured steps.

Mabel's room looked out over the city from at least seven stories high. No one would recognize me this far up. No doubt layers of magic prevented my escape off the balcony. I eyed several pots of tall flowering cacti placed a few paces apart near the edge. On the balustrade ledge behind the massive cacti sat smaller decorative pots.

I picked up a small cactus and inspected it. The dark red earthen pot matched the sands that seemed to stretch out to an eternal horizon in the east. A green spiked bulb sat in the fine dirt, as anemic as sand. The slightest hint of a bloom lingered on top. No doubt it had taken months for that little bud to sprout, inching toward the sun despite the soil's poor nutrients and lack of water.

"Merry part," I said under my breath as I tossed the pot off the balcony. An explosion sent me ducking for cover. Pieces of the shattered pot rained over me, freckling my hair with baby cactus spikes.

"Jikes," I whispered. Only a few remnants littered the balcony floor. I brushed a few shards off my shoulders, carefully untangling the cactus spikes from my hair and sleeves. *Well, so much for the idea of sending messages over the railing.*

Juba stood up, his hackles raised. I straightened, ignoring his throaty growl. "What? You think I'm going to jump off after that?"

He slowly lay back down, protected from the sun by the shade of Mabel's bedroom. But his slitted eyes remained on me, his paws lined up next to each other and ready to spring.

I sighed and leaned against the balustrade, peering down at the market below. Heavy canvas stalls stood in rows. Woven baskets piled high with dates, old books, leather water pouches, and shiny camel bells awaited buyers beneath the bulky material. An older woman with deep wrinkles from the hot Western Network sun sold spiny green bushes enchanted to bloom on command. The low bellow of gangly camels and the occasional shout of a merchant reached my balcony.

Just when I'd had enough of the heat, an odd witch standing beneath a braided blue canopy caught my eye. His yellow blonde hair—common in the Western Network—was pulled back into a ponytail, a few wispy strands curling out onto his wide shoulders. Nothing about him was unusual, but the confident way he stood with his legs braced and his head upturned to stare right at me arrested my suspicions.

"Zane," I whispered in relief. The Head of Protectors. Aside from Papa, no other witch was as talented or sneaky as Zane. He'd transformed his appearance to blend into the Western Network, but I knew it was him without a doubt. He must be here for me.

I gripped the hot stone in my palms and leaned forward to make sure I wasn't imagining it. A shot of white-hot pain ripped through my fingertips, down my body, and into my heels, flinging me away from the balustrade. My ribs hit the wall of the Arck with a crack. The cloudless sky swam between dark spots in my vision until the colors faded and everything turned to black.

"Ah, delightful. You tested the boundaries, didn't you?"

Mabel's voice moved in ripples through my buried levels of consciousness. I ascended them slowly, aware first of my throbbing head, then the burn of sun on my skin, and at last the still-smarting cheetah bite on my arm.

"It's a powerful little manacle," she said, her voice sounding further away, then closer, then further away again. "I told you it wouldn't allow you to leave the Arck."

Bit by bit, I put the pieces together. Zane. Leaning forward to see. Darkness. The magic of the manacle had thrown me back, preventing me from escaping. How long had I been lying there? Sweat coated my back. My skin burned. I would have moaned, but I didn't want to give Mabel the satisfaction of knowing I hurt.

When I opened my eyes to the blistering desert sun, Mabel was pacing back and forth, her arms folded and her fingers drumming a rhythm against her arm. Juka stood next to Juba at the balcony opening, watching her with an intent, tense gaze.

She stopped to stare at me. A slight breeze rustled her hair.

"I paid your father a little visit today," she said. I pushed myself off the floor, scooting backward into the shade with my good arm.

"You went to the Central Network?"

Her eyes gleamed. "Something like that. The wonderful thing about Almorran magic is that I don't even need to leave to go somewhere. I can be everywhere if I want. It's lovely."

Like a coward, I thought. *Frightened enough of Papa she won't see him in person.*

"What did you say to him?"

"I told him I will accept his full surrender in exchange for his beloved daughter."

"And his reply?"

Mabel smiled, slow and steady. "He told me to burn in the fires of my own magic."

So Papa had neither refused nor accepted her offer, which put both Networks—and the war—into a strange kind of limbo. I wasn't surprised. He was stalling for time, likely. Giving Zane and me a chance to figure out how to break free.

"Will you kill me now that he didn't give you what you wanted?" I asked.

"Are you afraid that I will?"

I paused, wondering if I should put on a brave front and tell her that nothing scared me. Deciding to stick with the truth, I said, "Yes."

She studied me for a moment, as if she were surprised, then turned her back on me, the gauzy fabric of her dress floating around her.

"I never expected Derek to agree to my terms. Not right away. There's time to drag this out. Besides, there's no reason to kill you just yet," she said. "Not until I get what I want."

"My father?"

She turned so I could see the profile of her beautiful face. "The Central Network."

The horizon had righted itself, making me feel more grounded. I stood but held onto the wall with a hand behind my back. My breath caught with a nervous flutter in my throat when Mabel started to leave.

"You didn't know it would happen, did you?" I asked, blurting out the question before I lost my courage. Mabel paused, her back to me. Several seconds passed in tense silence.

"No," she said. "Perhaps I didn't know that particular spell could allow you into my mind as easily as I entered yours."

I couldn't help but wonder if she underestimated the power of Almorran magic and hadn't known how to control it that night. What else had she not anticipated?

"Although, I should have known you to be a sneaky little lynx who goes where you aren't invited."

"You weren't invited into my head."

She bared her teeth. "I went there anyway."

Her hatred for me had grown. I could feel it in every word she spoke. The value of my life as Derek's daughter was the only thing keeping her from killing me.

"You were the one in control of the magic," I said, taking a step back to put some distance between us. The backs of my knees collided with the balustrade. "It wasn't my choice."

Her nostrils flared. The ebony folds of her dress billowed out in a plume as she whipped around, her eyes as red as blood.

"You know nothing about the magic!" she snarled. "Nothing!"

The tendrils of Mabel's mind called to me in whispers. In a flash, shadows of my time in her head resurrected themselves. They shifted, gaining ground until all I could hear was the tormented cry of young Mabel's voice in my head.

She left me.

"You'll die for what you know," Mabel hissed, advancing on me. "I'll have my revenge on you the same way I took revenge on Angelina. I am the most powerful witch in all of Antebellum. Thanks to the High Priests of Almorra, no one will hold power over me ever again."

I tried to mentally untangle myself, shaking my head to clear away the burst of darkness. As quickly as her sudden mania arose, it disappeared. The keen of her buried pain faded from my mind.

Mabel turned away, breathing fast. She clenched her jaw, as if striving to regain control. After what seemed like an eternity, she pulled her shoulders back, drew in a deep breath, and sashayed off the balcony and out of her room. Juka slinked after her. I watched her walk away, keenly aware of the desperation of my circumstance. I had to find Isadora and the *Book of Light* before the glimpses of madness I saw in Mabel's eyes took control.

Gathering Information

The sound of the bedroom door opening startled me out of my thoughts the next morning. I sat up. Juba lifted his head and sniffed. I peered around the corner, expecting to see Mabel, but found a maid of ten or eleven instead. She had short, black hair, a wide face with a pert little nose, and narrow almond-shaped eyes so dark they were almost black. If I hadn't known better, I'd have said she was from the lower tribes of the Southern Network. But why would she be working in the Arck? The castle in the Western Network was a far cry from what I assumed to be her homeland.

The little girl carried a tray into the room and set it in front of me. She bowed low to Juba and scurried backward out the door. When she returned, she lugged a heavy bucket into the room. Frothy water sloshed onto her dress and apron, spilling over the top of a heavy black-bristled brush. At her age, she should be able to use magic to levitate the bucket into the room. Unless she was from the Southern Network and couldn't do magic anymore, of course.

"Merry meet," I said, touching the sleeve of her simple dress as she walked past. "Thank you for the food."

She leaped away. Her bucket of water tipped over, sloshing across the floor in foamy waves.

"Oh, I'm sorry," I said, rushing forward. "I'm so sorry. I didn't mean to startle you. My name is Bianca. Let me help you clean that up."

She scrambled back, fear in her eyes. I stopped and held out my palms in a gesture of peace.

"It's all right."

She stared at me like she didn't understand, so I switched to the common language spoken through all the Networks.

"Name?" I asked.

Her lips pressed together. Her skinny shoulders, too scrawny to carry such a heavy burden, trembled. She looked back at the spilled water, and tears filled her eyes. I used silent magic to cast a simple incantation, and the water slid backward, gathering itself into the overturned bucket, which righted itself once the water and scrubbing brush returned. Her eyes widened.

"Hot," I said, motioning to the steaming water. The words and accent felt cumbersome, but her shoulders relaxed. "Be . . . uh . . . careful."

Juba stalked toward us, his teeth half-bared. She squeaked and ran out the door, a small silver manacle flashing off her ankle as she disappeared. Satisfied, Juba circled lazily on the spot and sprawled his long, supple body across the middle of the floor.

"You're a bully," I hissed. He licked his lips and yawned.

Perturbed, I returned to the breakfast tray to find a small, round loaf of bread and a few scattered seeds on a small plate. The bread was only the size of my fist, but when I picked it up, it was so dense I imagined it would fill me up for a while. Next to it sat several sprigs of parsley and mint and a thin, shallow jar of olive oil. I wondered if I was supposed to grind the herbs up into the oil.

Grandmother loved the smell of parsley, I thought, reminiscing with a little smile as I twirled the green twig. The flailing leaves gave me a moment of pause.

Parsley.

And mint.

"*When you can't sleep,*" Grandmother had always told me, "*just blend together dried parsley, mint, cinnamon, and sage to make a sleeping potion. If you combine it with the right spell and put a little sprinkle of it in your warm tea, it'll put you right to sleep.*"

I cast a sidelong glance at Juba.

Put you right to sleep, eh? I thought.

I slipped both herb sprigs into my undergarment. They'd dry out on a high shelf in the bathroom soon enough in the desert air. A few more days of herbs like this, and I'd have enough parsley and mint to start the potion. But where to get cinnamon and sage? I doubted they had much sage around here.

I'll find it, I thought. *Somehow.*

Because one never knew when a sleeping potion could come in handy.

The most unusual event caught my attention in the twilight hours that evening: Juba was snoring.

I stared at him for several minutes in disbelief. Could it be real? He didn't move from his lazy, post-dinner slumber. Not even a twitch. I coughed. Nothing. The soft patter of my bare feet walking across the stone floor didn't rouse him either. He stirred for a moment and resumed snoring.

"Suspicious," I whispered.

A sound on the balcony caught my ear. I turned toward it, my breath held. Though I saw nothing but a black velvet sky studded with stars behind the rippling red rock wall, I tensed. Something—or someone—was there. I crept out to the balcony and peered down.

"Zane?" I whispered. "Is that you?"

"Sure is."

I cast a wary glance back at Juba, who snored on. Zane worked his way farther up the wall, wearing a hooded garment the exact color of the rock. His piercing eyes met mine as he pulled himself up to come face to face with me, clinging to the rock wall with no rope to secure him.

"Good," he said with a pleased little huff. "I'm in the right place."

"Why are you free climbing?"

"Just in case Mabel's tracking the use of magic around here some-how," he said, only slightly out of breath. "I've often found that the easiest way to beat magic is to not use it at all. This way she'll have nothing to detect."

So simple and uncomplicated it could work.

His fingertips dug into the wall. His nostrils flared as he shifted, getting a more comfortable grip. Thankfully, his arms weren't trembling with fatigue yet, and a small lip in the rock provided an adequate rest for his feet, but we wouldn't have much time.

"I can't help you," I said, lifting my manacled wrist. "Or else I'd give you my hand. This stops me from moving past the balustrade. Last time I tried, it knocked me out. Probably just as well. I think the balcony is enchanted to blow up anything that falls too far over the edge."

"Ah, yes. Of course she has magic in place, as I suspected. Is it Almorran magic?" he asked, studying the manacle. I lifted it in the flickering torchlight.

"I don't know."

"It's not," he said under his breath, shaking his head. "I should have known right away. It's Cudan magic. I've seen it before. Actually used a few spells from the Cudans myself. For as strong as it is, the magic is pretty simple. But I'm still surprised she didn't use Almorran magic, which would have been even stronger."

"Cudan?" I repeated, vaguely remembering one of the books on Mabel's shelf. "I've never heard of the Cudans before."

Zane shrugged. "They were an old, conservative group of witches that lived in the Central and Eastern Networks eight hundred years ago, I think. They didn't like things like transportation or transformation—said it wasn't natural for witches to be animals and travel instantly. They didn't create a lot of spells, but the ones they did craft were reliable. Mostly defensive. Kept to themselves. Kind of a strange group, if you ask me."

A prickling sensation ran up the back of my neck.

"Did the Cudans create a spell that uses flames to protect a doorway?" I asked wryly.

"Yes," he said. "Many spells like that. If that's what Mabel's using, she's done her homework. The Cudans aren't well known anymore. Your father and I use their magic sometimes."

"Hmm," I said, not reassured by his appraisal of her skills. I'd have rather considered her a lesser enemy, but I knew she was thorough and intelligent. Zane's quick eyes darted around the balcony.

"It doesn't feel like any of this magic is Almorran."

His observation forced me to think back over my imprisonment. Why wasn't it Almorran magic? She was the Almorran Master, but she didn't seem to use it often. Or, in retrospect, at all.

"Seems odd, doesn't it?"

He looked at me with a serious expression, and I realized he meant for me to answer. "Yes," I said. "It is strange."

"How are you?" he asked. "Are you doing all right?"

"Yes," I said. "Tell Papa I'm doing all right. Really."

"Is your magic under control?"

I reared back, startled. Being kidnapped and trying to find a way out had kept me so occupied I hadn't even thought about my magic. It had only been two days, but I felt no building energy.

"Fine so far, actually," I said, brushing a lock of hair out of my eyes. "I suppose I've been distracted enough that it hasn't been too bad yet."

Zane stared at the healing bite on my arm. "What happened?" he asked, motioning to it.

"The cheetah, Juba, thought I was too close to Mabel my first night here," I said, keeping my response light and unbothered. No reason to worry him or, by extension, Papa. "It's not as bad as it looks. I'm surprised he hasn't come out yet."

"I drugged him," Zane said, his eyes inspecting the doorway to Mabel's chamber. Dim candles illuminated a few areas of her room, but the light was weak at best. "Put a small potion in his food before they brought it up here."

"Oh?" I asked, forcing nonchalance. "Seems like it worked."

What a novel idea.

"I've had run-ins with his type," he said, studying the layout of the balcony. "It never ends well." He pointed up. "Have you ever seen anyone on the balcony up there?"

I glanced up. "No."

"Hmmm. Also," Zane continued, with all the breeziness of someone who came for tea, "I can't tell if he's a witch who's transforming into a cheetah or just an exceptionally trained cat."

"I'm almost positive he's a transformed witch."

"Then it's likely he's been transformed for a very long time, as the magic is faint, which means he's becoming the animal he's changed into. A common mistake."

Zane whipped his head around to study the other side of the Arck wall. Despite his position grasping the stone like a spider monkey, he didn't seem to stop moving. His eyes narrowed on something inside while he murmured to himself, no doubt memorizing whatever he could see from his perch.

"How did you keep Papa from coming?" I asked.

"Stella made him sign a binding that he wouldn't come to the Western Network and try to save you."

I sighed with relief. If Papa lost his head and acted rashly, it would only result in greater devastation for all of us. I couldn't bear the thought of the Central Network losing the war because of me. Zane raised his eyebrows as if he agreed with my thoughts.

"That doesn't mean he's happy about it," he said, and I imagined Papa pacing across his office, tearing his hands through his hair until it stood on end.

"I'm gathering information before we act," he said. "I have a few ideas about how to break you out."

"Be careful, Zane," I said. "Mabel . . . she's . . . different. I don't know how to explain it." My hands wrung together until the knuckles blanched white. "I couldn't bear it if something happened to you while you were trying to save me. Please don't do anything risky."

"All the more reason to get you out."

A bead of sweat streaked down his face. His fingertips had turned white, and his arms trembled. He wouldn't last much longer clinging to the wall.

"What about Isadora?" I asked. "I'm worried Mabel will kill her, if she hasn't already."

"We're still looking," he said crisply, shutting down the conversation. A sore spot, no doubt, now that six weeks had passed, and Zane and his group of Protectors still hadn't been able to find her.

A commotion in the marketplace drew my attention. Two swarthy West Guards grabbed a witch by the neck and hauled him away from a tent. It suddenly seemed like Zane had been here an eternity. The idea of Mabel—or a West Guard—finding him made me physically sick.

"You better go," I said. "Before you're seen."

He glanced over his shoulder. His head tilted to the side, motioning toward the humming marketplace below. "All right. Well, hold tight, kid. I'll be back."

"Wait!" I said. "Can you do me a favor?"

"What?"

"I need two herbs."

His eyebrows rose. "Herbs?"

"Cinnamon and sage. Can you find me three sticks of cinnamon and a small packet of sage?"

He hesitated, his eyes narrowing. "What for?"

I swallowed. Zane would discourage my attempts. Scouting and spying on Mabel was his job. But he wasn't a prisoner locked in the very castle that I felt certain held the counter magic—and the old Watcher—that we needed. If I could get past Juba, I could likely gain access to things that Zane wouldn't be able to find. Like Isadora. The opportunity was too great to pass up.

"A little experiment," I said. He kept his bold gaze locked on mine, and when I didn't back away, he gave in.

"Fine," he said. "How am I going to get them to you?"

"Oh . . . I don't know. I didn't think that far ahead," I said, wracking my brain. "I . . . uh . . ."

He brushed it off. "Never mind. I'll figure it out." His eyes tapered, shrinking to mere slits. "Just don't do anything stupid, all right? I know you. You're just like your father."

"Of course not," I whispered, managing a smile. "Thanks."

"I'll check on you even though you may not see me. Don't attempt to contac—"

The sound of the bedroom door slamming against the wall made me jump. I stepped back to see Mabel striding into the room, her black dress waving in plumes behind her. Juka trotted at her side. My heart leaped into my throat.

"Niko, you fool!" she cried, throwing a glass at the wall. Wine sprayed on the red rock, and the glass shattered into a million prisms.

Juba started awake, instantly alert though his eyes were pinpricks. I doubted he even realized he'd been drugged.

"Foolish child!"

Mabel hurled a chair against the wall. She balled her hands into fists, stood in the middle of the room, and screamed at the top of her lungs. It echoed through the chamber, sending Juba running in his disoriented stupor. Juka slinked away, her tail tucked between her legs.

My heart took courage. Mabel's rage against Niko likely meant he'd finalized an alliance with Papa. *Good,* I thought with relief. At least things were moving forward.

When I looked back into the shadows, Zane was already gone.

Be Strong

"Come on, little troublemaker," Merrick taunted me from behind. "You can run faster than that."

A field of green stretched in all directions, littered with the pink and blue petals of spring flowers. Letum Wood loomed tall and dark in the distance, competing only with Chatham Castle for space. I sprinted through the Forgotten Gardens and onto a trail, cutting through the bracken like a swift wind.

"That's better," he called. "Run like something is chasing you."

"Something is chasing me!"

The sound of his deep voice laughing made my heart quiver. When I glanced over my shoulder, he winked.

I jerked awake from the dream with a gasp.

Was it a dream? No. A memory. When I concentrated, I smelled the subtle scent of evergreen that always clung to Merrick's clothes. Felt the warm dirt between my toes and the stones in the trail. When the recollection became too real, I forced it away. The last tendrils slipped away from me, and I rolled onto my side.

White stars poked through the inky sky outside the Arck, decorating the night with swirls of light. Darkness had long since settled over the castle. Mabel and Juka breathed softly in bed, while Juba lay on the floor, his tail twitching dangerously close to my feet. I fantasized about stepping on it.

Juba's head rose the same moment I heard the lightest scuffle on the balcony. Both of us looked outside. A second, subtle little *snuff* sounded. I sat up. A lone figure crouched behind the biggest cactus, trying to hide but failing. The edge of a sleeve glowed in the moonlight. My mind went immediately to Papa, but I dismissed the thought. He'd never make such a rookie mistake, and he'd promised Stella not to come. Zane wouldn't attempt anything while Mabel was in the room, and no other Protector would be assigned to me. No, this was someone else entirely. But who would crouch on Mabel's balcony?

Juba growled low in his throat, rocking his hind legs back and forth. The crouching witch remained motionless. The ridge of hair along Juba's back stood up, creating a supple, speckled line from head to tail. Mabel's breathing paused. She'd woken but hadn't moved.

The witch leaped out from behind the cactus the same moment a blinding burst of light filled the room. I recoiled, throwing my arms in front of my face. The light disappeared, replaced by a shrill scream of pain. When I regained sight, Juba had sunk his claws into the broad back of a male witch attempting to scramble back over the cacti on the balcony. The intruder hadn't expected Juba.

Extensive, detailed tattoos covered the witch's arms and neck, indicating he was from the clans of the Western Network. His clothes were shabby and torn, as if they'd been worn and washed too many times. I could see his ribs, bony elbows, and knobby knees. He screamed, his head snapping back from the force of Juba's body landing on his spine. His eyes met mine in horror. I stifled a yelp by sucking in a sharp breath.

Juba's jaws wrapped around the front of the witch's neck, silencing his desperate howls. Juka straightened from her position on the bed and stared, remaining close to Mabel's side.

"Good work, Juba," Mabel said, yawning. She shifted underneath the sheets and settled again with a little sigh, as if this were a frequent occurrence.

Stay here long enough, and you'll find out, she had said.

The gauzy drapes whispered in the room on a breeze from the open balcony door. A puddle of blood shone in the moonlight beneath the dead, desperate soul. The body faced the ground, face turned away from me. I closed my eyes, covered my ears with my hands, and buried my face in the floor, humming a lullaby Mama used to sing when

I had nightmares. The horror of the grisly death replayed in my mind until the sun rose in the early morning hours.

Juba licked his lips when I woke up, staring at me from only a few paces away.

A slight, almost indecipherable, drop in temperature ushered the Western Network out of summer and into the first month of fall. A week after Mabel kidnapped me, I woke, sweaty and sore, to find her towering over me, kicking my ribs with her pointy shoe.

"Wake up," she said, dropping a ball of fabric on my face. "We have things to do today. I want to show you something."

She'd given me a fresh linen dress with capped sleeves, a long waist ending at my hips, and a rounded neckline, just like the dresses the silent maid had brought me. When Mabel stepped away, I changed, grateful to slide into something fresh and longing for a tub of water instead of the pitcher baths with which I'd been making do.

"Where are you taking me?" I asked. She wore a radiant red gown with complicated black lace over the bodice. It highlighted the glow in her eyes. The familiar *Book of Contracts* rested in her thin arms, held tight to her side. I stared at it. Did she still carry it around all the time? Even under the protection of her own castle? Her paranoia knew no bounds.

Juba growled when he noticed my keen attention, so I took a step away from Mabel. He quieted, but still watched me. The fading bruises and still-healing teeth marks on my arm were warning enough.

"I thought you might like to see the extent of my power," she said.

Her lip curled in disgust when she grabbed my arm and transported both of us away. When I emerged from the pressure and darkness, I found myself in a cavernous room filled with witches. Voices, bells, and the occasional low bellow of a camel rang through the organized chaos. The room smelled like wet hay.

Mabel released me with a flick of her hand. "Witches are flocking to my side and swearing themselves to my power on a weekly basis, as you can see. Everyone wants a piece of the new life I offer, Bianca." She gave me a sidelong glance. "You should think about it."

Mabel loved attention, so I gave her none and acted as if I hadn't heard her.

Two small waterfalls drained from holes in the ceiling and trickled down the striated rock walls, forming a small creek that cut through the middle of the room and flowed out the southern end. A glass dome protected the water, preventing any witch from getting a drink that wasn't rationed for them. Desert life was more intensely restricted than I had anticipated.

A crowd of witches filled one side of the room, congregating in close-knit, family-like groups and speaking in hushed whispers. Their almond-shaped eyes and sun-wrinkled, cinnamon-colored skin indicated they were from the native tribes of the Southern Network, like the little maid. Wealthy witches like Mikhail had forced them to the mountainous outer reaches of the Southern Network, where it snowed most of the year. Discarded fur coats littered the ground. They wore leather pants tied to their legs and waists with cords of rope. The strange chatter of their language—one I'd never heard before— echoed off the red rock walls. Had the young maid been here once?

A skinny, frail witch with a white turban and wide nose walked up to Mabel's side and bowed until his forehead grazed the floor. Behind him, a cluster of West Guards formed a semicircle.

"Your Omniscience," the witch in the turban said. "It is a blessing to see you this morning."

"You may rise."

He moved slowly, keeping his eyes down. Mabel's foot tapped, making the hem of her dress dance.

"It is my deepest desire to swear these new witches into our way of life," he said. "Do I have your all-powerful permission?"

The phrase *our way of life* belied her claim that they swore the new witches to her power. Mabel handed him the tattered *Book of Contracts*. The leather on the front cover had torn in a strip down the middle, and the frayed corners sprouted hairs like baby spider legs.

"You have my permission," she said. "Please proceed."

A West Guard stood on a tall platform in the corner with a scroll in his hand from which he bellowed out names. Each time he read a name, a witch in the crowd stepped forward and put their hand on the *Book of Contracts*. Every male witch that cooperated received a small leather bag of water and a sword before disappearing into another room. The women received a bag and an apron and walked to the opposite side of the giant cavern to vanish through a doorway. I wondered if the married couples would ever see each other again.

As the strange ceremony continued without interruption, I bottled up my questions. Mabel would certainly feel good about herself if I showed any interest, so I didn't ask, although I drank in every detail.

"Ah, a little family," Mabel said, motioning to a young couple that stepped forward together. The girl appeared to be not much older than I. "Isn't it sweet? I'm giving them a life. Probably not together, of course, but that doesn't matter. I'm sure they'll be more comfortable under my reign than they were eating whale blubber in the horrid, cold regions of the Southern Network."

My stomach roiled. The boy—he could hardly be called a man with such young features—stood protectively in front of his slim wife. She clung to a baby hanging in a loose sling from her shoulders.

"The wife will work for me, of course. Her baby will go into service as soon as he's old enough to wash dishes," Mabel said in an idle, conversational tone, patting her lips with her fingers when she yawned. "Her husband will have the privilege of becoming a West Guard."

The young man had a steely expression, and the girl looked as if she were about to weep. I wanted to ask what would happen to them if they didn't swear loyalty, but I didn't. In the end, I didn't really want to know. The manacles on their ankles told me they weren't volunteering.

A West Guard stepped forward, ripping the young man from his wife before they could embrace. She let out a cry and clutched her baby tighter. Her husband said something in a low voice before they were torn apart. I didn't need to know their language to understand what he meant.

Be strong, he seemed to say. *It's not forever.*

That's what Merrick would say to me, I thought. When the girl clutched her baby and stumbled away at sword point, my throat thickened.

"Ugh," Mabel said under her breath. "This always takes forever. But you know how it goes, Bianca. I must oversee things, or they won't be done correctly. No one else should have power unless I give it to them. Witches can't be trusted with magic. That's why the Almorran system is so wonderful. I control the power and give it to those who are worthy, rich or poor, young or old. The rest work for the common good of the world."

Each recruit passed through an arch beneath us, bowing to Mabel before they left. None of them dared raise their eyes to her. I remained as far back as I could, hoping to hide in the shadows. No doubt my plain dress, braided hair, and the shining, heavy manacle on my wrist would make it obvious that I was just property like the rest of them, but I didn't want to run the chance that anyone would associate me with her.

Soon an old man approached the book. A West Guard escorted him, keeping a sharp knife jabbed into his curved spine. When the old man made no move to put his hand on the *Book of Contracts,* the West Guard grabbed his wrist and held it there. It trembled, rope-like veins crawling through his old skin like green ribbons. The old man shook his head again when the West Guard barked a command. Mabel straightened, raising one eyebrow.

"Interesting," she murmured. The West Guard slammed the old man's hand onto the book, but nothing changed. He shook his head again. A stoic strength came over his small, wrinkled body, and I saw hints of my father in his steely jaw and straight shoulders.

Mabel leaned back in her throne with a little sigh. "His choice," she said. "They can't complain that I don't give them agency."

She waved a hand when the West Guard looked to her for direction. The old man's chest arched forward as the West Guard stabbed a curved blade through his body. The tip protruded from his chest, gleaming bright red. The old man struggled; a few witches in the crowd cried out. Then, with his head held high, he turned his wrinkled face to Mabel. With a regal, proud nod, he slumped over in death.

I turned away, my eyes heavy with tears. Another name rang through the cavern.

"Lovely process, isn't it?" Mabel asked. "It gives me so much more power to have all these witches devote themselves to my magic. I can feel it in my blood every time we hold a swearing-in ceremony." Mabel bit her bottom lip, sinking lower in the throne, holding onto the armrests as if she were in danger of flying away. Her eyes glowed bright red. "And I do love power."

How scared she must be that she doesn't have enough. Papa never bragged about his abilities. He didn't even believe he was as powerful as most witches thought him to be, which was only part of his greatness. All of Mabel's gloating just made her seem . . . frightened. Desperate for more, but more was never enough.

"What are you hoping to accomplish with all this?" I asked, gesturing to the witches below us. "You'll never be stronger than Papa. Not through means like this."

Her voice grew cold with annoyance. "I'm bringing about a new world, of course," she said. "One in which magic is controlled."

"You sound like Evelyn."

Mabel rolled her eyes. "I'm smarter than that old fool. Evelyn wanted to establish a hierarchy based on wealth. I don't care who's wealthy. I care who is using magic and what they're doing with it. That's why the High Priests of old came up with Almorran magic, you know. The witches fighting the mortals, casting curses everywhere, endangering the lives of all concerned. The High Priests of Almorra were just trying to protect everyone."

"They ended up slaughtering mortals and witches," I pointed out. "You may think they had good intentions, but they didn't."

Mabel shrugged. "Things went awry. It happens. But it won't under my reign because I'm stronger than they were."

I wanted to ask her if things went *awry* when she killed my mother, but I held it in. Mama's murder had been deliberate. A choice.

Just like how much I hate Mabel. The thought took me aback.

Just as my confusion swelled to new heights, whispers from her mind replayed back through my head, flashes I barely remembered because they were buried so deep in the darkness.

Make the fire stop! a young girl screamed. *I'll get it right next time.*

The terror faded in a flash, but it left me feeling cold. What she'd endured as a child at her grandmother's hand had been horrifying. Is that what led her to such grand delusions? I tried to turn the thoughts away. I wanted to despise Mabel as much as she despised me, but I couldn't find the energy. I'd shared her pain for what felt like eternities, and a traitorous sense of pity chased away my loathing.

Mabel was still talking, as if she didn't really care whether I listened.

"Under my reign, witches won't be cursed," she said. "Magic won't be used to harm others unless it's in punishment for breaking my law."

"You're banishing the use of curses?" I asked. "How ironic."

"I'm stopping the use of magic unless approved." Her eyes gleamed. "I'm preventing waste and . . ." She trailed off. When she spoke again, her voice sounded forced. "Pain."

"So you'll establish a system that witches must obey, and if they don't, you'll punish them with magic?"

"Yes."

The faded memory of Mabel's screams surfaced in my mind again, only this time with more clarity. There had been agony. No, not just agony. Burning. Magical fire on her skin. But why? Oh. A missed homework question.

"Sounds familiar," I quipped.

Mabel responded with a sharp intake of breath. She clenched her hand around the chair until her knuckles blanched white. I held my breath, certain she'd turn and choke me at any moment. Her body trembled. She turned to look at me for the first time. Despite the terror of her glowing red eyes, I didn't look away. I wondered if she remembered everything she saw while in *my* head.

"You know nothing, Bianca Monroe," she hissed, turning back to her army. I let out my breath.

"Don't forget how powerful I am," she said, returning to her light, conversational prattle, as if we had never deviated. "You're only seeing the physical aspects of my growing influence throughout Antebellum. The magic is . . ." She released a long, slow breath. "Empowering. Fascinating. It makes me stronger than you could ever hope to be."

As the swearing-in ceremony continued, I lingered back, unable to watch the innocent witches choose between two terrible fates. Despite trying my hardest to merge the two Mabels in my mind—the tortured soul crying out in pain and the sadistic Almorran Master who stood before me—I couldn't reconcile them. Of all the things I'd experienced at Mabel's hand, nothing was so terrible and confusing as the realization that beneath all the indifference and evil and cunning, Mabel had once been a witch just like me.

I Am Nothing

The Cudan witches fostered a rare breed of paranoia during the two hundred years of their existence, which took place largely on the border of the Eastern Network and the Central Network.

Despite the enormous magical advancements of their day—namely transformation and transportation—which would later reform the entire world of magic as it had been known since the time of the Mortal Wars, the Cudans staunchly held to the belief that neither transformation nor transportation was "good for the witch," as it was "against nature."

Since neither transformation nor transportation were yet perfected, the spells at times produced separated bodies, witches who could not leave their transformed state, and a few well-known witches who wandered around with whiskers and tails.

The Cudans remained isolated, keeping the new-world magic well out of their borders through indifference and a strictly conservative culture.

I closed the heavy book's faded leather binding, my mind buzzing with thought. A group of witches so adamantly opposed to transformative magic might not have worried about transformation at all within their community. If the magic was new—and better yet, unfamiliar—they wouldn't have known its intricacies.

Which meant they might not have protected themselves against it.

I gazed at the doorway. I'd never get through it as myself, but what if I transformed into something else? Could I move through the doorway as another creature? It would have to be a native, local animal, of course. One that wouldn't alert the maids if they stumbled on it in the halls unexpectedly. I didn't want to draw attention to myself.

Juba yawned, sprawling across the cool floor, stretching his limbs to their limits. An idea percolated in my mind.

Something local like Juba.

"How very interesting," I said, setting the book aside when the little maid's familiar tap tap tap sounded at the door. After today, I'd have enough parsley for the sleeping potion if the cooks included another sprig in the meal.

The little maid stood in the doorway, a tray in her hand, like every day before. Only today her eyes darted to mine, then to Juba, then back to me as she set the breakfast tray down in the doorway. The usual round loaf of seeded bread sat in the middle of the plate, but it came with nothing else. My stomach fell in disappointment. No parsley. Her hands trembled as she backed away, and she pattered out on bare feet as fast as she could go. I watched her leave, stymied. The poor little thing had always been frightened of Juba but had taken to smiling shyly at me the past couple of days.

I reached for the small loaf of bread but stopped when I heard an unusual rustle. My heart sped up. The smallest corner of an envelope peeked out from beneath the bread. A hint of cinnamon wafted into the air.

Herbs from Zane.

No wonder the small girl was nervous. She must have known. I shifted to the left, stretching to grab a book just barely out of reach while also blocking Juba's view of the tray with my body. With my right hand, I slipped my fingers underneath the bread, wrapped them around the small brown packet, and slipped it into my undergarment just as my left hand grasped the book. When I straightened, Juba huffed and laid his head on top of his paws, none the wiser.

Good work, Zane, I thought with a surge of pride. *Now all I have to do is practice transform—*

Juba shot to his feet, his hackles high and his nose in the air. I startled, my heart racing. Had he noticed me grabbing the herbs?

He sniffed and stepped back uneasily. I straightened, the hair on the back of my neck standing up. Juba wasn't my friend, but he had uncanny instincts. Something must be happening. To my great surprise, Mabel sashayed into the room with bloodstains on her skirt.

She moved as deliberately as a hand fasting march. Juka trailed behind, her ears down, casting wary eyes on her master. Blood streaked Mabel's jaw and splattered across her cheeks in little red dots. Her unfocused eyes burned as red as coals. I stood and backed away, reaching behind my back for a mosaic-glass vase. If she had finally given in to her insanity, I wouldn't go down without a fight.

"It's an interesting thing, Almorran magic," Mabel said, her eyes wide and dilated. "Very interesting. It feels so wonderful. So strong. Without it, I am nothing. Nothing."

"Is that your blood?" I asked, swallowing. The sharp edges of the vase bit into my palm when I tightened my grip. It wouldn't make for much of a weapon against the Almorran Master, but I felt better with something solid in my hand.

She grinned but made no response as she stopped in front of the window and gazed out at the vast undulations of sand beyond the capital city of Custos. Heat lines wavered from side to side, breaking up the horizontal monotony. Juka disappeared between the gauzy curtains.

"There's so much Derek doesn't know," Mabel said. A slow, gradual laugh bubbled from her chest until she screeched with mirth, nearly doubled over. "He's a fool to stand against me. An ignorant fool!"

She's mad. She's finally snapped.

Juba's ear twitched. He looked outside and lifted his nose again. When I strained to hear, a familiar wail rang through the marketplace. Mabel's laughter ceased. She whipped around with a hiss, wild eyes on the balcony.

"Silence!" she screamed.

A cold feeling sank in my stomach. The same mournful chant had sounded through the West when their High Priest, Almack, died over a year earlier. The cries seemed to come from the camps to the east. Mabel clenched her fists until her knuckles turned white.

"He had to die!" she said, speaking in a steady, chugging cadence. "He was a danger. Watchers must die. They must die for what they see, for what they know. He was not powerful anymore. No, I am the only powerful one. They saw him as a leader. He must not be a leader. Must not."

Watchers must die? Her rage against Watchers wasn't new. Throughout history, many witches had feared their ability to see future possibilities, while others coveted it, sometimes imprisoning them and forcing them, under torture, to reveal what they saw. Isadora's likely fate now that Mabel had taken her. Limiting the use of Watchers to benign purposes, such as student placement in the Network School system, had been a peacemaking attempt during the formation of the Mansfeld Pact. But why was Mabel railing against them now?

Mabel ripped her hands through her hair and paced back and forth, the many layers of her elaborate green gown rustling with every step. Her words played in my mind.

They saw him as a leader.

He was not powerful anymore.

Since Watchers often kept their gifts secret, I only knew of one other Watcher.

"Dane," I whispered. "You killed Dane, didn't you?"

Dane—a Watcher not nearly as powerful as Isadora—had run the Western Network during Almack's illness. Once Almack died, Dane took over as High Priest and served under Angelina's direction during Mabel's imprisonment. I hadn't known what had happened to him once Mabel killed Angelina and returned to the West; he'd just seemed to fade into Mabel's shadow. That she'd killed a Watcher who served her surely meant Mabel had lost her sanity.

"No!" she yelled. "The magic killed Dane. Don't you see? The magic did! I'm just the vessel, the carrier of something far greater than myself. It's so strong. It does what it wants." She stopped pacing to laugh again, low, long, and deep. Her back curved, and she tucked her chin into her chest with a breathy laugh. "All this time I worked for control, and it does what it wants."

Juba had disappeared, no doubt hiding with Juka. Had Mabel finally broken? Would she—or the magic—decide I had lived long enough?

Mabel fell silent. She straightened and stared out the window, her jaw tight and eyes constricted. Her hands relaxed. She breathed easier. The hysterical energy abated.

"Get out of my sight, Bianca," she said, her voice weak with exhaustion. "Do not speak of this ever again, or I'll cut your tongue out."

I hesitated only a moment before making a wide arc around her, the vase still in my grip. I stepped out onto the balcony and sat with my back against the wall, staring at the horizon where the sky met the sand, desperately trying to remember everything I knew about transformative magic.

Tomorrow, I promised myself. *I will start practicing transformation tomorrow.*

I feared I had almost run out of time.

When I stood up the next morning and headed for the bathroom, Juba followed suit, glaring at me with narrowed eyes. Whether he sensed my nerves or was just being his usual, overbearing self, I couldn't tell.

"Calm down," I said to him. "I'm just going to wash up in the bathroom."

He slinked along behind me until he stood a few paces from the door, where he collapsed on the ground with feline indifference. I carried the white porcelain pitcher filled with fresh water into the bathroom and bolted the wooden door behind me. The bolt slid back, and I scowled. Mabel's protective magic wouldn't even let me lock myself in to take a bath.

Or *pretend* to take a bath.

A tub with tarnished clawed feet and a rounded lip ran along the wall. Next to it stood a shelf stocked with towels and washcloths. Unfortunately, Mabel wouldn't spare precious water for a prisoner like me, so I wouldn't have a lot of time to practice transformation before Juba became suspicious. No matter how good my acting job, I couldn't justify thirty minutes for a pitcher bath.

A long, thin wooden bench ran along one wall. I reached behind it, reassured when my fingertips brushed my stash of drying parsley. It would have to be enough, for no more had come today. Despite the hot, dry air, it would still be another day or two before I could grind all the herbs into a fine enough powder to blend with the slab of meat Juba received some mornings.

I used a spell to splash the water in the pitcher, making it sound like I was taking a sponge bath, and sat on the edge of the deep tub. Priscilla had taught me detailed work with transformative magic a few times, but she'd focused mostly on smaller objects, like my hair, nose, or clothing. Changing my entire body into a different creature was another matter, requiring a more precise execution of the magic. I'd never attempted such large-scale transformation. Unfortunately, my limited experience would have to suffice.

"All right," I whispered, blowing out one long, uncertain breath. I banished my lingering, hesitant thoughts. "I can do this. I have to do this. I'll start small and work up."

Only confidence, Priscilla always said during our transformation lessons. *Otherwise you'll be distracted, and your transformations won't come out perfect. The magic can sense any hesitation.*

I didn't have much margin for error. No, I had *no* margin for error.

Thankfully, transformation only altered the physical aspects, which would leave me full control over my mental capacities. For a while, at least. I shuddered at the thought of turning to the wild side, like Juba, and not coming back out of the magic. Of course, there were worse animals to change into. At least a cheetah could run fast.

I picked up a bar of soap and closed my eyes, conjuring up a clear image of Juba in my mind. Not difficult, considering we spent all day with each other. Once I had a mental image of him, I set the magic to work.

The bar of soap levitated in the air in a swirl of light. It rotated for a few seconds and began to elongate. A tail formed. A head. Two ears. Patches of fur sprouted along the long, elegant spine of a cheetah the size of my palm. Keeping all my concentration on directing the magic required a great deal of mental capacity, but I persevered until the baby cheetah let out a growl that sounded more like a squeak. He fell into my waiting hand.

"It worked!" I whispered in disbelief. He had several bald spots, his nose was purple, and one ear was long and floppy while the other was short, but he moved and breathed. A solid start. Now I knew I could make a cheetah. Next, I'd have to practice with parts of the whole.

The shuffle of Juba's paws outside the bathroom door drew my attention. He snarled and butted the door with his head. I clamped a hand over the tiny cheetah's mouth and paused.

"I'm hurrying," I said, forcing exasperation into my tone. "Jikes. A girl can't even take her time with a bath."

Juba paused. He sniffed under the door, and I held my breath. Did he detect my magic? Smell the tiny cheetah? With haste, I used the counter spell to reverse the transformation. Five seconds later, the cheetah pulled back together, forming a misshapen blob of soap that oozed through my fingers. Clearly I still had some work to do.

I splashed water on my face and hands just as the door blew open, slamming into my shoulder. Juba pressed his way in, his eyes narrowed and teeth bared.

"Calm down," I muttered, slinging the remaining soap back into the wooden box.

With casual ease, I rinsed the soap off my hands, wiped my face, and slipped past him into the main chamber, my heart pounding. Juba lingered for only a moment, whipping his head from side to side in search of something he couldn't find. I settled back on the divan, buried myself in a book, and let my muscles relax with relief. Putting difficult spells into work had settled some of my prickly, agitated magic.

First attempt down, I thought, looking down at my arms and imagining them with fur. *Next time I'll change myself.*

Slow, thudding footsteps moved down the hallway toward my prison the next day. Ten seconds later, a familiar pair of dark youthful eyes peered around the corner and looked right at me. The little maid was back.

I jerked my head toward Mabel's curtained-off bedroom.

"She's here," I mouthed.

The young girl disappeared back into the hall but reappeared with a familiar bucket and mop. I couldn't help but feel disappointed—with Mabel around, I had no hope of getting answers out of the little girl. A rustle behind the curtains announced Mabel's entrance into the open living space. She strolled forward, her bright red eyes trained on the maid. The girl froze, her eyes wide.

A wrinkled garment dangled from the tip of Mabel's finger. She stopped halfway across the room.

"Do you see this, Zoe?" Mabel asked.

Zoe, I thought with triumph. Finally, a name! Zoe tensed, her shoulders pulled back. Her eyes flickered to the doorway and back to Mabel.

"There's a stain on this dress," Mabel said, lifting it higher in the air. An oily, black substance smeared the fabric, as if someone had used it to try to clean up spilled ink. I looked at Mabel's desk out of the corner of my eye. A half-full inkwell sat a hand's-breadth from the edge.

"What is this stain, Zoe?" Mabel asked.

Zoe stood still, her eyes wide. She hadn't moved. The two of them stared at each other like a predator and prey about to run to the death. I braced my feet and scooted to the front of my chair, ready to spring at any moment. When Zoe didn't respond, Mabel spoke again in the common language. Zoe paled. She shook her head. Her left foot slipped back just a little, giving her a wider stance.

Mabel lifted an eyebrow. "You wouldn't know anything about the missing ink then, would you?" she asked in the common language again, her voice a sing-song. I translated in my head, frantically trying to recall the conjugated words.

"You didn't spill the ink one day while collecting my laundry, then ball the garment up and stuff it under my mattress?" Mabel's nostrils flared.

Zoe slipped back another step. Her hair swayed around her jaw as she swallowed and shook her head. Her knees knocked together.

"You did it!" Mabel screamed, stomping three steps toward the girl. "I know you did!"

I shot to my feet. "No," I cried. "I did it!"

Both Mabel and Zoe turned to me at the same time. Mabel's eyes narrowed. "No, you didn't," she hissed. "I know this pathetic brat is guilty."

Whether Zoe did or did not spill something on the dress didn't matter. She'd die if Mabel caught her, and enough witches had suffered that fate while I watched.

"Yes, I did." I started forward, stopping mid-stride when Juba growled from behind me. "It was me," I said, keeping a wary eye on him. "I used the ink the first day I got here."

Mabel's eyes became slits. "What for?" she asked.

"I . . . I was trying to grease the manacle and pull it off. It was the only liquid I could find. I panicked when I realized you'd figure it out, so I grabbed the dress, cleaned up the ink, and shoved the whole mess under your mattress."

"You would have used magic to clean it up," Mabel said, but her eyes lingered on me as if she wasn't quite sure.

"Why?" I countered. "It's not like I expected you to conduct regular checks under your mattress for anything. Besides, most cleaning spells require water, and you don't give me enough as it is."

Mabel straightened. "I don't believe you. You're annoying and self-sacrificing, and I won't let her get away with blatant destruction of my property."

She started toward the girl again, but I darted between them, shoving Zoe behind my back. I kept my eyes locked on Mabel's broiling red irises.

"Prove I didn't," I said.

Mabel slapped me. The smack of her palm connecting with my cheek rang in my ears a split second before I felt the pain. My body twisted to the side. It wasn't the first time I'd been slapped—Merrick and Papa had cracked me in the face while training before, though not with as much force. My right eye watered.

"You. Are. My. Prisoner," Mabel said through gritted teeth. "You don't get to make demands."

A shot of pain rushed through my body, anchoring my arms to my side, forcing my knees to bend and my spine to stiffen until it locked me into position. Even though I tried, I couldn't move. Any paltry attempt I made to counter the magic met with total resistance. In the face of her sheer magical power, I stood no chance. Mabel cracked me in the face again, breaking the spell before I fell to the ground. Tears leaked out of my eye when I climbed back to my feet to face her again.

"You still maintain that it was you?" she asked calmly, tilting her head back. Her chest heaved up and down. "You're sure?"

I swallowed. "Positive."

Mabel's mind tugged on mine just before a leaden wave of Almorran magic moved through the room.

"Run, Zoe!" I cried. "Run!"

Mabel dropped the dress. It hovered in a waterfall of silk before bolting through the air, wrapping around my neck, and tightening. Zoe darted away, disappearing into the hall.

"Foolish idiot!" Mabel screamed, slamming me into the far wall with a wave of power so strong that pieces of rock dribbled onto the top of my head. I wrestled with the fabric, clawing at it with my nails. The song of Mabel's mind started in my head again, so distant it was almost indiscernible.

"Why must you get involved in things that have nothing to do with you?" Mabel cried in the background, pinning me to the wall. "You're worthless. Utterly worthless! I have no use for you. You can't do the simplest magic the way I direct, and you'll pay for your foolishness!"

The dress inched tighter and tighter. My ears rang. My head pounded. White dots flashed before my eyes. Nothing gave way. Mabel's face had taken on a frightening intensity, as if she didn't even see me.

"You'll never be better than me. Never! You'll never amount to anything. I'll find someone else to do the work you can't do!"

Her screaming faded. The borders between my own mind and Mabel's had nearly merged again, resurrecting the steady, cold voice of Mabel's grandmother.

You'll never amount to anything, Mabel. Nothing.

"That's what you get for trying to be better than me!" Mabel said, slapping me across the cheek again. The voices in my head grew in volume and intensity. My fingers tingled.

I could never love something as ugly as you. Your whore of a mother left you because she couldn't love you either. You've always been a burden, and you always will be. Put your arms out. I'll teach you what happens when you don't listen.

A final surge of energy rushed through me. Although I didn't know the capabilities of the magic that connected Mabel's mind to mine, I only had time for one attempt.

If you kill me, Papa will destroy you, I thought. *You'll have no leverage against him. He will win, Mabel. You'll lose everything.*

The dress disappeared, setting me free. The voices in my head ceased. I dropped to my knees, drawing in gasps of air. I vomited twice and rolled onto my side, my chest heaving. Mabel was gone. Juba stared at me with bored curiosity but looked away and made no move to come closer.

Exhausted, I dropped my head onto the cool rock floor and closed my eyes.

I'm still alive, I repeated over and over, forcing myself to focus on a memory of Papa's face. *I'm still alive.*

News from Home

A faint ring of purple circled my neck the next morning. Fractured blood vessels littered my right cheek. Every attempt I made at swallowing resulted in a swollen, thick pain, like a heavy ball in my throat, so I left breakfast at the door. I used an incantation to make my allotted water ice cold and drank slow sips.

The day would be sweltering, just like all the others. For now, however, the sun remained behind the Arck. It wouldn't shine on the balcony until it reached its zenith, so I sat outside and enjoyed the morning air that, while not cool, wasn't broiling yet. A new melancholy gripped me, and I longed to see home again. What were Camille and Leda doing? Was Papa getting any sleep?

Was Merrick thinking about me?

"You."

The small voice came from behind me. I whirled around, reaching instinctively for Viveet, even though she wasn't on my hip. Zoe stood in the balcony doorway, her dark hair swaying around her jawline. She'd tied white rags around her hands, which held a broom taller than she was. She'd addressed me with the formal greeting of the common language.

"You," I said back, and her tense fingers relaxed. She blinked several times and put a hand on her throat.

"Did . . . *da montagna* . . . did she—"

While I didn't know the *Yazika* language of the Southern Network very well, I knew the accent. It bore similarities to our own language in the Central Network, so da montagna likely meant monster.

I pulled my hair out of its queue and let it fall around my shoulders, hiding my neck. Surely she already lived most of her nightmares in her daily life. I didn't want to let her know she'd barely missed a brush with death. Then again, she likely already knew. Perhaps she'd experienced Mabel's—or Juba's—wrath before.

"Nothing," I said, attempting to splice words from the common language together. My tongue felt awkward in my own mouth. "It was . . . nothing."

"You?" she asked pointing to me.

"Bianca," I said, putting a hand on my chest. "My name is Bianca."

She glanced over her shoulder and, seeing no cheetah sneaking up on her, set aside the broom and stepped outside. The moment her feet crossed onto the balcony, she stopped, drew in a deep breath, and closed her eyes. Her scrunched expression eased. When her midnight eyes fluttered open again, she blushed.

"Outside," she said, shaking her head. "Not allowed."

I smiled. Zoe's eyes narrowed, but she didn't say anything for a long pause. When she spoke again, it was halting, like she, too, couldn't quite find the words. "Vy did you . . . ah . . ." She mimicked a slap to her face.

"Why did I help?"

She nodded.

"I don't like *da montagna*. I . . . uh . . . like you."

A girlish smile lit up her face. "Shto?" she cried. She shook her head. "I mean, yes?"

"Yes."

I had the impression that she would have rushed into my arms and hugged me if she hadn't been so wary. I remained by the edge of the balcony so she had plenty of space.

"Sit?" I asked as I sank to the ground and pressed my back to the warm sandstone wall.

"Shto," she said. A second blush bloomed across her cheeks. "Ah, yes."

She sat a few paces away, but some of the fear had faded from her eyes. I wondered so many things. How old was she? How long had she been here? How long had she worked for Mabel? Was she separated from her family? My instincts told me she hadn't been here long.

"Your home?" I asked. She gestured to the south.

"Far away. Big . . . uh . . . village."

"Family?"

Her eyes filled with tears. "Gone. All . . . gone."

"I'm sorry."

She stared at me. "Vy are you here?"

I sighed. "*Da montagna* has taken me . . . uh . . . prisoner."

Zoe thought over the words for a long time, and when they seemed to click, she became concerned. "No!" she cried. "Prisoner?"

I nodded. Zoe looked away. "They take our magic," she whispered and held out her hands to study the blood-soaked bandages. "Then *da montagna* takes us."

After watching the swearing-in ceremony, I had no doubt that Zoe had endured some similar barbaric choice.

"Zoe, have you seen an old woman here?" I asked. As a maid, Zoe likely had access to most of the Arck. She might have seen Isadora or know something about her. She could drastically cut down—or narrow—the risk I was going to take sneaking out to search for the Watcher myself.

Zoe glanced at me from the corner of her eye. "Old voman?"

"Yes."

"No. Vy?"

"She's a friend of mine," I said carefully, trying not to show my desperation lest I scare her away. "She's lost. A prisoner here also."

At this point, any little clue could help us track Isadora down. Even though all odds pointed away from the Arck, I couldn't imagine Mabel allowing Isadora to be far away.

Zoe shrugged, her eyes trailing back down to my neck again. I rearranged my hair to make sure it hid the worst of the bruises.

"I need to talk to her. It's very . . . important."

The sentences took me time to work out, but in the end, I felt mildly confident she'd understood, though she made no indication except a guttural sound in her throat.

"Food?" she asked, bringing her hands to her mouth. "You vant food?"

"I can't." I shook my head and patted my throat. "It hurts."

She leaped to her feet. "I vill return."

Before I could call out, she dashed away, her bare feet running across the floor and disappearing into the hall. She returned less than ten minutes later with a clay teapot and a small cup that fit in my palm. She put the cup in my hand and poured a warm broth into it. It tasted salty and rich and smelled like chicken soup. I sipped at it.

"Thank you," I said, smiling. I gestured to my throat. "Much better."

Zoe beamed and nodded. She held up a finger.

"More," she said, grabbing a linen sack from behind her. She untied the twine around the top, reached inside, and settled onto her knees in front of me. "I bring," she said, twiddling her fingers. "Give me feet."

I obeyed, stretching my bare right foot out in curiosity. I was wary of any kind of shoe, especially in this hot weather. But I let her put a thin piece of leather against the bottom of my foot and lace a pair of leather straps around my leg all the way to my knee.

"Stand," she said, motioning with her hands. "You like?"

I held my skirt above my knees and walked, enjoying the way the soft leather of the sandal followed my foot, conforming to each ridge instead of boxing my toes in. I wiggled my toes, still free to the open air. Juba glanced our way, huffed, and lay back down.

"Yes," I said, jogging across the room. "I can barely feel them."

"There are . . . others," she said haltingly. "More, uh, styles?"

"Of sandal?"

She nodded.

"Are all of them this simple?"

"Yes," she said, tilting her head to the side. "Less string, sometimes."

"Zoe!" I said, spinning in a circle. "These are perfect!"

She clapped, her eyes lighting up. "Good, yes?"

"Very good."

"More clothes."

She motioned to a pile of linen the color of pearl. Western Network females mostly wore short sleeves and low waists, with rounded necks and skirts that hung in layers. I tried one on to appease the little maid. The dress flowed around my ankles, tapering just below my left knee and revealing only one leg. Despite the four layers of cloth, it felt light and airy. The fabric bunched around my waist when Zoe tied it a certain way, reminding me of the female witches I had watched in the market below.

Zoe glanced over her shoulder, saw that Juba's eyes were closed, ducked her head, and crooked her finger to bring me closer. "I bring," she whispered with a conspiratorial smile. She pressed a finger to her lips, reached into the bag of clothes, and pulled out a scroll.

"Find on the ground," she said, gesturing. "Your . . . Netvork? No?"

I pushed the clothes away from the scroll with a gasp, hardly daring to believe. Zoe had found a *Chatham Chatterer* scroll in the Western Network!

"Zoe!" I whispered. "This is wonderful!"

She straightened up, checked Juba again, and hunkered back down. "You read ven you are very . . . ah . . . bored? Hide it," she said, her eyes widening. "Very sneaky."

I would have scooped her into a hug, but she kept all witches at arm's length, so I settled for a beaming smile. "Thank you, Zoe! Oh, thank you. This is wonderful!"

"I must vork," Zoe said with a reluctant sigh. She pointed to the *Chatterer* in the bag and lowered her voice. "No show *da montagna*."

I winked. "Our secret."

"I go," she said, walking backward to the door. "I clean later. You vill be here?"

"Yes."

A small smile spread across her face, and she left me alone on the balcony with my cup of broth and the warm feeling in my heart that I'd just made a friend.

CLAVAS ATTACK BORDER TOWNS

In a sudden, unexpected show of force from the Western Network, reports of Clavas attacking Eastern Coven villages along the border have been pouring in since morning.

The border villages of Buckley and Saxon have fallen to the West Guards that followed the Clava attacks. Those unable to transport away or flee for their lives have been slaughtered. Early reports indicate that no one remains in the small village of Jamesport. A few witches have said that the Clavas appear to be hydrophobic, though this hasn't been confirmed through Chatterer journalists.

This is the first time the Clavas have attacked civilians. They are not taking prisoners.

Shelters have been set up on the eastern edge of the Western Covens. Other safe areas are under construction in the Letum Wood Covens. Updates will be published as they become available.

URGENT NOTICE TO THE WITCHES IN THE SOUTHERN COVENS

This is an official evacuation announcement given through the Ambassador under orders from the High Priest. Evacuate immediately. Transport to Chatham Castle or neighboring covens. Leave behind anything you cannot transport with. Clavas and West Guards continue to invade.

DO NOT DELAY. EVACUATE IMMEDIATELY.

The Southern Network

The sound of Juba's paws pacing back and forth in front of the bathroom door rang through my ears. Hurry. Hurry. Hurry, they seemed to say. My left arm stretched in front of me like a furry, spotted rope. As far as cheetah tails went, it wasn't bad. A bit short, but I couldn't expect much more from my first attempt. My eyes flickered to the small gap of light at the bottom of the door when Juba's shadow passed by again.

One more attempt, I thought. He hadn't banged his head impatiently against the door, which meant I had just enough time. To solidify the ruse, I reached my other hand into the porcelain bowl and splashed it in the water.

Using a spell, I pulled the transformative magic back in. Patches of fur gave way to skin. Five fingers formed from the fuzzy end of the tail, separating back into my familiar appendages. I let out a sigh. It was always a relief when my body returned to its usual state.

Just as I restarted the magic, a knocking sound reverberated through Mabel's chamber, so loud I heard it in the bathroom. A visitor? Juba threw his shoulder into the door, rattling it. Ah. I had no time after all.

"I heard, I heard," I muttered, pulling the door open. Juba eyed me with suspicion but had no time to conduct his usual sniff check before he hustled away. I stepped out, peering around the corner to see a spindly messenger boy standing in the doorway to the hall. He waved an envelope in the air, a wary eye on Juba.

"A-a-a m-m-message!"

Mabel burst into the room from behind him, nearly knocking the poor boy over. The envelope flew into her outstretched palm. By the time it reached her, the messenger boy had disappeared down the hallway. The envelope opened itself, ejecting a small piece of parchment that floated up to her eyes. Her jaw clenched. The message exploded into a bright flame, burning until it dribbled to the floor in a pile of ash.

"Fool!" she cried. "Mikhail, you bloody fool."

For once, Mabel and I agreed. Mikhail, the High Priest of the Southern Network, was a fool. She disappeared into her walk-in closet, emerging five minutes later in an ice-blue gown with elbow-length sleeves and a long bodice.

"Come," she commanded as she walked past me. A chain appeared in the air, locking onto my manacle and jerking me toward her. I stumbled, falling twice before gaining my feet. She snatched my arm and, without warning, pulled both of us into a transportation spell.

Without time to prepare myself for the pressure and time of a long-distance transport, I found myself gasping for breath when we landed on the castle steps in the Southern Network. The air felt crisp, carrying the promise of fall. Without snow banking the castle and coating the evergreen tree branches, the Southern Network bloomed a surprising shade of deep green.

"Compose yourself," Mabel snapped. "I won't have you blubbering while I'm reigning Mikhail back in."

The cool tingle of a silencing incantation wrapped around my throat. My head still spun, but I righted myself just as Mikhail's Ambassador, Dmitri, stepped onto the porch. The past few months had not been kind to him—his eyes sank into his once-stout cheeks, leaving sagging skin and deep wrinkles. Stains marred the front of his shirt. His sharp gaze fell on me, but he said nothing. I'd met Dmitri at the end of winter earlier this year, on a trip with Marten before the Southern Network broke the Mansfeld Pact. I hadn't made a good impression then. I had little hope of making one now.

"Where is he?" Mabel demanded. "I need to speak with Mikhail immediately."

Dmitri flew back, colliding with the door with a sickening thud. "He is in a meeting, Your Greatness," he said, falling to his knees and bowing until his nose touched the floor. This clearly wasn't his first encounter with Mabel.

"Pull him out of it. I'll be waiting in the throne room."

She plunged into the castle without invitation, dragging me with her. Dust had overtaken the windowsills and obscured several old paintings, one of which hung crooked. The long hall, once filled with white and blue banners, lay empty. Only one banner remained, and its ends were burned. A mouse scampered across our path as I struggled to keep up with Mabel's stride. Whoever Mikhail employed as the Head of Housekeeping needed to be replaced. Just like last time, not another witch was visible in the castle, leaving it in an eerie, unbroken silence.

Dmitri followed us for a few moments but disappeared to the left when we took a right. Mabel plowed into Mikhail's throne room—a disorganized place on a good day—and threw herself into the golden throne. The inlaid rubies sparkled as red as her burning eyes. She filled the chair better than fat little Mikhail—at least her feet touched the floor.

I swallowed. She'd insulted Mikhail's greed and pride by overtaking his throne and demanding his attention. They both had nasty tempers. Surely this wouldn't go well.

In the absence of concubines to fawn over him—and someone to clean the place—Mikhail's throne room looked like an abandoned storage area. What wasn't coated with dust was hidden by dirt. Tangled knots filled the polar bear rug. A gruesome tapestry on the wall had frayed in two corners. Most of the precious gems that normally littered the room were missing.

Mabel's fingers drummed on the armrest. She sat back, shifted forward, and moved back again.

"Where is the little rat?" she hissed.

When Mikhail came into the room, I didn't recognize him. The fat, bawdy, disrespectful witch I remembered had faded into an aging, thin old man with a squashed face and an unattractive scowl. While the word *meek* could hardly apply to a witch like Mikhail, I couldn't think of any other word to describe him now.

"Mikhail," Mabel said, her voice ringing over the room. "You have disappointed me yet again."

He stood in front of her but remained out of reach. The lapels in his half-untucked shirt spilled over his pants. The opal in his beard hung crooked, and two braids had come unraveled. He smelled like ipsum but didn't appear drunk. Then again, his eyes were tucked so deep into the folds of his face that it was hard to tell.

"Vy is this so, Your Greatness?"

Mabel rose up from the throne and towered over him. "You lost the city of Husseldorf in the Eastern Network! Derek and Niko now have an advantageous position near the Central Network border."

She pulled a scroll out of her pocket and threw it on the ground. It unfurled itself in front of him. The headline across the top flashed in bold letters.

Central Guards Obtain Key City

"Derek now holds the bridge," she said, slapping Mikhail across the face with the back of her hand. She must have strengthened the blow with magic, for Mikhail flew back head over heels and slid across the floor.

"Your Greatness," he said, his arms trembling as he pushed himself to his feet. "The situation vas bad. Ve didn't have Vest Guards. My vitches have no magic!"

Mabel pointed at him. "Do not blame your weakness on me! You should never have agreed to the attack if you were short on supplies or staff. I want to speak with your Head of Guardians."

Mikhail waved a hand as if to dismiss the idea, but I wondered if he was protecting his Head of Guardians.

"He is busy," Mikhail said. "You deal vith me."

Mabel's eyes glowed blood red with pleasure. "Oh," she whispered. "I will deal with you. Derek has remained one step ahead of you ever since the fighting began. If you will not prove yourself to be an asset to the cause, I will find a High Priest who will!"

To his credit, Mikhail didn't cower. His ruddy face reddened further. "I vill take care of it," he said.

Mabel studied him, pulled in a deep breath, and sat back on the throne, forcing herself to calm down.

"And the troubles we previously discussed?" she asked, her eyes flickering briefly in my direction. "Do they continue?"

"They're under control," he snapped.

"What does that mean?"

"It means you do not vorry about my problems. I need more pover."

"I'll have new West Guard recruits to send to you next week," she said with a wave of her hand. Mikhail's scowl grew.

"No," he said, his massive nostrils widening. "*I* need more pover."

I kept my eyes averted, staring at a stain on the floor. My heart pounded. Mabel released a long-suffering sigh and pinched the bridge of her nose between her thumb and index finger.

"Must we go over this again?" she asked, her tone suspiciously even. "I've given you plenty."

"You've taken avay plenty," he said, leaning forward. "I need magic to get done vhat needs to be done. You want Husseldorf? Give me pover! I can't fight a vitch like Derek vhen I don't have pover. You're holding back!" He stomped a foot on the floor. "You agreed!"

Ah, I thought. The relations between Mabel and Mikhail went deeper than a mere Network alliance. When they broke the Mansfeld Pact, Mikhail's whole Network had lost their ability to use magic for the duration of their lives. Perhaps even children born to their witches in the future would be stripped of power—no one knew. But he was somehow using Mabel to borrow magical power, and I had no doubt she was loaning him Almorran magic. I tried to imagine a life where I couldn't produce what I needed with a spell or transport where I wanted to go, and the idea made me sick to my stomach. No wonder he sounded so desperate.

"You'll receive more power when it's needed to fulfill my purposes," she said.

Mikhail recoiled. "*Your* purposes? Vhat happened to our agreement?"

"Yes," she hissed, baring her teeth. "Mine! You're too foolish to be trusted with any more power!"

No wonder he looked at her with such hate.

"I agreed to vork vith you because ve vere supposed to vin," Mikhail said, tilting his bulbous chin in the air. "But ve are not vinning. Derek is strong!"

A bolt of black fire appeared from Mabel's hand and slammed into Mikhail's chest. It doubled, then tripled, expanding until it formed a ring of fire around his little body. He screamed. The air thickened with the power of Almorran magic.

"Stop!" Mikhail cried. "It vill kill me!"

"Derek is not stronger than me!" she screamed. "No one is stronger than me! The magic is all-powerful. You will not question its strength!"

My ears began to ring with the familiar strains of a small, agonized voice.

Make the pain stop! I'm sorry I missed the question.

I pressed my hands to my head, resisting the pull of her mind. The fire stopped. The song of her mind receded. Mabel curled her fingers into her palms while Mikhail lay on the floor, moaning and writhing. If he hadn't been such a horrid little witch, I would have felt sorry for him.

"He's not stronger than me," Mabel said again, though her voice trembled. "You'd do well to remember that. I will not give you any more power until you accomplish the tasks I've set for you. All of them."

Mabel started forward, and I scrambled after her.

"Get your Network under control." She kicked Mikhail in the stomach as she passed him. "Or I'll take the Southern Network and make sure you live long enough to watch a voman win the war without you."

His agonized groans rang through the empty castle as we transported away.

"Jikes," I muttered under my breath. "That will never feel normal."

Fur sprouted from my two hands and climbed all the way to my shoulder. Where fingernails had once been, I now had claws. Black spots filled my pale yellow fur. When I flexed, long, gleaming claws spread out from my paws.

"Nice."

The sound of Juba's dinner hitting the floor echoed through the chamber. He stood, padded away from the bathroom, and immediately returned to stand just outside the door. I spoke the counter magic under my breath. If there was anything Juba couldn't tolerate, it was waiting to eat, and he was too stubborn to leave his post, the mongrel. The fur shrank, retreating into my pores. The claws grew long, thin, and jointed, becoming fingers again. Luckily, transformation didn't hurt; it just tingled.

"I'm coming!" I called, hoping to buy myself a few seconds before he barged in. "I heard your meal."

Trying to secretly perfect a new skill used some of my cooped-up magical powers, although I still jogged around in circles every day to keep them at bay. While I wasn't about to explode, I didn't feel calm either. After putting the magic into motion, I felt less on edge.

Juba's head slammed into the door. I stood and pulled it open before he could force it. He surveyed me with a snarl, sniffed the air, and trotted over to his food once he was satisfied I'd done nothing suspicious. The knot in my stomach unraveled. Every attempt at transformation was a risk. If Juba caught me, who knew what he'd do? My only chance to find the *Book of Light*—and possibly change the direction of the war—would be gone.

Juba ate his dinner, stretched out for a lazy catnap, and started snoring. I perked up. Was Zane coming back? Perhaps he knew a way to break me free. The longing to return home overwhelmed me, sending my powers into turmoil. I paced across the balcony to burn them off.

A moonless night fell—no accident, certainly. With less light came less risk of being seen. Zane free climbed again, wearing the same garment as before. I waited between two blooming cacti.

"How are you?" he asked when he surfaced, as down-to-business as I'd expected. His tight jaw and the creases in his brow meant he wasn't in as lighthearted a mood this time.

"Fine," I lied. "Nothing has really changed. Have you found a way to bring me home yet?"

"I can remove the manacle, and I can transport you back to the Central Network, but I can't safely get you out of her room. I have a few ideas, but . . ." He trailed off. "They're risky, and Derek has made it abundantly clear that I have no margin for error."

"Oh." I rubbed the tip of my finger along the cool surface of the manacle. Papa would never approve of my plan, but if Zane hadn't found another way out, transforming into a cheetah might be my only option. *What about Isadora?* I thought. *And the Book of Light?* I didn't want to leave the West until I had searched for both of them. Mabel's unhinged visit to Mikhail replayed through my mind. I didn't have much time.

My stomach lurched, nervous over what I was about to propose.

"Well . . . what if I told you I think I can get out of the room?"

Zane lifted his eyebrows. "You have my attention."

"I won't tell you the details," I said, swallowing. "Because then you'd be held accountable to Papa. You'd have to tell him what I plan to do, and you'd be obligated to stop me."

He hesitated. "I'm not sure I like this."

"Can you put Juba to sleep again tomorrow?" I asked. I felt pretty sure that Grandmother's sleeping potion would work, but it wouldn't be as strong as I'd like. Also, since I was a little short on parsley, it might take longer to take effect.

"No. It won't put him to sleep unless there's time between the doses."

I bit my bottom lip. I'd have to make do with Grandmother's. *What if it doesn't work because of Zane's sleeping draught?* As if I needed one more thing to dilute its effects.

"Fine. Let's just plan on meeting somewhere in the Arck tomorrow."

He sucked in a deep breath. "Tomorrow?"

I nodded.

"Are you sure?"

"No," I said. "But Mabel's losing sanity with every passing day, and I want to get out of here. There's a chance."

"If you get out of the room," he said, "I'll get that manacle off your wrist and get you home."

My stomach fluttered with hope. "Consider it done. Tell me where to meet you. Describe how to get there as best you can."

He leaned forward. "Get to the kitchen first. It takes up half of the second floor. When you reach the bottom of the stairs, you'll see a large pantry off to the left that witches rarely go into. Hide behind the flour barrels."

"Noon?" Juba's breakfast arrived at ten. That would allow enough time for the potion to put him to sleep and for me to explore the Arck before I met up with Zane. Juba should sleep at least two hours if all went according to plan.

Zane nodded. "Noon."

"If I'm not there by 12:30, I won't be there at all."

He pressed his lips into a thin line. "Don't let that happen," he said. "For both of our sakes."

Although Papa was usually an understanding witch, I couldn't imagine the pressure he must be putting on Zane to break me free, especially if he couldn't come save me himself.

"I'll try," I said. Zane shifted, as if he were about to leave. "Wait!" I cried. "I've seen a few things I think you need to know about. They could be important. I have to tell you now in case things go badly."

He readjusted his grip. "You have three minutes."

"I met a maid named Zoe. She's young, about ten or so, and is the only staff member I've interacted with. She was kidnapped from her village in the Southern Network and forced into servitude here. Her family is gone. They might be dead, but they might just be working for Mabel, too. She hasn't said."

"Forced into servitude here?" he repeated, the skin between his eyebrows wrinkling. "From the Southern Network?"

"Yes!" I cried, all my suppressed angst spilling out in a single word. "Mabel is forcing people to give up their agency and swear loyalty to Almorran magic. I've seen the swearing-in ceremony. If they don't support her, they . . . they die."

His eyes glimmered. "Interesting. I knew they were swearing their lives to the magic, but I didn't realize she'd brought them up from the Southern Network. It must be recent, or I would have recognized them in the West Guard ranks."

"That's not all," I said. "Mabel took me with her to the Southern Network, and I think something is going on there as well."

Zane listened without interrupting while I recounted the visit, including the small details I'd been puzzling over ever since, like Mikhail's dirty castle and their cryptic conversation about something going wrong.

"I think Mikhail's staff left the castle. Everything was filthy. Even he was unkempt. Something there isn't right."

"There have been many revolts against Mikhail," Zane said, his eyes tapering in thought. "Most of the witches in the Southern Network are livid that he took away their magic. He's survived many, many assassination attempts."

"So my suspicions are right: There are witches in the Southern Network that want nothing to do with Mabel or Mikhail. Right?" I asked. "And that's not the only case I've observed. The other night, a young man from the Western Network clans tried to break in and kill Mabel."

"The West?"

"Yes!"

"You're certain?"

"Of course. From the outer clans, if his tattoos meant anything. Look, this means her own witches are trying to get rid of her. We need to get them on our side! Think of all the witches that may be willing to fight for revenge. What if they fought alongside the Central Network?"

He gave no response, which I took to be a good sign. Juba's soft sighs hadn't stopped, but their intensity had lessened. Zane's arms shook.

"I'll look into it," Zane said, readjusting his grip. No doubt he'd transport to the Southern Network as soon as he left and do what he did best—spy.

"How's Papa?" I asked quietly. What I wouldn't give to smell the spearmint and forest on Papa's clothes, to hear his deep, exasperated laugh when Marten gave him a report on my argument with a Border Guard who thought the Eastern Network was spying on them through a sack of potatoes.

"He told me to tell you to pay attention and don't run your mouth."

I laughed under my breath. "That sounds like him. Have you found out anything about Isadora?"

"No."

I waited for more, but nothing came. The sound of West Guards walking below silenced both of us. Juba stirred with a low huff, and his front paws twitched.

"You'd better go," I said.

Zane bit the inside of his cheek. "She actually took you with her to the Southern Network?"

"Yes."

"Any mention of going back?"

"Not that I know of."

"Any mention of traveling anywhere else? Like maybe the Northern Network?"

"The North? No, definitely not the North. Going to the Southern Network was a spur-of-the-moment thing. She didn't plan it."

He stared off into the distance for a minute. "I'll be nearby," he finally said, shaking off whatever thoughts had plagued him. His eyes drifted back to my neck. "And make sure you pay attention."

My breath caught in my throat. Although the bruises were fading and I'd kept my hair down, he must have seen that I'd been injured. I nodded, grateful he didn't inquire about it. Zane let go of the wall and plummeted downward, transporting as he fell.

"Merry part," I whispered into the breeze.

I turned and faced Mabel's chamber—my prison—again. Because I had to. Because this was a game, and I—the High Priest's daughter—was the most valuable pawn on the board.

And the next day, I planned to make my grand escape.

Don't Give Up

I ground up the dry sleeping potion early the next morning, just after Mabel left.

Juba's morning meal—usually a partial rack of ribs fresh from some poor animal—would arrive promptly at ten. At 9:50, I sat on the divan, faced the door, and clutched the brown packet that Zane had sent the sage and cinnamon in. The dry sleeping potion, which I'd activated with the right spell, filled the little envelope. Over the top of my book, I watched for the meat to come while Juba lay in the shade, his lidded eyes half open.

The moment the heavy sound of approaching feet neared the door, I stood up, raising my arms far above my head in a luxurious stretch reminiscent of Juba himself. My heart beat hard and fast. Everything hinged on this action—me getting the dry potion onto the meat.

The plate clattered on the floor, and the ribs slid into the room on a silver platter. Juba's ears perked up.

"Oh," I said, feigning dizziness. "I stood up too fast."

I sat down on the floor between Juba and his meal, my right hand on my head. My left hand squeezed the envelope, forcing it open. I used a scattering spell, sending the herbs airborne. With careful control of the magic, all the little specks drifted toward his food, as if in a wind, and fell on top of the raw meat.

Juba prowled past me, his eyes narrowed in question. Either he sensed my magic—which I doubted, given the appetizing scent of raw meat nearby—or he smelled my fear. Ignoring me for the time being, he approached his food, sniffed it, paused, and sniffed it again. My heart leaped into my throat. What if he could smell the herbs? What if he didn't eat it?

Juba licked the top of the carcass and paused. He growled deep in his throat and tore into one of the ribs with savage delight. Relieved, I pressed my back against the wall, hid my face in a book, and waited.

Juba finished his meal at 10:30. With a full belly, he collapsed in a sunbeam, cast a glance at me, and settled in with a sigh. The hands of the clock continued to tick in perpetual motion.

10:55.

11:15.

He lay on the floor, drowsy in the sunshine, his tail and ears twitching. I shifted, testing his alertness. His head popped up, his groggy eyes on me. Still awake. Panic, pure and hot, ran a long circuit through my bloodstream. If this waiting game continued, I wouldn't be able to look for Isadora or the *Book of Light* before meeting up with Zane. Or, worse, what if Juba didn't get drowsy enough for me to slip away? I longed to pace back and forth across the floor to work off all my nervous energy.

When the minute hand moved to 11:43, I heard the first light snore. With nearly silent movements, I set the book aside and tiptoed to the bathroom. Juba didn't stir.

"Here we go," I whispered, straightening my shoulders. Since it had taken so long for Juba to fall asleep, I might only have an hour before he started to wake. If all went according to plan, I'd be back in the Central Network by then. Likely without the *Book of Light*. I grimaced. Was escaping worth it if I couldn't find the counter magic?

The transformative magic fell over my body one wave at a time, first coursing through my right arm, then my left. Heat flowed down my fingertips and through my legs, ending in swirls at my feet. The beginning of a tail began to pull out of the small of my back. Hair sprung out on my skin. I kept my eyes closed and the magic at the forefront of my mind. Half-transforming would be worse than not transforming at all. Once the heat abated and I'd completed the spell recitation, I opened my eyes to find the floor only a breath away. When I awkwardly hobbled out of the bathroom—uncertain how to use four legs instead of two—I found the closest mirror a few paces away and stared into the golden eyes of a cheetah.

The whiskers were a bit skewed, the fur wasn't very lustrous, and I knew the ridge between Juba's shoulders was thicker, but I'd at least come out with four legs, a tail, and the right color of spotted fur. The lines below my eyes were too thin to be Juba's, and I was significantly smaller. Juba must have been a massive witch to become such a large cheetah. Although transformation changed the witch to fit the magic, vestiges of personality and body still shone through. I couldn't change my leaner build and shorter tail.

Relief flooded through me first, and then I faced the disconcerting realization that I had to learn how to walk with four legs. The manacle weighed heavy on my paw, but its dull color faded into my fur. Unless I stood in direct sunlight, the manacle would likely go unnoticed.

Or so I hoped.

I stumbled over my feet on my first attempt to skulk to the door. Coordinating all my paws was, at first, confusing. But I fell into a workable rhythm within a few runs of the room. Juba's snores deepened.

Hurry, hurry, I thought, slinking toward the door. *No time to waste on perfection.*

So much could go wrong. Mabel could return unexpectedly. I could get lost, caught, or stepped on. But if I found the *Book of Light* or Isadora, I could make so much right. Keeping that at the forefront of my mind, I held my breath as I approached the door, ready to vomit a nervous hairball. No burst of fire exploded from the seams. When a little flame flared, I bolted through it as fast as I could. The fire ebbed.

First obstacle complete.

I glanced over my shoulder into Mabel's room. Juba slept on. The clock said 11:53. Zane would only risk waiting until 12:30.

Sounds from the hall filtered past my sharp ears. Walking. A sweeping broom. My sense of smell was better too—without even trying, I detected burnt bread, steel, and dust behind the nearest door. I could tell which direction a slight wind was going just by the scents it brought.

What would a walk in Letum Wood be like from a cheetah's perspective? I wondered. *Focus. Focus on the goal.*

The hallway stretched in two directions. I headed to the right, the way Mabel always did, grateful that my paws seemed to find their natural stride.

The heat, which I'd found burdensome and oppressive enough as a witch, startled me with its intensity. *Must be the fur.* Panting, it turned out, was inefficient, and I longed for a cool pool to lounge in. The Arck, which had seemed a little damp before, suddenly had a thousand different scents. Mold. Decay. Fresh linen. Hints of spices. How did Juba handle this all day long? I shook my head and was startled by the unusual sensation of my ears flapping.

Strange.

The hard edges of each paw gave me a firm grip on the stone floor as I padded down the hall, trying to orient myself to my lower-than-usual vision. I recognized the pulse of muscle as I ran, the ease of movement that came with bone and sinew, moving the many small parts of the body as one great whole. Running was running, and it satisfied a flare of magic in my chest that had been antsy and itching. If nothing else came of this adventure, at least I'd have some reprieve from the demanding magic.

I remained a cheetah while creeping through the halls, panting in the heat, exploring the world from knee height. I moved from shadow to shadow, keeping low, out of sight, moving almost without sound. Maintaining the unfamiliar magic tired me, but after days of pent-up magical energy, I *needed* to be tired.

It didn't take long to familiarize myself with the basic layout of the Arck or find the stairs. Most of the doors in the hallway were closed. My thick, strong tail served as a decent sort of arm to reach up and test the doorknobs, but nearly all the closed doors were also locked.

That won't work, I thought with increasing nervousness. Perhaps I'd never find Mabel's office. Or Isadora.

The scent of blood drifted in on a breeze, activating bells in my cheetah mind. A thudding pulse of hunger took over me, drowning me in the desire for the rich juiciness of a rack of—

Hold on, I thought, mentally retreating out of the haze of instinct. *Cheetah taking over.*

Once I reoriented myself, a new idea occurred to me. Seeing my way through the Arck wouldn't be easy as a cheetah. But my strongest asset wasn't my vision.

It was my nose.

I scurried from door to door, sniffing. Mabel's floral scent would be punishingly strong to my ultra-sensitive nose. Minutes passed. I crept along the hall, waiting in the shadows for maids to pass by and hurrying along the walls in the quiet until, finally, I smelled Mabel's floral perfume. With an eager trot, I followed it until I came upon a set of double doors. Light spilled from one that stood ajar. I paused, ensuring that no one waited inside, slipped in, and pushed the door closed behind me with my tail.

It was a large room, nearly as big as Mabel's personal chamber. A balcony filled one wall, admitting a hot breeze. In the middle of the room lay a table that was as long as the ceiling was tall. On top of it, papers fluttered in a little breeze. Inkwells were stationed at varying intervals, surrounded by stacks of blank scrolls. A small shelf of books stood against the back wall.

Mabel's office. It had to be.

A clock on a natural stone shelf said 12:19. My heart leaped with a little thrill. I'd done it. I'd found Mabel's office with only a few minutes to spare.

I headed for the bookshelf while I released the transformative magic. Thumbing through the books would be difficult with claws. Reversing the transformation released a heavy burden, and I turned back into an exhausted version of myself.

I pulled the books off the shelf with a spell so I could look at them all at once. *Dark Arts. Network Governments. In Defense of Black Magic.* Nothing that could be the *Book of Light.* Despite my depleted magical reserves, I used a revealing incantation, but none of the books changed. My heart sank, and I slumped back against the bookshelf.

Frantic, I searched all her drawers and peeked under the couches to no avail. Tears sprang to my eyes. I couldn't fail!

"Tell Daemon I want to meet with him in the morning," Mabel's voice said from just down the hall. My blood froze. I straightened in disbelief. *No!* With another taxing spell, I sent all the books back to the shelf, closed the drawers, straightened the pillows, and stood against the back wall near the door, my heart pounding.

12:26.

"His performance has been unacceptable," Mabel said, her voice growing louder. I glanced around in a panic. I couldn't jump out the window because I still wore the manacle. Juka would surely recognize me as false right away, even if Mabel didn't. In one last-ditch effort, I transformed my hair into short, blonde locks, smudged dirt from the dusty books on my face, and transformed two quills from the desk into a mop and bucket. The door to the office flew open, and Mabel strode inside.

"The West Guards in contingent thirteen need to start training with—"

I remained pressed against the wall, my eyes averted. Mabel stopped two paces after she passed me, her expression twisted in confusion. Juka walked on her other side, her ears perking up. Her head swung my direction when I slipped by, murmuring what I hoped sounded like an apology. I darted into the hallway, the water in my transformed bucket sloshing onto my dress.

I didn't wait around to see if Mabel or Juka had detected my magic or not. I half-walked, half-jogged out of the hallway. *Now, how to get down to the kitchen without raising questions . . .* Once I turned the corner, I dropped the mop and bucket and whispered the transformation spell. Twice as fast as before—no doubt the result of my panic—the magic twisted me back into my cheetah shape. I could hide more easily as a cheetah.

Before my tail had finished elongating, I sprinted for the stairs, bounding down them so quickly they blurred together. One of my four legs slipped, and I plunged forward, smacking my front leg, jaw, and head into a wall. The impact reverberated through my skull. I blinked, dazed, before righting myself and starting down the stairs to the second floor again.

Don't give up on me, Zane, I pleaded as I started to navigate the stairs. *Don't give up!*

The smell of baked bread rested heavy in the air when I slinked onto the second floor with a sigh of relief. I'd made it! I was going home!

A familiar, high-pitched cry stopped me. I had only enough time to suck in a deep breath before a spotted body tackled me, its razor-sharp claws digging into my shoulders.

Juba's weight sent me flying back to the staircase where my head hit again with a resounding thud.

Dafina

I woke to the metallic smell of death.

It took me only a few seconds to register that Juba stood over me, panting. I turned away with a grimace, revolted by the smell. My stomach threatened to empty itself on the floor. He snarled, so close to my face I could feel the movement of his whiskers.

A hot trickle rolled down the back of my neck and shoulders, and I recalled the pain of his claws in my flesh. I put a hand to my bloody neck, surprised not to see fur. Had Juba dragged me back to Mabel's chamber by my neck? I must have still been a cheetah when we crossed the threshold, or the flames would have killed us both. I supposed the transformative magic had dissipated over time since I hadn't been awake to keep it going.

Juba loomed over me with undisguised menace for an eternal minute. Hostility rolled off him in long waves, and I realized that I'd risked his life by sneaking around. The fact that Mabel wasn't openly laughing at me meant she hadn't returned.

Which also meant she probably didn't know.

Juba's eyes narrowed. He pressed his paw into my ribs, leaned his weight on me, and forced the air from my lungs, making clear what he couldn't say in his feline state.

Not a word.

With a growl, he backed away to stand near the wall like a tall sentry, his gaze as steady as death. If he hadn't been so vicious, I would have found his feline grace beautiful. A deep disappointment surged through me. I hadn't found the *Book of Light*, I still had no idea where

Isadora was hidden, I wouldn't be going home, and I'd just made a greater enemy out of Juba.

I forced the bitterness aside. For now, I had to focus on repairing my cuts and hiding the blood. At least Juba and I had one mutual purpose.

Mabel could never know that I had escaped.

After my escape, life with Juba changed dramatically.

I woke the next morning to find Mabel gone and the manacle attached to the bedpost. When I tried to move, it resisted, tightening by a few links and pulling me closer. At this radius, I barely had enough room to stand.

"What is this?" I demanded. Juba glared at me, his head cocked to the side as if to say, "*You did this to yourself.*" He'd probably replaced the chain after Mabel left.

"I have to use the bathroom."

The chain disconnected from the bed and shot across the room, jerking me with it. It linked itself to a spot on the wall near the bathroom. I slid across the floor and collided with the wall. The jostling opened the puncture marks on my shoulders and neck. I ground my teeth together to keep from screaming. Blood oozed onto my collarbones. I cast a numbing incantation and stood up. Just enough chain remained to allow me to use the bathroom and come back out. When I glared at him, I could have sworn he smirked. He screamed when I tried to shut the bathroom door, so I swallowed my dignity and left it open.

For a cheetah, Juba exhibited impressive magical strength. After transforming into an animal, I could understand the forceful drive of instinct. But Juba's use of magic made it clear that he *liked* being a cheetah and chose to remain in that form. I shuddered when I recalled the delighted way in which he'd eaten the Western Network witch that attempted to murder Mabel.

I took my time cleaning my wounds and washing my face. Juba

prowled in the doorway, alternately growling and banging his tail against the doorframe.

"Can I sit on the divan and read, Your Highness?" I asked him imperiously when I left the bathroom. He bared his teeth and stood on top of the book I'd reached for.

"Fine," I said, shrugging. "I'll sing. All day long."

I caterwauled at the top of my lungs, horribly off-pitch. After a few moments, Juba hissed and moved off the book. The chain slid over to the leg of the divan, wrapping around it several times. I'd learned my lesson—I hurried toward the divan before the chain pulled me in.

No sooner had I settled into *History of the Networks Volume Three* than I heard a strange little cry. I peered over the top of the book to find Juba stretched across the balcony on his belly, his front paws trapping something that glowed red. He growled, his nostrils flaring open and closed. He moved his paw to look at his prisoner, and the light twitched to the side. A high-pitched bellow of rage rang through the air. Only one creature was that small, that bright, and that bossy.

"A fairy?" I whispered in disbelief, setting aside the book. "In the West?"

Juba pressed one of his nostrils to his paws and sniffed, setting off another round of hysterical displeasure. The light intensified.

"Set Dafina free!" screamed the fairy, her voice shrill. "The wrath of the fairies be upon you!"

I'd just stumbled upon a most fortunate—and rare—situation: a fairy in need. If I could save her, she would owe me a favor that fairy law dictated she must fulfill. If she didn't, she would lose her natural beauty. A true tragedy.

"Let her go," I called, standing up. Juba ducked his head down and snarled, his golden eyes compressed and his nose wrinkled. He snapped his teeth at me.

"Fine," I said, shrugging. "Eat the fairy."

The red light flashed frantically underneath his paw. "No!" she wailed. "Dafina is not your meal!"

Juba hadn't taken his eyes off me. His lips pulled back, revealing his back teeth in a low hiss. I met his gaze, feigning confidence.

I'd already made a lifelong enemy out of him—this wasn't going to help our relationship at all. Still, a favor from a free-roaming fairy was worth Juba's wrath.

"If you eat her, I'll tell Mabel that I escaped," I said. "If she needs proof, I'll transform back into a cheetah. Although I doubt she'll need me to convince her with all the holes you left in my neck and shoulders."

His ears flattened against the back of his head. He growled.

"What's it going to hurt me if she knows I escaped?" I asked. "I'm her only leverage in the war. She can't kill me."

But she can certainly torture me.

I forced the thought aside and continued with forced casualness.

"But she can kill you. Although, knowing Mabel, I doubt she would. No, she prefers pain over death. She doesn't like it to end too easily, now does she? She killed her own mother, remember?"

While Juba's nose twitched and his tail shifted back and forth, I sat back on the divan, taking pains to straighten my skirt with exaggerated nonchalance. After a few minutes, I glanced over at him. He hadn't moved. He panted in the hot air, but his paws remained still. Even the fairy had quieted.

"Ah. No treat, then?" I asked. "Smart move."

Juba leaped toward me with a scream but stopped short of my legs and retreated, whacking the terrified fairy across the room with his tail. She tumbled, heels over wings, and smacked into the sandstone wall. As soon as Juba turned his back, I scrambled forward as far as I could. The chain barely allowed me within reach of her.

"Are you all right?" I asked.

The fairy shot away from my touch and into the air like a tiny firework. She was nearly naked, clad in a tight dress that stretched from her bosom to the middle of her thigh. Her fast-moving wings created a radiant glow that matched her scarlet hair but left a choking trail of smoke in their wake. She bared her razor-sharp teeth, tinged red with blood. No doubt she'd just returned from hunting before she, herself, was hunted, trapped, and brought to this lifeless land of sand.

"Daughter of the Central Network," she hissed with a scowl, hovering a breath away from my face. "Why are you here?"

"Why are you here?" I countered. "You're far from Letum Wood. Did my father send you?"

The little fairy scowled. "I work for no one, and I know no witches, daughter of the Central Network."

My hope, though small, shrunk smaller still. Fairies had earned their reputation as vain little beings that hated anything not fairy. While some used false innocence to draw in their prey, and a few associated with witches, most were vicious creatures obsessed with blood. They hunted in family packs that stayed together for decades and fiercely guarded their territory. The scorn in her voice told me all I needed to know.

"Why are you in the West?" I asked.

She hesitated. "Many reasons."

I studied her. "You were caught by a West Guard, weren't you? They brought you back to show you off to their friends, and you've escaped."

She narrowed her beady eyes on me. Her lips curled up in a snarl. "I recognize you," she said.

"I hear that a lot. I'm the High Priest's daughter."

"High Priest's daughter?" She tilted her head back. "What does this mean? You are not of the forest?"

"You don't know who the High Priest is?" Fairies were conceited, but I hadn't known they were clueless.

Her long wings fluttered. She folded her arms across her chest. "No. We care not for witches and mortals. Or your war."

The war between witches and mortals had ended thousands of years earlier, when the five Networks were first formed, but I didn't feel like giving her a history lesson.

"Ah," I said. "I see. Well, if you don't know my father, how do you know me?"

"The forest."

"Letum Wood?"

"It knows you."

"Why?"

"The forest recognizes its own." She zipped around my head, her lips twisted as if she'd just sucked on a lemon. Demeaning herself to speak to a witch clearly pained her. "I am Dafina, fairy of the Mytack pack of Letum Wood. Since you prevented my demise, I shall grant you a favor."

"What can you do for me?" I asked, although I already knew the limits of her magic.

"Wealth, power, guaranteed love." She held out one hand. "Tell me your desire, and I shall grant it."

I considered using the fairy to free myself. How wonderful to beat Mabel with such a horrible little creature! The irony alone made me want to laugh. But my amusement at fate faded. Would saving myself be the best use of such an opportunity? Besides, there were so many layers to Mabel's magic. I likely couldn't peel them back enough to escape with just one favor.

Dafina looked at my manacle. "Freedom?" she asked, one eyebrow raised. "It is a wonderful gift, is it not?"

"A wonderful gift indeed but not the one I seek." I swung the manacle behind my back. Juba remained within earshot, so I lowered my voice. "I want you to find my friend."

"You seek a friend?" She put one hand on her hip and cocked her head. "You desire nothing for yourself?"

"This is my desire. You'll know her already. She's an old woman named Isadora."

Dafina's lips pulled down. "The Watcher of Letum Wood?"

"Yes."

"She is missing?"

"Mabel kidnapped her. I think she's here, in the Western Network, but I don't know for sure. I need to find her. It's a matter of life and death for all of us. Your pack as well."

The red aura of Dafina's wings intensified. She made chubby fists with her hands. "You desire me to stay here, daughter of the Central Network?"

A temper in such a small being didn't really frighten me, though perhaps it should have. Although they were tiny, their magical abilities were not. Still, I showed no fear. "Yes."

"I shall not!"

"Then give up your beauty. I'm sure the fairies in your pack will welcome you back when your hair falls out and your skin wrinkles like an old hag."

Her face turned beet red, matching her fiery hair. She let out a hiss. "You know our magic?"

"I do."

"Fine," she spat. "I'll seek the Watcher of Letum Wood."

"No," I said, holding up my hand. If I wasn't precise in my request, she'd take advantage of *seeking* Isadora for all of five minutes. "You'll find the Watcher, not just seek her, and return to tell me where she is. Also, you'll want to leave this room through the door, not the balcony. The balcony is enchanted to destroy anything that goes off the edge."

Dafina's wings moved so fast they hummed. She tightened her fingers, bending them as an old woman would.

"I shall find the Watcher of Letum Wood to fulfill the favor," she hissed, spitting every word with a wave of disdain. "But you, daughter of the Central Network, are no friend of the fairies."

She disappeared through the door in a streak of light.

A Strange New Land

The next morning started too soon—I woke with the earliest light of sunrise. Although Mabel's chamber still lay quiet under the subtle blanket of night, the rustle of movement sounded in the background.

"Are you going mad here in this cavern yet, Bianca darling? If you are, I have good news. We're going to take a little trip this morning."

I sat up to find Mabel standing in front of a gilded, full-length mirror, inspecting her reflection with a shrewd eye. Torches along the wall illuminated the room. She wore an elegant dove-gray gown with sleeves that fell to her wrist. Her hair spilled onto her shoulders in a golden waterfall of curls. Her eyes were blue, so I knew she was calm.

"We're going to the Northern Network," she said. "I'm sure you don't want to miss this opportunity."

I held my breath to keep myself from gasping. "The North?" I finally asked. She eyed me askance, amused.

"You heard me."

For one long, silent moment, I couldn't think. The words *Northern Network* whirred through my mind on repeat. Just like Marten had taught me, I shut my mouth and waited for the situation to unfurl.

"Don't look so surprised," Mabel said, watching me in the glass. "Witches have always lived in the Northern Network. They're just exceptionally good at hiding themselves. They don't particularly like us, you see. I can't say that I blame them."

Which would make them a fabulous ally. A tingle of fear shimmied down my back. Hadn't I been telling Papa to do this all along? To search out the North to see if it was really inhabited or not?

"You mean to negotiate with them?" I asked, turning around. Although I tried to force indifference, my mind raced. What would we find when we arrived? Were they a strong Network? How would Mabel transport us safely into such a treacherous, mountainous world? The idea was so foreign I felt confused. On so little sleep, my still-muddied brain tried to sift through all it meant with limited success.

"I do mean to negotiate with them, though it will be tricky. The High Priestesses have answered my request, granting me an audience with them. A rare circumstance."

"High Priestesses?" I repeated. "There's more than one?"

"Yes."

"How do you know?"

Her teeth sparkled when she smiled. "Because I do my homework."

"Do they know we're coming?"

Mabel rolled her eyes. "Of course they do. I'm not entirely sure what to expect when we arrive. They're notoriously paranoid. But rest assured—we'll speak with those in power eventually. Three women run the largest Network in Antebellum. Don't you like them already?"

The lower Networks—which included all the Networks except the North—all had a similar hierarchical structure: one High Priest and one High Priestess, with variations in who did the governing and who held the most power. After three hundred years of separation from the lower Networks, differences in government hardly surprised me. But three High Priestesses? The Northern Network already exceeded my expectations.

"I see," I said, striving to keep my tone neutral while my head spun with all the new information. As usual, Mabel saw right through it.

"No," she said, her eyes gleaming. "You don't see. You have no idea how much power lies in the North, Bianca darling. But you will soon. Oh, you will soon."

My right arm rose. The manacle glowed so brightly I turned away. Piece by tiny piece, a chain grew from the manacle until it attached itself to a similar manacle on Mabel's right wrist.

"Added security," she said. "Your father may be able to transport another witch, but no one in Antebellum can transport three. And, just in case . . ."

A cold, prickling feeling wrapped around my neck. When I attempted to speak, nothing came out.

"You have a notorious reputation for speaking when your opinion is not wanted," she said. "This shall prevent any unwanted communication, I think. Come. Let us transport there now. I will not be late for my destiny."

Darkness overtook me, along with the pressure of transportation that pressed on my face, hands, and eyes. Mabel held my arm so tightly it throbbed. The stress pushed into the sinews of my skin. I'd never transported for such a long time. Just when the intensity threatened to obliterate my body, Mabel released me. I fell onto rocky ground, slamming my shoulder into a boulder. Mabel landed like a feather while I lay on my back, gasping.

Mabel craned her head, studying a copse of evergreen trees surrounding the dirt road we'd landed on. We were high on the side of a rocky, lush mountain. I stood up and brushed the dirt from the back of my dress. Mountain after mountain waited behind the trees, stacked back to back like sentinels. Their rocky crags rose into the sky. A skirt of snow held on to their peaks, giving way to waves of undulating green hills. There was no leaden humidity, nothing but a delightful freedom of breath and wind, like we'd entered a perpetual spring day. Unlike in the Central Network, where the canopy of Letum Wood blocked the sky, the mountains hugged the world with arms of stone.

"They should be along soon, I would imagine," Mabel said, the chain between our manacles jerking me to the other side of the road when she spun. "They will have detected us."

She must have seen the question in my eyes.

"Whom do I speak of?" she asked merrily. "Well, the North has a complicated welcome party for witches who transport into their land.

None of that will matter, of course, as they're expecting me and will grant me a diplomatic pardon. You'll see soon en—"

"Halt!" an unknown voice shouted. Ten witches materialized in a circle around us, arrows nocked, three of them within a breath of my face. All of them had a thick purple rope tied around their right forearm. Swords dangled from their hips, and thick pads of leather protected their necks and chests. Most of them had dark brown skin, just like the gypsies in the Central Network, but I noticed three fair-skinned warriors in the group.

A towering, dark-haired witch stepped forward from the ranks, his sword drawn. He had long legs, chocolate skin, and a vibrating, deep voice.

"Hands up," he commanded. I obeyed. "What is your business crossin' over our boundaries?"

His voice was husky and deep, with thick rolling r's and a heavy burr. I could barely understand him.

"I'm here to speak with the High Priestesses," Mabel said, her arms hanging at her side. "They're expecting me."

He barked a command in a different language and lowered his sword, holding his chin high. "So you're the visitors from the lower Networks that we're to be expectin'," he drawled, looking us over from top to bottom. He sneered. "You can keep your war where it belongs and go home."

Some diplomatic pardon, I wanted to say to Mabel.

Mabel's eyes tapered. The Guardian jerked his head toward us. "Tie them," he called, "under the authority of High Priestess Farah."

The word *Farah* purred like thunder off his lips. From the respect in his eyes, I had a feeling that Farah would be an enemy worth contending with. Mabel didn't fight when two Guardians grabbed her wrists and bound her hands in front of her, but her eyes became slits as thin as her lips.

"Be careful what enemies you make," she said with a cold smile.

He cast an arrogant look over his shoulder as he sauntered away. They tied my hands behind my back and tossed a burlap bag over my head. The smell of dirt filled my nostrils. Only a few pinpricks of light shone through the coarse material. I refused to panic. Instead, I

focused all my attention on listening to the sound of wheels clatter-
ing over the cobblestones as the North Guards led us further into a
strange new land.

We rode downhill over bumpy roads for hours.

Every jostle sent my body swaying from side to side. My skull
smacked into a metal bar so many times a headache pulsed in the
back of my neck. My hands burned from being tied together, and
I longed for my sword. *Couldn't she have transported us any closer?* I
hoped Mabel was as uncomfortable as I was.

Just as the ride evened out, the bustle of a village drowned out the
clop of hooves. The aroma of fresh-baked bread made my stomach
growl. We'd moved into a shadow—I couldn't feel the sun. The jostling carriage stopped fifteen minutes later. My heart took off like a
hummingbird. We'd arrived.

The North Guards grabbed my arm and yanked me out of the back
of the wagon, pulling Mabel with me. I stumbled and pitched forward,
but a hand caught me, stopping me from falling onto my face.

"Easy," a familiar voice murmured, so low I could barely hear it.
My entire body went rigid.

Merrick.

His firm hand squeezed my arm in silent command. *Be quiet,* I
imagined him saying. The tips of his fingers brushed against the inside
of my arm, sending a bolt of fire across my skin. Luckily, the hood
bought me time to gather my wits without giving anything away.

"I'll take this one," Merrick said in the same low burr. It sounded . . . natural. My heart pounded, and I strained to hear their conversation. Questions fluttered through my mind like a flock of birds.
Why are you here? I wanted to ask. *How is this possible?*

"Follow me," Merrick called. "We're takin' them inside Balmberg
Castle."

Whether he said that for my benefit, so I'd know where I was, or
he was some kind of leader, I couldn't discern. Maybe both. Was this

the mission Papa had sent him on? My frustrations doubled. I wanted to say so much!

Mabel lengthened the chain between us while we ascended several flights of stairs and walked through a maze. The world had darkened, which meant we'd likely moved inside. Cool air filtered into my burlap hood, clearing away some of the dusty stink. We turned a sharp corner and stopped. The ropes around my wrists fell away.

Merrick stood just behind me, his chest nearly touching my back. Our proximity made me lightheaded. I closed my eyes and resisted the urge to spin around and throw myself against him. He let go, but the tips of his fingers trailed across the small of my back before he stepped away. I listened to his departing footsteps with a sinking feeling in my stomach. The air seemed colder without him behind me.

Come back, I wanted to shout. *Please, come back.*

"You may remove your hoods," an unknown voice said from across the room. "Forgive our less-than-charitable welcome, but Her Majesty is careful when it comes to protectin' the Network."

I reached up and pulled off the hood. A burly witch approached us with a confident stride. He had short brown hair chopped off in an erratic fashion, as if he'd attempted to do it in the middle of the night with no light. A cluster of pink scars on the right side of his face pulled his eye down and twisted half his eyebrow in a perpetual grimace. A well-groomed beard covered the parts of his face that weren't scarred.

"The name's Wolfgang," he said. "I'm the Head of Guardians in the Northern Network."

Mabel's scowl didn't ease, but he ignored her.

"Such poor treatment is inexcusable," Mabel said. "The High Priestesses were expecting me."

"Still are," Wolfgang said, stopping a breath away from Mabel. Her jaw tightened. "But this is our Network," he continued, the deep brogue of his accent more pronounced. "We'll be doin' this our way, not yours."

Mabel's nostrils flared, but she said nothing. I rolled my lips together to keep from laughing. What a delightful place the Northern Network had turned out to be so far. Wolfgang cast a sidelong glance at me, my manacle, and the chain anchoring me to Mabel.

"Who are you?" he asked.

"This is my prisoner, Bianca Monroe," Mabel said.

He didn't acknowledge her response. His shrewd eyes remained on me. "Can't you speak?" he asked. I shook my head.

Mabel watched him intently, her head tilted back. "She's the daughter of Derek Black."

Ah. That's your game. She'd brought me along to buoy her social power. To gloat. To win the vote by showing superior force. Wolfgang grunted.

"Don't care. Why are you chained to her?"

Mabel's smile tightened. "She wanders off on her own a lot."

"Better figure somethin' else out. You can't go into the throne room wearin' that."

Mabel lifted an eyebrow. "And why not?"

"It's a weapon, stupid witch," he cried. "I'll not let you near Their Majesties with a metal chain. Are you daft? What if you tried to choke them? Or hit them?"

Mabel recoiled. "I'll not be separated from her."

"I didn't say you had to be," he said. "Just get rid of the chain. She doesn't have to leave your sight. Don't be so scared."

"I'm not afraid of anything," Mabel retorted.

Wolfgang grinned, which twisted the distorted half of his face into a scowl. "Sure you aren't. Now, lose the chain, or I'll escort you to the dungeons until you do."

The manacle around her wrist disappeared, taking the chain with it one link at a time. She glanced at me.

"Stay close, Bianca darling," she hissed through her teeth. "You wouldn't want another little shock to knock you out again, would you?"

Passing out would reduce my chances of spotting Merrick again, so I shuffled closer to her.

"Come on then," Wolfgang said, already halfway across the room. He muttered under his breath, "Stupid foreigners always take forever."

Beams of light streamed in long ribbons through the hallway. The air had cooled inside the heavy stone walls of Balmberg Castle, reminding me of Chatham. Balmberg sat in the middle of a close ravine.

Craggy mountainsides vaulted out of the earth around us, climbing so high I could barely see the sky. Water thundered down the rock ledges in bursts of froth, spinning a lacy design of falling mist. Several stories below, a bridge ran from the castle entrance to a road that wound up the steep mountainside. The river flowed around the castle before it dropped into the village and disappeared.

Wolfgang stopped to gesture at a window. "The Balmberg waterfall is considered the jewel of the North. The castle was built around it so our first High Priest, D'Artagnan, could see its beauty whenever he wanted."

Mabel cast an idle glance outside and yawned. A faint chime rang in the air from far away. I cocked my head to hear it better, drawing Wolfgang's attention.

"The Mala bells," he said, noticing my curious expression. He pointed to the bridge below. Hundreds of strings filled with tiny bells ran across it in a glittering canopy.

"Whenever a witch dies, we set them free on the river to complete their journey," he continued. "When they pass under the bridge, we put up a white bell about the size of your smallest fingernail. The wind immortalizes them forever. No two Mala bells look or sound the same. They're all unique, made by a witch in the high mountains named Hezba."

The Mala bells created a sweet, beautiful symphony that rode on the wind. I had to settle for smiling my thanks at Wolfgang.

"Can we continue?" Mabel asked in a chilling tone. "I have business to conduct back at home."

Wolfgang's forehead puckered. "Cheeky monster, aren't you?" He turned to continue on, speaking mostly to himself. "And a High Priestess at that. I'd start a war with you, too, if I had to put up with your attitude."

Mabel gritted her teeth.

I pulled myself away from the view with great reluctance. A fair-skinned witch in a fuchsia turban drifted by us, wisps of blonde hair coiling to her shoulders. She nodded wordlessly to Wolfgang and met my gaze with a curious smile. I returned her smile, eyeing her bright yellow dress. I'd seen so many bright colors in the Northern Network that I wondered if the people were somehow related to the gypsies, who dressed in a similar style. Could they be some kind of descendent? A splinter group?

A low-arched entrance of gray and black rock welcomed us into the East Wing. Wolfgang reached up and slapped the top of the door as he passed underneath. I felt a reverberation in the air.

"Here we are," he cried. "The East Wing, where Their Majesties do all their best work. The throne room is just ahead on the left."

Mabel's shoulders eased back. She closed her eyes, drew in a deep breath, released it, and opened her eyes again. They were as blue as a summer sky. Wolfgang stopped at a door, casting a look at Mabel and then at me.

"You ready, Miss Attitude?"

Mabel sneered. "Just let me into the meeting already."

"Act like that with Her Highness Farah," he muttered, returning Mabel's glare, "and I'll never have to talk to you again."

I Am Farah

A sprawling window dominated the throne room, overlooking a particularly beautiful segment of the Balmberg waterfall. Panes of sapphire, ruby, and emerald glass sparkled in the windows, and panels of mahogany wood gleamed along the walls. The elegance was simple, grounded in earth tones and wood. Portraits of past leaders, male and female, hung in clusters of three along the wall. *So the Northern Network isn't always ruled by women,* I thought, suppressing a flash of disappointment.

Wolfgang lifted an arm to the right, where three thrones sat in front of a wall of pure glass. Light from the cascading waterfall flashed behind the glittering gold thrones.

"Her Highnesses await," he said.

The three High Priestesses sat quietly, regarding us with striking differences in their expressions, which ranged from annoyance to curiosity. Their piercing stares surprised me. I wondered how Mabel would approach such a tough crowd. *It never hurts to appeal to their vanity if you can,* Marten had once instructed me. Vanity, however, required a careful balance of searching and sincerity. I hadn't yet mastered it because I didn't have the patience to flatter other witches.

Wolfgang escorted us to the back of the room, far enough away that it would take several seconds to reach the High Priestesses should we decide to attack. Mabel shoved me behind her, near a window with floor-length curtains, but kept a polite smile on her face.

"Your Highnesses," Wolfgang said, standing between Mabel and the thrones as he dipped into a bow. "Allow me to introduce our hon—our guests, High Priestess Mabel of the Western Network and her prisoner, Blanca. I mean Bianca."

The witch in the middle had spirals of ebony hair and coffee-colored skin. A ring in her right nostril glinted when she shifted forward. She stared at me, her eyes calculating. When I met her gaze, she didn't pull away. We remained locked in a silent stare for a full ten seconds before she turned back to Mabel.

"I am Farah, High Priestess over the Guardians and Defender of our Network," she said. Her commanding tone rang over the room, making it clear why she ruled over security. She had the businesslike countenance of a leader. I didn't see much room for forgiveness or error in her eyes.

She motioned to the black-haired witch on her left. "This is my sister, Samantha." Her right arm rose toward the third High Priestess, who wore her hair wrapped in a turban. "And Geralyn. They rule the Northern Network at my side."

None of the sisters seemed remarkable in appearance. Geralyn and Samantha had the same thin, hawk-like nose and solemn countenance. As soon as Farah said their names, I forgot which one was which, for both sisters seemed to blend into each other. They wore variations on the same outfit, with jewels in their ears and full-bodied skirts of glaring fabric. The three High Priestesses had the same coffee-colored skin as many of the Northern Network witches I'd seen so far. Farah, however, shared no other characteristics with Geralyn and Samantha. I wondered if they were truly sisters or just bound under a powerful magic to rule the North as such.

"A pleasure to meet you," Mabel purred with a smile, bowing low. I fought the urge to roll my eyes but did the proper thing and bowed with Mabel.

"What have you come here for?" Farah asked. "We granted you an audience only because we are curious. I assume you're here to discuss the war simmerin' in the lower Networks?"

"I am."

"And our participation in it?"

"Not quite."

"We don't consider ourselves part of Antebellum," Farah continued, "so this war has nothin' to do with us."

I listened in quiet fascination. They were so close-minded. So certain.

Mabel gestured to me with an outstretched hand. "As your Head of Guardians mentioned, this is my prisoner, Bianca Monroe. She's the daughter of the High Priest of the Central Network, Derek Black. He's rumored to be the most powerful witch in Antebellum," she said, leaving a pregnant pause. "But here I have his daughter, whom he was unable to protect and clearly has not been able to recover."

"We know who she is," Farah said.

Mabel appeared surprised. "Do you?"

"We have our ways. To what end are you pointin' out the lineage of this girl? I don't care who your prisoners are."

Mabel's cunning smile bloomed on her face. "Proof," Mabel said. "Derek Black is not the witch of great power he's reputed to be should you ever be tempted into an alliance with him."

Farah's eyes narrowed. "An alliance?" she asked. "I know nothin' of what you speak."

"I've come with a proposition," Mabel said. "One I believe you'll like very much."

"And what is it?"

Mabel spread her hands. "I've come to offer you freedom."

Farah braced her hands on either side of her throne and leaned forward, her nostrils flaring. She kept her voice cool. "Are you insinuatin' you've taken our freedom away?" she asked in a low, dangerous tone.

"No."

"Explain yourself."

"I understand your hesitation to join the lower Networks, so I won't ask for an alliance or even support," Mabel said. "I ask only for your indifference. If you make an agreement to not assist Derek in any way, I will swear a binding that the Northern Network shall be left alone."

Farah's eyes tapered. Geralyn and Samantha showed the first signs of life, exchanging unreadable looks.

"Explain what exactly you mean by alone," Farah said.

"Exactly what it sounds like. No one shall bother you. The isolation of the Northern Network will continue under my reign."

A more perfectly crafted proposal didn't exist. Mabel didn't even ask for their help. No cost. No loss. In a rush of horror, I realized that I'd vastly overestimated her goals. She wasn't doing this to rule Antebellum. Unlike Evelyn, she didn't want to advance herself politically or financially. Until now, I hadn't appreciated that Mabel's sole motivation flowed from one desire: to claim the Central Network as her own. I wondered briefly if she even cared about the South or the East. Had she just used them as a means to get what she really wanted?

Farah straightened. "Interestin'," she murmured. "I wasn't expectin' that."

Mabel smiled, as if Farah had given her a compliment. "If you are willing," Mabel said, withdrawing a scroll from her pocket. Wolfgang started toward her but stopped when he saw the paper. "I have a *non actio concensi* binding drawn up. I'd love to discuss the particulars with you, if you're interested."

Farah sucked in a deep breath through her nose. "I am," she said, releasing the air with one *whoosh*. She turned to her sisters, murmured something to each, and all three stood. Samantha and Geralyn cast one last glance in our direction before exiting through a side door, their bright dresses rustling. Farah held out her hand.

"Let me read it," she said.

Mabel turned around to face me, blocking my view of the room with her body. "Kneel," she commanded in a low voice. I obeyed. She grabbed my lower jaw and squeezed until her fingertips dug into my bone. My nostrils flared. "Don't. Move," she hissed. "Don't even sit. Stay on your knees where you belong. Unless you want to pay for it later."

She released my face with a flick of her wrist, giving me a quick glimpse of Wolfgang before he looked away, a thoughtful expression on his face. Mabel glided to the other side of the room, binding in hand. Farah remained near her elevated throne, standing at least a head taller than Mabel. They fell into conversation. I released my breath in relief, shifting my jaw from side to side. Kneeling on the cold stone floor wasn't even embarrassing as long as I didn't have to endure Mabel's company. Besides, I had other things to think about. I scanned the room. Where had Merrick gone? Had I been dreaming? Perhaps I was finally going mad, falling victim to Mabel's insanity.

No, I told myself, feeling the burn of his hand on the small of my back again. He had been real, and so was the hope I felt.

To my surprise, a tea tray drifted to the floor in front of me. One shiny silver cup sat in the middle of a matching plate. It reminded me of Isadora. Small biscuits lay in a petal formation around the steaming teapot, but I had no appetite. I watched Mabel out of the corner of my eye. She still spoke with Farah but kept her body angled toward me.

With a sigh, I leaned forward to smell the tea. In the reflection of the silver pot, I saw Merrick standing just behind my left shoulder, hidden on the other side of the floor-length window curtains. Strands of sandy blonde hair had fallen out of his queue and hovered around his face. Our gaze met in the reflection, taking the bottom out of my lungs. His eyes were no longer a beautiful emerald but a livid, verdant fire.

"Are you all right, B?" he asked, low and quiet, without the thick accent of the North to disguise him. This was my Merrick. My best friend. While his presence comforted me, I felt more confused than ever. Had Papa been using him as a spy? It seemed impossible—Merrick was the youngest Protector in the Brotherhood. Perhaps Papa had already made an alliance with the North that I didn't know about. It wouldn't surprise me. Papa had always been one step ahead of everyone else.

Despite my overpowering questions, Merrick's voice still sent a thrill through my body.

I nodded. Technically, I was fine. Stressed but not hurt.

"Can you speak?"

I shook my head. He huffed. The light behind him highlighted the profile of his face as he looked away, setting fire to the golden stubble on his cheeks. The need to speak to him filled my throat with a heavy weight. How I'd missed my best friend! I kept my eyes riveted on the teakettle, drinking in every detail.

"Your father wants me to tell you to hold on a little longer," he said. "We have a plan. A solid one. It's going to work."

His voice sounded like a song. I would have closed my eyes to drink it in, but I didn't want to take my gaze off him. *When?* I wanted to ask, but I knew he wouldn't tell me. It would be better for me if I didn't know.

"When I saw you on the back of that wagon with her, I—" His throat bobbed as he swallowed. "I'm sorry this happened. Has she hurt you?"

I shook my head. Mabel glanced over, checking on me over her shoulder. I returned her icy stare, satisfying her curiosity. She looked back at Farah, none the wiser.

What are you doing here? I wanted to ask. *Did Papa send you on a mission? Have you missed me as much as I've missed you?*

He ran a hand through his hair. "I wish I could set you free now, but we have to wait. Do you understand?"

I nodded and curled my fingertips into my palms until my nails bit into the sensitive skin. Tears filled my eyes, and I was grateful he couldn't see them. The sweet, tangy scent of evergreen filled my lungs. Though he stood only an arm's-length away, the distance between us felt eternal. I yearned to throw my arms around him, to laugh when he made a quip about my wild hair, to know home wasn't far away. The magic silencing my voice burned heavier than ever.

"Do you trust me?" he asked.

I nodded. Of course I trusted him.

"We'll get you out of here. You can do this, B. You're made of steel. If anyone can survive Mabel, it's you."

In that moment, when I didn't believe enough in myself, Merrick's faith in me quieted my doubts. I nodded so he'd know I'd heard.

"I'll see you soon, little troublemaker."

The curtains rustled as he transported away. I swallowed back the rest of my emotions. His promise rang through my mind, giving me strength.

I'll see you soon.

"I will not make such a decision in one day," Farah said to Mabel, rolling the scroll back together but keeping it clasped in her hand. "I will discuss this with my sisters. We will summon you when we have an answer."

Mabel's neck twitched, but she nodded. "Very well," she said, the lack of a respectful title such as *Your Highness* ringing in the air. "I shall await your decision."

Farah's eyes lingered on mine for a half-second.

"Go," she said, turning away. "And do not return until you are called."

"Daughter of the Central Network," snapped a familiar voice in my ear several days later, on the eve of my third week as Mabel's prisoner. "You have not left yet."

I whirled around, suppressing a gasp. Dafina hung in the air behind my shoulder. I pushed myself away from the balustrade and turned my back to the bustling marketplace far below.

"You're back already," I said, not bothering to disguise my surprise. Her crimson wings fanned even faster.

"A fairy is very fast," she said, baring her teeth. Her once-vibrant hair had faded, and now its ends looked jagged and torn, uneven on both sides. She'd already changed so much since our first meeting four days earlier that I hardly recognized her. If her wings hadn't been such a bright red, I would have thought her a different fairy.

"You started losing your beauty," I said. "Is it because you haven't fulfilled my favor yet?"

"Favor?" she hissed. "You think fairies are fools?"

She zipped around my head, choking smoke trailing behind her. I ducked away, coughing until it cleared out of my lungs.

"What are you talking about?" I asked, waving my hand in front of my face to clear the air. "I never said you were a fool."

She flew toward me, her bony, thin arms outstretched. "Send me to find the Watcher!" she screeched. "When she's here all along! I am no fool!"

I dodged her attempt to rip strands of hair from my head. "Dafina, what are you talking about?"

She hovered a breath away from my face. Her cheeks flared a hot crimson that flowed down her neck and onto her arms.

"The Watcher!" she cried, pointing inside. "The Watcher is with you every day! You send me on a fool's errand—flying all over the Network, speaking with witches, sneaking into the Arck. All for nothing! You make a fool of the fairies!"

I followed her arm to see Juba lying in the sun.

"No," I said in a low voice. "Absolutely not. Juba is not Isadora. Juba's a bully and ornery and ate a witch. Have you been sipping from ipsum bottles?"

Dafina trembled with rage. "Not that one," she cried. "The other. The other! The one that follows the other daughter of the Central Network. The other animal is your friend, the Watcher. I know the magic. I sensed it while hiding in the castle. The Watcher passed me. I know her magic!"

I reached out to hold onto the wall. "Juka?" I whispered. "You're trying to tell me that Isadora is Juka?"

Dafina hissed, like a snake about to strike. "Yes!" She grabbed a fistful of hair in her hand. "For your ignorance, I lose my beauty! You, daughter of the Central Network, will pay for what you've done to the fairies. What you do to one, you do to all!"

The past few weeks whirred back through my mind. Juka had always been with Mabel. Except for when Mabel journeyed to the Southern Network and the Northern Network, Juka never left Mabel's side. Unlike Juba, Juka interacted with no one else. My heart nearly stopped. Isadora had been under my nose all this time.

"Dafina, I didn't know, or I never would have sent you," I said, exultant. "I didn't know! But how wonderful!"

She regarded me through narrowed eyes, her arms crossed over her chest. "You lie," she said, but the vehemence in her tone had lessened.

"No! Why would I waste my favor and your time?"

Dafina hesitated only a moment, blinking rapidly. "You did not make a fool of the fairies?" she asked. I shook my head.

"No, of course not."

Now that I knew where to find Isadora, I had to tell Zane. Writing a message wasn't an option, and I couldn't afford to wait for him to come back to check on me. He had to know immediately. My mind raced with ideas until Dafina cleared her throat, her hands on her hips and her eyebrows raised in expectation.

"Oh," I said, shaking my head. "Right. Sorry. Your bondage to me is released. You have fulfilled the favor under fairy law. Reclaim your beauty and be free."

Dafina bobbed in the air. Her sharp tone faded. "You are still no friend of the fairies, daughter of the Central Network," she said. "But . . . you are no enemy, either."

As close to a compliment from a fairy as I was likely to ever get. I paused, staring at her. "Dafina," I drawled, "what are you going to do now that my favor is fulfilled?"

"Leave," she said, folding her tiny arms. "I will return to my forest home."

"Can you go wherever you want?"

"Of course."

"Can you deliver a message?"

She paused, hovering in one spot, and tilted her head back. "Why does the daughter of the Central Network ask?"

"I need you to tell my friend Zane that the cheetah with Mabel is Isadora. Can you do that?"

"No!" she hissed, balling her hands into fists. She flew around me in a fury. I dodged her attack, holding my breath to keep the red smoke out of my lungs. "You have asked enough of the fairies!"

"Wait! Let me finish!"

"I will never help you, ungrateful daughter of the Central Network," she screeched, zipping around me in fiery agitation. "Never! May the war kill you and all your family! May the winds of the West tear all the hairs from your head! May your eyes—"

"Stop, Dafina!" I cried. "I'll owe you a favor!"

Her crimson wings, humming so fast they appeared a mere whir of red light, slowed until she hovered in one spot. She glanced back over her shoulder.

"What?"

I swallowed, already regretting it. Having a fairy in my debt was one thing, but being in debt to a fairy was another. Her request could get ugly. She could fly back to her pack, tell them the news, and ask any sort of strange or outlandish favor. I'd be obligated to fulfill it. Dafina seemed to know what she was doing, which didn't bode well for me.

"If you deliver the message to my friend and can prove that you did it, I will owe you a favor."

Dafina dropped until she floated right in front of my face, so close I almost went cross-eyed.

"Does the daughter of the Central Network swear on the magic of the fairies?" she asked, one eye narrowed.

"I swear."

"'Tis done," she said. "I will fulfill your request."

Once I told her about Zane and gave her a question to ask him so that his answer proved she'd found the right witch, she flew away without a sound, leaving me in stunned silence.

"Desperate times," I said, shaking my head. "Desperate measures."

High Priestess of the Western Network,

Your presence is requested before Their Majesties Farah, Samantha, and Geralyn immediately.

Sincerely,
Wolfgang, Northern Network Head of Guardians

Don't Provoke Her

An aged butler with flecks of gray in his reddish-brown hair met Mabel and me on the outer wall of Balmberg Castle when we transported to the Northern Network for the second time. As it was our second visit, we weren't forced to go through the usual formality of being tied, tossed into the back of a cart, and bounced over endless roads. The butler bowed when he saw us and motioned to the hall with a white-gloved hand.

"Their Majesties await," he said. "Please, follow me."

The moment I stepped into the throne room, trailing just behind Mabel, the hair on the back of my neck stood up. An uneasy pit opened in my stomach. Mabel clenched her jaw and drew in a deep breath, her fingers tapping a staccato rhythm on the folds of her dress. I searched for Merrick out of the corner of my eye but found only rose-colored window panes and gilded mirrors. Disappointment weighed on my heart.

Farah, Samantha, and Geralyn sat on their thrones, as regal and indifferent as I remembered from our first visit. Wolfgang escorted us into the room, dressed in a metallic armor that gleamed in the sunlight. He kept one hand on the hilt of his sword. There was no small talk—no tour—this time. In fact, Wolfgang didn't speak at all. The air in the room felt thick and awkward with latent tension.

"Odd," Mabel muttered under her breath, staring right at Wolfgang. Her gaze moved to Farah, then Samantha. The silencing magic burned in my throat, preventing me from asking her what she meant.

"Mabel," Farah called. "Thank you for respondin' so promptly."

"As promised, Your Majesty," she said in a halting voice.

Farah didn't shrink away from Mabel's silent challenge but instead matched her with an equally intense gaze. For a long minute, neither of them spoke.

"I have come for your answer," Mabel finally said. Her hands stopped moving, remaining stiff at her side. "I'm sure no one wants to waste time with forced trivialities."

"Agreed," Farah said. "I'll get right to our official response. We are not willin' to join a *non actio concensi* bindin' with you."

She threw the binding scroll on the floor. It landed with a *thunk* and rolled to Mabel's slippered feet.

"We do not feel it's in our best interests."

Mabel's eyebrow arched. "Indeed? And why not?"

The question Mabel didn't ask seemed to hang in the air: *Did Derek get to you first?* I certainly hoped so.

Farah's gaze turned cool. "You forget yourself," she said. "I don't answer to you. You are a tyrant and a fool, resurrectin' an ancient magic responsible for the deaths of so many in the annals of history. We shall not support a witch with such a dark agenda."

Farah's display of force, while impressive, sent a bolt of fear shooting through my body. *No,* I wanted to say. *Don't provoke her.*

But it was too late. Mabel smiled in a coy, sultry way that only meant trouble. Her darkness tugged at my mind. I pressed a hand to my head, frightened by the chaos I could feel building within her. Wolfgang took a step forward. Farah didn't move.

"A tyrant and a fool?" Mabel said. "We shall see who the fool is."

The fragile strings holding Mabel together shattered. A stream of black smoke burgeoned at her feet and slithered across the floor. It wrapped around High Priestess Samantha, smothering her. Geralyn leaped from her throne and grabbed her sister, but the smoke swallowed her as well.

"You shall die with your sisters, Farah, you fool!" Mabel screamed, her fingers outstretched like long tentacles. "I warned you!"

The weight of the air felt so heavy I could hardly breathe, an indication that she was using powerful Almorran magic. I backed as far away as I dared, turning away from the smoke. Farah stepped back, putting the throne between herself and Mabel.

A familiar whisper surged in my consciousness with such strength and clarity that I lost myself in it for a moment, remembering the horrible eternity of pain and darkness I'd endured in Mabel's mind.

She left me.

Almorran magic compressed the air as the black fog crawled with lightning speed toward Farah's throne, disintegrating it into dust in moments. I shook my head, trying to force the encroaching darkness and all its familiar whispers away, to no avail. The pain sucked me back into Mabel's mind. The whisper grew to an agonized cry. I was losing.

Make the fire stop!

Mabel's gaze snapped over to me. The smoke hovered a few paces from Farah, who hadn't moved. Taking advantage of her momentary hesitation, I threw my body into Mabel's, knocking both of us to the ground. The black smoke faltered. Farah disappeared. I was sucked away, back to the darkness of Mabel's mind again.

Voices exploded in my head, drowning me in a sea of pain again. Instead of encompassing darkness, I floated in a red current of rage. A bone-deep fatigue, so strong it overcame everything else, weighed me down. There was no room for hatred here. The only thing stronger than exhaustion was an insatiable desire to win. The voices of the past didn't haunt Mabel now. Her own voice chattered in the background, alternating between weary fatigue and fanatical madness.

It's too much.

I will prove I am stronger than them. I will prove I am stronger than them. I am more than my mother. I will prove I am stronger than them.

But I can't do this. The magic is so strong.

I must see it through. That's all. I will see it through to the end. I will prove that I am stronger than them. I will.

A faint whisper persisted, a haunting response to her own declarations.

It's too much.

Images flashed through my head at an alarming rate. West Guards. A woman with black hair and cold eyes. The arm of a young girl, bleeding and swollen. An unmarked grave. A dark room with no candle. The *Book of Spells* open on a desk.

The delineation between Mabel's mind and my own started to evaporate. Whatever life I'd had before this moment faded, and I melded into the images. Blood dripping off a wrist. A dark forest at night. Angelina smiling, her arms open. Her cold embrace, so foreign.

I'm so tired.

I'll show them I'm strong, I said in response, and it sounded like Mabel. *Because she left me.*

Above the fatigue and uncertainty swam a beautiful light, a wave of gold that danced back and forth. I sought it, trying to capture it, but it didn't want to be caught. On and on I tried, seeking the thin thread until it broke, spilling its strength on me. Power. Excitement. I knew it from the first moment it filled me with strength and renewal.

Almorran magic.

Just when the bliss of Almorran magic bore me above the fatigue and desperation, a lingering voice in the background called out. The voice beckoned, and I answered, falling into a memory hidden in the deepest darkness.

"You're a stupid girl, Mabel."

The woman stood in front of a warm hearth, facing a window that looked out on a snowy winter night. Snow fell in soft drifts, collecting on the windowpane in tufts like lines of melted marshmallow fluff. My arms smarted, but I didn't look at them. I stared at the soft snow in the safety of silence instead.

"You failed your exam."

Grandmother. The witch I hated more than anyone, with her thin face and voluptuous black hair. She held a homework scroll in her hand. When the firelight flickered across her severe features, she reminded me of a raven. She threw the small scroll into the fire, causing a spray of bright blue sparks.

"Put out your arms," she said, reaching for a long stick near the fireplace. "You shall receive your just punishment."

Impassive indifference had become my forte, even though the ball of heat in my stomach flared with such strength it made me sick. I lifted my arms. She wanted me to flinch, but I stared at the window with steely determination instead.

Prove how strong you are, I thought. *Prove it.*

I heard the hot crack of the stick tearing through the sensitive flesh of my arms before I felt the burn. Tears rose in my throat, but I pushed them back. May wanted me to show weakness. I would never give her what she wanted.

The thin piece of wood had a stringy end that wrapped around my arm with every blow. Once she finished with the right side, she moved to the left. A trickle of blood dripped from my elbow. I slid my foot over to catch it before it hit the floor. I didn't fancy scrubbing again this week. Except for the crack of the wooden stick and the burn of the fire, no other sound joined the bitter symphony.

Once May finished, she stepped back and surveyed her work.

"Go to bed," she said, using a spell to send the stick back to the fireplace where it rested, waiting. "I have nothing more to say to you."

Always waiting.

The memory faded, leaving me in the agitated burn of my—no, Mabel's—mind. I sifted through the hatred, finding a sense of comfort in it. Hatred was familiar, after all. Hatred. Agony. It was all I'd ever known.

Leave, Mabel's voice hissed. *Leave my mind!*

But why would I leave? Where would I go? Was the anger not my home? My saving grace? What else was there for me to know?

"You came," Mother said, meeting me with outstretched arms. Letum Wood proliferated around us in a world of green ivy and wildflowers. The heavy humidity of summer rested on my shoulders.

"Yes," I said, stopping just short of her embrace, imagining that her foreign touch would burn my skin. She folded her hands together with a small, understanding smile, the way any normal mother would. Then again, Angelina wasn't a normal mother. No normal mother met her daughter for the first time in the forest when she was fourteen years old. Although I didn't want to acknowledge it, we shared many facial characteristics. Without a doubt, she was the witch I'd always sought. And now that we'd met, I wished I hadn't looked so hard. The disappointment rang through my chest like a hollow bell.

"Well, thank you for coming," she said. "I didn't know if you'd respond when I sent you that letter, but I was so happy when you did. I know this isn't easy for you, but I've wanted to explain why I haven't been in your life for the last fourteen years."

I wore a long-sleeved, white muslin dress that Celia had just finished sewing. It fitted to my wrist, covering my ugly scars. The slightest bit of sleeve moved up Angelina's arm, revealing a hint of puckered, scarred skin. So it wasn't just me that May tortured with whips and magical fire. My stomach hardened in a cold knot of anger. How I already hated her, this false mother.

But perhaps she could be useful. If she'd wanted to meet me badly enough to risk May's wrath, maybe she would take me away from this life. Away from the pain. I'd happily endure Angelina's desire to be my mother if it meant escaping May.

When I said nothing, Angelina motioned to a log. "Would you like to sit down?"

"No."

"Shall I just . . . go ahead and explain?"

"I need to be back in twenty minutes," I said, surprised at how easily the lie came. I didn't want to be in the forest with Angelina, whom my grandmother called a whore. The witch who had dropped me off in a torturous prison and never looked back.

The mother that left me.

"I'll make it fast, then," Angelina said, rubbing her lips together. Her eyes shone with affection. "You are very beautiful, Mabel. Very beautiful, just as I knew you'd be."

Her hand twitched, as if she wanted to reach up and touch my hair, but she kept it at her side.

"Anyway," she continued. "I owe you an explanation for why I left you with your grandmother instead of keeping you myself." Her eyes softened. "Has she been terrible?"

The tone of her voice told me that she knew, firsthand, the horror of May's parenting. She knew the cutting remarks, the impossible expectations, the days without food, the nights without candles, and the lingering burn of magical fire dancing on her skin.

"Why did you do it?"

"I had no choice." She spread her arms in a helpless gesture. "I was pregnant, alone, abandoned by your father, with no currency. I gave birth to you by myself in the forest and almost died. I tied you to me and crawled through the bracken because I was too frightened and weak to transport with you. What if I hurt you? I loved you too much to do that."

Love. The disgusting, horrid emotion that I'd fought for every day but never found. For a moment I wanted to lean into it.

No, I thought. *She left me here. If she loves me so much, let her prove it by taking me away.*

She looked at the forest, swallowing a lump of emotion. "I went to the only place I knew: my home. But Mother had forbidden me from returning, so I left you on the porch and hoped for the best."

I swallowed. Why hadn't she just let me die in the woods? Why hadn't she just taken me with her? The questions overwhelmed me.

"I see."

"No, Mabel," she said, stepping toward me and taking my hand. I jerked it away. Pain flickered in her eyes. "Please, let me make it up to you."

"Take me away from here."

"I can't," she whispered, pressing a hand to her chest. "Oh, Mabel, I want to. I love you very much. But I have another family now."

I reared back. "What?" I hissed.

"I have children back at home and a wonderful husband who loves me. I have a life, and I can't . . . I can't reveal to them who I really am, or all will be lost. They can't know you, and for the time being, it's best that you don't know them."

Her excuses felt like a slap in the face. *She's leaving me again*, I thought. *She's sending me to hell to stay. She is no mother.*

"Why are you here?" I asked, trying to control the rage bubbling from deep within. "Why are you here if not to take me away?"

"Because I have a grand idea," she said, an eager smile spreading across her face. "A goal, if you will, to enact justice on all those who have wronged me. And those who have wronged you, of course, for you are the best part of me."

A shining light glimmered in her eyes. Although brief, the force behind the gleam piqued my interest. Revenge? As much as I hated her, I wrapped my mind around the idea and felt a stirring of hope. While I could never trust Angelina, I could use her.

Achieve my own ends.

"You have my attention, Mother dearest," I said with a brittle smile. She beamed, adoration and relief in her gaze. She didn't even notice the loathing behind my smile. *She doesn't want to see it,* I thought. *Good. All the easier to manipulate her.*

"Good," she cried, her eyes alight. "For I have a marvelous plan to take over the Central Network and then all of Antebellum, and we shall do it together."

The memory blurred, returning me back to the agony. *Angelina.* How wonderful it had felt to see her die. To enact the retribution she'd always dreamed of herself. The irony had been delightful.

Just delightful.

"Competitors, line up."

Three other students stood apart from me in a line in the dark yard of Miss Mabel's School for Girls. Torches flickered on the rails of the fence, making it look like the bushes were rustling. I curled my right hand into a fist when the quiet chatter of the other girls met my ears in the chilly night.

"I can't believe she's competing. She's just a first-year! What could she know?"

"This'll teach her not to be so arrogant. She'll lose, for sure."

"She might be beautiful, but that doesn't mean she's better than we are. I think she's just doing it so she's the only first-year to ever win."

"She's related to the Head Witch. I hope she doesn't get shown favoritism because her grandmother runs this school."

I scoffed. Favoritism? May would kill me before she allowed me to win. She'd be furious if her fifteen-year-old granddaughter beat her at her own game.

Which was just what I planned to do.

"Students!" May stood near the old estate with four envelopes in her hand. "Your challenge lies within these envelopes. The first two girls back will advance to the next round."

I shook my head. May was so cold, so businesslike in all her dealings. Why couldn't she be charming? Warm? Alluring? Surely there was more safety in pretending to be nice than blatantly refusing to be. I promised myself—not for the first time—to never be like her.

The envelope soared through the air and into my waiting hand. Once it opened, a gauzy, ethereal butterfly with wings of red and black slipped out from the folds of paper and spun around my head. It disappeared into Letum Wood. I watched it go, my eyes narrowed. A butterfly? What was May's angle? With May, nothing was ever what it seemed.

Find your butterfly, the note said. When I looked up, two girls had already left, following the disappearing trails their butterflies left behind. I crumbled the note in my hand, let it burn into ashes, and plunged into the forest.

Letum Wood held me in a constricting tunnel of dying leaves for hours. Everywhere I looked, all I could find was darkness. No moon. No stars. Nothing pierced the high, haunted canopy.

"Ridiculous," I muttered, the tips of my fingers numb. I'd been walking the forest all night, attempting every incantation possible, to no avail. Surely two other girls had already returned, but I couldn't quit.

"Won't quit," I said, steeling myself. "I won't quit."

Just as I started to wonder if there was no butterfly, a flicker of red caught my eye. My butterfly bobbed up and down in the air in front of me in a beautiful taunt. I started forward, but it moved away. Frantic to win, I ran after it.

At the crest of a hill, my leg gave way beneath me. I slid down the hillside, my shoulders slamming into rocks and my back scraping against exposed tree roots, to slam into an old oak at the bottom of the slope. I tried to breathe, but pain shot through my side with every attempt.

"Damn," I whispered, my breath billowing out in front of me. I braced an arm around my midsection, certain I'd cracked a rib. My right ankle throbbed, and shots of heat ran through my legs. I shifted aside my dress to find the bone in my lower right leg oddly askew. The discomfort intensified. I gasped.

"I figured as much," May said, appearing in front of me. "I knew you'd never win."

Shame burned hot and fast in the back of my throat, almost as strong as the burn of my broken bone. Of course she'd be here.

"You set me up," I said. "You enchanted the butterfly to fly over a hidden hole so I'd fall."

Her eyes sparkled. "Maybe I did, and maybe I didn't. Either way, it proves you don't pay attention the way you should. You were so focused on the butterfly that you weren't watching your surroundings. You'd fail as a High Priestess because you're too focused on proving yourself to me. You allow too many emotions to control you. A smart witch uses logic. If you'd been thinking with any kind of strategy, you would have used magic to capture the butterfly instead of chasing it like a fool."

No, I thought. *I'm too focused on how much I hate you.*

"I broke my ankle," I said, shifting. The pain overwhelmed me. I could hardly breathe. "And a few ribs. I need . . . I need help getting back. I can't transport while I'm in so much pain."

Admitting my need nearly choked me. May raised an eyebrow.

"Good luck." She stepped backward. "If you haven't returned by tomorrow evening, I'll send Celia looking for you."

I stopped the memory in a rage. How dare that surface? How could it come up now? I'd buried it too deep for that.

Angelina peered at me from across the room, a slight smile on her lips. As always, her radiant beauty was without competition—porcelain skin kept bright by the sea air, dark curls resting on her shoulders, and a striking gaze softened by affection, yet firm with control. A look she reserved only for me . . . and that stupid second family she spoke of. My lip curled back in bitter annoyance. Love that she gave to her "family" freely. Love that kept her with them and away from me.

No bother. I hadn't needed her then, and I didn't now at almost thirty.

"Well?" she asked, the corners of her lips tilting upward. She raised her hands with a breath. "Can you believe that the day has finally come? That horrid witch is gone. May can haunt us no more. Executed for treason. What a wonderful phrase."

I smiled stiffly at her because that's what she expected. Even now, years after our first meeting, she never noticed the loathing behind the gesture. She didn't want to. Her face fell.

"Are you not happy, dear daughter, to be rid of May?"

"Ecstatic," I said, forcing a blithe smile. *But not as happy as I'll be when you're dead, you horrible old crow.*

"Good," she said, her eyes gleaming with a terrible, dark light that spurred me to a moment of jealousy. No witch would be terrible and dark with power except me.

Eventually, I reminded myself. *Be patient. My time for greatness will come after I've exacted my revenge on Angelina. After all, she left me.*

Angelina strode over to the bookshelf. She ran her fingers along the alphabetized titles until she stopped on a thick volume and pulled it from the shelf. It sank in her grip. Her gaze shone.

"Here it is," she whispered with reverence. "The beloved Book of Spells. I knew May had it, although she tried to hide it from me. She failed in her quest to become High Priestess and resurrect the ancient magic, but we shall not." Angelina's eyes lifted to mine. "Don't you think so, pet?"

"Of course, Mother dearest," I said, managing to keep the bite out of my tone by sheer willpower. I smiled. "We shall be great together."

Angelina's face brightened. She closed the book with a snap of her hands.

"Delightful," she murmured. "I am the more powerful of the two of us, so I shall take the Book of Spells first. It will take many years for me to master such a strong, wonderful magic without drawing attention, but then I shall teach it to you. We shall have to be patient while Mildred is in power. But she won't last forever, will she? Once a new High Priest or Priestess takes over, we shall act before they learn what they need to know. In the end, we'll be great together, a true mother-daughter pair."

I smiled. "Yes, we shall be together."

As soon as I am strong, and things are set into motion, I shall take your life, I thought with a thrill of excitement that she mistook, as always, for love. *The magic will be mine.*

And so will the Central Network.

Leave now, said a familiar voice, pulling me out of the memory. I experienced a moment of disorientation before I remembered that I wasn't Mabel.

Leave, Bianca. I cannot bear it.

The voices faded. My power dimmed. One minute I swam greedily in the sweet, delicious anger, and then it disappeared, like I'd slammed into a stone wall. The exhaustion took over.

My eyes fluttered open.

The War of the Networks

A quiet murmur of voices filled the background, all of them vague and distant. I surfaced through the layers of consciousness slowly, my head throbbing in sync with the slow plod of my heart. I blinked. I lay beneath a stone ceiling with a beautiful arch in the middle. Sun streamed through the windows, warming my face. A familiar brown gaze hovered just above me.

Papa, I thought, staring at him in surprise. *Why is Papa here?*

"B," he said, tapping me on the cheek. "Wake up."

"Papa."

"Hey," he said, his brow furrowed into deep lines. "Are you hurting anywhere?"

I pressed a cool palm to my head to stop the room from spinning. "I . . . I don't think so. Where am I?" I asked, glancing around us. Vague details replayed in my mind. Mabel's burning red eyes. Black smoke. A throne disappearing.

"You're still in the Northern Network. You connected with Mabel's mind again, I think. You've been out for a few hours."

Blinking cleared my blurry vision. Merrick stood near a window off to the right, his profile illuminated by the buttery sunlight. He kept one hand on the hilt of his sword, his concentration on something outside. Wolfgang crouched next to Papa.

"Feeling any better?" Papa asked. The heavy weight of his hand on my shoulder felt like a reassuring dream. Was I really in the North? Was Mabel gone? Although my head still pounded, it banged with less gusto now. My whole body felt sore.

"A little better," I said.

"Do you want to sit up?" Papa asked, and I nodded. He slid an arm under my shoulders. The room spun, but it settled when I leaned against him. His arm felt firm and strong behind my back. The comfort of his presence seemed almost too good to be true.

"What are you doing here?" I asked.

"I transformed into Wolfgang before you arrived so I could be here in case things went wrong," he said. "We suspected Mabel would act rashly once the North refused to cooperate with her, so Wolfgang transformed into Farah to protect the High Priestess."

"What about Samantha and Geralyn?" I asked. "Did the black smoke kill them?"

The muscles in Merrick's jaw flexed as he looked down. Wolfgang let out a heavy sigh.

"Yes, but they were two of my best Guardians, not Their Majesties," he said, hanging his head. "My best. But they died with honor, protecting their High Priestesses and Network."

With a flicker of pain on Wolfgang's behalf, I recalled Mabel's intent stare. "She knew something was wrong," I said. "She must have sensed your magic."

"She may have sensed something, but I doubt she knew exactly what it meant, or who was hiding behind the magic," Papa said. "She couldn't have been surprised that the High Priestesses weren't here in person to reject her. We had to hope that her desperation for the North's neutrality would motivate her to continue even if she grew suspicious, and so it came out. If she had known I was here, I think she would have left right away. Anyway, it doesn't matter now. We have you back. That's all I care about."

"Where is she?"

"Back in the West," Papa said. His eyes drooped a little, looking dimmed and fatigued. Like usual, his hair stuck out at many angles, but I noticed that he'd lost weight. The war, or perhaps my kidnapping, had taken a heavy toll on him.

"We tried to kill her before she left," Wolfgang growled. "She was too fast. Once you knocked her down, she managed to untangle herself from you and escape, but only barely."

"And she just left me?" I asked.

"Well, she didn't have a choice," Papa said, glancing at Merrick. "Merrick came after you when you fell, and I attacked Mabel. She transported within moments. She seemed to be on the verge of losing consciousness as well, but I'm not sure."

Time passed so differently under the Almorran spell. Within seconds Mabel and I had shared years' worth of memories, just like before. Or had the connection maintained even over a wide distance? Perhaps the link between our minds had strengthened after a second time.

"How did this happen?" I asked Papa. "I connected with her mind again, only this time it was . . . different. Stronger. She didn't come into my head. It was like she pulled me into hers."

"We aren't sure," Papa said, exchanging a look with Wolfgang. "At least, not with certainty, but Zane had a theory that I think is right."

"That you hoped was right," Wolfgang said with a snort. Papa agreed with a wry, pained nod.

"Yes, and we were lucky," he said. "Zane believed that Mabel accidentally created a connection between your minds that night in the Eastern Network caves. A connection that regenerates whenever you're in Mabel's presence and she's using Almorran magic."

"How did he figure that out?" I asked, rubbing my temples in a circular pattern.

He gestured to my wrist. The manacle was gone.

"Her use of Cudan magic. And Zane said that the magic protecting her chamber wasn't Almorran either. We believe Mabel was forced to use a lesser, non-Almorran magic so you couldn't see into her head."

"A theory Mabel just proved," Wolfgang said.

Pieces of my time in the Western Network clicked together. "Zane was right," I whispered, running through all the instances when I'd mentally heard her voice.

"Your description of what happened in the Southern Network really clued Zane in," Papa continued. "You said Mabel lost her temper and started to torture Mikhail with Almorran magic, and you heard her voice again."

"So, you hear voices in your head, eh?" Wolfgang asked, watching me dubiously.

"Yes," I said. "I'm half-crazed."

He nodded, appearing impressed.

"We took a calculated risk," Papa said. "But I had a gut feeling we were right, and my gut is rarely wrong. To my eternal gratitude, Their Majesties here in the North were willing to help me get you back."

Farah, Samantha, and Geralyn were nowhere in sight, and I was glad. I wanted some time to absorb all this information before meeting new witches. My head hurt too much. I'd sort through all the threads of this complicated tapestry later.

"I see," I said, grimacing.

"Want anything for the pain?" Wolfgang asked, lifting a jeweled goblet. I waved it away.

"No, thank you. It will go away on its own. Potions don't help. At least, they didn't last time."

His eyes narrowed, changing the structure of his face even more. "This really has happened to you before?"

"Unfortunately."

The deep, reverberating blast of a horn rippled into the room from outside. Wolfgang and Merrick looked out the window.

"What's that?" I asked.

"A call to war," Wolfgang said.

"War?"

Wolfgang let out a long, drawn-out sigh, exchanging a dark look with Papa. "Her Royal Highness Farah has declared that the Northern Network is going to war."

"Against Mabel?"

He nodded. "Against Mabel."

The two of them were grim-faced and dour. "But this is a good thing, right?" I asked. "We have help. Our chances are better with the North on our side, aren't they?"

"There are *no good things* when declaring war on other witches," Wolfgang said.

"And no sign of the *Book of Light*." Papa ran a hand through his hair. "Without it, I fear we don't have much hope. We have no way to subdue Almorran magic."

Their stony silence left nothing but the dying resonance of the war horn.

"So all of Antebellum is going to war against a magic we can't stop wielded by a witch who has nearly lost all sanity?" I asked.

"Yes," Papa said, squeezing the back of my neck. "It's the war of the Networks."

"Merrick will bring you back in the morning when you're feeling better," Papa told me a few hours later. "I don't want you transporting until some time has passed. You need to regain your strength."

Papa, Merrick, and Wolfgang had worked out the particulars of the North's involvement in the war. The North would send two thousand Guardians to join the fight. Considering they had no time to prepare, they gave far more than expected and their aid would be a boon. A hearty meal of potato stew and fresh bread sat heavy in my belly, a welcome variation from my diet of seeded bread in the West.

Although Papa could transport me so I wouldn't have to do the magic, I felt too wrung out and exhausted to deal with the extended stress of transporting back home. While I longed for the close comfort of the Witchery and the sound of Reeves puttering in our apartment, I wanted to sleep until my next birthday.

"I'm sorry. I need to go back," Papa said, pitching a stack of letters he'd just answered into the fire. "Zane is reporting increased activity in the Western Network. He said West Guards are pouring into Custos City."

"What does that mean?" I asked.

Papa set his jaw. "Mabel's lost her leverage and is sufficiently angry; she's preparing for battle. Don't worry. Nothing's going to happen overnight, so you stay. Recover as best you can."

"Thanks," I said. "I think that's a good idea. I'd like to spend a little more time at Balmberg anyway." I glanced around at the thick wooden beams and rose-colored windows. "Seems like a lovely place."

Papa put a hand under my jaw, turning my face up to meet his intense gaze. "I almost lost you, B," he said, his eyebrows wrinkling over his dark eyes. "I would never have been able to live with myself. I'm glad it all worked out. Good job staying calm under pressure. I'm proud of you."

I managed a crooked smile. This wasn't the first time we'd had a conversation like this. "It seems like we're always stressing each other out, aren't we? But it always works out in the end. You saved me."

He looked away, his lips turned down like an old man's. "Not this time. This time was different. Or it could have been."

I put my hand on his wrist. "I'm alive, Papa. Let's not worry about it. You have a war to win."

He grabbed my neck and pulled me against his chest. I wrapped my arms around him and breathed deep, smelling spearmint and leather and safety.

"I love you, Bianca," he said in a husky voice. "More than anything. More than the Central Network. Once this bloody war is over, you and I will go find a place to hide in Letum Wood for a month and live off the land."

I laughed. "Sounds like heaven."

"Wild child," he muttered, ruffling my hair.

Tears of relief surfaced in my eyes. "I love you too, Papa," I said. When he pulled away, he cleared his throat, blinking fast.

"You'll be safe here with Wolfgang and Merrick," he said, his deep voice indicating he'd switched back into High Priest mode. "I can't ask for better protection for my daughter than a Head of Guardians and one of his Assistants, can I?"

The words *one of his Assistants* rang through my head. I stared at Papa. "I'm sorry. What did you say?"

Papa froze.

"His Assistant?" I repeated. "What do you mean?"

Papa closed his eyes. "Jikes." He ran a hand through his messy hair. "I forgot, B. I'm sorry. You don't know."

"Don't know what?"

"Merrick," he said, gesturing toward my best friend with a nod. "Merrick's from the North. He works for Wolfgang."

My heart sank into a cold pool of water. I glanced past Papa to see Merrick talking with Wolfgang near the door, his arms folded across his chest. Shock rendered me momentarily mute. I shouldn't have been so surprised. I recalled his perfect accent, his unexpected presence in the North, and the strange way he'd never really spoken of himself.

"He'll explain everything to you later tonight, all right? I need to head back." Papa paused, shifting uncomfortably. "Don't . . . er . . . be too hard on him."

With that, Papa chucked me softly on the jaw and transported away, leaving me standing alone in the middle of the room. Both Merrick and Wolfgang looked up when Papa left. Merrick met my gaze, swallowed, and let out a heavy sigh. Wolfgang clapped him on the shoulder and disappeared.

My heart pounded when Merrick closed the distance between us with a slow, deliberate stride.

"You lied," I said.

Merrick's nostrils flared. He looked down at his hands. "Yes," he said, and this time his voice carried the heavy burr of the North. "I did."

I looked away, unable to bear the remorse in his eyes. Too much had happened for me to even know how I felt. Elated? Betrayed? Confused?

"I don't know what to say," I admitted.

"It's pretty simple, really," he said, meeting my gaze without flinching. "I grew up in the Northern Network. My boss, Wolfgang, sent me to the Central Network so we'd know what was happenin'. There's more to it than that, of course."

Mabel's memories still spun through my head in long, complicated ribbons, clogging my rationality. I was free. The Northern Network was fighting the war with us. Merrick wasn't who I believed him to be. My bones felt limp with fatigue. Grogginess overcame me in the wake of fading adrenaline and a warm meal in my belly.

"Can I have a little time before you tell me everything?" I asked, putting a hand to my head. "I just . . . I need sleep. Then we can talk all you want."

He nodded, but I could see the disappointment in his beautiful green eyes. "Of course. I'll show you to your room. We promised your father that Wolfgang or I would be with you at all times. Wolfgang is going to take the first watch."

Though I craved it, sleep remained elusive.

Farah had ordered their grandest room prepared for me, and so I stretched out in a sprawling bed large enough for four grown witches. The opulent chamber was easily as big as the apartment I shared with Papa at Chatham. I left the double doors to both balconies open to the mountain breeze and lay on my side, a light blanket pulled over my shoulders. Wolfgang snored from where he sat just inside the main door, and three North Guards stood in the hall outside. Merrick had not returned.

I stared at the rocks on the mountainside across from Balmberg, listening to the replay of Mabel's memories again and again. The quiet became too lulling. I slipped into vague dreams of Clavas and Mabel and Angelina and the *Book of Spells*. When I felt the cool metal of the manacle slamming back onto my wrist, I jolted upright out of sleep with a gasp.

The room lay quiet and dark, sweetened by the cool air. No heat. No Juba. No Mabel. I grabbed my empty wrist. No manacle. A heavy feeling of relief rippled through me. I fell back onto the mattress, turned my head into the pillows, and let out a long, slow breath.

"The rosemary doesn't go here. What were they thinkin', rearrangin' my pots?"

Who was speaking so quietly outside? Startled out of my thoughts, I pushed myself off the mattress and pattered over to the balcony, clutching my borrowed wrap dress. Wolfgang continued snoring.

"Parsley, that's better. Parsley goes before rosemary in alphabetical order. Nutters."

The mountain wind brought goosebumps to my skin when I stepped outside and looked to my left. To my great surprise, a thin figure stood with her back to me. Farah. Her nightgown, a rich ivory color, rippled in the wind. She bent toward her potted plants on a balcony parallel with mine.

Clucking, she shook her head. "Need more thyme."

I watched her for a moment. The ring in her nostril glinted in the residual light of two torches burning on the wall just behind her. She reminded me a little of Jackie with her dark skin, coiled hair, and long eyelashes. I couldn't help but wonder again about a connection between the gypsies and the North.

"Farah?" I asked, hoping to alert her to my presence.

She didn't even look up. "Yes, I am talkin' to my plants at three in the mornin'," she said. "I find that's the only time I can guarantee them I'll check in, and they're the only thin's in the Network that really listen to me."

"You have your own garden?" I asked. Several herbs bloomed in the clay pots. I recognized mint right away and lifted my face to smell the sweet scent on the wind. I thought of Grandmother. How comforting that something so small and familiar could still be found so far from home.

"Yes, I do," she said with a wan smile. "I love to garden, especially after a difficult day. Interactin' with plants and the earth—even if it is contained in pots and not wild the way I prefer—grounds me. I think today could be classified as difficult. Don't you?"

"Yes, of course."

"I thought you'd never come out," she said, plucking a shriveled oregano leaf. "I've been hopin' to talk to you."

"Me?"

"Yes. You're of great interest to me."

I folded my arms across my chest. "Why is that?"

"Because you know the witch that I just decided to go to war against better than any other witch on Antebellum does." Her dark chocolate eyes met mine for the first time. "I'm secretly hopin' you can help me understand her better. Your father told me what happened the night Isobel died."

While it made sense that Farah would be aware of all that happened in the lower Networks, I realized I hadn't expected her to know about Isobel. I shifted, biting my bottom lip. She smiled softly.

"I have my ways of stayin' up-to-date on the news," she said, anticipating my thoughts. "Besides, your father and I have just agreed to go to war together. He's told me everythin' I need to know."

"I see," I said, not sure of what to say next. She was right—I did know Mabel best. But I wasn't sure what that meant. Nor was it a burden I wanted to bear.

"You're restless tonight, aren't you?"

"I'm struggling to slow my thoughts," I admitted, folding my arms over my chest.

"A restless mind is a busy one," she said, straightening. "Would you like to talk about it?"

I hesitated. I didn't know Farah at all beyond her steel cage of an exterior. Tones of Mildred ran through her strong personality. But the last High Priestess I'd trusted had turned out to be my mortal enemy and tried to murder Papa. Farah held up her hands. The tips of her fingers were smudged with black dirt.

"You don't have to, of course. Just an offer."

The zesty tang of a tomato plant filled the air, making my stomach growl. It seemed ages since I'd eaten the thick stew.

"You know, for an eighteen-year-old girl, you seem quite . . . unbothered by the traditional ways of your Network," she said, and I was grateful to change topics. "I've often had the impression that witches from the Central Network are sheltered and close-minded. I don't see that in you."

She spoke in a musing way, as if trying to add together a strange new arithmetic.

"I'm probably not the best witch to represent other girls my age."

"Yes, I hear you don't enjoy wearin' shoes or dresses."

My eyes narrowed. That seemed like an odd tidbit for her to know. "Did Papa tell you that?"

"No. Merrick."

"Oh."

"I think it impressed him."

She flicked a handful of weeds off the side of her balcony, sending them to plummet tens of stories until they fell into the raging river below. The breeze whipped my dress against my legs.

"Do you mind if I ask you a few questions about Mabel and her mother?" she asked. "I believe war is more of a mental game than a physical sport, although it's arguably both. By understandin' her better, I'd like to think I could anticipate what she'll do. Protectin' my Network is my life, you know. I take it very seriously."

I shook my head. "No, I don't mind."

"What was Angelina like?"

While Mabel exuded a sultry, fluid kind of beauty, like burning desert sands, Angelina had been reserved and as strong as steel.

"Angelina? She was cold. Calculating. And the best liar I've ever met in my life."

Farah tilted her head back. "No doubt the daughter learned all she knew from the mother."

"No," I whispered, recalling Mabel's memories. "Well, not exactly. Mabel was mostly raised by her grandmother."

"Ah."

"But May was . . . worse. She was—" I shuddered, pulling my arms more tightly around my middle. "Horrible."

Farah studied me but didn't ask me to elaborate, for which I was grateful. The sting of Mabel's memories still ran deep, and I had a hard time separating her pain from my own.

"That kind of thing tends to run in families," Farah said, "which means Mabel must still be bitter."

"You have no idea."

"What was it like?" she asked, her voice lowering a notch.

"Being in Mabel's head?"

She nodded.

"Dark. Full of pain. So much pain. Hatred, too. Her hatred gives her an unbelievable amount of power."

Farah rubbed her thumb and forefinger over a downy strawberry leaf. "I suppose someone dedicated to the dark Almorran path would have to be guided by such ideals. It opens Mabel up to incredible weakness, which is likely why she's so defensive. I'm not surprised. I'm frightened by it, of course, but not surprised."

She's a witch just like us, I wanted to say, but the words choked me. Was Mabel just like us? Or had she allowed herself to fall so far that she'd lost her humanity? Rather than risk sounding too compassionate toward Mabel, I said nothing. It wouldn't look good to spout sympathy toward the witch who wanted to annihilate us.

Farah eyed me with fresh curiosity. "You bear the mark of Almorran magic, do you not?"

I'd gotten the scar behind my left ear months before, in my first encounter with Mabel's mind. I reached up to touch it with the tip of my finger.

"Yes."

"Your father has one as well."

"Can you sense it?"

She nodded.

"May I ask you a question now?" I said, hoping to divert the conversation.

"Of course."

"Why didn't you take Mabel's offer?"

Farah folded her hands in front of her. Her casual air struck me as odd. She had been so distant and cold in the throne room. I wondered if her sisters were as compartmentalized and easy to talk to.

"A fair question," she said. "What Mabel was askin' of us was certainly appealin', and I have no doubt she meant to honor her agreement at first. But it would only be a matter of time before what she'd gained wasn't good enough, and she'd fight us for the North as well. Knowin' her, she'd find a way around the bindin'. Even if she didn't, the agreement would make trouble for future generations. Almorran magic used by a governin' power would not benefit any Network."

"I believe you're right," I said. Winning wasn't enough for Mabel. She strove for total domination. "Are you afraid of her?"

"Of course I am. I'd be a fool not to be. She may not be invincible, but she is the Almorran Master. She wields power we can't change or control. But fear isn't always a weakness, you know. It's an indicator. It means somethin' isn't right." She looked away, her profile regal in the soft moonlight. "I have a hard time reconcilin' a world that requires death to achieve peace. But I suppose I don't have a choice, do I?"

"No," I said. "None of us do."

"Which is why we shall fight," she said sadly. "And hope that goodness prevails after all."

I sensed no relief or vindication in her declaration. Instead, I felt an overwhelming flood of regret that conversations like this had to happen at all.

She forced a smile. "I have no doubt your father can lead us to victory, Bianca. I have a feelin' you believe in him as much as I do."

I smiled. "I do.

"Now, you look tired. Try to get some sleep. I'll save the conversation with my plants for another time so I don't keep you awake."

"May I ask you one more question?"

She smiled. "Of course."

"The gypsies, in our Network, bear many similarities to your people. Are you . . ."

Farah nodded. "Yes, I know of your gypsies. They were once Northern Network witches who fled before we closed our borders. Their ancestors didn't want to be stuck in the mountains, so they traveled down into the lower Networks to live as nomads."

"Really?" I asked. "That's incredible."

She smiled. "We are all connected, whether we know it or not."

I didn't regret my reticence to tell Farah more about what I'd seen in Mabel's mind. After Isobel's betrayal, it would take time for me to trust strangers again. Besides, I didn't understand it all yet. But I was glad to speak with Farah on a more intimate level, to feel some semblance of trust in our new ally.

"Thank you, Your Majesty," I said with a curtsy. "I appreciate you taking the time to speak with me."

She smiled, and her eyes sparkled in the moonlight. "Good night, Bianca."

"Good night."

I slipped back into the opulent chamber, falling into a dreamless sleep.

The Real North

I slept in well past lunch the next day, waking up with a clear head and a mind free of Mabel's voice. The distance strengthened me, and I felt more like myself as I rubbed the sleep from my eyes.

Merrick stood on the balcony nearest the bed when I woke, his arms stretched out and his weight on his palms, as if he could lean into the mountains. He wore a simple white shirt and brown breeches. The broad expanse of his back faced me, drawing my eyes to the muscular, attractive cut of his shoulders. Strands of his golden hair shimmered in the sunlight. I sat up, an unwanted tickle of anticipation in my stomach as I slipped out of bed, ran a hand through my unruly hair, and joined him in the sunlight.

We didn't look at each other or speak at first. The distant sound of the waterfall filled the background. Like Merrick, I studied the lines and grooves in the mountains across the ravine. They were so close and majestic I wanted to reach out and touch them.

"I brought something for you," he said, unlatching a second belt from his waist and producing a familiar sheathed sword from a clip on his belt. Next, he lifted a familiar oblong case off the ground in front of him and handed both of them to me. I gasped.

"Viveet! The Volare!"

The moment I touched her, Viveet glowed a bright, familiar blue. The metal hissed as I pulled her out of her sheath, laughing when her blue flames danced merrily, as if she'd missed me. It felt wonderful to hold her in my hand. I swung her, enjoying the movement of the muscles in my wrist again. Merrick smiled in an offhand way, but it remained a little distant, as if he were afraid to commit to being happy for me.

"I thought you'd want her back," he said.

"My muscles are weak," I said, rubbing my wrist. "I need to start practicing again. Build my strength back up."

The Volare slipped out of its case on command, growing longer once it burst free of its magical house that kept it to a manageable size. It hovered in the air next to me. I sat down with a laugh, excited to feel the familiar carpet beneath me.

"Thank you," I said, leaning back. "It feels wonderful to have them with me again."

For a moment, it felt as if no time had passed between us at all. I strapped Viveet to my waist, feeling better with her at my fingertips. The air between Merrick and me shifted back to uncertain awkwardness. A worried shadow fell over his face.

"Care for a little hike?" he asked.

"A hike? Uh . . . sure."

"It would be easier to explain why I never told you about where I was from if I could show you more of our Network."

"All right."

He met my eyes. The turmoil stirring in his irises surprised me. "It's . . . my family," he said. "I want you to meet my family. And I want you to see the real North. But only if you want to, of course."

"Your family?" I repeated, sliding off the Volare. "Really?" The Volare rolled up and slipped back into its case at my silent command. I slung it over my shoulder, letting it fall across my back. Being armed had never felt so empowering.

Merrick nodded. "Yes," he said.

Merrick hardly ever spoke of his family. Whether they were protected by his silence or he simply didn't want anyone to know about them, I'd never known. Extending such an offer showed incredible trust. Saying no to his offer could create a fissure in our relationship too great to repair. Besides, I didn't want to say no. I wanted to meet his mother. It seemed like so many of my questions would be answered if I could find out more about his life.

"Will you meet them?" he asked, drawing me from my thoughts.

"Yes, of course," I said. "I would like that."

He straightened and relaxed his shoulders. "Then let's go," he said, a hint of a sparkle in his eye. "We have a long climb ahead of us."

Merrick's family lived higher than any witch had business living.

To reach his house, he led me to the back of the castle, where a bridge started at Balmberg Castle and connected with the sidewall of the ravine. I glanced down as we crossed, watching the frothing white river rapids swirl beneath us until they gave way to another section of waterfall. Mist collected on the ends of my hair. Above us, the Mala bells sang on a light breeze, filling the air with a whispery chorus.

"The air is thinner here, so take it easy on the speed," he said as we moved onto a narrow road that wound up the steep mountainside in a zigzag pattern. An old peddler with a cart full of knickknacks waved to us as he passed. He wore a bright orange cloak around his thin shoulders, and his cart swayed back and forth on the pebbled road.

"Right," I panted, although we had only walked a short distance. "I . . . noticed."

As we climbed higher, I glanced over the side of the crumbling trail at the needle-sharp tops of pine trees in Balmberg Village. The temptation to pull the Volare out and spare my energy flitted through my mind only once. I feared I'd miss too many little details of the North if I rode—the rocks in the trail, the wildflowers scattered along the path, the way Merrick seemed unusually at ease, even happy.

In the distance, a vast array of glacier-white mountaintops, interspersed with rocky peaks, filled the vista. Clouds floated near the tops of the highest mountains, blocking the sky. Not far away, a burst of snow billowed into the air in the wake of a high avalanche.

"Just wait." Merrick leaped on top of a boulder to gaze out over his homeland. "The view will be worth the climb."

The higher we ascended, the more glorious the views of the mountain ridges became. The craggy rocks split the sky in two, like combs of teeth and snow and granite. Some of the peaks spiraled into the clouds, decorated with frills of snow. Others hung just below, half-rock, half-tree.

"Just about there," Merrick said. "Up here it'll even out onto a plateau."

He moved with a quick, easy limberness I hadn't seen from him before. The serious, no-nonsense Merrick had disappeared, and I rather liked this more carefree, happy side of him. I drew in another breath and kept going, setting aside the tension that persisted between us.

"It's beautiful up here," I said. "This road takes us to your family?"

"Yes."

"Did you have to hike this often when you lived here? Or did you transport?"

"Hiked. Northern Network witches are tied to the mountains," he said, moving deeper into his natural burr. "It's a point of pride in our culture that we don't use magic to travel much in near areas. Most of us enjoy the challenge of the trail."

"No wonder you outrun me," I muttered, still puffing along, the back of my throat cracking in the dry air. As promised, the steep trail leveled off onto an even plain. Buildings were clustered together off to the right, near the outer edge of the open field. Other houses spread out on the surrounding hills, which led up to even higher mountain peaks.

"*This* is home, the real North," he said, gesturing around him with open arms. "This is what I work for."

The Northern Network rolled around us in undulating ribbons of dark green. "I can't believe you grew up here," I said. We couldn't even see Balmberg's waterfall from this high up.

"Come on. My family doesn't know I'm bringin' you. We'll surprise them."

My chest tightened. Among all these natural beauties in the unknown North, I'd forgotten why we were climbing in the first place. "When was the last time you saw them?" I asked, forcing nonchalance.

"I've seen them almost every day since your father sent me back."

His response reminded me that we had a lot of catching up to do. "Did you ever see them when you were in the Central Network?"

His shoulders tightened. "Yes. Sometimes on the weekends."

Tracking Merrick's schedule would have been as useful as keeping tabs on a butterfly's path, so I had never bothered to try. But I hadn't once thought during his unexplained absences that he was visiting his family. Nor that his family lived in the North.

He motioned to a trail on the left that led away from the village. "That house," he said, indicating a cottage so far away I could only see smoke rising from the chimney, "is where my mother and sister live."

"Mother and sister," I repeated, glad to have some idea of whom to expect. All I'd known was that his father died when he was a teenager.

We walked along the edge of a field and through tall grass that grew up to my thighs. I ran the tips of my fingers along the silky strands, soaking in the quiet majesty of the mountains. A small house built with crossed logs came into view. White mortar held the cottage together, insulation against what must be cold winters. A girl appeared in the doorway. She stumbled out of the house with a bucket, saw us, and called over her shoulder to someone inside.

A graceful woman with long, slender arms and a bright smile appeared next. Like Merrick, she had sandy blonde hair with deeper brown tones. My stomach twisted in a nervous spasm.

"Don't worry," he said. "They'll love you."

It frightened me more that I desperately wanted them to.

The girl waved from the cottage door and started toward us through the field. Her blonde bun loosened, unwinding onto her shoulders as she rushed up to us.

"Hullo! You must be Bianca!" she cried, taking my hand. "I'm so excited you came! I'm Jacqueline, Merrick's sister."

"It's nice to meet you, Jacqueline," I said with a smile.

"Are you and Merrick just friends?" Jacqueline asked. "I mean are you his—"

"Friend, yes. My father," I said, clearing my throat. I tried to compose myself with a smile. "He, uh, works for my father."

"Ah," she said, winking. "Right. Your father, the High Priest."

Merrick's mother strolled down the path. She wrapped her arm around her son, inhaling a deep breath as they embraced.

Merrick turned to me. "Bianca, this is my mother, Kalli. Mother, this is Bianca. The girl I told you about."

I couldn't help but notice his use of the word *girl* instead of *friend*. Kalli smiled warmly at me and took both my hands. Her eyes gleamed a warm umber, like the deep forests of Letum Wood.

"It's good to finally meet you," she said, squeezing my fingers and pulling me into a hug. "I've heard a lot about the High Priest's daughter. I suppose I owe you a debt of gratitude for keepin' my son in line."

The scent of roses wafted up from her clothes, and for a moment, I lost myself in the embrace of a mother again. What I wouldn't give to have Mama to talk to right now. I returned Kalli's soft hug, already liking her more than I had expected.

"It's good to meet you too," I said, meaning every word. "In fact, it's wonderful to finally meet someone from Merrick's family." I pulled away, motioning to the mountains around us. "I only just found out about all . . . this. It's magnificent."

Jacqueline grinned with the conspiratorial smile of a little sister. "Oh, I know all about you. Merrick said that—"

"Come, Bianca," Kalli said, looping her arm through mine and shooting a discreet glare at her daughter over my head. "We have some talkin' to do, and Merrick has some firewood to gather before dinner starts. Jacqueline will give you a little tour of our humble cottage. It's not much, of course, but it's home."

"This is Merrick's old room," Jacqueline said, bouncing onto a bed. "Merrick has the attic to himself—when he's here, anyway—and Mother and I sleep downstairs. It's cooler in the summer."

Merrick's room reminded me vaguely of my own—sparse, functional, and utterly without decoration. Dust had settled on the floor and along the windowsills. One pane of glass had cracked. A narrow bed jutted into the middle of the room, covered with a quilt and a pillow but nothing more. I looked out a side window to see a large garden patch thriving with tomatoes and peppers.

"It's a very normal room."

"Merrick likes it." She shrugged. "It's not as glamorous as yours, probably, since you live in a castle and your father is the High Priest."

I laughed under my breath and sat next to her on the bed. "Glamour is a relative term. Not everyone enjoys it."

She looked dubious. "But you live in a castle. I'm sure everything is glamorous."

"Yes, I do live in a castle. However, your room downstairs is still more decorated than mine. My room is simple," I said, lifting my hands. "Like this."

Her eyes widened. "You're lying."

"No. I don't decorate it much."

"Why not?" she cried, straightening. "Think of what you could do!"

Reeves would certainly love to help me spritz the apartment up a little. I looked up at the thick rafters overhead. Cobwebs had gathered in the corner. The simplicity made me think of Grandmother, of home. This was the world that I grew up in, the one I yearned for. Not a cold, drafty castle.

"I'd rather live in a normal house," I said. "I grew up in a cottage a little smaller than this, and I miss it."

Jacqueline didn't seem convinced but let it slide. She reached over and touched Viveet's sheath. "Merrick told me you have a sword. Can I see it?"

"Sure."

I stood up and unsheathed Viveet. She glowed light blue in a beam of sunlight that streamed through the four-paned window. Jacqueline's mouth dropped open.

"Whoa. He wasn't kidding."

"Would you like to hold her?" I asked. "She's not heavy."

"Can I?"

She leaped to her feet and took it from my outstretched hand. Viveet's carved blue ivy faded when she left my touch. She looked like just a regular sword in Jacqueline's hands, but Jacqueline didn't seem to care.

"It's beautiful."

"Has Merrick taught you to sword fight?"

She shook her head. "Not yet. He says he wants to, but I don't really care about sword fighting. Besides, we hardly ever see him. He stops in for lunch most days now but sleeps at the castle except on the weekends. Before then, he lived in your Network." She sighed. "We don't see him much."

"Really?"

"He said he can't leave his job without raising suspicion, and when he first went down, he was afraid that they'd follow his transportation magic whenever he left, so he didn't come at all." She handed Viveet back to me with a little smile. "Thanks for letting me look at it. My father was an expert swordsman."

"Has it been hard to share your brother with the Central Network?"

Jacqueline's nose crinkled. "I never thought of it like that. Sharing him, I mean. It was just . . . just what he needed, Mother said. When we see him now, he seems much better. He used to be really irritable." She grimaced. "We argued a lot."

"Do you remember when your father died?" I asked, hoping to find common ground.

"A little. I was young at the time. I remember when Ana died better. I had to go live with the neighbors for a week so I didn't get the sickness too."

"Ana?" I asked. "Who was Ana?"

Jacqueline looked puzzled. "My sister, Ana. Hasn't Merrick told you about her?"

I shook my head. "No, he hasn't. He didn't even tell me about you."

She rolled her eyes in true little sister fashion. "He's weird like that. Mother says he gets it from our father."

"I lost a parent too," I said. "It's not easy. I bet you miss him and your sister a lot."

Jacqueline's green eyes, so similar to Merrick's, sobered. "Merrick told me about your Mama. I'm very sorry."

For a moment, she seemed much older than fifteen, and I realized that though she was still a bouncy teenage girl living in an isolated meadow, something of an old soul lived within her. She'd certainly faced a lot of loss for her age. In that moment, I felt a kindred bond with her.

Kalli called up the stairs. "Girls! Dinner is ready!"

I smiled to dispel the sadness in the air. "Let's head down for dinner. I'm starving."

"There," I said, releasing the end of the small scroll. "A note to tell Papa to expect me tomorrow morning."

The scroll disappeared when I sent it with a transportation spell. A full dinner of fresh garden vegetables, cow's milk, and a hearty brown bread smeared with butter filled my stomach. The warm ambiance of home gave me a groggy, content feeling.

"Come on," Merrick said, grabbing my wrist and tugging me back up the ladder toward the attic. "I want to show you somethin'."

I obediently followed, held captive by the startle the heat of his skin gave me. We'd been politely distant throughout dinner. Being in his home made it abundantly clear that Merrick wasn't a sneaky witch by nature, so I'd already forgiven him for not telling me he was from the North. The good gods knew I'd kept plenty of my own secrets in the past.

His long fingers maintained a firm hold on my arm, distracting me as we climbed the ladder. Kalli and Jacqueline remained behind, talking about meals for the next day. Jacqueline had plagued me with questions about the Central Network throughout dinner. She asked about the war, Chatham Castle, learning sword work—anything that popped into her head. She was clever and quick-minded, just like her older brother. Kalli seemed content to observe and smile. She responded when appropriate but largely just watched. I saw a lot of Merrick in the quiet mannerisms and movements of his mother.

"I didn't spend a lot of time in the attic as a kid," Merrick said, opening the side window and swinging one leg over the sill. "But I did sit out here. Come on. If you put a foot on the bottom of the window, you can shimmy onto the roof."

Somehow he folded his shoulders and lean body through the window. I followed his example and found him sitting at the peak of the sloping roof, one hand extended. After I slid my palm into his, he pulled me up with ease. The shingles felt warm and gritty through the thin leather of my sandals, still half-baked from the sun.

"This was my favorite place to go at night," he said, stretching out his legs and leaning back on his palms. "My father used to come up here with me."

"Just to talk?"

He nodded, stacking his hands behind his head and lying back. He was so relaxed, so . . . normal. I wished I could take this Merrick back with me. Bottle him up to keep in the Central Network.

The mountains grew cool as the sun disappeared into the horizon. Crickets chirped in the distance in a sweet symphony of summer and nighttime. I drew in a deep breath. My gaze traveled up to the dusky, velvet sky.

"The stars," I whispered, my head tilted all the way back. "They look different up here."

"They may seem so different because your position has changed."

His comment reminded me of Isadora. Hadn't she alluded to something like that before? The passage of time changed what the future could be, so she often just waited to see what would happen. Maybe life was just about changing perspective in order to understand. Even though I'd looked at the stars thousands of times, seeing them from a different angle made them almost new. Kind of like glimpsing Mabel's mind.

"You're probably right," I said with a sigh, content to feel small under the vast expanse of sky. The soft breeze soothed me, and we sat together without speaking for a long time. My thoughts drifted in and out, flittering from place to place, never settling. I'd missed this most about Merrick—saying nothing because we didn't need to say anything.

"Thanks for comin'," he said, startling the quiet. "To meet my family, I mean. It . . . it means a lot to me."

"I should be the one thanking you," I replied. "Your family is wonderful. I can't imagine why you don't talk about them more."

"To protect them," he said, and I wasn't surprised. We fell into another easy silence until he broke it with a heavy sigh. He shifted forward, leaning his arms on his loosely bent knees and staring into the distance.

"I owe you an explanation," he said.

"You don't owe me anything." I picked a twig off the roof and bent it in half. "But I would like to hear your story, if you want to tell it."

Our eyes met.

"I do want to tell you."

I smiled. "Then I want to hear it."

"I was fifteen when my father died. My anger spiraled out of control, so Wolfgang, my father's best friend, took me under his wing. Both of them were Masters—a lot like the Protectors for the Central Network, only we allow women in, and we're a force of twenty instead of fifteen. My father wanted me to be a Master, and so did I, so he had been teachin' me how to sword fight for years."

"So you're basically a Protector for two different Networks?" I asked. "Impressive."

He smiled in a lopsided, boyish kind of way that stole my breath. The cords of muscle in his arms shifted when he moved, and I swallowed back a lump in my throat. Why did he have to be so ruggedly attractive?

"Somethin' like that. Anyway, once my father died, Wolfgang continued my trainin'. It helped a little. I wasn't as depressed, but it didn't fix anythin'. I had two little sisters," he said, picking up a twig like mine and twisting it into a knot. "Jacqueline and Ana. Jacqueline is a normal little sister. She's loud, rambunctious, and annoyin'. But Ana was different. She never spoke, not once in her entire life. She just watched everythin'."

His shoulders tightened, and his eyes darkened. His use of the word *was* made my heart ache.

"How old was Ana when your father died?" I asked when a silence stretched between us. He shook his head.

"Eight. She took it hard. She'd crawl into bed with me every night with tears on her cheeks. I think she had nightmares. If she did, she never made a sound. She always fell right to sleep next to me. Sometimes I found her standin' at my father's grave in the middle of the night, holdin' wildflowers in her hand. They weren't flowers that grew anywhere near our house."

"How did she get them?"

Merrick shrugged. "I think she made them with magic. Although she was mute, she was smart. All I'd ever really seen her do was draw, but I think she figured out how to do silent magic without bein' taught. She had an incredible talent with charcoal."

My stomach clenched even though I already knew what was coming. "Had?" I asked. The twig in his hands snapped.

"Ana died two years after my father passed."

He fell quiet, into memories I had no access to, and I waited until he decided to continue.

"She contracted a fever when she was ten. We tried everythin'. Wolfgang even requested help from the Masters who were stationed in the lower Networks, but nothin' worked. After three days, I held her while she died."

My heart lurched. All the angst and turmoil of losing Mama rushed back over me. I had to sort through the emotions I felt on his behalf for a full minute before I could speak.

"Merrick, I—"

"At first I couldn't handle it," he said, as if he had to get the words out. "I couldn't sleep, could barely function. I didn't want to eat or talk. Wolfgang threw me in a lake in the middle of winter and told me to snap out of it. After that, I trained even harder and made it into the Masters at eighteen. Wolfgang came over one winter night and presented a plan to my mom. He wanted to send me to live in the lower Networks, to monitor what was going on, to make sure no one posed a threat to us. It would be my first real task as a Master, and a relatively easy one. Mother agreed. She said I'd remain lost among the ghosts if I stayed."

"So you left your family and moved down to the Central Network."

"Yes. I watched, listened, reported back to Wolfgang. Nothin' traitorous or bad. We have Masters in all the Networks, keepin' eyes open, watchin' to see if there are any threats to us. But I ended up likin' the Central Network, the freedom of bein' on my own. When a chance to join the Guardians opened up, I decided to take it."

My eyes widened. I already knew this about him—he'd had to be a Guardian before he could be a Protector—but I felt as if the information was new. Like the stars, my perspective on Merrick had shifted.

"You just up and joined?" I asked, my mouth slack. "Did Wolfgang allow that?"

Merrick nodded. "He thought it was a good idea. There was enough quiet turmoil in the Central Network hidden beneath the surface to justify goin' deeper into it. It's pretty easy to get into Guardian trainin'. It's harder to stay in. Shortly after startin', I met your father. Even though I tried to hide my skills, I couldn't entirely. Tiberius became suspicious of me."

"Is that why he hates you?"

A slight smile slipped across Merrick's face, filled with sardonic amusement. "We had a few spars durin' trainin' that angered him, yes. Anyway, Derek noticed my abilities, and I made it into the Brotherhood at twenty-two. Here I am at twenty-three, back home."

My chest tightened again. Merrick had infiltrated the most selective squad of witches in the Central Network. *How is that possible? Wouldn't Papa have known somehow?*

"Did you . . . I mean as a Protector, you—"

"Never gave Wolfgang any information protected by the creed of the Brotherhood," he said, already anticipating my question. "No. Wolfgang wouldn't have wanted it unless it affected our safety. But the North has lain quiet for so long that I rarely heard information regardin' us, just the rumors of war comin' from the West."

"Oh."

"Mabel attacked with the Clavas the very night I made it into the Brotherhood, makin' it more important than ever that I stay. Wolfgang wanted me there as a semi-permanent set of eyes so we didn't get important information too late. Farah takes the security of the Northern Network seriously."

I let go of the breath I'd been holding. No wonder Farah was so informed on events in the lower Networks.

"I noticed that," I murmured.

The North's isolation was a blessing and a curse. It protected them but could leave them in the dark until it was too late. Keeping tabs on the lower Networks made sense. I shook my head, hardly able to sort through the conglomeration of emotions.

Merrick rubbed his hand along the back of his neck. "Trust me, B. The last thing I wanted to do was lie. You weren't even . . . you weren't even in my plans."

The way he said it, with a touch of vulnerability in his voice, lit a fire in my stomach. I stared at the stars, my knees pulled into my chest. It was difficult to know what to say. I felt like I'd lost my best friend and replaced him with someone infinitely more complicated. In the end, Merrick was a Northern Network witch. After the war ended, he'd likely return to his original loyalties. Where would that leave us? Was there even an us to worry about?

"I couldn't tell you, B," he said, his voice low. "I had signed a bindin'. Wolfgang gave me permission to break it when things escalated with Angelina, but only to your father. I wanted to tell you everythin'. I even asked permission to tell you at the same time, but Wolfgang denied it."

I turned my head, biting the inside of my cheek as I studied his face, thrown into sharp shadows in the darkness. When it came to secrets and bindings, I well understood the weight of secrecy. His eyes, a deep emerald now, looked wary and uncertain in a way I'd never seen.

"I know, Merrick," I said. "It was out of your control. There's nothing to apologize for."

He smiled, slow and quiet, like the drip of rain on a summer day. His whole story formed a tie between us, like two ends of a rope pulling a knot closer together, making it stronger.

"Thanks, B."

"Thanks for telling me. I mean . . . I-I'm just glad it's worked out between us," I said, biting my bottom lip with a sheepish smile. "I, uh, missed you more than I expected."

A warm breeze stirred my hair, whisking it out of my face. His gaze drifted toward my lips and flickered back up to my eyes. It wasn't a pithy romantic gesture but a charged, intense moment that made my stomach flutter.

Katie Cross

"Me too," he said.

"So what now?" I asked. "Where do we go from here?"

His jaw tightened. "You go back home to the Central Network," he said. "And I'm goin' to the West."

My back stiffened. "What?"

"Zane wants me to join him in the mornin'." He looked away, out at the dense network of stars overhead. "He said he needs help keepin' track of everythin' goin' on there now. Mabel's furious. She's appointed a new Head of Guardians. Advance West Guard teams are startin' to show up in the Borderlands, likely to prepare for an invasion."

Oh, fate. That tricky devil. Not only had I provoked Mabel into an invasion, but Merrick would be in enemy territory.

"That's great for you," I said, swallowing back the hot rise of fear. "This is the kind of mission every Protector—and Master, I suppose—dreams about, right? Infiltrating enemy territory. Spying on the opposition."

"Maybe," he said, and his breath caressed my cheek, making me aware of how close our faces were. "Maybe for Protectors who don't have somethin' to lose."

"Do you have something to lose?"

"I hope so."

He grabbed my chin with one hand and wrapped the other around my neck. Our lips pressed together in a heated, hard kiss. My eyes closed as a shot of fire spiked through my limbs like lightning. He smelled like evergreen and forest and freedom. With his strong arm around me, I'd never feel frightened again. Once the kiss ended, his lips hovered just a breath away from mine.

"I've been wantin' to do that for a while," he said. My hand was tangled in his hair. My lips burned. I wanted to press a hand to them to make sure they didn't fly away.

"Took you long enough," I quipped, breathless.

His expression sobered. "I like you, B. More than I should. You're different. Strong as hell. Not to mention you're probably the only witch I know who could put up with me. Let's try this out. You and me."

His words didn't exactly ring with romantic tension, but when he dragged a soft knuckle down my cheek, it left a line of fire.

"I suppose courting between two witches like us would never really be romantic, would it?" I said with a wry smile.

He laughed. "I'm not sure either of us knows how. Is this your way of letting me down?"

I grinned. "It's my way of saying yes."

"It's not just because every other guy is scared you'll beat him in a sword fight, is it?" he asked as he lifted my chin with a bent knuckle.

I laughed. "Definitely. My options are very limited. It's either you or Tiberius."

The lazy, slow grin returned. "Good," he whispered, stretching his coiled fingers out to frame one side of my face. "Because I've already beat him."

I melted into his kiss, pushing aside all thoughts of him leaving, the Northern and Central Networks, and our place in them. The feel of his warm skin under my fingers and the hot shingles of the roof at my back momentarily erased my fear that I was growing attached to someone who would just leave in the end. Although I couldn't predict the future, I knew, in the deepest part of myself, that Merrick wasn't a witch who would leave.

The underside of a velvet canopy hung above us, reminding me that sometimes life was all a matter of perspective.

I'm Back

The air in the Central Network hung over my head like a wet, muggy blanket. The climate was nowhere near as pleasant as the Northern Network, but it had never felt so much like home. I drew in a great lungful of the humid air early the next morning after transporting to Stella's balcony from Balmberg Castle.

"I'm back!" I cried, spinning in wide circles with my arms flung out. Letum Wood flashed in the distance, alternating with the gray wall of Chatham Castle and the blue sky soaring overhead. "I'm back!"

High Priestess Stella waited for me, standing off to the side with her hands folded in front of her. She spread her arms and rushed forward. "Bianca!" she cried. "We are so happy you're back safe!"

I hurried into her embrace, grateful to feel her warm hug, like my grandmother come back to life. Her light auburn hair shone in the bright light. She wore a long-sleeved dress with a high neck ruffled by lace. As always, she looked lovely. Mildred had never had the true appearance of a High Priestess in terms of apparel or grace, but with Mildred it didn't matter. She commanded respect with her no-nonsense attitude. Stella brought a regal dignity back to the role. She pulled away, looking me over from head to toe.

"And you're not hurt?" she asked, running a hand down my hair. "You came out of it all right?"

"No, I'm fine," I said, holding onto her hands. "Just fine."

She let out a steady breath, smiling. "That is wonderful news."

"Bianca?"

My boss, Marten, the Ambassador, appeared just behind her. He hurried toward us with an eager, relieved smile, his bald head gleaming in the morning light.

"Marten!"

He pulled me into his wiry arms, drawing in a heavy breath. "It's wonderful to see you," he said, holding me close. "I've been so worried."

"I appreciate you taking care of Papa." I pulled away, giving Marten and Stella a knowing look. "Thank you for putting up with him. I'm certain it was the two of you that kept him sane."

Stella motioned to Marten with a hand. "It was all Marten," she said. "He knows how to deal with stubborn witches. There's a reason he's been Ambassador for so long."

"Thank you," I said, squeezing his hand one last time. "I was so worried he'd do something rash."

Marten lifted his eyebrows, showing the worry lines in his forehead. "He almost did. We all almost did. But sanity prevailed. I believe the habit of thinking things through logically instead of emotionally is a side effect of loving Mildred all my life," he said with a wistful smile.

Stella chuckled, pulling away with a step toward the balcony door. "We'd love to keep you to ourselves all day and hear about your little trip to the West," she said, "but we have a few things to take care of, and you have two anxious friends waiting for you."

Her eyes darted to the glass door. Leda and Camille impatiently waited on the other side. Camille wore a light pink summer dress, her hair cascading in dark blonde ringlets. Her apple-red cheeks blazed with color. Leda wore a tasteful blue dress, her hair swooped into a bun, like usual. They had never looked so beautiful.

"Your father is in a meeting, but he'll be out soon. I'll inform him that you've returned." Stella smiled, squeezing my fingers. "I'll tell him you're in the Witchery."

"Thank you, Stella," I said. "I appreciate that."

"I must go as well," Marten said. "I'm meeting with Niko to update him on the recent developments with the North. I'll see you at work tomorrow?" he asked, offering his arm to Stella.

"Yes, of course."

He smiled warmly, stepping toward the glass doors. "It will be wonderful to have you back. I look forward to hearing you complain about all the letters I left unopened for you to sort through. I've never hated my quiet office so much as when you weren't in it, complaining about not being able to run."

I laughed. I'd been gone for over three weeks. Surely he hadn't hoarded that much correspondence. "Sure, Marten, sure."

He exchanged a sober glance with Stella. "I'm quite serious. I know how much you love sorting the mail, so I left all of it for you."

My joy plummeted.

"What?"

He winked and continued on his way, humming a bright tune under his breath and dispelling my fears. The glass doors burst open, spilling my two best friends onto the balcony.

"Bianca!" Camille cried, her arms outstretched, tears already on her cheeks. She collided with me so fast it nearly knocked both of us to the ground. "I was so scared!"

Leda encircled both of us with her skinny arms. When they pulled away, Leda managed a smile. While she'd always been pale, she looked white as a sheet. Her normally bright eyes—one brown and one olive green—were muted and fatigued. I reached out and touched her fraying hair with a little breath of surprise.

"You look terrible, Leda. Is everything all right?"

"I know," she said with a sigh. "It's been a madhouse since you left. But that doesn't matter. You're back."

"She's been trying so hard to see what could happen to you," Camille said, wiping at her tears with her fingers. Her lips tightened. "Among other things."

Leda pulled a handkerchief out of her pocket and handed it to Camille. "I didn't try as much as she's making it sound," she said. "But I have been trying. You were too far away, and Mabel's too strong. I'm no Watcher, that's for sure. I just have the Foresight Curse, but I thought I could help. I just . . . couldn't bear the thought of you not coming back."

"Doesn't matter now," Camille said with a dismissive wave. "Isadora's back! She can help out more. Well . . . if she wakes up, anyway."

"What did you say?" I grabbed Camille's arm. "Isadora's back?"

"Yes!"

"Zane freed Isadora?"

Camille beamed as if it were her own personal victory. "While you were in the North with Mabel the second time, he went after Isadora. Perfect, isn't it?" Her voice lowered. "Although we aren't supposed to tell anyone. Leda and I overheard the news a few minutes ago while we were waiting for you to arrive."

"Isadora just returned yesterday," Leda said, frowning. "She hasn't been here long, and she hasn't woken up yet. Zane said that transforming back into a witch shocked her old body. They're not sure she'll wake up at all."

"She'll wake up," Camille said, but it sounded forced. "She has to. We need her."

My head spun with questions. How did Leda and Camille know about my visit to the North? How had Zane rescued Isadora? I brushed the questions aside to deal with later. For now, I was home.

"Let's not talk about that now," I said, taking Camille's hands. "Can we just . . . go to the Witchery and stuff ourselves full of food? I want to hear everything that's happened while I was gone."

"I'd love to stuff myself full of food," Leda said, putting a hand on her stomach. "It's hard to come by anything that isn't porridge or dry bread anymore. The fighting Guardians are taking most of the food from the castle."

In a rare turn of events, Camille took over the situation. "Don't you worry," she said, pushing her sleeves up to her elbows. "I'll get us some food. Just give me twenty minutes. Leda, you stay with Bianca while she cleans up, and I'll meet you in the Witchery."

Camille disappeared, transporting to some unknown place, leaving just Leda and me on Stella's private balcony. Behind Leda's usual sharp expression lay a slight sheen of moisture.

"I'm glad you're back, Bianca," she said, running a hand over her face. "I wasn't hopeful. How you've managed to escape Mabel so many times, I'll never figure out."

"Me either."

"Are you going to tell us about it?"

"Of course."

She looked at me with narrowed eyes and a suspicious hesitance I wasn't sure how to read. "I mean . . . was it bad? Did she . . . ah . . ."

"Torture me?"

She blushed. "Yes."

For a half-second, I remembered the sting of Mabel's slap, her hands around my throat, the agony of entering her mind, and the sheer terror of waking up to her cheetah drooling just above me.

"Not really," I said, sensing that Leda didn't really want to know the truth. "She didn't hurt me."

"Good," she said, her face relaxing.

"You must tell me now instead of making me wait," I said, leaning forward. "I've been dying to know what happened with you and Rupert ever since I left. Is he still working with you? Has he asked you to be hand fasted to him again?" My eyes widened. "You haven't agreed, have you?"

Leda sighed. "Old Rupert left, the poor chap," she said. "He only lasted a week after I turned him down. And no, I absolutely will not marry him."

Poor chap? Since when did Leda ever show compassion for Rupert?

"Are you working as Jansson's Assistant?"

A stricken look crossed her face. "No," she said, looking at her hands. "I . . . I don't have a job right now."

"No?"

She hesitated. "No. I've been helping care for the wounded ever since Jansson let me go when Rupert left." She sucked in a deep breath. "My . . . my brother died."

My heart faltered for a moment with a painful flutter in my chest. Tears filled her eyes. She sniffled.

"Your brother?" I whispered.

"The one who joined the Guardians this summer. In a battle in the Southern Covens. He choked under one of those red clouds the West Guards send. He didn't even make it off the battlefield."

"Leda . . . I'm so sorry."

Her eyes shone, but she swallowed the emotions back. "Ever since it happened, I've just . . . I can't bear to sit in an office." She looked away, entwining her hands together in front of her. "I want to, but I can't. It feels too soon. Anyway, nothing is the same. So I've volunteered all my time helping the Apothecaries when wounded Guardians come in. I can always work later, once things have settled down. Working with the wounded makes me feel like maybe I'm . . . I don't know . . . helping my brother."

Leda's deferral of work shocked me, but for her to volunteer with wounded witches—with germs and blood and remnants of Almorran potions? That astounded me. Her Foresight Curse would wreak havoc on her in such a teeming crowd. Three weeks ago I would have expected her brother's death to make her hyper-focused and more sarcastic, but it hadn't. She had changed. I could see it in her sad eyes.

That's grief, I thought. *It alters and molds us all.* I wanted to reach out and heal her aching heart, to take away her pain so she didn't have to face the darkness I knew so well. But I couldn't, and the helplessness prickled in my chest.

"I can't bear to talk about it anymore," she said. "I feel like it's taking over my life some days."

Although she spoke gently, I understood the command. *Don't bring it up all the time,* her wary gaze seemed to say.

"I understand."

A ghost of a smile crossed her face. "I knew you would. Come on. Let's go get you into some of your clothes." She glanced down at my new sandals with a raised eyebrow, blinking her tears back. "What are those things?"

I grinned. "They're wonderful," I said. "A slave girl in the West brought them to me. They fit my feet and feel like I'm going barefoot. I'm going to keep wearing them."

"They're a fashion choice from our enemies," she pointed out, as pragmatic as usual.

"They're functional," I countered. She opened her mouth to argue but couldn't. She gave in with a light huff and a lift of her nose.

"Fine," she said, looping an arm around my waist. "But don't be angry if it never catches on."

"Isn't it fabulous?" Camille asked, spreading her hands to indicate the bounty of food on the Witchery table. "I went to Brecken's mother's house. Tabby has been storing up a massive pantry for years, and they're living the high life."

Slices of cheddar cheese—a rarity since the destruction of the dairy farms in the Western Covens—lay on a plate around thinner slices of sourdough bread. We drank water, as there was no sugar to spare for lemonade or Fina's famous fizzy drink. A few pickles and a small bowl of cucumbers rounded off the meal. Simple, but better than the same bread I'd been eating for a month in the West.

Leda had been grilling me with questions ever since I had finished my bath, checked in with Papa, and climbed the beloved winding stairs to our turret home. I didn't mind a willing audience. Despite the nature of my visit, there was much about the Western Network that I could have enjoyed if I hadn't been a prisoner. Talking about it made it seem less like a horrible place and more like a place in horrible circumstances.

Camille leaned back in her chair. "What did you miss the most about home?"

"Papa," I said. "And my friends, of course."

Camille beamed. "That's what I thought."

"Where's Priscilla?" I asked, glancing around. Clothes spouted from Camille's side of the turret in a veritable disaster, which meant Priscilla hadn't been helping her organize her wardrobe.

Leda grinned in a sly way. "Probably in the Eastern Network. I think there's a budding crush between her and Niko. Your father sent her over as part of the alliance to help teach the East Guards transformation. They're terrible at sword work, apparently, so Priscilla is teaching them a different way to fight that uses other strengths, like disguising themselves during battle. Anyway, the young High Priest and our lovely Priscilla get along really well."

"Really?" I asked, mulling the news over as I chewed. "How very interesting." Priscilla would make a lovely High Priestess, and all the witches in the Eastern Network would fawn over her red hair. She wasn't a local commoner for Niko to hand fast, the way tradition in the East dictated, but I had a feeling a lot of traditions would change in the East after the war ended.

Camille had loaded her plate with a couple of slices of bread but hadn't touched them yet. She stared at the table, biting her lower lip while her fingers fidgeted with her napkin.

"You all right, Camille?"

She jumped. "What?"

"Calm yourself," Leda drawled, popping a crispy slice of cucumber in her mouth. "Why are you so jumpy?"

Camille hesitated before she pulled something out of her pocket and slid it over her wrist. My eyes widened.

"That's a cord of engagement," Leda whispered, stricken.

"That's exactly what it is," Camille said, covering her face with a happy squeal. "It's a cord of engagement. Oh, girls! I'm not supposed to tell you yet, but I can't help it. I'm not engaged . . . I'm *married*!"

Among her many words, which sank into my brain with all the weight of a boulder, came a strange kind of comprehension. Leda and I shared a glance of utter disbelief.

"What?" Leda snapped. "You're . . . you can't possibly . . . I mean . . . you're—"

"Married," I said, finishing what Leda couldn't. "You're . . . you're married?"

"Yes! Don't act so surprised," Camille said, breathless from laughing. "Well, I guess you should be at least a little surprised. We didn't say a word to a single soul."

"When did this happen?" I asked, scrambling to recover my wits. "How . . . where?"

"Two days ago. We didn't tell anyone we were going to do it! We just slipped away to Newberry and had the High Witch there perform the hand fasting ceremony."

Leda's forehead ruffled. "How did you keep it from me? I never saw anything!"

"We decided it on a whim. It wasn't planned. We just . . . we just did it. Besides, you were occupied trying to see Bianca's future and with all the sadness over your brother. It may not sound like it would be, but it was an incredibly romantic hand fasting, running away and not telling anyone."

"But what about all your plans?" Leda asked, gripping the edge of the table and leaning forward. "You had your hand fasting all planned out. The flowers and recipes and . . . your dress! What about your dress?"

She shrugged. "I helped Michelle with her hand fasting, so it's like I was able to enjoy one of my own. Besides, does the dress really matter?" Her cherubic face, spattered with freckles, grew sober. "We don't even know if we're going to make it through this war alive. I don't care about flowers or trellises. I almost lost Brecken once, and I would never have had the chance to be his wife. Dresses seem a bit . . . I don't know . . . ridiculous when you think about it."

"That's the most adult thing I've ever heard you say," I said. Leda stared at the table, wide-eyed.

"It's the most adult I've ever had to be," Camille said with a smile, but it wavered. Her eyes flickered momentarily to Leda. "This war is asking a lot of sacrifices from all of us. Some witches are giving up their lives. I figure I can forgo a beautiful hand fasting ceremony to spend this time as Brecken's wife." Her voice dropped, and she looked at her hands. "I'm lucky to still have him."

I glanced around, seeing the Witchery in a new light, one that cast long shadows without Camille's bubbly, disorganized presence. What would it be like with just Leda up here? No more clothes scattered on the floor or perfume bottles littering the fireplace mantle.

"Where will you stay?" I asked.

She cast her eyes around with a heavy sigh. "I don't know yet. Brecken had a lot going on with the West Guards gathering near the Borderlands, so he had to leave right after the ceremony and hasn't been back." A blush filled her cheeks. "We haven't exactly had any time together as husband and wife."

Leda's spine had gone stiff. Her cheeks barely moved when she spoke. "When are you going to tell his family?"

Camille didn't seem to notice the change that had come over Leda. I kicked Leda's shin. She glared at me.

"We're going to tell his parents when he returns this morning," Camille said, oblivious to—or ignoring—Leda's life crisis.

"I'm sure his mother will be ecstatic," I said.

Camille beamed. "Yes! Yes, I think so too. Now I finally have a family that wants me around and a mother to share things with. I'm the luckiest girl in all of Antebellum."

"I'm very happy for you, Camille," I said, propping my chin on my hand. "It's wonderful."

Leda mumbled something incoherent.

"I'm a little worried about where we'll stay since we can't live in Chatham City," Camille said, "and I certainly can't stay with him and all the other Guardians in the Wall. I may ask Mrs. L if there's a small room that Brecken and I could have until . . . well, until we know what's going to happen with the war and everything. But I think I'll just end up moving in with his mother and father. It's safer in Newberry."

"Newberry isn't too far," I said, taking her hands and squeezing them affectionately, even though the idea of Camille moving to Newberry sent a dozen cold pinpricks through my heart. "I wish I could have been there, but I'm glad you did it. So glad."

"Thank you."

We embraced, and I felt the soft texture of her dress against my arms. I held her extra tight, inhaling her floral scent. When she pulled away, she swiped a stray tear off her cheek.

"Angie and Bettina will be furious, of course," she said with a little laugh, "but I don't even care. Brecken is all that matters now."

"Your name will be different," I said. Camille grinned.

"Camille Jameson," she said. "Isn't that a wonderful name? Camille Jameson. It's perfect."

Leda stood up. "I have to go," she said. "I . . . I have to go."

She transported away, leaving us in stunned silence. Camille's eyes filled with tears.

"I thought that would happen," she whispered, leaning back in her chair. "I knew Leda wouldn't take the news well, especially after her brother's death. She's terrified of losing someone again. It's why she tried so hard to see your future, even when she knew she didn't have the power."

Leda's gaunt emotional state stood as a chilling reminder of the cost of war. "She just loves you," I said, putting a hand on her shoulder. "And me. Besides, you know Leda better than anyone. She doesn't handle change well, and you've been her friend all her life. She probably just needs to get used to the idea."

Camille smiled through her tears. "It's a sign of how much she loves me."

"Leda loves you more than she loves anyone else, I think. She just doesn't know how to show it. I know how she feels," I said. "I went through the same thing when Michelle got engaged, remember?"

Camille nodded. "She'll come around," she said with a sweet smile.

"When are you going to go see his parents?" I asked. She glanced at an old clock on the wall, the color draining from her face.

"Oh, dear!" she cried. "I need to get ready! I'm supposed to meet him right now."

Her hands flew to her hair, but I pulled them away.

"You look lovely."

She smiled, letting her hands drop to her lap. "Thanks. We're going to stay the night in Newberry. Will you tell Leda not to expect me back? If you see her again. She's probably hiding in a closet somewhere. She does that when she's upset."

"Of course." I flashed her a saucy grin. "Enjoy your night."

A fresh flare of color flooded her cheeks. She pressed her lips into a prim smile. "Yes, of course. I'm sure dinner with his parents will be lovely."

"Right," I drawled. "Dinner. Lovely."

She smiled with a coy twinkle in her eye. "Merry part, Bianca. I'm so glad you're back. Have a good evening. I know I shall. Eventually."

With a little whisper of wind, Camille disappeared in a transportation spell. I stared at the spot where she'd been standing with twin feelings of joy and loss.

"Good for you, Camille," I said with a little smile. "Good for you."

She Sought the Darkness

fter visiting with my friends, I returned to the apartment, grateful to see my canopied bed again. I ditched the Volare and Viveet in my room, took a luxurious bath, and slipped into my own clothes with a contented sigh. Reeves bustled in the background, cleaning all the places I'd touched since I returned home. I detected a happy tilt in his usual straight-lipped expression.

Ten minutes after I settled on the divan to peruse the Chatterer, a heavy hand on my shoulder startled me out of an article about the retreating South Guards in the Eastern Network.

"Hey, B," Papa said. "Isadora just woke up. She's asked to speak with the two of us."

I twisted around to look into his eyes. "Really?"

He nodded. "We need to go now. The Apothecary doesn't think she has much longer to live."

"Of course," I said, setting aside the newsscroll and standing. "Let's go."

A fire crackled in the background of Stella's private chamber despite the hot summer air, and the Apothecary stood near it, several glasses set out in front of him. A small cauldron brewed over the hottest part of the flames. Sweat trickled down his face. His eyes narrowed in deep concentration.

Papa and I approached her bed with quiet steps. Isadora didn't look any different, except she seemed thinner and weary-looking. Her foggy, different-colored eyes gazed our direction with her usual keen intelligence, though her movements were weak. Her time as Juka didn't seem to have had any lasting effect on her, and I wondered if she had fought it in ways that Juba didn't.

A heavy blanket covered her torso, tucked snugly under her chin. Firelight danced on her pale, nearly translucent skin. Sanna lay next to her, her eyes closed and breathing even, their shoulders pressed together and hands intertwined. The red dragon's tail drooped down from the roof outside. Her gleaming talons dug into the shingles, sending a spray of dirt skittering to the ground when she shifted. The snap and hiss of her two children playing as they circled in the air filled the quiet in an oddly reassuring way.

"Isadora," Papa said, half-sitting on the mattress. He reached out and enveloped her tiny, arthritic hand in his. "I am so glad to see you awake."

She managed a tired, thin-lipped smile. "So am I. It's all thanks to Bianca, I believe."

"A fairy, actually," I said, recalling my agreement with Dafina with a bitter taste in my mouth. No doubt the fairies would come calling any day now. Papa shot me an odd look.

"Can we do anything to make you more comfortable?" he asked, turning back to Isadora. She shook her head, her white hair shining.

"No," she said. "I'm old and ready to die. I haven't much time. Only allow me to speak with both of you." Her eyes drifted to me. "And then with Bianca alone. She and I have much to discuss."

Papa nodded, a glimmer of curiosity in his eyes. I flinched. Isadora might speak casually about death, but I couldn't take it so easily. What would we do without her to help us? She'd seen the Central Network through many rough times. Heading into the future without her guidance felt like walking into a dark tunnel.

"Of course," Papa said. "Have you seen something that could be helpful to the Central Network?"

"Perhaps." Isadora squeezed his hand. "There is more you have to learn, and it is not mine to tell. Soon, however, you will know."

"Do you have any advice for me?" Papa asked.

To my surprise, she smiled. "Do what you do best, Derek Black, and listen to those instincts of yours. Trust me. You may be surprised at the avenues salvation takes."

A knock sounded at the door, and Stella slipped inside. She smiled warmly at Isadora and me before turning to Papa, her hand still on the doorknob.

"Tiberius is requesting your presence, High Priest. Mabel is advancing the front line. The entire West Guard army is moving through the Borderlands toward the Western Covens."

Papa stood, covering Isadora's hand with his. "Thank you, Isadora. I'm glad you're back home. Try to get some rest."

"Oh, Derek?" Isadora called out. He paused halfway to the door and spun around, his eyebrows lifted in question. "I know you've wondered about the location of the *Book of Light*," she said. My heart nearly stopped. Papa froze.

"Yes," he said.

"I believe you've had it all along."

Her frosty eyes bore deep into his. A thousand questions rose in my throat. Where was it? What did she mean she believed he'd *had it all along*? Impossible! I'd personally scoured Chatham Castle—and Papa's office—at least three times.

Isadora smiled gently. "Good luck to you, Highest Witch." The flicker of confusion in Papa's gaze lingered for only a few moments before it softened into uncertain surprise.

With one last bow, Papa exited, his brow furrowed in thought. Isadora turned to me with her queer eyes as soon as the door closed behind Papa. Her eyebrows lowered, giving her a solemn, pained expression.

"I saw what was going to happen to you that night in the caves, Bianca," she said, delving right into business. When Mabel killed her mother, Isadora had been the only other witch present, the only one who could truly understand how horrible it had been to watch Angelina's death.

"I didn't warn you beforehand about what Mabel could do because I thought I could prevent it," she continued, "but I wasn't strong enough. Now I think I wasn't supposed to stop it from happening. Fate has a funny way of taking her own course."

"Did you see Mabel's mind too?"

She shook her head. "Only that she formed a connection with

you through Almorran magic. Your thoughts are your own. She has created darkness and confusion in an already grieving, troubled heart. That's all I can detect."

"My thoughts are not my own anymore," I said bitterly. "Mabel sorted through all of them. She knows everything about me, I think."

Isadora's eyes narrowed. "You have done the same to her on some level recently, haven't you?"

I swallowed and nodded. "I didn't plan it," I said. "It just kind of happened. Both times. The pull of her mind was . . . strong."

"You may have had such a strong connection with Mabel in the cave because you're both very powerful witches. You perhaps more so than Mabel."

My eyes popped wide open. "What? I'm not stronger than her. She's the Almorran Master. She helped resurrect a dark, ancient magic. I—"

"Power is more than just the ability to do magic," she said. "Your natural talents—and extensive training—have kept you alive so far. I call that powerful."

"Oh. I hadn't thought of that."

She smiled. "Don't disregard who you are—the lines of your family are strong, Bianca. Powerful magic has run through your blood for decades. I knew that the moment I met you."

"I don't know my family. Except for Papa, they're all gone."

"Not all."

"What do y—"

"It's not for me to tell," she said, and though my curiosity urged me to press for details, I knew she'd say no more. She drew in a shaky breath, her eyes half closing. She didn't have much time. I didn't want to waste it bugging her with questions she wouldn't answer.

"You interviewed Mabel, right?" I asked, leaning forward and wrapping my arms around my knees. "She attended Miss Mabel's School for Girls, which means you must have put her there."

"I did. She grew up at the school, but that didn't guarantee her admission. May privately tutored Mabel until I interviewed her."

"What was the interview like?"

"Come," she said, beckoning me closer. "And I'll show you."

She put her soft, wrinkled hands on either side of my face. The effort seemed to exhaust her, so I moved in as close as possible. Her hands trembled against my skin.

"We Watchers have been feared for many centuries because of what we see and what we can do with that information. But what I've found through the years is that it's not so much the possibilities I see that empower me but the details I remember."

She closed her eyes, and so did I. Instead of darkness, I saw Mabel's old office at Miss Mabel's School for Girls. When I jerked back in surprise, Isadora held me firm in her grasp.

"Be calm," she said. "I cannot see into your head. I am simply giving you the chance to see a memory in mine. Parts of what you see will be blurry, but disregard them. My powers as a Watcher cannot be accessed or shared in any form. What you see is the memory I keep; it is true in its entirety. Pay attention."

I relaxed. Unlike Mabel's memories, Isadora's felt calm.

It began with Isadora sitting in a familiar office—what would eventually become Mabel's office. The lackluster decorations—gray drapes, a single wooden chair, and no paintings on the walls—meant it was May's office, not Mabel's. Every detail of the memory felt crisp with color and precision, right down to the scratches on the bottom of the desk and the dust motes floating in a sunbeam.

Mabel sat across from Isadora in a wooden chair. "This school means a lot to you, doesn't it, Mabel?" Isadora asked, beginning the interview. Isadora's mind moved quickly, in a blur I couldn't distinguish, the way she'd warned me. A thought or two trailed out of the madness, running through my mind in Isadora's voice, which wasn't quite as creaky back then.

Very serious for such a young girl. Not much levity in her future.

Mabel's face didn't betray much, even as a young woman. The same glistening gold hair, like threads of sunshine, fell on her shoulders. Her features were softer, younger, less defined, but she still carried herself with an air of confidence far beyond her age. Looking at her in a less powerful state made me uncomfortable. I wanted to pull away from the memory, but I didn't understand why.

"No," Mabel said. Her voice rang clear, almost innocent, without the coy undertones that colored it now. "It's not the school I care about."

There's no indication in her future that she cares about anything, Isadora thought in surprise. *Nothing consistent moves through her paths. Her personality is difficult to decipher; I'm not sure she even knows who she is.*

Isadora's thoughts shifted in the memory, moving forward into another great blur of color. *Her future is decidedly set around the school,* Isadora thought. *Differing faces, seasons, and times but a sense of attachment that can't be denied.*

"And you don't care much to make friends," Isadora said. Mabel hadn't moved.

"No," she said.

"Why not?"

"I don't need friends."

"Everyone needs friends."

Mabel didn't even flinch. "I'm not everyone."

She's a lonely child. The loneliest I've ever met. She must suppress her emotions, pretend they don't exist through indifference. Perhaps being with other girls her age could change that. Or it may make it worse.

"You're very beautiful," Isadora said. "Is that important to you?"

"No."

"What is important to you?"

Mabel paused to think, showing her first sign of interest in the interview. *Her emotions move so quickly,* Isadora thought. *There are so many. The greatest of which I can sense is anger. No, not anger. Rage. A penchant for choosing the darkness. I see very little light in her future.*

"Justice," Mabel finally said.

"Justice?" *A queer response.* "Why justice?"

Mabel shifted, looking uncomfortable for the first time. "Because it proves there is balance in the world. For all the bad that happens, justice provides a path of retribution. Redemption, if you will."

Odd, Isadora thought. *Such an abstract idea for a young girl. She's very intelligent. Her grandmother's school could continue to foster such difficult lines of reasoning.*

"Interesting," Isadora murmured.

Mabel waited, staring at Isadora with an unnaturally steady gaze, her hands folded in her lap, her back straight. Her perfect features and impeccable manners lent a tense air to the room. Isadora's mind spun into another wild blur, leaving the room in silence.

She will almost always choose the darker path in the future, Isadora thought. Even when an option for good presents itself. She seems to find comfort in anger.

Isadora shifted in her seat, staring at Mabel, who seemed unbothered by the direct attention.

There's much I cannot see, Isadora thought. I don't know what that means. So many stops, so many blocks in her future that I cannot move around. So much frustration. Where does her path lead? There is so little happiness, so much loneliness.

But there's a chance. There's a small chance she could make friends. She could choose to be happy. Surrounding her with other girls could lead to competition, of course. She may feel even lonelier. But if there's even a possibility for such a lost child to find her way to light and good, I must give her the opportunity.

Isadora broke the silence. "You hold on to your emotions with uncanny strength, Mabel. And you have a self-confidence that borders on arrogance. Although you act indifferent, I can sense that you care about many things."

Mabel's thin fingers curled into a fist on top of her dress. The cheap fabric rustled with the movement.

"You also have a habit of nurturing your anger," Isadora said. Her brow furrowed. "I cannot understand why."

A question lingered in Isadora's statement, but Mabel made no response. Although I knew it was a memory, my heart pounded. Isadora waited, feeling the situation out, but Mabel offered no answer.

"You are admitted to Miss Mabel's School for Girls," Isadora finally said with a weak note of fatigue in her voice. "I feel it could be a good opportunity for you."

Mabel's lips curled into a cold, distant smile. She inclined her head, her blonde hair swaying. For the first time since the interview started, she looked pleased.

The memory faded when Isadora pulled her hands away. Her

peaked, ashen face fell back onto the pillow with a sigh. I shook my head, blinking.

"Are you all right, Isadora?"

She gave me a weak smile. "Just tired. That required more energy than I remembered. Of course, I'm quite old now. It was much easier to do when I was young."

I processed the memory in silence. "I don't know what to think," I said. "Everything you observed about her is consistent with what I know from her mind. Angry. Distant. Selfish."

Isadora peered deep into my eyes. "And what do you think of your deeper understanding of your greatest enemy?"

I swallowed, afraid to say what had burdened me for months. "I'm surprised," I said. "She wasn't born horrible and evil. I guess I'd always assumed she had been."

Isadora shook her head. "No one is born bad, Bianca. They arrive there through complicated paths."

I fiddled with a loose thread in the blanket. *But why did Mabel have to take the path that killed members of my family? And why do I have to understand her at such a deep level? One that makes me feel a traitorous sense of pity.* My deep-rooted hatred and newfound compassion for Mabel tangled themselves again. Only this time, I didn't know which one was stronger.

"Mabel and I connected a second time," I said. "In the Northern Network."

"It was different this time, wasn't it?"

"Very."

"A second connection with such a powerful magic would likely produce something deeper. I'm going to guess you saw more than last time."

"Yes."

"And?" she asked. "What did you see?"

I related Mabel's memories in full. Isadora listened quietly until I finished.

"It's as I suspected," she said. Her brow furrowed. "I find it interesting that Mabel replicated her own first challenge when you signed up for the Competition. The challenges are supposed to be new every year. I'm willing to bet she saw something in you that piqued her curiosity. Perhaps she was testing you, seeing what you'd do under similar circumstances."

"I won," I said. "She didn't."

Isadora nodded. "But she could have if May hadn't gotten in her way. Have you ever thought about the similarities between you and Mabel? Both of you were only children. Both raised by women. Both largely without father figures on a day-to-day basis—although Derek arguably was as good a father as his job allowed him to be. Both of you are extremely intelligent and capable with magic. You have a natural determination to succeed."

Isadora's running list thickened the knot in my throat. I hadn't analyzed Mabel and myself on such a level, although I wasn't surprised. Likely I'd already sensed some of our similarities but didn't want to admit it.

"One thing, however, separates you and Mabel," Isadora continued. "You always choose the light. Again and again. While Mabel, in her unloved, vulnerable state, more often sought the darkness. I'm willing to bet that she saw in you what she could have been if she'd chosen differently or if life had given her different circumstances."

"That explains why she hates me."

Isadora nodded. "Part of the reason. Remember, Mabel was an intense young girl when I first met her. After a time, she didn't just choose the darkness. She pursued it. I don't think she feels the need to have a reason to hate anyone."

"Well, she found the darkness."

Isadora nodded. "Yes. And the darkness found her."

"What did you see when you looked into my mind?" I asked, unable to bear another moment discussing Mabel.

Isadora smiled, dispelling some of the tension. "Nothing that will surprise you," she said. "I saw a pair of smiling gray eyes and a cottage with a little herb garden. I saw trees and branches and Derek and bare feet running down a trail."

Tears welled up in my eyes. Could there be any better representation of my soul than Papa, Letum Wood, and Mama's eyes? Isadora covered the backs of my hands with her wrinkled fingers. Her touch left a chill on my skin, but her eyes peered into mine with deep, searching intent. A bluish tinge lingered around her lips.

"You were stronger than Mabel had been when I interviewed you for the Network School, but in a different way," she said with strained breaths. "That's why I worried for you. I didn't know if you'd fight the grief or embrace it like Mabel. You have the ability—and you choose—to love, which explains your tendency toward self-sacrifice and loyalty. It's something Mabel has never understood, but it is one of your greatest strengths."

A single tear slid down my cheek. "Strength or no, it doesn't matter. She's threatening to destroy everything. It's too late."

"I don't believe in too late. I believe in the inherent power of goodness over evil. Fate—"

"Often takes her own course," I finished for her, and we both smiled.

"In the end, Mabel was a child," Isadora said. "Any girl or woman forced to live under the circumstances that she endured could not emerge unscathed. Her life was a perfect storm. She had powerful blood, a poor environment, and the inclination to choose darkness over light. Underneath all the bad decisions she's made is a girl who's not so different from the rest of us."

"She's a witch."

"A witch who ached for love," Isadora said. "And never received it."

"Is it possible to feel compassion for someone who has caused me so much pain?" I asked, wiping away a tear.

"Yes, it is. And it demonstrates the differences between you and Mabel to a sharp degree."

"I feel such sadness for her."

"As do I."

Speaking with Isadora relieved a heavy weight from my chest, and I breathed a bit easier. While I hadn't truly sorted out how I felt about Mabel, I no longer feared my pity.

Isadora released a rattling, strained breath. "No matter how dark the night," she whispered, "morning always comes. And deep inside of you, greater than all the sadness and pain, is a girl who loves the light."

Her eyes fluttered closed. She turned her head toward her sister. Sanna's shoulders moved with her shallow, infrequent breaths.

"My time here is done, Bianca," Isadora said with a note of relief, as if she'd been waiting. I cupped her cold hand in both of mine.

"Are you afraid?" I asked.

"No. Death is something to respect, not fear. There are witches waiting for me. Witches I love very much. I've . . . I've missed my father and mother for a long time. I . . . look forward to seeing them and Maximillion again."

Maximillion? I supposed I hadn't known Isadora as well as I'd thought. She had a story, a history, just like anyone else. Being present to close the final chapter of her impressive tale felt like a great honor.

"And Sanna?"

"She'll be along," Isadora said with a sigh. "She never did do things well without me there to supervise, you know. I was always . . . always the responsible one."

Her breathing faded into a staggered rhythm with long gaps between each breath. Every now and then she'd murmur quietly, as if she spoke to someone I couldn't see. Her twitchy movements slowed until her breath ceased and her hand grew limp. I detected a glimmer of light in her eyes at the moment when our world made way for another.

"Oh, Papa," she whispered, slipping away with a peaceful smile on her face.

"Sister," Sanna said, twining her quivering hand through Isadora's. "I . . . I see you again."

Sanna pulled in one last ragged breath and settled into the same eternal slumber. Outside, the red dragon let out a keening wail. Dust rained from the ceiling.

My heart ached with the familiar pain of loss, only this time it was sweet, not frightening. I thought of Isadora's words.

Death is something to respect, not fear.

For as little as I knew about death, I imagined something wonderful must lurk behind this life, waiting to welcome us into a better world, if both the sisterwitches died with such fearlessness.

"Merry part, my friend," I whispered, my eyes glimmering as I placed Isadora's hand on her chest. "How I shall miss you."

We laid Isadora and Sanna to rest outside Sanna's small cottage the next day.

Papa allowed only a few witches to know of Isadora's rescue and passing. Leda, Stella, Tiberius, Camille, and a few trustworthy Council Members came, all wearing white.

"Let Mabel think we still have her," Papa said when I asked him about it over breakfast. "She doesn't need to know her advantage."

Dragons ringed the outer meadow, hiding in shadows. The red dragon took Sanna's death the hardest. She lay in front of the cottage door, snorting fire and keening deep in her throat. I watched the skies but saw no sign of the blue dragon. Perhaps he slinked among the trees with the rest, mourning in solidarity with the great beasts of the forest. The other dragons circled the castle, flying wide over Chatham City, their yellow eyes narrowed and black scales glinting in the hot sunlight. The rapid approach of the West made them nervous. Losing their Master made them furious.

Nicolas had already stepped into the role of Dragonmaster with confidence and ease. Considering how little time he'd had to learn from Sanna—just over a year, really—he exuded remarkable certainty.

"It doesn't seem fair," Leda said. We stood side by side, staring at the two mounds of fresh dirt hiding the sisterwitches. No mourner chanted the final farewell. No headstones marked the graves. Such an unobtrusive end to lives so filled with purpose. Stella stood in the middle of the small circle we'd made around the graves and spoke about Sanna. Stella was the only witch who could kindly summarize the brawny old woman's brazen personality.

A pervasive kind of numbness had taken over my heart. I'd been through this scenario so many times now, with so many people I cared about, that it seemed like an old, rote memory I kept reliving. At least Isadora left Antebellum yearning for the other side.

My mind kept pulling me back into the caves of the Eastern Network and to the Northern Network throne room. Away from Isadora's calm departure and into the darkness of Mabel's mind. Even Isadora's reassurances couldn't banish my confusion. How could I feel compassion and rage for the same witch?

"It's hard to believe Isadora's gone," Leda murmured once Stella finished speaking, dispelling the dark memories I'd been cycling through in another futile attempt to understand. "She's always been here."

Two Protectors milled around the clearing, although I couldn't imagine we'd come to any harm with all the dragons stomping, unseen, through Letum Wood. Papa stood to my left, his hands folded in front of him and his eyes narrowed.

"Where are the West Guards now?" I asked Papa, watching as Camille led a group of witches in collecting two summer flowers, one for each grave. Their low murmurs evoked a reverent feeling in the meadow. Leda still hadn't spoken with Camille, though she kept eyeing her, as if she longed to but didn't know how.

"Standing in formation at our border," he said. "They've taken over the Borderlands. The battle over the Western Covens will begin tonight."

He stared deep into Letum Wood, his gaze so distant I couldn't be certain that he saw anything at all.

"And what do you think of it?" I asked.

He looked at me, one eyebrow raised. "I think we're going to fight a crucial battle very soon."

His wry tone startled me until I realized he was trying to make light of an intense situation for my benefit. I hazarded a smile, but it didn't last long.

"Isadora mentioned the *Book of Light* to you last night," I said in a low voice that no one else could hear. "What did she mean?"

"Don't worry about it."

"But Pa—"

"Do you trust me?"

"Of course."

"Then leave it at that."

Although I longed to argue with him, I didn't. I could see in his gaze that he'd say no more. For now.

"Can Tiberius hold the West Guards at the Western Covens?" I asked, giving voice to my other greatest fear. "Are we strong enough to keep them away from Chatham City?" If Chatham City fell, I feared we'd lose Chatham Castle.

"I'm not sure. Marten, Zane, Tiberius, and I are meeting about it tonight. But one thing is certain: We won't give up. We'll make a stand, no matter where it leads. Peace isn't free, Bianca."

A heavy lump rose in my throat. What if Isadora hadn't told Papa what future possibilities she saw because we were destined to fail? Perhaps she didn't want to scare us earlier than necessary, to fill our last days in Antebellum with despair and hopelessness.

"Yes, Papa," I said, forcing my dark thoughts into the deepest recesses of my mind.

He pulled me into his side in a warm, tight embrace. "Don't worry, B. We can't predict the future. Not even Isadora knew it with certainty. Come on. Let's head back before witches start wondering where all the leadership has gone."

Unexpected Visitors

If the witch I passed in the hall later that day hadn't been so sickly thin, I probably wouldn't have even noticed her.

Her ramrod-straight back and pinched nose caught my eye. Another woman shuffled along beside her, draped forward, looking almost like a gargoyle. I smiled, but as they seemed to know where they were going, I said nothing as I walked by.

Ten minutes later, I came to a fast halt at the top of the Witchery stairs, gazing around in wide-eyed shock. Half-packed bags littered the table and chairs. Clothing and lace clotted the floor in a vast array of material. Garments, books, and trinkets flew across the room, no doubt under a sorting incantation. Camille ran from her dresser to her valise, heaping all the clothes she'd just packed back into the dresser drawers.

"Bianca!" she cried, panting. "Oh, I'm so glad you're here. Can you help me out by straightening up a little? I'm trying to make it look like I still live here, and I don't want it to be a mess. Maybe just . . . just make it look like I've been doing homework?"

Paperwork littered the desk in a disaster of half-opened scrolls, books, quills, and old ink bottles. "Camille, it already looks like you've been doing homework."

Objects moved so haphazardly around the room that I had to duck to avoid a flying shoe. I blocked a vase from falling off a bookshelf when a comb collided with it.

"What's going on?"

"Ridiculous old bat," Camille muttered, dodging a book as she grabbed another armful of clothes. "I never asked her to come!"

"Who are you talking about?"

"Bettina! My horrid Aunt Bettina is coming. She simply can't know that I'm married. Oh, I'll never hear the end of it. She'll probably lecture me for hours, never mind that I'm nearly eighteen."

Camille dumped a pile of clothes onto Leda's bed, sliding the curtain closed behind her.

"Leda will be furious if she sees all of your stuff on her side of the room," I said, grabbing a fork that whistled through the air and nearly stabbed me. "Are you sure you want to do that?"

"Not if she doesn't know! Please help? I don't have time to fold all of them and put them away. Bettina won't look on Leda's side of the room. She's a huge stickler for privacy. Oh, please!"

"Of course I'll help," I said, grabbing a dress off the back of a chair. "But you can't hide your marriage forever."

"Oh, yes I can!"

"Camille—"

"I know!" she wailed, wringing her hands. "I know. I'm just . . . I'm not ready to tell them yet. My parents were hand fasted when my mother was seventeen, and Bettina was adamantly against it. She didn't even go to the ceremony! And now she'll never stop lecturing me. Even though it was terribly romantic."

"It'll be all right, Camille," I said, moving into action. Just as we finished tidying things up—or more aptly, putting all Camille's loose belongings on Leda's side of the room—I heard feet climbing the stairs. Camille threw herself into a chair at the table and grabbed a quill.

"Look busy!" she hissed. I grabbed a book but didn't have a chance to sit down before a knock sounded at the door. Camille's hands flew to her hair, which had come undone in the chaos and looked like a tattered bird's nest. I cast a quick spell to straighten it, readjusted a pillow, and indicated all was ready with a satisfied exhale.

"Don't mention Brecken," she whispered, pleading with her wide hazel eyes. "Please."

I agreed with a quick nod. Taking courage, she used an incantation to open the door, facing Bettina with a bright smile.

"Merry meet, Bettina! It's so good to finally see you here!"

The sickly woman I'd passed in the hall stepped into the room. Bettina's narrow expression and thin lips made the crotchety housekeeper Mrs. L seem like a warm grandmotherly type. I couldn't imagine how vivacious Camille had survived under such a rigid guardian. *No wonder Camille never goes home.*

Bettina inclined her head in greeting. "Camille." Her dark eyes slipped over to mine in silent question. Camille, picking up on the glance, shut the door with a spell. "This is my best friend, Bianca," she said. "I've told you about her before."

"Yes," Bettina said, looking away, her nose tilted back. "I know all about her."

I felt dirty at the way the words rolled off her tongue, like she felt a moral obligation to make me feel small. I would have responded with a sharp retort if not for Camille's harried, apologetic glance. I smiled to reassure her instead and stepped back, giving them a wide berth.

"So this is the Witchery," Bettina said, enunciating every word as if she wanted to flick them off her tongue one letter at a time. "It's much cleaner than I expected."

She clasped her hands in front of her wiry body as she sauntered around. If she'd been any stronger in attitude, I would have asked her if she had a relative named Scarlett.

Bettina ran her finger along the top of the mantle, which, thanks to a last-second collection spell, remained dust-free. Camille made a sheepish noise under her breath, but her flared cheeks gave her away. Fortunately, Bettina was too busy scouring the room to pay much attention to her niece. I used a spell to straighten a crooked painting on the wall just before Bettina turned to face the spot. I smiled when she gave me a suspicious look. She glanced out the window, and I fixed Camille's rumpled bed skirt with another spell.

"It's a lovely view," Bettina said. "I'll give you that."

"Yes."

"What's this? Your personal closet?" Bettina asked, reaching for the curtain that separated Leda's area from the rest of the Witchery. I blithely slid into her path.

"That's Leda's personal space," I said. "She keeps the curtain drawn all the time. I'm sure you remember what a private person she is."

Bettina's hand stopped just short of the curtain. "Oh. I see."

From the other side of the room, Camille blew out a long, relieved breath. Thank you, she mouthed when Bettina faced away from her.

"Well, Camille. It certainly is . . . livable," Bettina said. "From your lengthy letters, I expected it to be a bit less . . ."

"Hot?"

"Shabby." Bettina pursed her lips. "But then, you are still quite young. Who did that awful sign above the fireplace? It looks like your work. You've never been talented at sewing."

Bettina gestured to the embroidered sign that hung over the fireplace. Camille had stitched it shortly after she first arrived at the castle. She'd meant it to say The Witchery, but all she'd managed was *The Wits*. It had hung there ever since. All the color drained from Camille's pretty face.

"That's mine," I said, clearing my throat. "Camille has been teaching me how to sew. Thankfully, she celebrates my accomplishments and not my failures."

If Bettina caught the subtle jab, she didn't let on except for a quick flash of her eyes aimed in my direction. Like most bullies, she seemed to back down when I fought back. Camille's breath came so fast she was close to hyperventilating. I walked behind her to sit at the table, brushing her shoulder as I passed. When I whispered a calming blessing, the tightness in her body seemed to release.

"I expect you're behind in your school classes like usual," Bettina said, stepping forward.

"No, Aunt Bettina. In fact, I'm on track to graduate by the third month of winter."

One of Bettina's thin eyebrows arched halfway up her forehead. The other didn't even move. "Oh?"

"Miss Scarlett has helped me, and her Assistant, Priscilla, has been my personal tutor."

Bettina stared down her long nose. "I see. And what else are you doing to fill your time?"

"Oh," Camille said, her voice wavering. She swallowed. "This and that. I started working with Henrietta, the castle seamstress. She employs me three days a week now. I used to go into Chatham City, but, well, you know how it is with the war. Nothing, er, too exciting."

Her strangled nonchalance couldn't have gone unnoticed, but Bettina drew no attention to it. She'd turned her attention to a portrait of the first High Priestess, Esmelda, that I'd dragged from the depths of the castle for our little lair.

"Where is Aunt Angie?" Camille asked, filling the vacuum of awkward silence.

"She couldn't make it up so many stairs, as I'm sure you're aware. All this traveling has weakened her fragile temperament."

"Speaking of traveling," Camille said. "Why *are* you here, Bettina?"

Bettina sucked in a sharp breath, her limbs rigid. "We came to see you."

"But why?"

Bettina's eyes closed, and her lips rolled together, betraying the first sign of emotion I'd seen from her. "Hansham was attacked by West Guards a few nights ago," she said. "Our house was destroyed."

Camille's eyes popped wide open. "Hansham?" she whispered. "What about Leda's family?"

"Their house remained untouched, thankfully. I don't know what else they'd do with all those children. The apothecary was burned, along with one or two other places."

I expected Camille to burst into tears at the news of the devastation, but she didn't. She gazed calmly at her aunt, her hands clasped in front of her. Bettina cleared her throat, her austerity back in place. She whirled around.

"Everything is gone. We need a place to stay. I was . . . that is . . . Angie and I were hoping you could direct us somewhere." Bettina shifted her shoulders back and cleared her throat. "You seem to know a few more witches than we do these days, especially with Angie's ill health."

"Of course," Camille murmured. "A place to stay . . ."

"We don't expect a room at the castle, of course," Bettina said, sniffing. Her voice became small and a little shrill. She didn't look Camille in the eye. "But we haven't, ah, we haven't the funds for an inn. Nor is there any availability."

Camille looked at me. "Do you know anywhere safe, Bianca?"

I nodded, hoping Camille wouldn't hate me for what I was about to suggest.

"My friend," I said. "Tabby Jameson. She lives in Newberry."

If Bettina hadn't been standing there, Camille would have hexed me for even suggesting it. Her arms tensed at her side, and she looked for a moment like she'd pass out. The strange expression on her face faded before Bettina took note of it.

"Yes," Camille said, swallowing. "That's a . . . a wonderful idea. Tabby is a very kind witch."

"Who is this witch?" Bettina asked. "I won't stay with just anyone, you know. I don't like strangers. They're not safe. Angie and I need to be safe!"

Camille's gaze lingered on mine, searching desperately for strength. I smiled and nodded. She drew in a deep breath, pulled her shoulders back, and turned to Bettina.

"The Jamesons aren't strangers," she said. "They're . . . they're my family."

"What are you talking about?" Bettina snapped. "This is no time for games, Camille. We don't have any family. If we did, I certainly wouldn't be here."

"Aunt Bettina . . . I'm married."

Bettina's eyes tapered to slashes. "You're what?"

"Married. I eloped with a Guardian named Brecken Jameson a few days ago. His parents live north of here, in Newberry. They have a large house, and I'm sure they would allow you and Angie to stay until we can find you a more permanent residence."

Bettina paled. Camille braced herself, her jaw clenched, but Bettina's sudden show of bluster faded. Her arms relaxed.

"I should have known," Bettina said, gazing away, disapproval staining her tone. Though if I had any talent at reading witches, I'd say she looked wounded behind all her raging disapproval. "Married at seventeen. Just like your mother. The pear never falls far from the tree, they say."

"It was a last-minute decision."

"Of course it was!" Bettina snapped. "Just like your mother's hand fasting. She didn't even invite me."

Camille paused. "Mama said you didn't approve." Bettina's shoulders shifted back, as if she couldn't quite reach an itch.

"I didn't. Your father was as young and childish as your mother, plus he had no real income to support her. But . . . she still didn't invite us." Bettina's voice stretched into a little squeak. "We would have gone."

Camille blinked several times in astonishment. "Bettina, did you want to go to my hand fasting?"

"Well, it's too late now!" Bettina snapped. "Whatever I did or didn't want doesn't matter, does it?"

A half-smile stretched across Camille's lips. "I didn't know you cared."

Bettina shot her a withering glare. "Of course we care, Camille. We may not be as vivacious as you, but we did raise you, and we loved our sister."

"I . . . I'm sorry, Bettina," Camille said. "I didn't know."

"Well, you've already done it. The past can't be changed," Bettina said, rallying with admirable aplomb. She dabbed at her eye with a bent knuckle. "This is a very dusty room. Angie is waiting downstairs and losing energy by the moment. If you're willing to help us, let's go. If not . . . we'll find something."

"Of course, Aunt Bettina," Camille said, rushing forward. "I'll take you to meet Brecken right now, and we'll send him to ask Tabby."

Bettina cast one more disapproving glance around the room, glossed over me, and headed down the stairs with the sedate energy of a walking stick. Camille shot me a look filled with gratitude, mouthed the words *thank you*, and disappeared down the turret stairs in silence instead of with her usual, comforting prattle. No doubt Bettina didn't appreciate anything that didn't have a purpose, and I imagined it would take Camille some time to really get her bearings around her aunts again.

"Good riddance," I muttered as soon as they left. I put several spells into motion that repacked Camille's bags and cleaned Leda's side of the room. Once I finished, I grabbed the book on potions Leda had requested and headed back to help take care of the wounded Guardians.

Marten rubbed a hand over his head that afternoon, his eyes clos-ing with weariness. A *Chatterer* scroll flashed new headlines behind him almost every twenty minutes, describing the tens of thousands of West Guards preparing for the invasion of the Western Covens that evening. He gazed into the distance before yawning.

"You look exhausted," I said.

He ran his hand across his face. "No more than everybody else, I'm sure."

"Were you and Papa up all night planning?"

He nodded but said nothing more. I leaned back against my desk because I couldn't tolerate the thought of sitting behind it for another moment. The bright outdoors drew my gaze, and I stared out with longing, feeling the pull to run under Letum Wood's high canopy. I felt empty without the whispers of the forest, but I didn't dare leave the castle. If Mabel caught me, she'd kill me on sight. Not to mention that it would be selfish to run while witches prepared for imminent death in the castle.

A message flew into the room, stopping right in front of me. I recognized the seal of the Eastern Network.

"Marten," I said, ripping through the thin paper. "I think it's from Niko."

Please come immediately. I have a strange thing to show you.

I handed the note off to Marten. He glanced at the clock. "I have a meeting with your father soon, but I should have time. Would you like to come?"

"Of course."

"I'm sure your father won't mind you going if I'm with you," he said, glancing out the window toward the West. "Besides, it's safe to say Mabel has other plans on her mind."

I snorted. "You make me sound like a toddler who needs parental approval to go anywhere."

"I imagine you were a very precocious toddler," he said, laughing. His face dropped for a moment, as if he considered saying something more, but he shook it off. "I should probably warn you: Magnolia Castle has sustained heavy damage over the past few days. What you're going to see won't be pretty."

Wounded and dying witches flooded the halls of Magnolia Castle in the Eastern Network. We walked down the corridor without an escort; there were no Guardians standing sentry to stop us. Countless East Guards reached out as we passed, blood seeping through their bandaged hands. Their skin was black, bruised, or mottled. They moaned, crying out in pain and confusion, suffering from the same barbaric wounds I'd seen in Chatham Castle. Deadly byproducts of Mabel's Almorran magic. I whispered a calming incantation as I walked. Hardening my heart to their pleas required concerted effort. I breathed through my mouth and strode down the hall at Marten's side, mourning their pain inside my broken heart.

"This way," Marten said, guiding me down the same path Niko and I had once taken on a tour. Ahead of us loomed another wing of Magnolia Castle. I stopped in my tracks. Instead of a graceful white structure surrounded by eternally blooming magnolia trees, a burnt skeleton of corridors and hallways remained in the aftermath of the fire. Charred wood and black stones littered the ground. The smell of smoke lingered in the air.

"Jikes," I said. "What happened?"

"The war."

I whirled around to see a stocky, familiar little man approach. Niko's Assistant, Hector. Tufts of coarse black hair billowed from the top of his shirt and onto his neck. His scrunched face glowered at the damage as if he was seeing it for the first time.

"When?" I asked, clearing my throat and regaining a degree of composure. "I had no idea the fighting had come so close."

"It's been close to home. The flames died down two days ago after burning for several hours. We moved His Highness back in last night once we deemed it safe. Or relatively safe. In truth, there is nowhere else in the Eastern Network to put His Highness that would be safer than here."

I had so many questions. Safe? Move back in? Who had done this? I swallowed back most of them, lest I flood him with my curiosity.

"The South?" Marten asked. Hector shook his head.

"The West *and* the South."

Not even the sea air felt good anymore—it tasted like ash. I swallowed, looking back at the ruined structure. The smell of charred wood and smoke wafted through the open windows, overpowering the usual scent of salt.

"Take us to Niko?" I asked. He grunted.

"Follow me."

Hector led us to a sprawling room filled with marble columns and inlaid with gold filigree. It had once been grand, I imagined, but now it looked pell-mell and broken, as if it had been looted or abandoned. Only a few pieces of furniture remained in the room, and I wondered where most of it had gone. The walls lay bare. Only a tall standing clock filled one corner, ticking with reassuring regularity.

Niko sat behind a makeshift desk made of . . . driftwood, perhaps? His chin rested on his chest, which moved up and down in soft, regular intervals.

"Niko?" Marten asked, venturing forward a few steps. Hector had disappeared. For an Assistant, he spent impressively little time with his High Priest, at least whenever I'd been around.

Niko's hands jerked to the armrests, and his head snapped up, his hair rumpled and his shirt half buttoned. He seemed to have aged thirty years in the past few weeks. I hardly recognized him for the old man in his face now.

"Oh, Marten. Miss Bianca," he said, breathing fast, one slender hand on his chest. "I did not hear you come in."

His lilting accent was still soft and gentle, though it seemed more wary. The state of affairs on his desk, which looked as if it molted scrolls, didn't look much better than Niko himself.

"We received your letter," I said, stopping in the middle of the room at Marten's side. Niko rushed to his feet, blinking rapidly, as if he'd forgotten where he was.

"Oh, Miss Bianca, how wonderful to see you again. I'm very happy you returned safely. It is kind of you to come so quickly," he said. No smile graced his lips. He gestured a bit helplessly with uplifted hands. "As you can see, we are not well."

"What happened?" I asked.

Niko scowled, his nostrils flaring.

"The West Guards are supporting the South Guards with Almorran magic, as you know. They threw burning balls of fire as big as my head into our villages and homes. The smoke burns red instead of gray and chokes those who breathe it in. They attacked Magnolia Castle." His lips formed a thin line. "They murdered half of my staff."

My fingers curled into a tight fist. The Central Network had only avoided such a fate, surely, due to the vigilance of the dragons.

"Oh, Niko, I'm sorry," I said. "I knew it must be bad over here as well. I just had no idea—"

"I have asked you to come to show you a strange sight," he said abruptly, "and to speak with you concerning the impending battle. Will you follow me?"

"Of course," Marten said.

Niko led us outside, walking us through patchy, dying gardens and onto the sand. He stopped short of the beach, where the surf whispered up and down in gentle foamy rolls.

"I woke up this morning to find this," he said, gesturing to the ocean. "I don't know what to make of it. Do you know, Marten?"

At least twenty abandoned ships sat on the water, bobbing up and down with the movement of the waves. Not a single witch stirred on any of them. The scorpion flag of the Western Network flapped in a heady breeze that brought in a bank of gray clouds off the ocean.

"Mabel ordered the West Guards back," Marten said, squinting. "She's gathering all her forces together to try to invade the Central Network. Thousands of West Guards are transporting to the Borderlands. Likely that's what happened here."

Niko's hair shifted in the wind. "Considering our conversation yesterday, Marten, I am not surprised," he said, his jaw tightening. "That is why I ordered my Guardians to burn the ships on the water."

He gestured to the closest ship, where a contingent of East Guards appeared, torches burning bright. A line of archers stood on one side of the ship, shooting flaming arrows at the ships closest to them. Other East Guards transported from ship to ship, setting fire to the sails and sending flammable potions into the bellies of the vessels. Smoke, thick and black, billowed from at least three boats.

Marten clapped Niko on the back. "A smart move, Niko," he said. "You're leading this Network into war even better than you think."

"The Eastern Network is prepared to help the Central Network," Niko said, brushing aside Marten's compliment. "We are not talented on land or with the sword, and we don't have much skill in magical fighting, but those of us who are still alive will do what we can."

Marten's eyebrows rose. "Are you sure?" he asked.

"I can only give you what I have—a little more than a thousand Guardians—but we fight with a lot of heart. Give us orders," Niko said. "We will fight alongside the Central Network."

Marten smiled, but it drooped with weariness and a permeating sadness. "Thank you. Every pair of hands helps."

"How are you really doing, Niko?" I asked. The day I'd seen him fighting on the water replayed in my mind. He'd been so certain and confident. Where had that witch gone?

"I am surviving," he said, his gaze dropping. "That is all I can do."

"Is there anything we can do to help?" I asked. The question was empty at best, but I felt it had to be asked. Niko managed a struggling smile.

"No, Miss Bianca," he said, his accent thickening. "But I thank you for your friendship in such a time as this. It is a light in my deepest darkness."

Something behind us drew Niko's gaze. His shoulders dropped, and he let out a long, easy breath.

"My other light in the darkness," he said, motioning behind us with a nod. I twirled around to find a familiar redhead standing at the edge of the gardens, her mint-colored dress flapping in the wind. I'd know that crimson hair and pale skin anywhere.

"Priscilla!" I cried, jogging toward her through the sand. She threw her arms around my shoulders, rendering me momentarily paralyzed with surprise. While our friendship had come a long way in the months before Mabel kidnapped me, Priscilla rarely touched anyone.

"You're alive!" she said, pulling away. "I'm so glad you made it out of the West. Camille has been keeping me updated, but I never dreamed I'd see you here."

When we parted, I couldn't help but notice freckles on her nose. Her hair, normally so lustrous and silky, poofed around her face in undecided, frizzy waves. I could scarcely believe the red blemish on her chin. A light seemed to radiate from within her, banishing the sadness that had always lingered in her haughty gaze. She'd never been so beautiful before. The less-than-perfect edges that transformation normally hid actually gave her a natural appeal far greater than her usual perfection. At least I thought so.

"How are you?" I asked. "You seem so . . ."

"Different?"

"Happy."

"I am happy." She tucked a strand of hair behind her left ear. "I love it in the Eastern Network. It's different, and I'm of great use here. Not to mention that it's far from my parents, who would never dream of coming to the beach," she added with a wry smile. "Mother wouldn't like the ocean. She'd think it dirty and unbecoming of a well-bred witch."

I couldn't help but laugh. Who was this new bright girl?

"Strange, isn't it?" she asked, motioning to the empty ships. Flame billowed from almost all of them now, clogging the pristine sky with black clouds of noxious smoke.

"Not so strange," I said, folding my arms across my chest. "Looks like Mabel's just putting her plans into motion. When are you coming back?"

Priscilla bit her bottom lip. "I don't know," she admitted, looking over my shoulder to where Niko and Marten stood in discussion. "I love it here, and I've been able to help so many of his Guardians. I'm not as useful in the Central Network. I hated feeling helpless and . . . bored. Scarlett was wonderful, don't get me wrong, but I was never very interested in education."

"I'm sure your job is all you love about this place," I drawled, letting my eyes trail toward Niko.

Priscilla grinned, a light blush on her cheeks. "It's a lovely place," she said lightly, as though she didn't want to say *yes* but couldn't say no. I laughed.

"You and Niko would make a great match. Both of you enjoy etiquette, which is strange."

Priscilla's face fell into an expression of deep thought. "Niko and I are good friends. We're also in an emotionally charged environment, so nothing concrete has happened." Her tone changed, softening. "He's been through a lot and needed a friend. I'm in a new place and needed a friend also. It turns out we have a lot in common, and that's where we're at. And that's all. For now."

"Ah," I said. "There's the Priscilla I know. Careful and cautious."

She lifted her eyebrows. "Can you blame me?"

"No," I said after thinking about it. "Not at all." She'd lived a strict, structured life with her parents, drowning in riches and rules. Trust and unconditional acceptance had never been her forte.

Marten and Niko approached us, walking slowly through the sand, their conversation laden with the vocabulary of war—phrases like *show of force* and *anticipated casualties.* Niko greeted Priscilla with a deep warmth in his eyes, but they made no move to touch. She smiled, her red hair wind-tossed and beautiful. Niko's abiding sense of passion and Priscilla's need to be loved without rules could—and hopefully would have the opportunity to—make them a lovely pair.

Marten and Niko clasped arms. "Gather your witches," Marten said. "I'll be in touch after Derek and I sort out a plan this evening. We'll give you your orders then."

I embraced Niko and Priscilla in farewell and transported away, leaving them standing together on the beach.

Chatham Castle had never felt like home before. Not with its stiff-backed servants, elaborate decorations, and chilly stone walls.

But when I sank into my bed that evening, not even I could deny how wonderful it felt to be back at the castle.

The fact that I could lose all of it loomed in my mind, but I forced the depressing thoughts away. A *Chatterer* scroll lay open on the floor, flashing the headline *Battle over the Western Covens Begins*.

A small scroll the size of my thumb waited on my pillow. I pulled it open to find a familiar scrawl on the inside.

I'll be back soon, little troublemaker.

"Merrick," I said with a smile, a warm flush rippling over my skin. The note didn't really say anything, but it told me everything. It was his subtle way of communicating that he was all right. And, just maybe, that he missed me.

"Bianca," Papa called, his deep voice reverberating down the hall of our apartment and into my room. "Come out here. We need to speak with you."

I slipped out of my bedroom and came to a halt. Marten, Stella, and Papa stood around the table. Dripping candles held open a yellowing map of Antebellum. Stella's eyes glowed from more than the candlelight—something wonderful must have happened. A definable current of excitement ran through the air.

"This better be good, Derek," Tiberius muttered as he strode into the room from the hall. Reeves sent him a disapproving glance when he didn't remove his shoes. "I don't like being pulled off the front line. It's mine."

"Trust me, old friend," Papa said, clapping him on the shoulder. "This is good news."

"What's going on?" I asked.

Tiberius shoved me into the wall. "Good to see you too, rotten child," he said, covering my face with his hand when I tried to fight back.

Papa spread his arms and leaned his palms on the table. "We have the counter magic."

My heart leaped into my throat. "What?"

Stella's foot tapped a cheery little rhythm while she exchanged a delighted glance with Marten.

"You were there when Isadora said to me, *I suspect you've had it all along*," Papa said, straightening. "What did she say next?"

I wracked my brain. "*Good luck.* She said *good luck,* didn't she?"

Papa shook his head, his eyes shining. "No. She said, *Good luck to you, Highest Witch.* Remember now?"

"Yes . . ."

Papa tapped his fist on the table. "I should have seen it earlier, but I've been too busy, too distracted with the war to really make the connection. The magic of the Book of Light is contained in one of the two Esmelda Scrolls."

My mind spun. The ability to read the Esmelda Scrolls was a privilege only given to the Highest Witch of the Network—currently Papa. The scrolls contained the law of the Central Network as set forth by Esmelda after the formation of the new government. And, apparently, the counter magic that could save the world from Almorran fire.

Papa anticipated my thoughts. "There are two scrolls," he said, holding up two fingers. "One of them holds the law and writings of Esmelda. The other?"

"The *Book of Light*?"

He grinned. "Yes. The *Book of Light.* I'd perused it before but never paid much attention. Mildred had just died and Mabel attacked. It wasn't pertinent in the same way the law was. But now it all makes sense. Esmelda had just brought a Network out of war," Papa said, gaining more energy with every word. "She'd seen the destructive power of Almorran magic and knew the harm it could do, so she preserved the counter magic in the second scroll just in case. She must have known that the *Book of Spells* wasn't destroyed."

"And she provided an extra layer of protection for it by ensuring that only the Highest Witch had access to the scrolls," Marten said. The puzzle pieces began to come together in my mind, and I felt a thrill that seemed a lot like hope.

"What does this mean?" I asked, breathless.

"It means it's time for domination," Tiberius growled, slamming his fist onto the table. "Let's go show Mabel who's in charge now!"

Alarm rippled through Stella's face until Papa put a hand on Tiberius's shoulder and shoved him into a chair. "Sit down and calm down," he said. "We aren't going to throw away this opportunity to destroy Almorran magic by acting on rash emotions. Marten and I have developed a plan."

Marten motioned to the map. A tiny Central Network flag lay across the Western Covens, and a Western Network flag lay near the Borderlands, a thin tract of unclaimed, desolate space between the two Networks.

"As all of you know, Mabel has assembled her West Guards here," Marten said, running a finger down the Borderlands, "and is currently in control of the Borderlands. I believe her plan is simple: She's throwing her entire West Guard force into the invasion of the Central Network. The Eastern Network, even with our help, is on its dying breath. Their Guardian force is small and weak. Mountains protect the Northern Network. Their witches live too far north for her to worry about invading there yet. Worrying about them would be a waste of her time at this point in the game. If she beats the Central Network, however—"

"She wins everything," Stella murmured. Marten nodded.

"We want to preserve as many lives as we can while still winning." Marten moved the Central Network flag a step back toward Chatham Castle. "So we're going to continue putting up a convincing fight at the Borderlands for a few more hours, then retreat."

Tiberius scowled.

"Your men will set up fire traps, dig giant holes, and wait in ambush for our Western Network visitors as you go," Papa said, nudging Tiberius with an elbow. "When they follow our Guardians, they will fall."

A grim smile stretched across Tiberius's face, widening his scraggly red beard. "I like it," he said, sobering. "But that won't be enough. She has at least fourteen thousand South and West Guards fighting for her, not including Clavas. We only have nine thousand with the Eastern and Northern Network helping. Mabel hasn't had half our casualties."

"It's not meant to be enough. It just needs to buy us time," Marten said. He moved the Central Network flag all the way to the ink drawing of Chatham Castle on the map. "Or, more correctly, it will buy Derek time. He'll familiarize himself with the counter magic while we draw Mabel into Chatham City."

"Chatham City? But she'll destroy it," I said. "If we let her come all the way to the castle, we won't stand a chance."

Papa shook his head. "No, B," he said, folding his arms across his chest. "It's our only chance. We have to accept some loss in war. Bringing Mabel to us will minimize the deaths of our witches. If we continue to fight her at the Borderlands, we're sacrificing Guardians, which weakens us for the final push. The city? We can rebuild."

The Eastern Network flag and a royal purple flag—the color of the Northern Network—appeared next to the castle.

"We'll concentrate our forces," Marten said, leaning back. "The Eastern Network is giving us a thousand Guardians. The North will supply at least two thousand, along with their Masters. Because we possess the counter magic, we have a chance. A small one, of course."

Tiberius studied the map with one narrowed eye, a fist pressed to his mouth. "This is all dependent on the counter magic working, Derek Black," he said, staring at Papa. "Can you do it?"

"Yes," Papa said without hesitation.

"But the counter magic will only work against pure, active Almorran magic cast by a witch. That doesn't cover the lesser magical properties of the flesh-eating potions or choking smoke," Stella said. "And we'll still face hand-to-hand combat. Not to mention that allowing them so close to Chatham City means we risk Mabel overpowering us and taking the castle."

Papa put his hands on the back of a chair and leaned forward. Firelight from the candles cast dark shadows on his face. "It's not foolproof," he said. "We're tossing the dice. But I feel it's the best plan. What do you think, B?"

"What?" I asked, jerking out of my thoughts.

"What do you think of the plan?"

"You're asking me?"

"Yes."

Tiberius and I exchanged equally befuddled expressions. "Why are you asking me? I don't know anything about planning a war."

"You know Mabel better than anyone," Papa said. "And it's Mabel we're fighting. How do you think she'll respond?"

"Oh," I said, dropping my arm to my side.

"What do you think?"

I searched my mind, wondering if my journey into her subconscious had given me any clues to her war plans, but I found nothing. I thought of my conversation with Farah on the balcony.

I believe war is more of a mental game than a physical sport, although it's arguably both. By understanding her better, I'd like to think I could anticipate what she'll do.

Instead of sorting through the bog of memories I'd stuffed away, I relied on my instincts. "I think Mabel's going to be focused solely on defeating the Central Network. In doing that, she'll make mistakes."

Papa leaned his hips against the table and folded his arms across his chest. "Why?"

I paused, feeling my initial reaction out. "Because she wants the Central Network. She's obsessed over it, almost irrationally."

"Not all of Antebellum?"

"Well, maybe. But she wants the Central Network the most. It's all she really spoke of. She isn't as interested in ruling the world, I think, as proving that she can. Not to mention she's probably livid. Unhinged with rage. She walked a fine line after Angelina died, but I'm sure she'll be out of control after I . . . after what I saw. What I did is likely to make her snap."

"What'd you do now?" Tiberius growled.

"The same thing she did to me: I searched her memories. I think she'd locked all her most painful memories away, and I . . . well, I sort of resurrected some of them."

"What did you see?"

"Things she didn't want me to."

Tiberius tapped his sausage-like finger on the map, drawing the conversation away before I was forced to explain further. Although Mabel's memories were not my own, I couldn't bring myself to share the details. They were too personal, too horrible.

"While I take my witches and fight on the front line, who will guard Chatham Castle?" he asked. "What if Mabel sends West Guards ahead?"

"Zane is sending reinforcements," Papa said. "He said to expect them in the early morning hours."

"Who?" Tiberius asked.

"They're probably witches from the Southern and Western Networks," I said, straightening.

Tiberius snorted after I explained what I'd told Zane in the Western Network. "You're expecting untrained witches to keep you safe?"

"Not exactly," Marten said. "The dragons will keep the castle safe. I've already spoken with Nicolas. At least ten dragons will patrol the air above the castle and Letum Wood."

Tiberius opened his mouth to protest but stopped. "Fine," he said, looking sheepish. "That'll do."

"Think this will work, Papa?" I asked, staring at the map until the lines between the Networks blurred together.

"It has to," he said on a long breath. "It has to."

The Antebellum Army

The drawn-out bugle of an unfamiliar horn broke through the morning mists, waking me from a restless slumber. I jumped off the divan, where I'd fallen asleep while Papa and Marten finished crafting their plans, and ran to the balcony doors. The sun broke on the horizon, rising in bursts of yellow, orange, and pink. Far below, a teeming crowd of witches filled Chatham Road, flowing into the lower and upper baileys. New witches appeared every moment, walking, running, or transporting. The numbers multiplied in the distance, filling every available space, even into Chatham City. My breath caught in my throat.

"Zane and Merrick," I said. "The reinforcements. It has to be."

After braiding my hair at lightning speed, I slipped into a fresh dress, strapped Viveet to my thigh, threw the Volare on my back, and transported to the Wall. My braid flopped between my shoulder blades when I landed near the Gatehouse, which housed Zane and Tiberius's offices. Papa was already standing outside of it, deep in discussion with Zane, who boasted an ugly scar across his right cheek. A keepsake, I suspected, from an ornery kitty named Juba.

"Bianca!"

I whipped around to find Merrick striding down the Wall toward me, his sword swinging on his hip and his sandy hair loose on his shoulders. I collided with him, wrapping my arms around his solid chest in relief.

"You made it," I said into his neck. "I've been so worried."

He lifted me off the ground. Strands of white wove through the blonde hair I knew so well, souvenirs of the Western sun. He smelled like sweat and leather and fresh air. When he set me down, I spotted a crooked grin on his face.

"It's good to see you again," he said in his Northern accent. Now that I knew the truth, he didn't force an accent, and I wouldn't have had it any other way.

"I—"

"Ahem."

The sound of a witch clearing his throat interrupted my reply. My arms dropped to my sides, and I turned to find Papa glowering at both of us. I gave him a sheepish smile.

"Oh . . . uh . . . hi there, Papa."

"Mind if I speak with my Protector?" he asked, his eyebrows raised in a can-you-do-this-somewhere-else expression. I stepped to the side.

"Nope."

Papa shot me a look of fatherly long-suffering and proceeded to speak with Merrick while I tried to control the butterflies in my stomach. After a minute, Papa sent me one last exasperated glance before transporting away. Once he left, Merrick and I looked at each other and burst out laughing.

"Come on, troublemaker," Merrick said, hooking an arm around my neck. "Zane spoke with Ijet and Nan and convinced the gypsies to come back and fight. Your father wants me to take Ijet his orders." He winked. "Then I can show you what Zane and I have been up to."

Merrick led me straight into the heart of the chaos swarming Chatham Castle.

"We're callin' it the Antebellum Army," he said, keeping a heavy hand on the small of my back as we navigated the tight crowd. "They aren't fightin' for the Central Network or even for their homeland. They're fightin' for Antebellum."

I sorted through the strange, unfamiliar faces as we moved closer to Chatham City. "There are so many," I said, dodging a bull led by a rope tied to a ring in his nostril.

"We think there are about two thousand witches joinin' the fight, most of them male, although the Western Network has a good number of women with some . . . interestin' weapons instead of heavy swords and shields. They've come from all over the Western and Southern Networks," he said, glancing behind him as two young boys ran past us.

"And they're willing to fight with us?"

"They want freedom. This is what it will take to get it, so . . . yes."

"What will you do with all of them?" I asked, studying an overweight witch from the Southern Network. He smiled, and his eyes disappeared in the rolls of his face.

"Right now we're puttin' them to work preparin' Chatham City for the West Guards. Most of them aren't skilled with swords, but they have their own weapons. Since a lot of them aren't trained, they're goin' to occupy Chatham City and support the trained Guardians. A lot of the witches from the West are good archers. We'll put them in the buildin's. It's a lot easier for an archer to kill a West Guard from a third-story window than from down on the ground."

My eyes flickered up to the windows. The smell of campfire and smoke drifted down the road. A goat, escaped from a group of Western Network witches, ran by with a bell jingling on its neck. I watched it in amusement. At least three different languages chattered on in the background, the individual words indistinguishable in the great mass of noise. The Southern Network witches spoke so fast I could barely see their lips move, but the Western Network folk seemed more deliberate, quiet, even fixated.

"And the Southern Network witches?" I asked. "What will you do with them? They can't do magic, which makes them more of a burden than an asset, doesn't it?"

"They'll do what they can," he said. "Since they can't do magic, we're havin' most of them get the ambush spots ready. We'll reserve them until the end, or else it'll just be one big slaughterhouse."

"Not to mention they'll be fighting their family members," I said, remembering the ceremony I'd attended in the West. Merrick's thin lips echoed my grim thoughts.

An extended family from the tribes of the Southern Network stood off to the side of Chatham Road, near the gate that led into the city, distinguishable by their thin eyes and clothes made from the finest silk in Antebellum. Although they were preparing for war, most of the male witches wore elegant white silk shirts—made with magic in their cold Network—which couldn't have been comfortable in the heat. For these Southern Network witches, however, fine silk was a point of pride, even survival. After the wealthy class banished them to the far reaches of their Network, silk became their greatest trading tool. No doubt they wore it to the battle to represent their home.

"They want revenge against Mikhail for takin' their magic," Merrick said, following my gaze. "Part of our agreement with them is that the witches of the Southern Network get to decide Mikhail's punishment if he survives the final battle."

Several smoky candles dripped greasy wax around a makeshift table, and a lone lantern burned bright with whale oil, casting a yellow glow in the fading darkness and making their entire camp smell like fish.

My eyebrows rose in amusement at the thought of these witches enacting their revenge and regaining control of their Network. What a lovely turn of events for them. "Really?"

"I don't blame them," Merrick said, and the firmness of his rolling voice sent a cool chill down my spine. "They'll never be able to do magic again because of his selfish actions, and no one knows yet if their children will be able to either."

The power of the Mansfeld Pact had been underappreciated until it was broken and its penalties unleashed, leaving an entire Network crippled and without magic.

"Most of them seem to know the common language, which I believe they use when they trade with the other tribes, so talking with them hasn't been too difficult. Some of the older witches only know their tribal language."

One of the Southern Network witches grasped a double-sided ax. He spun it around, inspecting the blades, which flashed in the morning light. Another witch near him held a spiky wooden club in his hands. Old bloodstains darkened the wood, and metal prongs jutted in every direction.

"Jikes," I said. "The gory business of war."

"Kill or be killed," Merrick said. "It's particularly desperate for them since they can't use magic to protect themselves."

I shivered. "It's like fighting as a mortal. Can you imagine?"

Merrick pressed his lips in a grim line. "No," he said. "It's barbaric."

The sound of a familiar voice piped up from behind me.

"You?"

I whirled around to see Zoe a few paces away, a goofy grin on her face. A middle-aged witch stood next to her with similar thin eyes, graying hair, and a simple blue silk dress. Zoe wore a silk dress just a shade lighter.

"Zoe!" I cried. "You're safe!"

Her grin widened. "I have family," she said in the common language, pointing to the witch. "My . . . uh . . . aunt? Vitch with no hair came." She curled her hand into a claw and slashed it through the air.

"He fought Juba?"

Zoe nodded, her eyes animated, and she gestured to her manacle-free ankle.

"Freedom," she said.

The gaps in the story weren't hard to fill in. Zoe must have been present when Zane fought Juba, so once he won, he removed the manacle from her ankle and transported her back to the Southern Network, somehow either tracking down her family or finding someone who would.

"I'm so happy for you, Zoe," I said, smiling at her aunt, who held tight to Zoe's hand. "But you can't stay for the . . . uh . . . the battle."

Zoe turned around and pointed to Letum Wood. "Ve hide," she said. "Deep in forest."

While not the safest place to be, it wasn't the worst either. Letum Wood itself wouldn't harm the innocent witches, but it housed plenty of creatures that the forest didn't control. The thought of offering her shelter in Chatham Castle crossed my mind, but it was already packed full—overfull, really—and was the biggest target in the

Central Network. She wouldn't be much safer there. Letum Wood would have to do.

"Be safe," I said with a warm smile. "And thank you."

Zoe nodded, smiling. With a tug on her aunt's hand, she disappeared into the crowd. Merrick stared after them.

"Friend from the West?" he asked. I nodded.

"Yes," I said, grateful to release one of the worries that nagged at me. "She worked at the Arck."

"Come," he said, his hand drifting to the small of my back again. "Let's find Ijet."

We passed a pile of old shields that maids and fireboys had carried or levitated out of the bowels of the castle. Witches surrounded the heap, testing the weight and height of the shields. I missed my old shield. It had irreparably cracked when I fought Mabel in the ballroom what seemed like ages ago.

A flash of bright color caught my gaze. We'd found the gypsies. "Here they are!" I cried under my breath, glancing beyond the Southern Network witches at a familiar sight—vivid fabrics, eccentric carvings, and beautiful caramel skin.

"I want to find Jackie," I said, lengthening my stride. I rushed forward, raking my eyes through the crowd. After all I'd seen in the North, I had so much to tell my old friend from Miss Mabel's School for Girls. Last I'd seen her, she'd been mourning the loss of her people and had left with her Nan to go to Gypsy Wood, a chunk of Letum Wood protected by magic and given to the gypsies by the Mansfeld Pact. A nearby gypsy with horizontal green lines painted across his thin chest caught my eye.

"Jackie?" I asked, grabbing his arm. "Is Jackie here?"

He recoiled, distrust in his eyes.

"Ijet?" I asked him. "I'm a friend of Jackie, Ijet, and Nan. Do you know where Ijet is?"

Another gypsy turned around, a male with black hair that sat like a pillow on top of his head. "You are Bianca," he said, his face lighting up. "Da High Priest's daughter."

"Yes."

His wide lips spread in a bright smile, the whiteness of his teeth highlighted by his dark skin. A colorful, painted dragon crossed his chest, roaring with smoke and flying with wings made of fire. "I know ya," he said, his voice thick with the gypsy accent. "Ya helped with da fires."

"Yes. Is Jackie here?"

He waved a hand, and several bracelets on his wrist clinked together. "Come," he said. "I take ya ta her."

When I turned around to make sure Merrick would follow, I ran into his chest. "Right behind you," he said. Together we plunged through the crowd that streamed with fabrics, the scent of cloves, and the chants of their strange music. I spied a pair of dark eyes and a familiar head of spiraling curls only a few moments later.

"Jackie?" I called. Her eyes widened.

"Bianca?"

She rushed toward me, nearly toppling me over in her enthusiasm. Paint covered her skin. Purple and green flames danced across her cheeks, winding around her eyes and hiding her eyebrows. When she blinked, I saw that the flames had been painted on her eyelids as well. With her high cheekbones and natural grace, she was a stunning masterpiece of art.

"You're alive!" she cried, pulling away. She put her warm hands on either side of my face. "You're so crazy I thought for sure ya would have done something ta get yourself killed."

Merrick snorted behind me.

"I'm fine, I'm fine," I said, looking her over. "Are you all right? Is Nan?"

"Nan is still in the homeland," Jackie said, the strength of her gypsy accent fading, "where it's safe. We've appointed two more elders, but they don't have as much power or experience as she does. We want to keep her safe as long as we can."

"And your brothers?"

She smiled. "They're running around somewhere."

"What's all this paint?"

Jackie ran her fingers along the coral flames on her arms. Tendrils of yellow and orange snaked all the way up to her shoulder. "Protection," she said. "The magic we use while applying it shields us in battle."

My throat tightened. "Are you going to fight?"

She grabbed a wooden club hanging from her belt and held it up. A thick, spiked ball at the end of it would tear apart a grizzly bear. Bite marks in the wood indicated she'd either been practicing with it, or someone had tried to fight her already.

"Jikes. You could take down any West Guard with that thing."

She smirked. "I know how to use it."

"It's going to be dangerous. Will your father let you fight?"

Jackie mimicked my skeptical look. "Will yours?"

I laughed and gave her another hug. "He doesn't have a choice. I'm going to be out there ready to fight the moment I see West Guards in the city."

Jackie grinned. "Me too."

She'd always been lighthearted and fun—when the Factios weren't killing her family—so seeing her animated again made it feel like the war hadn't taken everything away.

"Who is this?" Jackie asked, looking beyond me. "He's beautiful."

"Oh," I said, blushing. "This is Merrick."

He opened his mouth to respond, but a deep voice like rolling thunder interrupted our conversation.

"Jackie."

Ijet, Jackie's father, approached us from behind. His dark, towering frame loomed above us like a moving pillar. While Jackie had skin the smooth color of melted caramel, Ijet was as dark as cocoa powder. He loomed over his daughter, laying a massive hand on her shoulder. Swirls of dark blue, green, and black and little specks of white mimicked the night sky across his wide chest. He wore a string of tiny beads around his neck. They sang when he moved, like wind chimes in a summer breeze, though in the heavy air they sounded hollow and off-key.

"Ijet," Merrick said, stepping forward. The two of them clasped forearms in a grip that would have broken my bones. He handed a small scroll to the gypsy leader. "This comes from Derek. He asked me to deliver it in person."

"We are ready ta fight," Ijet said, thumping a fist over his heart. "We are part of Antebellum. We will fight as Antebellum."

Merrick nodded. "Derek thinks the West Guards will make it to the city by this evening." He gestured to the scroll. "He wants your witches just inside Letum Wood, surrounding the castle. If any West Guards try to sneak into the forest, you can take care of them."

Ijet nodded. Jackie met my eyes.

"Ya ready?" she asked, giving me a wicked smile. Her blind confidence would have been contagious if I didn't already know what Mabel was capable of. *No,* I wanted to say. *And neither are you. Neither is any witch here. You have no idea what we're up against.*

Instead, I smiled. If Jackie had confidence, let her keep it. We could all use a little more.

"Let's save our world," I said, and we embraced again. I held her an extra moment longer, hoping it wouldn't be for the last time.

Later that afternoon, Leda and I strolled across the lower bailey, her light pink dress trailing in the breeze. Murky, gray clouds hung in the sky. *Blast this humidity.* Sweat soaked my arms and back until my braid lay sticky and hot on my neck. Leda had been brooding ever since Camille's surprise marriage announcement, although she tried to blame it on a headache. I had underestimated Leda's attachment to our vivacious, frizzy-haired friend.

"Are you ever going to forgive her?" I asked gently. Leda cast me a sidelong glance. Even though we hadn't been talking about Camille, I knew she understood.

"Yes," she said with a sigh. "I will. I have. I mean . . . it's not like she's done anything that I need to forgive. I just . . . I don't like surprises."

"You love Camille, and you're sad she's going to leave," I said. "Seems pretty normal to me. Camille isn't mad, you know."

Leda's shoulders slumped. "Yes," she said, resigned. "I know." I waited for a snappy retort, but nothing came.

"That's it?" I asked.

Leda *humphed* and looked the other way. I considered our little pep talk a success and felt a small margin of relief that a bit of her old verve had resurfaced.

"I see you're wearing pants," she said, motioning to my legs. "That might not be a bad idea."

I followed her gaze with a wry smile. "It's a lot easier to manage a sword when I'm not tripping over my own skirts," I said. "Want me to find you a pair?"

For a moment she seemed to contemplate it, but then she shook her head, as if she couldn't quite break that barrier of propriety, even during a war.

"I'm not planning on sword fighting tonight," she said. "I'll pass." She tilted her head back, contemplating the sky with an expression that mimicked the storm. "We need to get all these Guardians inside before it rains."

Countless Guardians lay on cots in a grid structure around us. Apothecaries ran by, supervising the levitation of Guardians into the castle. Other less magically talented witches carried the Guardians on makeshift stretchers.

"The rain?" I retorted. "We need to get them inside before the West Guard invasion." I motioned to two Guardians leaning against the Wall, their faces pale. "Let's help those two. They look like they can walk with some aid."

Leda was a creature of logic and rules, so her compassion for the wounded had been surprising, even endearing. She followed behind me, but both of us stopped short after only a few steps. A familiar witch with a small flock of children clinging to her skirt appeared on the stairs leading into the bailey. Leda's mouth dropped.

"Mama?"

Leda's mother, Lara, saw us at the same moment and let out a breath of relief. She waved, holding a young child on her hip.

"Leedee!" she called.

"Oh, no," Leda murmured, starting forward. "Something else must be wrong."

I followed close behind. Lara met us at the bottom of the stairs and threw an arm around her daughter. Tears filled her exhausted eyes. Strands of ragged brown hair fell from her disintegrating bun.

"Mama?" Leda asked, pulling away from her embrace to pick up a little girl with two blonde braids. "What's wrong?"

A brown-haired girl the same height as Leda stepped forward. She had to be Bronwyn, Leda's younger sister. "Hansham is empty," she said. "We were the only ones left."

"I couldn't stay there alone," Lara said, swallowing. She trembled but forced her expression to remain composed, I supposed for her children's sake. "What if the West Guards came again? They'd—" Lara glanced at her younger children. "Well, they wouldn't spare us a second time, that's for sure. Your father is out trying to find us a place to stay in the city, but there isn't anything. There must be something here in Chatham Castle. Is there?"

Lara looked between us, walking that fine line between desperation and blatant panic. Her children, some weepy, some fidgeting, remained close and kept their wary eyes on all the commotion in the bailey. They were the saddest casualties of this war, stripped of innocence. No young children should see the horrors they'd witnessed.

Leda's lips tightened. I knew what she was thinking. Hansham would have been a much safer place. Chatham Castle was an overcrowded broiler of sickness and death. Not to mention the imminent approach of the West Guards.

"Mama," Leda said, stumbling over the words. "I . . . I don't know where there's room in the castle. I—"

I put a hand on Leda's arm.

"I do," I said, looking at Lara. "You can have the apartment I share with Papa."

Lara reared back. "Bianca," she said with a sharp intake of breath. "I couldn't possibly—"

"Yes," I said. "You can. Besides, our butler will be ecstatic to have so many little ones to help take care of during the battle. He needs a job, but he's old and can't really fight. You'll be safer there than anywhere else in the castle, although it's not really all that safe anywhere. I'd send you into Letum Wood, but your children are too young."

Leda eyed me with a deep look of gratitude. "Thank you," she whispered.

"It's not like we'll be using it," I said under my breath. "Take them there now." I turned to Lara. "There's an extra room that Reeves knows about. It has no windows. Lock yourselves in there until the battle is over. It will be the best protection for you and your children."

Lara's eyes filled with tears. "Thank you, Bianca. Oh, thank—"

The deep, booming reverberation of West Guard drums echoed in the bailey, cutting Lara off. My heart nearly stopped. Leda and I looked at each other.

"Are they that close?" she asked, paling.

I transported to the top of the Wall. A moving mass of black filled the horizon, seeming to overtake the world in a sticky maw of death and smoke. My stomach churned when I transported back down.

"They're outside the city," I said. "Take your family to the apartment. Reeves will take care of them. I want to find Marten and see what's happening."

Leda pursed her lips and nodded, grabbing one of her younger siblings by the shoulder. I clutched her arm before she left.

"Can you meet me in the Witchery?" I asked. She paused.

"Yes. Once I get my family settled."

"Can you send a message to Camille, Priscilla, and Michelle to meet there as well?"

Leda studied me. "You want to say *merry part,* don't you? Just in case."

I hesitated. "Yes. I do."

"Me too," she said. "I'll send the notes from your apartment. That will give you time to find Marten." Leda turned back to her family, a little one still in her arms. "Follow me," she called. "Don't get separated!"

Once I helped the two wounded Guardians into an old room in the lower levels of the castle, I transported to Marten's office, but it was empty. I went from place to place in the castle, but I couldn't find Marten or Papa. A wild thought crossed my mind, and I transported into Chatham City. When the darkness of the magic dissipated, I found myself in the heart of town. Most of the Antebellum Army had taken up residence on the outskirts and would fall back as the West Guards pressed in. Except for two witches standing in the middle of the square—Papa and Marten—I saw no signs of life.

An old newsscroll drifted by on the same tepid breeze that carried the scent of the West Guards' fires, tumbling across the cobblestone street end over end. The door to Miss Holly's Candy Shop stood open, its windows shattered by looters. It creaked and groaned in the breeze. The fountain in the circle outside had run dry. The stark, silent city left a deep hole in my heart.

I walked up to Papa's side.

"They're advancing," Marten said. Both of them stared down the street toward the West, although nothing could be seen but the columns of fires that followed on the tail of the West Guards. Billowing clouds of smoke filled the sky, heralding an early darkness.

"This is it," Papa said. "Mabel's shown no sign of resting. She'll push through the city tonight."

I crossed my arms over my chest to hide a shudder. Despite the thick, hot humidity, I felt cold and numb. The driving sound of the Western Network's drums of war nearly drowned out Papa and Marten's conversation. The rhythmic *thud thud thud* rang in my ears, dull and heavy, like a heartbeat. A reminder.

Chatham City had never been perfect. Parts of it flowed with disease and rats and sewage. But there were beautiful districts and historical places too. Above all, we took pride in it. No matter its imperfections, it was still the heart of the Central Network. If Mabel obliterated it, much would be mourned and missed.

"Are you ready, Papa?" I asked, thinking about the Esmelda Scrolls and the counter magic. He'd had so little time to practice.

He let out a long breath. "I have to be."

We fell silent, listening to the approach of the drums. I knew, deep in my heart, I'd never see the same Chatham City again.

Now We Fight

When I transported to the Witchery, my turret home lay empty and combed over. Soon after Camille moved out, Leda had followed, unable to stay in the Witchery alone. She slept in a closet in the bowels of the West Wing, where the quiet was loud and the air chilly, just the way she liked it.

Seeing pillows strewn about, the table bare, and papers littering Leda's once-organized space made my eyes sting. If Leda's area was messy, it was the end of the world. The disorganization of the Witchery brought home an awful truth: No matter what happened, things would never be the same. No more cozy Witchery evenings, playing the game Networks with Leda and always losing. No more meals at our old broken table or staying up until the early hours talking to Camille about her dream wedding.

"Daughter of the Central Network," hissed a familiar voice in my ear. "I have returned."

I whipped around to find Dafina hovering in the air behind me, her svelte good looks restored and her bright wings humming in a red cloud. My heart plummeted.

"Dafina," I said, forcing a smile. "How . . . nice to see you again."

She folded her arms across her chest, drumming her tiny fingers. "You owe me a favor. Have you forgotten?"

"Yes, I did forget."

Her little body flew back, recoiling. "You do not deny it?"

"No." My brows furrowed together. "Why would I?"

"Because witches are sneaky and unfaithful!"

I rolled my eyes. "No, we're not."

"Then why are you fighting yet another war?"

My mouth opened to respond but quickly closed again. She had a point.

"You've come to collect on your favor, I assume?" I asked, hoping to get rid of her before Leda or Camille found their way back. There was no telling what the vain creature would ask for. Getting more witches involved would agitate Dafina, and the last thing I needed was a wild fairy darting around the castle.

"Yes," she said, baring her teeth. "The witches are destroying our home. Our trees burn under strange flames."

"Black fire."

"Yes!"

"I know. So what's the favor?"

Dafina eyed me askance. "Save my pack."

"Excuse me?"

"Save us!" she cried, her voice shrill. "We must find a new home." She stopped flying and landed on my shoulder. "You must find us a new home."

"Find you a new home?" I repeated, tilting my head to study the small features of her face. "Now?"

"Immediately!"

"I can't do it now!" I said, gesturing outside. "The final battle is about to start. The world may come to an end shortly, so I'm not all that worried about your fairy pack, to be honest."

Her eyebrows drooped low in a glare of surprising power for something so small.

"You refuse to fulfill your vow?" she asked, her voice a careful, quiet hiss.

I hesitated. In a way, delaying would constitute a refusal. I didn't get to set the terms of the favor, and it wasn't like finding Zane had been convenient for her. But where would I put a pack of fairies? They were violent and destructive in large numbers.

Dafina tilted her head back. "The magic of the fairies will come against you!" she cried, her wings moving so fast I could barely hear her. "We will pull out all your hair! Maytar will rip your eyelashes out one at a time while you are sleeping! We will poke out your eyes and tear your fingernails in ha—"

"Calm down!" I said, plucking her from the air. She twisted and writhed in a poor attempt to kick my wrist. "I'll help, all right? Just relax."

She settled, distrust in her eyes. "You will help the fairies?"

"How many of you?" I asked, glancing at the door. Camille and Leda would arrive at any moment.

"Five hundred in my pack."

"Five hundred?" I cried. "Are you joking? Where am I going to put you?"

She leaped into my face, gnashing her fangs. "Dafina never jokes!"

I leaned back, batting her away. "Fine. I'll find you somewhere safe."

"Where?"

My mind raced. Nowhere was safe, not even for these tiny, narcissistic monsters. Letum Wood was out of the question—if they moved, they'd encroach on another fairy pack's territory, and an epic bloodbath would ensue. The Eastern Network was too far, and fairies didn't like water. They'd need someplace sheltered, away from the fight, and big enough to house them until the battle ended. Unless they became attached to their new home, of course, and decided to stay.

"Where?" she asked again, flying in a circle around my head. "Daughter of the Central Network has no answer! The fairies have no time!"

"Here!" I said, spreading my arms. "In the Witchery."

Dafina stopped her annoying buzzing. Her eyes trailed over the walls, the belongings cast aside and left without an owner.

"Hmmm," she said low in her throat, her eyes tapering. She zipped from place to place, searching the nooks and crannies. Cracks littered the stone walls, and the fireplace was much too small, but those things wouldn't necessarily matter to something so miniscule. Or five hundred somethings so miniscule. She inspected the room, overturning every discarded sock, opening each book, and flying underneath the furniture.

"Under whose authority do you bestow this parcel of land to my pack?" she asked as she approached me again.

"My own," I said. "I placed the magic that protects this turret."

"Yes," she said, humming. "I sense that."

"It's mine to give."

Dafina studied me. I held my hands at my side and rubbed my fingers together. Surely Leda would burst in. She'd never forgive me for giving up the Witchery to a pack of fairies, never mind that she'd left it behind. The bloodthirsty creatures would probably bring the turret down. Although maybe they'd frighten away any Clavas or West Guards who had the misfortune to stumble upon them.

"'Tis done!" Dafina cried, levitating above my head. "I shall find my pack immediately."

"You can't move in for at least an hour," I said. She hesitated in the window, sending me a piercing stare of annoyance.

"An hour?"

"Yes."

She huffed. "Fine, daughter of the Central Network. An hour."

Dafina left, and I heaved a giant sigh of relief. Their arrogant little bodies would fill the Witchery soon enough. I wondered if they'd bring back the small rodents they hunted and have a fairy feast on the same table where we had dined so often.

"I guess the Witchery definitely won't be the same anymore, will it?" I murmured to myself, running the tips of my fingers over the top of our tattered floral divan, wondering what I'd done.

"No. It won't. We won't either."

I whirled around to find Leda shuffling into the room. Her hair hung in limp tendrils around her pale face. Her shoulders were bony beneath her loose dress, but she still looked lovely in her own tired way.

"What did Reeves say?" I asked. A hint of a smile lingered on her face.

"He was polishing the silver when we showed up. Although he acted a bit stuffy, he picked up two children and started giving orders right away, so I think he was relieved."

I smiled. "Good."

We stood in the middle of the room in silence. Now that she was here, I didn't know what to say.

"What happens now?" Leda asked, swallowing.

"Now? Now we fight."

My words echoed in the empty room.

"And if we lose?" she asked.

The door to the Witchery opened. "Bianca?" Camille said, step-ping inside. "Leda? Everything okay?"

Her eyes fell on the messy room and the two of us standing in the middle. Outside, the drums of the West Guards continued their rest-less thud thud thud. Camille pressed her lips together so tightly they disappeared.

"Oh," she whispered. "I . . . I see. You sent that letter to get us here one last time together, right?"

"We were just . . ." Leda's voice broke. She looked away.

"Yes," I said. "We were hoping for one last moment in the Witchery together, just in case."

Camille's eyes sparkled. She nodded.

The idea of saying *merry part* to my friends—my sisters—was so unbearable that I changed the subject.

"Where are you going when the battle begins?" I asked, looking between the two of them. "I want to make sure you're safe."

"Brecken wants me to stay with his family," Camille said, lowering herself onto a chair near the table. She looked down at her fidgeting hands. "Bettina and Angie are living in the attic of Brecken's house for now. Tabby is ecstatic to have someone to talk to, and Angie is happy to tell her about all her health problems. I think it takes Tabby's mind off of . . . well . . . everything."

"Really?" Leda asked, one faint eyebrow rising. "Your aunts were willing to leave their house? I thought for sure they'd stay put."

Camille smiled, her freckles pressing together. "Yes," she said, chuckling softly. "It literally took an act of war to get them to leave."

The joke, so light and whimsical—almost fragile—broke some of the awkward tension. Leda's shoulders relaxed. Leda and Camille had been so distant she hadn't even known that Bettina and Angie had come to the Witchery.

"Camille," Leda said, her voice husky. "I'm—"

Camille silenced her by throwing her arms around her. Leda re-turned the embrace with shaky hands.

"I know," Camille said. "I love you too."

Leda closed her eyes, holding onto Camille's dress. "I'm so excited for you," Leda said. "Truly. I hope you and Brecken will be very happy."

"We will," Camille said. "I promise we will."

"You'll be safer at Brecken's than here," I said, relieved. "I'm glad."

Camille bit her bottom lip as she pulled away from Leda's embrace. "Oh, no. You misunderstood. I'm not going to Brecken's house," she said. "His mother wants me to, and so does he, but I'm going to stay here and help fight."

Both Leda and I started to protest, but Camille stopped us by holding up a hand.

"Brecken is here fighting, and he's my husband. I won't be parted from him. I will fight. We will win. Besides, he's not my only family, is he?" A tear fell from one of her wide eyes. "You, Michelle, and Priscilla are my family, the sisters I never had. I won't leave you here to fight while I cower in the country. I won't do it!"

Her voice rose with a fervor I'd never heard before, reaching a frantic pitch. Leda and I exchanged astonished glances.

"Camille," I stammered. "Are you sure?"

She raised her chin. "Absolutely."

My mouth bobbled open and closed for want of words. The defiant gleam in her eye said she wouldn't be swayed. The three of us moved at the same time, colliding in a warm embrace. Their arms felt heavy and reassuring, draped across my shoulders.

"Whatever comes," I said as we pressed our foreheads together, "let's agree to celebrate the good times."

"All the wonderful memories," Camille said.

"We'll never forget," Leda said.

"Never."

With one last reassuring squeeze, we parted. Tears sparkled in Leda's eyes. I swallowed mine. Emotion and grief could—and would—come later. Later. When we won or when we died.

We heard a rustle in the middle of the turret. Michelle and Priscilla transported right next to each other in the middle of the Witchery floor.

"Michelle! Priscilla!" Camille cried.

"Oh," Michelle said, sounding relieved. "We were hoping you'd still be here. Priscilla and I just ran into each other in the kitchens. We both got your message, Leda."

"Good timing," Leda said.

Michelle held a hand to her belly, where the smallest budge could be seen through her dress. She kept her hand there, as if trying to protect her unborn child. Priscilla gazed around the Witchery with a frown. She looked lovely, her red hair shining around her shoulders.

"I haven't been here as long as you four," Priscilla said, "but it still breaks my heart to see the Witchery so . . . lifeless."

Just wait an hour, I thought. "How is Niko?" I asked. Worry flashed in her green eyes.

"Ready to fight," she said. "The Eastern Network Guardians are protecting the northern section of Chatham City. He's leading them into battle there. I wanted to come fight with the Central Network." She let out a long breath. "Although I love the East, the Central Network will always be home."

"Oh, I have something for all of you!" Camille said. "I was going to track you down one at a time, but this is so much better."

She reached into her pocket and pulled out five silver lockets, all shaped like a diamond and about the size of a thumbnail.

"It's not a memento," she said, "because none of us are going to die. The Central Network is going to pull through. It's a keepsake. A reminder. No matter what Mabel tries, she can't take our memories. She can't take our friendship." Camille looked each one of us in the eye. "Remember that."

The five lockets levitated into the air when Camille cast a spell, dropping over our heads and onto our shoulders one at a time. They glinted in the dim light, like a sentinel against the encroaching darkness. I clasped mine in my fist.

"I'll be keeping Clavas out of the kitchens with Brecken," Camille said, sticking a hand in the middle of our circle. "Once we've won the fight, come and find me there. I'll probably be eating any chocolate that's survived the battle."

"I'm going to help the Apothecaries with the wounded," Leda said, extending her hand forward and placing it, palm up, on Camille's. "I better not see any of you there."

"I'll be with Miss Scarlett." Priscilla placed her hand on Leda's. "We're protecting the orphans and small children in the West Wing."

"I'll be with my husband." Michelle put her hand on the bottom, underneath the others. "And the dragons."

They all looked at me. I placed my hand on top, palm down, to seal the pile of hands together.

"I'll be with my father," I said. "Where I belong."

"No matter what," Camille said, "we'll always be best friends."

"Always."

The five of us pulled together in a long embrace. The collective beats of our hearts worked in sync for a few seconds. I held my breath, marveling that I could hurt so much with anticipated pain. Losing any one of these girls would be torturous. The thought alone terrified me—something I would never have imagined the first time I met Priscilla or Leda.

The long, mournful tone of the bugle sounded for the first time, and my heart leaped into my throat.

"What was that?" Priscilla asked.

I put my hand on Viveet. "The bugle," I said. "It means the West Guards are approaching Chatham City. When it sounds again, it means the invasion's begun."

"It's the beginning of the end, ladies," Leda said, with the snap and vinegar of her old self. "Now let's get to work. We have a castle to save."

Many Powerful Witches

A frantic, desperate bustling had overtaken the castle, with Mrs. L at the center. She moved through the chaos, hurrying from place to place, her cheeks flushed as she shouted orders and directed traffic. Fireboys slammed windows shut and hammered boards across them. Maids used spells to light all the torches to ensure they didn't go out. A small kitchen maid carrying buckets full of water sloshed by, tears streaking her frightened face.

"We need another bucket here!" called a lad with soot on his face. "In case the Clavas come around the corner!"

Hoarding water to fight the undead. An ugly testament to our desperation.

The vague notion that these witches would soon be fighting for their lives plagued my mind, but I let it go, intent on finding Papa. The door to the throne room stood ajar, admitting a single ray of light into the dark hallway. Papa's armored body filled the throne. His dark eyes stared at the wall, and his hair stood up on end as if he'd dragged a hand through it over and over again. I put my fingertips on the door and pushed it open.

"Papa?"

His eyes flickered to mine. For a moment, he regarded me in confusion. The Dragon Throne sprawled out behind his shoulders, making him seem more indomitable and powerful than ever.

"I thought I'd find you here."

"I was just thinking about your mother," he said with a wistful smile. "Then you walked in, and for a moment, I thought I'd imagined her back to life. You look so much like her, B. It's uncanny."

Only the *slip slip* of my leather sandals sounded in the room as I walked to his side. "I think about her all the time too."

"Never more than when I need strength and courage," he said, and his face sobered. "Never more than right now."

"Are you scared?" I asked.

"Terrified. You?"

I nodded.

"I want you to promise me one thing, B," he said.

"Don't make me promise to stay away from the fight," I said, bristling. "I won't. If this is the end of the world, I won't spend it holed up in Chatham Castle waiting for someone else to save me. I'll die fighting." I paused, holding his gaze. "Just like you. I want to be at your side."

Papa hesitated. "You're a stubborn witch, you know that?"

"Witch?" I said with a grin. "Not a girl?"

He put a hand on my shoulder and squeezed it, his lips dropping into a frown. "Unfortunately not. You've been a woman for some time now, I think. I just don't like admitting it."

I swallowed. "You'll let me fight, won't you Papa?"

Our eyes met again, and he seemed like an old, tired man. I wished we could go back to the days when we played games in Letum Wood until the sun faded and Grandmother called us back into the house, where warm lanterns illuminated the windows and the smell of fresh bread drifted on the breeze.

"You are in charge of your own life now, Bianca. I can't tell you what to do."

The idea of so much autonomy seemed foreign. Wouldn't Papa always be overprotective and certain of my impending demise? "Really?" I asked.

He smirked. "I don't like to admit it, but I can't protect you from everything forever, can I? Besides, if I tell you not to do something, you're just going to do it anyway."

"What if I mess it up?"

"You will."

I snorted. "Thanks."

He shook me lightly. "You're supposed to mess up, B. It's part of the process."

I smiled despite myself, but it soon faded. His face remained as calm as usual, despite my own building hysteria. The last time we'd been in the throne room together was when Mildred empowered him as High Priest. He studied me for several long moments, then leaned forward and wrapped me in his arms.

"I love you, B," he said against my shoulder. "You and your mother are all that ever mattered. If I don't make it, I need you to know that."

Tears filled my eyes. "I love you too, Papa."

A knock sounded at the door, reverberating through the room.

"May we come in, High Priest?" Marten called from the doorway. I pulled away from Papa's strong arms.

"Of course, Marten," Papa said. "Bianca and I were just . . . gathering our thoughts."

Marten and Stella entered the room, drawing our attention to the door. It closed behind them.

"Forgive our intrusion on your conversation," Marten said, stopping a few paces short of the elevated throne. "But Stella and I wanted to discuss a few things with you before the final battle."

The serious register of Marten's voice caught my attention. One hand, resting at his side, trembled. This was no idle conversation. Papa seemed to have noticed the same thing. He straightened, leaning forward.

"Go ahead."

"We have some . . . important information. About you."

"Me?" Papa said.

"Yes. You."

Something in the slow, even cadence of Marten's words made me uneasy. Marten paused, meeting Papa's narrowed eyes with new determination.

"We hope the truth will give you strength and me peace," he said, adding quietly, "In case I fall tonight."

I gripped the smooth, carved wood of the Dragon's Throne to

anchor me. A few sculpted teeth bit into my palm. Marten glanced at Stella, drawing strength from her nod of encouragement.

"Two years after Mildred defeated Evelyn and took over as High Priestess," Marten began, "she came to Stella and me with the greatest secret of her life. She was pregnant with my child."

My heart stopped in my chest. Mildred, pregnant? The most by-the-rules, severe witch I'd ever met in my life? No, it couldn't be. She'd sworn her life to the role of High Priestess. Tradition dictated she remain childless. My mind whirred through what I knew from reading *Mildred's Resistance*, but the shock muddied my mind.

Is it really that surprising? Marten and Mildred had loved each other so much, and it was only a tradition—not a law—that the High Priestess be unhindered by marriage or family. Papa slid to the edge of the throne, his hands pressing into its armrests. I held my breath.

"The Network was still unstable at the time, and witches remained distrustful of Network leaders," Marten continued. "Mildred had made great strides in cleaning up the mess of the Dark Days, but it would be many years before stability was really achieved. In order to spare the Network another shock, she kept her pregnancy an absolute secret."

"Of course, Mildred refused to take a potion to kill the pregnancy," Stella said. "We went to extensive lengths to hide it. In the final months, she stayed at a small house in Letum Wood under the ruse of needing a mental health break after the Dark Days. She delivered her baby there in secret."

Marten stared at the floor. My lungs felt tight. Something uncomfortable loomed in the air, something I couldn't avoid but didn't want to see.

"We couldn't keep our child, obviously," Marten said, picking the story back up. "I took the baby away after the birth. He was a beautiful, healthy child with dark brown hair. Mildred's brother Jorden and his wife Imogen tended him until I found a trustworthy family in the Northern Covens to take him. Mildred, by necessity, had to distance herself, or she would have risked the stability of the entire Network. She didn't know anything about the baby, not his gender nor the color of his hair or eyes. She lived without knowing she had a son. I, on the other hand, watched him grow from a distance. He was happy until—"

"The adopted family died from a plague," Papa whispered, his face pale.

"Yes," Marten whispered. "Jorden removed our child from the house before he could contract it, and the family died."

The devoted way Marten spoke the words *our child* sent a chill down my spine. Clearly, his loyalty was absolute despite the horrible circumstances. But Papa's knowledge frightened me more.

There was only one way . . .

"So the child went to an orphanage in Newberry," Papa said. His breathing sharpened, coming in fast, short bursts. Marten gazed at him with teary eyes.

"Yes," he whispered. "I did everything I could for our adventurous, rebellious son but could not intervene without drawing suspicion. He lived in an orphanage until he turned fifteen, when he lied about his age and joined the Guardians. To be honest, I was so excited to finally be his mentor that I didn't care he was too young to join."

The muscles in Papa's jaw pulled so tight I could see the tension in the thick, muscled cords of his neck. "The witch in the forest?" he asked. "Was that you?"

Marten chuckled under his breath. "Yes. I caught you pickpocketing when you were twelve and made you return the stolen items. I transformed my appearance so I wouldn't be recognized."

"We wanted to tell you, Derek," Stella said, her dress rustling as she stepped forward. "But we agreed to a vow with Mildred to never disclose what we knew. Mildred released us from the vow the night of her death. We both wanted her to know, and she agreed. Marten told her about Derek before the Anniversary Ball, which means she died knowing who you really are." Stella turned to face me. "And she died knowing she was giving her life for her granddaughter."

Their words clicked together in my mind like puzzle pieces. I thought back to the last conversation I'd had with Mildred and the sad expression on her face, so cryptic and fleeting. She'd known. Papa had rarely spoken of his life before he met Mama, except for a few references to his rebelliousness. He had mentioned that he'd lied and joined the Guardians at fifteen.

"Papa is your son," I said.

"And Mildred was his mother."

If an army of Clavas had spilled into the room, I couldn't have been more shocked. It felt as if I'd fallen a long distance and couldn't regain my breath.

"But . . . that means—"

"You are my granddaughter."

Hearing the words caused something to shift inside my chest. I paused, uncertain what to say.

"Mildred didn't know until just after Derek's empowerment ceremony," Stella said. "She didn't knowingly appoint her son as High Priest."

Papa still hadn't spoken. His eyes were distant and fixed, as if he were reviewing every memory. Did he remember leaving his childhood family? Did he remember Jorden?

"So what does this mean?" I asked, forcing back all my whirring thoughts and seeking the steady ground of reality. "Why . . . why are you telling us now?"

"Because he deserves the truth," Marten said. "And now, of all times in his life, he needs to have confidence in the powerful magic in his blood. Derek did not come to the Dragon's Throne by an idle chance." Marten stared hard at Papa. "He is the most powerful witch in Antebellum, just like his mother was."

A long moment passed in silence. Papa stood and cleared his throat. "Thank you for telling me," he said, firm and businesslike. "I . . . thank you."

A hint of disappointment lingered in Marten's eyes, but he nodded, his lips pressed into a line. The sound of the second bugle resonated, distant and weak. My stomach plummeted. The West Guards were here.

"If you'll forgive me," Papa said, stepping off the platform. The Dragon Throne looked oddly small without him filling it. He took three steps forward, stopped, and turned around. I held my breath.

"I have one request," Papa said.

Marten opened his hands. "Anything."

"Once this war is over, I want all of us to have a long conversation." Papa looked at me, then back at Marten. "A very long one."

The corners of Marten's lips turned up. Relief flooded his features. "Of course, Your Highness. I would like that very much."

Stella followed in Papa's wake, but I remained behind, my feet frozen in place. Marten stayed, as if by an unspoken understanding. Was I supposed to call him Grandfather now, or was he still Marten? Knowing we were related by blood made everything awkward. I tugged at the ends of my sleeves, unsure of what to do with my hands and even less sure of what to say.

"I've dropped a heavy burden on your shoulders tonight," Marten said, breaking the silence first. The compassion in his tone overcame my rising barriers, reminding me that whoever Marten was to me, he was a good witch.

"May I ask you something?" I asked.

"Of course."

My throat thickened. "What did she say? What did Mildred say when she found out I was her granddaughter?"

He smiled warmly, as if it were a special memory. "She just stared at me at first. She had gone quite pale when I told her about Derek. After a length of time, she cleared her throat and said, with a tear in her eye, *Yes. Yes, I believe that wild Bianca is my granddaughter. Spunky, foolish girl.*

I laughed. I couldn't help it. It bubbled out of me with pain and annoyance and the feeling that even though it was all so unfair, it was right.

"Even though Mildred didn't know your father, she loved her child with a strange and fierce love," Marten said in a reverential tone. "It plagued her every day. I caught her staring into nothing many times. I never had to ask her what she was thinking about. I always knew."

"It's not fair that we should never have known," I said. A surge of gratitude, even happiness, took me by surprise. Was there any other witch in Antebellum I would want as my grandfather? No. Just Marten.

"No, it's not fair. But many things in Mildred's life weren't fair;

this was just the greatest of them. As it is with all of us." He reached out and put a hand on my shoulder. "I don't expect you to adjust to this revelation right away. Nor your father. I have no expectations for an instant family or for you to even call me *Grandfather*. If you want, I can still be just Marten. I wanted you to know the truth so it didn't die with Stella and me if things go badly today."

His lack of demands softened the building knot of uncertainty in my chest. I relaxed. Marten's face, though exactly the same as it had been before, seemed new to me, like I could sort through his features and see pieces of myself in him.

"Thank you, Marten. I'm grateful to know the truth," I said with a smile, glancing at the doorway. "Perhaps we should go."

Marten smiled wryly. "Or should we say it like Mildred?" His tone sharpened. "Pull yourself together, Bianca Monroe. We have a war to win."

I tilted my head back and laughed, amazed at his uncanny impression of the late High Priestess. It felt good to experience an emotion other than fear, even if for just a moment.

Marten's expression dropped into a half-frown when he followed my gaze to the empty doorway. "I hope it wasn't too much of a shock for Derek. The last thing I wanted to do was distract him. He needed to know he comes from a line of stubborn, powerful witches. He possesses the ability to win this war and control the counter magic."

"Papa will be fine," I said, hoping to convince myself. "Nothing can distract him when he's pursuing a goal."

"I hope so," Marten said. "Because we'll never win without him."

We Are Mighty

Thirty minutes later, Merrick and I stood on top of the Wall, staring out at the remains of Chatham City.

The fading heat of the day radiated off his skin and onto mine. Night had started to fall, coating the hazy air in another layer of darkness. I gripped Viveet, comforted by her smoldering blue flame. Sweat streaked down my palm. Merrick had found an old set of half-armor in the Guardian storage room. After a few magical incantations to adjust it, it fit me like a glove. Despite the weight of the thin metal plates, I felt as if I wore nothing more than a jacket. The leather was soft and pliable but enchanted to withstand sharp objects.

"Damn Westies!" Tiberius roared from where he paced in front of the Gatehouse, barking commands at every turn. His small eyes darted around us, constantly assessing the situation. Blood oozed from a cut on his shoulder that had been hastily sewn together with uneven stitches of black twine. His beard had been burned off on just the right side, and he smelled like singed hair.

Crowds of Guardians and witches from the Antebellum Army fled Chatham City, rushing down Chatham Road toward the castle gates and signaling the final retreat. A knot formed in my throat as I watched them hurry, trying to outrun the long fingers of death not far behind. Some limped as they carried other injured Guardians, dragging them or using levitation to float them back. The rest transported in. A low buzz of voices hummed in the high and low baileys.

"So this is it," I said, staring at the smoke-clogged sky. Chatham

City burned—the black flames consuming the bakery, Miss Holly's Candy Shop, and the pub.

"Yes," Merrick said. "This is it."

Chatham Castle had her own protections—magical spells that prevented witches from climbing the Wall on the outside, false hallways leading to nowhere, and main doors impervious to magic. Contingents from the North worked with our Guardians to secure the inside of the castle, where Wolfgang and five of his Masters roamed the halls. But that didn't make Chatham Castle impenetrable, and as I watched the West Guards advance toward us with their black fire, I had a special appreciation for our mortality.

"You're not going to stop me from fighting?" I asked Merrick.

"What's the point? I'd rather have you fighting next to me than somewhere else. Besides, I've given up hope that you'll ever listen to anything other than your own sense of right and wrong."

A grin stole across my face. I'd been preparing myself for a long argument, so it was a relief to win so easily. "You've given up hope of controlling me? That's the most romantic thing you've ever said."

He wrapped his fingers around my wrist and yanked, slamming me into his chest. There was nothing tender or sweet about the way he crushed me in his tight grip, pressing his lips to mine. When he pulled away, his eyes were a stormy green.

"Shall we save Chatham Castle together?"

I kissed him once more, refusing to believe it might be the last time. "Let's do it."

The front doors to the castle slammed open, and Papa strode out, carrying himself with long, sure steps. Light from the floating torches along the walkway flashed on his half-armor. Dark crimson flames shot high and bright from his sword, so dazzling I couldn't look straight at it. He blithely leaped up the Gatehouse stairs two at a time. Despite the shocking news he'd just received, he didn't seem at all distracted.

Papa nodded once as he clapped Tiberius on the shoulder. "I believe it's time to win a war, old friend."

The Guardians and witches in the baileys behind us cheered. Tiberius's massive shoulders slumped, as if relieved that the weight of maintaining control had shifted to someone else.

"High Priest," he said, gesturing to the West Guards with a sweep of his arm. "Your party is ready to begin. We'll follow you wherever you take us." He put a fist over his heart in the Guardian sign of unity. "We await your orders."

Papa scanned the sky, the woods, and the last stragglers limping toward the castle. "Has Mabel shown up?"

Tiberius shook his head. "No sign of her."

"Very good," Papa murmured. "Let her hide until she's desperate. In the meantime, we'll take the fight to them."

Papa climbed to the top of the Wall and raised his sword. Great flames leaped skyward, drawing every eye. He used a spell to project his voice over the baileys, Chatham Road, and Letum Wood, where thousands of witches awaited his command.

"Witches of Antebellum," he called, his mighty voice rippling over the tightly packed bodies. "I am honored to lead you to victory tonight. Tonight we fight for our right to live free. Tonight we fight for our homes, our families, and our children. We fight against an evil power that has not been seen in thousands of years. But should we fear? Never! We shall never fear, for we are strong. We shall prevail!"

A rousing chorus rose from the castle and the forest surrounding it. Two dragons snorted fire. Michelle sat on the back of an umber dragon that hovered high above the fight, no doubt to protect her and her unborn child. Nicolas rode the red, who knocked the hats off two witches on the Wall when she soared over the baileys.

"I cannot promise you that you'll live," Papa continued, "just as I do not know that you will die. But do not shrink away. Fight as if we are going to win, and fight as if today shall be your last!"

A deafening cry of agreement, led mostly by Guardians, rose through the crowd. Movement just behind Papa caught my eye, nearly stopping my heart. A thunderous black cloud raced toward Chatham Castle with stunning speed. I grabbed Merrick's arm, the tips of my fingers digging into his skin.

"Are those Clavas?" I asked, tilting my head in their direction.

"The good gods," Merrick muttered. "There must be thousands of them."

"Papa!" I cried, pointing behind him. "The sky!"

A cloud of half-dead, half-living entities flew toward the castle, born from the depths of hell to fall on us in a gruesome massacre. Interspersed in the midst of the Clava ranks were bats, the Clavas not yet transformed into their ghoulish state. They emitted an unnaturally high-pitched shriek that made my ears ring. Only Mabel could conjure a cloud of such size and power. And only a force of such excessive proportions and nightmarish strength could siege Chatham Castle.

"There's no way we can fight off that many," Merrick said.

"We don't have a choice. I'm not going to let one of those sticky buggers be the last thing I see on Antebellum."

"I'd kiss you if we weren't under attack."

"Save it for later," I said. "I'm busy."

"Witches!" Papa shouted, his sword pointed at the sky. "Prepare for attack!"

Five dragons circling overhead released giant plumes of fire so hot they singed the hair on the backs of my hands. The green and blue dragons hovered protectively over the baileys, scattering debris and dust with every pump of their mighty wings. Their black scales gleamed despite the cloud of Clavas blocking the moonlight. Screams of fire and rage came from the purple and silver dragons as they circled through the turrets.

"Well," Merrick said, his head tilted back, "at least the dragons are ready to fight."

My heart didn't take much courage. Five dragons couldn't fend off so many Clavas. What about all the witches from the Antebellum Army in Letum Wood? I braced myself for the worst.

The Clavas approached Chatham Castle with unnatural speed, their twisted faces becoming visible all too quickly. After a moment, they were nearly upon us, their white fangs gleaming and their ethereal black cloaks only seconds away. The blue dragon grabbed the first Clava near the lower bailey and tore it in half. Black blood trickled from his snapping teeth when he screamed, sending fire at fifteen bats and turning them to cinders.

A familiar sliver of wind brushed my cheek, stirring up magic in my chest and drawing my eyes to Letum Wood. Vines shot out of the trees, yanking Clavas and bats into the dark canopy. The high branches swayed, twisting around the ghoulish bodies and breaking them in half.

"The forest," I said to Merrick. "It's fighting."

Three massive creatures shot out of the treetops, headed toward the Clava horde with breathtaking speed.

"Dragons!" a nearby Guardian cried. "Look at the dragons!"

Seven more dragons bolted from the depths of Letum Wood and took to the sky, tearing into the Clavas with ferocious teeth. Eight, nine, ten, and finally too many to count filled the night. By the time the Clavas and bats descended on the castle as one entity, countless dragons clogged the air, incinerating and swiping at the ghastly beasts.

"Jikes," Merrick said, dodging a wounded bat as it screeched by, one wing bitten off. "Where did these dragons come from?"

A bat flew at my braid, gripping it in its talons and wrenching my head forward. Merrick swung his sword high, cutting off half my hair and killing the creature with swift justice. The bat fell to the ground with a meaty plop. I stepped on its head for good measure, my hair swinging around my jaw.

"Thanks for the haircut," I muttered, blowing my new bangs out of my eyes. "Wasn't exactly the style I had in mind."

"Looks good on you," he said, winking.

"I didn't know there were this many dragons." I ducked another errant bat wing and jabbed upward with Viveet. A morphing half-bat, half-Clava screamed in pain and toppled to the lower bailey. Corpses dropped from the inky sky, casualties of the vengeance of the dragons and the forest. When one of the undead wraiths made it through, a Guardian felled it. The two baby red dragons stood on the section of the Wall above the high bailey, scorching any Clava that made it to the ground.

With the dragon attack well underway, the Clavas hesitated. Every attempt at challenging the castle was met with pearly dragon teeth and searing fire. The red had never been so surly or so pleased. She snapped, growled, and hissed, mauling each Clava with moans of pleasure.

"Think the dragons can hold them off?" I asked, kicking a fallen corpse off the Wall.

"Don't know," Merrick said, his eyes on Chatham Road. He

dodged another bat, grabbed its wing, and twisted it until it cracked. "Where's Mabel?"

"Waiting."

"For what?"

"For Papa to weaken. She'll arrive once victory is assured. She's lost too many times in recent history, and I doubt she wants to face Papa if there's a chance someone else can kill him first. She's a coward who can't afford to lose again. She'll fight him only after he's used up most of his energy against the Clavas and West Guards."

West Guards started spilling out of Chatham City, surrounding the castle by filtering into Letum Wood, which meant we couldn't determine how many we faced. The Clavas focused their attention on distracting the dragons from the West Guards rather than overpowering the castle.

Papa transported to a different segment of the Wall, fighting the heaviest concentrations of wraiths and bats. He moved from place to place, saving witches when he could and assisting weakened Guardians. Tiberius disappeared from where he'd been pacing back and forth on the Wall and reappeared near Papa, bombarded with a surge of undead wraiths. He roared, fighting with a smooth finesse that looked like a dance. Marten and Stella stood on the High Priestess's balcony, Marten fighting with a sword while Stella fended Clavas off with spells that sprayed water.

The dragons rose higher and higher, pushing the Clavas back. Just when I thought our luck had changed, a second wave of wraiths appeared over Chatham City, heading toward us. I tightened my hold on Viveet as cries of alarm rippled down the Wall and through the forest. Tiberius stopped fighting long enough to take in the oncoming cloud of death. He cupped his hands around his mouth.

"Prepare yourself," he shouted, using magic to project his voice over the war raging in the sky.

"The castle won't hold long if the Clavas breach it," Merrick said, lopping off the head of a bat. "Not even with Wolfgang and the Masters defending it from within. And we won't make it through a second wave with enough strength to fight both the Clavas and the West Guards."

"I know," I whispered.

The blue dragon let out a piercing scream of pain when at least fifteen Clavas swarmed his wings, biting and tearing at them. Unable to buck them off, he crashed into the Wall, sending a spray of rocks and rubble into the lower bailey.

"No!" I cried, rushing forward.

Clavas swarmed the dragon, blanketing him in a writhing mass of black. I gasped, frightened by the stunning *thud* as the blue dragon fell to the ground. Guardians rushed forward, yanking Clavas off the beautiful beast, but it was too late. He died within moments, his blood spilling onto the stones. My heart dropped.

"Let it go, B," Merrick said, jerking me away. "Don't think about it now. We have more friends coming in from the West."

I forced myself to face the oncoming foe, though my heart hurt.

"Ten seconds," Merrick said, his eyes on the approaching swarm. He grabbed the ankle of a descending wraith and killed it with a swift stab to the abdomen. I sliced a bat in half. Another bat soared by, slicing my cheek and neck with the edge of its wing. I put a hand to my stinging face. Only a small amount of blood dribbled onto my palm, not enough to be concerned about.

"We'll never make it, Merrick," I said. "The second wave is twice as big."

"Five seconds."

A burst of light streamed from the balcony of Stella's apartment and broke the hazy fog, cutting through the smoke. Once it pierced the haze, the light grew, spreading outward in little specks. The specks bubbled, forming lines and circles that elongated into witches made of light.

"Papa's using a counter spell!" I cried, grabbing Merrick's arm. "Look! He moved up to the balcony with Stella and Marten."

"Old Guards," Merrick said, ducking a falling bat. "See the red patch on their left shoulders? That's only given to Old Guards—witches who died serving as Guardians. They're buried with the patch as a symbol of honor."

The witches of light continued to grow and change, taking on the stern faces and familiar half-armor of Guardians. They sent the Clavas screeching and scattering into the sky. The dragons followed, shooting bursts of flame at the fleeing horde. Old Guards marched around Chatham Castle with impressive speed, standing sentry in front of the doors and windows. They moved inside with confident steps, burning vengeance in their eyes.

"It's the counter magic," Merrick said. "Mabel has an army conjured by magic, and now so do we."

"Yes," I said. "But such a massive force will have cost Papa a lot of power and energy. He can't maintain magic like this forever. Mabel's had time to build up her magic; Papa hasn't."

Through the brightness, I could just see the outline of Papa on the balcony, surrounded by light. Clavas flailed away from him, shrieking. Every wraith the Old Guards touched fell to the ground in smoke.

"Are they actual Old Guards, do you think?" I asked, watching in fascination. The suffocating globe of wings and wraiths began to disappear, opening the castle up to the sky again. "Were they actually Guardians once? They all look different."

"I think so," he said, his eyes tapered. "Some of them seem familiar. I think . . . I think they're Guardians who fought in the Southern Covens. I recognize a few of them."

"Archers!" Tiberius screamed. "Now!"

Arrows flew into the black Clava cloud and exploded, spraying water. The wraiths recoiled, shriveling and screaming. The Old Guards moved up and out, forming a bubble of light that encompassed Chatham Castle. The wave of Clavas soared away with livid hisses. The tide turned in our favor, the dragons gained ground again, and the Guardians cheered. We battled on until the dying Clavas retreated, leaving the air empty and thin in their wake.

"Don't celebrate too much yet," Merrick said, nodding to Chatham Road, which stretched from the portcullis out to Chatham City. West Guards marched onward, sparking black fire that raced toward the castle, causing our witches to flee. The flames consumed those who didn't run fast enough.

"Archers!" Tiberius called. "Let's give the West Guards a friendly Central Network welcome."

Guardians with dark crimson sashes tied around their right wrists stepped forward and formed a line along the outer sidewall. In one synchronized motion, they grabbed their arrows and nocked them.

"Release!"

Despite our distance from the invading army, the first wave of arrows hit their marks, but the West Guards and the Antebellum Army diffused into each other with increasing speed, making it difficult for the archers to distinguish their targets.

"Contingent twenty-three . . . advance!" Papa bellowed. He stood on the Wall again, near Tiberius. Zane transported next to them, his chest heaving and blood dripping from his nose. Three continents of Guardians transported onto Chatham Road. The black fire split into three directions, heading right and left for Letum Wood and continuing toward the castle.

"Merrick, I'm not waiting up here while West Guards burn my forest," I muttered, my blood boiling.

"Go. I'll follow your magic," he said, and I spat the transportation spell already on the tip of my tongue. Less than a blink later, I was on the ground, Merrick at my back, hiding behind a sprawling tree covered with moss. Thick, humid air greeted us where we stood, halfway down Chatham Road, just within the tree line. A few wide-eyed witches from the Antebellum Army crouched in the bushes around us. They held their weapons with trembling hands.

We fight with you, whispered the magic of the forest, and I glanced up to see the tree tops swaying back and forth, although there was no wind.

"Keep close to the trees," I said to Merrick and those nearby. "They'll help. The forest will protect you if you don't harm it."

Merrick looked skeptical but knew better than to question me. The members of the Antebellum Army straightened, gazed up at the treetops, and seemed to take courage.

"Hey, I was wondering if you wanted to spend a little time together tonight," Merrick said, forcing levity, his eyes on a group of West Guards heading our way. Four in all. Burly, which would slow them down, and tall, which would give them a higher center of gravity.

"Oh?" I asked. "What did you have in mind?"

"A little sparring. A little gore." He grabbed my arm and pressed our backs together, swinging his head from side to side as he assessed the oncoming threat. "Maybe dinner afterwards? I hear Fina has stale bread in the kitchens."

"Will there be brownies?"

He scoffed. "Of course there will be brownies. Well . . . eventually. There isn't much butter these days."

"Then I'm in."

Viveet burned bright blue when I lifted her higher. The four West Guards were twenty paces away.

Merrick spun around, grabbed my face, and pressed his lips to mine in a rough kiss. "Make me proud, troublemaker."

I grinned. "Always."

The West Guards, their broad shoulders clad in armor of leather and steel, arrived with shouts of violence, and Merrick and I fell into the melee as a single fighting unit.

The battle for Chatham Castle and Letum Wood passed like a dream. Each moment seemed to happen in snatches. Witches fell to their knees, gurgling with death. Vines wrapped around West Guards, plucking them from the ground. Tree branches fell without warning, eliminating whole groups of West Guards. Smoke clogged the air. Dragons roared. Blood dripped down my lips. I existed from one second to the next, focusing on my breath, the sturdy feel of Viveet in my palm, and Merrick's back against mine. He never faltered, and neither did I.

After what felt like an eternity of fighting, a West Guard sprinted toward me, sword held above his head. My legs stumbled clumsily in my attempt to escape, tripping over a dead vine. I hopped around, trying to gain my footing. There wasn't time to swing Viveet around and block his weapon. Just as I freed my left ankle and prepared to kick up with my right leg, a swish moved past my right ear. The ground moved far away from me. My fingers dug into the rich carpet of the Volare as it carried me above Letum Wood. Merrick whipped around, stabbing the West Guard in the throat.

"Oh!" I cried, holding onto the sides of the carpet. "Good work. But you must take me back! I can't leave Merrick."

The Volare hovered for just a second before obeying my command, as if it didn't want to release me back into the jaws of hell. When my feet touched the ground, it curled back up, sliding back into its case on my magical command.

Merrick grabbed my arm. "What happened?" he asked, motioning to my face. His hair fell in sweaty clumps, sticking to his neck and forehead. Soot, sweat, and blood streaked his face. He panted, just like me, unable to draw breath under the weight of the Almorran magic in the air. I reached up to touch the blood on my upper lip. My nose ached.

"I don't know," I said. "I don't remember being hit. How long have we been fighting?"

He whirled around, fending off an approaching West Guard. I cast a tripping curse to delay the enemy, but the Almorran magic absorbed it. The two of them sparred before the West Guard fell on Merrick's burning sword.

"I don't know," he said, bucking the dying Guardian off. "But I get the feeling we aren't winning."

My arms ached, and my lungs hurt. Viveet's flame wavered, quenched with blood. A West Guard had tripped me at some point, rolling my ankle. A scratch bled down my shoulder, staining my half-armor. I ignored it. I ignored everything but the next fight, the next West Guard, the next threat.

The wings of a dragon soared overhead, cloaking me in a moment of darkness. I glanced up to see the umber dragon. Michelle still rode on top. With most of the Clavas gone, she couldn't have found a safer place.

"I need to go check on my friends," I said to Merrick, glancing at the few remaining Clavas flying in and out of Chatham's windows. "I need to know they're all right."

"Now?"

"Yes," I said. "Now."

He studied me for half a second before nodding. "I'll follow."

We transported to the kitchens to find Camille. Chaos reigned supreme. Pots and pans were flung aside, cluttering the floor. Water coated every surface, caking loose flour into doughy clumps. Three Clavas soared down the stairs and darted toward us. Merrick and I moved into action, ducking their open mouths and slicing at them. A bat flew overhead, screeching with a high trill that raised every hair on my arm.

"Camille?" I yelled, ducking a falling Clava arm. "Camille?"

Merrick and I shuffled through the wreckage to the other side of the room. Two pairs of feet stuck out from behind a long table.

"Bianca," he called, his uncertain gaze meeting mine. "Come here."

He swallowed and closed his eyes. My heart leaped into my throat as I darted toward him. Camille lay on the floor next to Brecken. Her eyes, wide and glassy, stared at the ceiling. She didn't move. A trickle of blood ran out her left ear. Water coated her dress and arms in tiny droplets.

"Camille?" I whispered. I dropped to my knees at her side, shaking her. "Camille! Wake up. Wake up!"

Neither she nor Brecken moved. I stumbled back, my mind screaming. A bundle of rage, grief, and terror unwrapped itself in my chest, reaching around my heart with long, ugly tentacles. The shock paralyzed me. Camille was the best of us. The happiest. The most innocent.

"No," I said. "Not Camille. Not—"

A firm hand on my shoulder jostled me out of my trance. "Bianca!" Merrick said, shaking me. "Pull it together. This is not the time, all right? We can't save Camille, but we have to keep fightin'."

"No! I can't just leave her."

"Where will you take her?"

"I . . . I don't know! I have to do something. I . . ."

"She's with Brecken. She wouldn't want you to focus on her, would she? She'd want you to win the war."

"We're losing, Merrick," I cried. "It's not going to matter!"

"Don't say that," he said, wincing. He held his sword in his left hand instead of the right. "We have to keep fightin'."

Fight for what? I thought, gazing at the dead bodies littering the ground. *Fight now just to die in a few hours?*

"For what?" I snapped. "What's left? They're killing everyone."

"We just . . . we have to keep fightin'," he said, sounding wooden and uncertain. "That's what you're supposed to do in war. Just keep fightin'! Camille died fightin'! Are you goin' to give up? Do you think she'd want you to do that?"

I remembered Camille's words. *Brecken is here fighting, and he's my husband. I won't be parted from him. I will fight. We will win.*

"No," I said, my eyes stinging. "She wouldn't."

He squeezed my shoulder. "Don't think. You can't afford to think right now, B. You have to fight."

His sharp tone jolted me back to reality. He was right. This was war. I didn't have time to think. I only had time to act. I mentally shut the door to my throbbing heart, forcing my concentration away from my best friend.

"Then let's go," I said. "Transport back to where we left. We can keep helping the Antebellum Army."

I transported away, but instead of going directly to Letum Wood, I went to the middle of the ballroom. The makeshift hospital teemed with chaos. Old Guards stood at the windows to prevent Clavas from breaking in. They walked behind the Apothecaries and their Assistants, watching over the witches who kept their brothers-in-arms alive. Wounded Guardians trickled in from the battle in a near-constant stream. Apothecaries ran from patient to patient, frantic and harried, blood staining their clothes. Injured witches were draped over every surface, taking up every spot on the floor.

"Make way!" a thick voice shouted. "Make way!"

Wolfgang and two other North Guards bolted into the ballroom, a thin figure held in their arms. My heart nearly stopped when I saw a familiar, bloodied face.

Stella.

"She was fightin' in the West Win' with the children," Wolfgang said, panting as they set her on a cot. Apothecary Assistants swept dirty bandages aside to make room for her. "A few West Guards approached the windows with those smoke bombs. Her Highness stopped them, but I don't think she'll make it."

I turned away, unable to bear it. Not Stella. Not Camille. Not the blue. Not any of them.

Don't think. Don't think.

I grasped for something good, something to fight for when everything seemed to be crumbling. In the distance, Leda hurried from cot to cot among the dying, still in the dark about Camille. An Old Guard followed close behind her, a young man with a head of familiar white-blonde hair. My vision went blurry. Her brother protected her.

The sight sent a jolt through my body. I had to go back; I had to keep fighting. Grasping Viveet, I balled the seething wrath in my body into a tight bundle right at my heart, ready to unleash it on the West Guards and Clavas that had taken Stella, Camille, and the blue dragon.

As soon as I landed back in Letum Wood, Merrick grabbed my neck and pulled me to the ground. A potion bottle soared over our heads, right where I'd been standing, and exploded in putrid smoke on a nearby West Guard. He screamed as the liquid burned through his skin. I turned away, suppressing the need to retch.

We stood at the edge of Letum Wood, right next to the Wall. Snatches of the castle were visible through the trees. Falling bodies, screaming Clavas, black smoke, livid dragons. It all looked the same. The foul blood of the Clavas streaked the ground, making it difficult to walk without falling into the hot black acid. The war spun with wild abandon around us. I could hardly bear the stench of blood, death, and fear.

A group of West Guards shot ten arrows at a yellow dragon all at once. Two struck her heartscales, bringing her down. The red screamed fire when a horde of Clavas headed for her two children. Gypsies attempted—to no avail thanks to Almorran magic—to spout fire from their fingertips as West Guards stormed through the front doors. Even the smallest fireboys scampered over fallen bodies to recover unbroken arrows for the archers.

Where had Papa gone? Could he stop this death with the counter magic?

But this isn't just Almorran magic at work, I realized. *This is war. Bloody, filthy war.*

While Merrick and I had been helping the Antebellum Army, the Almorran fire had almost completely consumed the section of the

Wall beneath the Gatehouse. Burning stones teetered precariously on unstable ground, groaning as they started to sway. Once it gave in, West Guards would pour into Chatham Castle, unconstrained by the portcullis or stories-high Wall.

"Merrick! The Wall!" I cried, ducking. The Gatehouse crumbled in a deafening roar, sending a flood of dust and rubble into the forest. Once it settled, Merrick grabbed me by the arm and jerked me to my feet. Dust covered his face and chest.

"Your father!" he said, pointing to a segment of the Wall that still stood.

I whirled around to see Papa's face strained and taut as he fought with two West Guards. Sweat dripped down his neck. He clenched his teeth and squinted, struggling to maintain the counter magic while physically fighting. Tiberius kept himself between Papa and a third West Guard as large as he was. On Papa's other side, Zane battled three West Guards. The West Guards in the forest clambered over the stones that had once been the Gatehouse, flooding Chatham Castle. They'd only need a half hour to overtake the castle and destroy the Central Network at this rate.

The heavyset West Guard fighting Tiberius grabbed him by the throat, forcing him to his knees. Tiberius's arms swung for purchase, but the West Guard used magic to conjure a black cord that snaked around Tiberius's thick body, pinning his arms to his side.

"Tiberius!" I screamed.

The West Guard slammed his shoe onto Tiberius's face and pushed. Tiberius disappeared over the side of the Wall. He fell into the undergrowth just as his opponent advanced on Papa, who didn't see him. I dropped to one knee, held Viveet in the air above my head, and transported. I appeared in front of Papa just as the massive West Guard swung his sword. Instead of killing Papa, the sword connected with Viveet. I sent a rush of power through her metal body, and a burst of hot flame rolled through the air. Both weapons shattered in an overpowering rush of magic, sending the West Guard and me flying in opposite directions. A painful shock reverberated through my arms, into my shoulders, and down my body.

I will win.

I hovered in a moment of darkness, disoriented. The chant of Mabel's mind beckoned to me. In my weakened state, I couldn't fight her. The staunch voice wavered just slightly, pulling me into her silken darkness.

I . . . will win.

Papa, I thought, trying to force myself back into my own mind. *I cannot leave Papa.*

Using all my strength, I jolted out of the current dragging me into Mabel's madness and jerked back into the battle. Merrick appeared, put his foot on the West Guard's neck, and stabbed him through the heart.

"Viveet!" I cried, scrambling through the bits of metal to grab her intricate hilt.

I had no time to mourn the loss of my loyal weapon. The darkness of Mabel's mind overpowered me until I felt lightheaded. The air grew heavy, so thick I could barely breathe. Her voice rang through my mind with stunning authority.

I will win.

I looked up at the sky.

Mabel was here.

I Will Win

Mabel descended from the clouds on the bent backs of three Clavas.

A silky black dress enshrouded her, undulating in midnight waves. The battles below ceased one by one, leaving an eerie quiet on the baileys as every eye turned to Mabel. The Clavas hissed but retreated to the skies, forming a cloud behind her. Papa stepped forward, toward the burnt hole that had once been the Gatehouse, his chest heaving and his body smeared with blood. The Clavas carrying Mabel stopped, hovering just above the Wall, a few paces away from Papa.

"Merry meet, Derek Black," Mabel said with her usual coy smile, her eyes flaming bright red. "I've come to accept the terms of your surrender."

"Antebellum will never surrender to you," he said. "Will you run away to let other witches fight your battles like usual?"

She tipped her head back and laughed, her blonde curls cascading down her back in a golden dance. All at once, her mirth faded. She dropped all fake pretenses of amusement.

"You want to fight me?"

"Yes," he said, gripping his sword with a smile. "I do."

I started forward, a cry of protest lodged in my throat. Merrick grabbed my arm and hauled me back.

"No, Bianca," he whispered. "This is your father's fight. He has the counter magic, not you."

"I won't take the chance. I won't lose him!"

"You have to," he said in my ear. "What are you going to do? You can't save the Central Network. You'll be nothing but a distraction. Derek can do this."

I didn't know how to answer. Mabel regarded Papa through cruel, haughty eyes. Her hellish Clava minions writhed beneath her in pools of black. They seemed to absorb the light, bringing a nightmarish sense of darkness to the castle.

"Are you ready to give your life for this Network, Derek?" she asked.

"I already have."

The Clavas beneath her dispersed with wild howls, leaving Mabel on the top of the Wall. Merrick tightened his hold on my shoulder.

"Merrick," I whispered, digging my fingers into his arm. "I can't lose Papa."

"Just believe in him, B. Give him a chance."

"I can't lose him."

"You won't."

"Oh, Derek," Mabel crooned. "I've destroyed the Central Network despite your best efforts. You'll never be more powerful than I. Submit yourself to my will and fall to your knees."

She sent a percussive wave of black shadows at Papa. They rippled through the air, knocking down everything in their path. The shadows slammed into Merrick and me, sending us flying into the Wall. A crack of pain ricocheted through my spine when I collided with the stones and collapsed to the ground. When I scrambled back to my feet, Papa remained untouched. A familiar witch stood in front of him. My breath caught in my throat when I saw her short, stocky frame.

"Mildred," I whispered.

The late High Priestess had a wispy, thin quality, like millions of pinpricks of light made up her form. Somehow Papa—or the counter magic—had conjured her to protect him. She stared at Mabel while the Clavas wheeled away, writhing and shrieking in the intense glow of her light.

"Do you doubt me now, Mabel?" Papa asked, his voice booming. "Do you have the strength to fight against the one who holds the counter magic?"

Mabel's jaw tightened when Papa reached inside his armor and extracted a set of small scrolls. Their brilliance dazzled me. I shielded my eyes with a hand, blinded by the light shooting from the scrolls. They floated high in the air. The strength of the Almorran magic faded away, allowing me to suck in the first deep breath I'd taken in some time. My vision sharpened. Everything appeared to be more vibrant and have more precise detail, right down to the shades of gray in the stones beneath my hand.

Ten Clavas zipped in front of Mabel, obscuring her face, their mouths gaping in high-pitched screams of pain. Their bodies shriveled into dust. More Clavas flew up to replace them.

"You'll never win!" Mabel screamed from behind the protective wall of the undead. "Never!"

A horde of Clavas gathered in the low bailey and flew at Papa. Mildred dissipated in a glittering cloud and reformed into a dragon that spewed white-hot fire. The Clavas were incinerated in seconds, vanishing in black smoke.

"Merrick!" I cried, grabbing his arm. "That dragon! That's the blue!"

The dragon of light hovered in front of Papa. His distinctive face and fierce expression gave me a moment of strength. Mabel barked commands in the Almorran language from behind the Clavas, and a third collection of screeching wraiths headed toward Papa. The blue dragon breathed a plume of glimmering light and flew in a circle, spewing lines of light around Papa that repelled Mabel's curses until they sparked and fizzled into nothing.

Her scream tore through the air. "I don't care how!" she cried. "Just kill Derek Black!"

The West Guards hesitated, their eyes averted from Papa's glowing form.

"Cowards!" Mabel yelled. The Clavas and West Guards nearest her began to seize in pain and fell to their knees. "Must I do everything myself?"

A black arrow appeared in her hand. She threw it, striking the glowing dragon right in the heart. The magic scattered in a million prisms of light, falling on the baileys below, leaving Papa open and unprotected. A great pressure seemed to fall on his shoulders, as if she was trying to force him to his knees.

"Bow to me, Derek Black!" Mabel said. "Give me your allegiance and your power!"

Papa's legs trembled as he resisted. His nostrils flared. The light glowing from within him wavered for just a moment as magic battled magic. His left knee buckled, but he caught himself before it dropped. Mabel's face flickered in the darkness, lit by the flames of the scrolls hovering above.

"No!" I cried.

A line of light burst out from Papa's chest and spread outward, striking Mabel in the heart. She flew back, toppling head over heels before righting herself by hovering in the air. Papa sprinted forward, swinging his sword, but Mabel transported away, leaving him to slice through vapors. In the distance, the Clavas howled. Mabel appeared behind Papa, a second black arrow in her raised arms.

"Papa!" I yelled. "Behind you!"

Thousands of specks of light appeared between Papa and Mabel, sending Mabel flying back again. A form took shape in the light. A familiar willowy witch with restless black hair stood in front of Papa, her wide eyes intent on Mabel. Though she was made up of fractals of light, her eyes were still a warm, cloudy gray. Mabel paused, her eyes narrowed in surprise.

"Mama," I whispered, my throat tight. "That's . . . Mama."

Mabel's fingers fluttered as another black arrow formed in her hand. "No," I whispered, stepping forward. Mabel was going to destroy Mama, just like Mildred and the blue dragon. They hadn't come back. Mabel threw the arrow.

"No!" I shouted, but it was too late. The black arrow struck Mama in the heart. The glowing dots dissipated. I fell to my knees when another siren call from Mabel's mind threatened to pull me in.

I must win.

The certainty in Mabel's chanting had faded. She was tiring. *No,* I thought, pulling myself away with all my strength. *I won't be part of your madness anymore.*

Papa attempted to conjure another protection spell, but the

glowing dots fizzled into nothing. He pitched forward, barely catching himself. His shoulders bowed under great pressure again. He was losing. Mabel's eyes glowed with maniacal fury.

I will . . . I will prove my worth.

Despite the weight pressing on him, Papa pushed himself off the ground, his legs trembling as he struggled to stand.

"He won't make it," I whispered, pushing away the darkness that tried to suck me in again. Merrick made no response. Mabel's voice cut through my mind with increasing tenacity, as if she meant to take over my mind by pulling me into hers.

The Central Network is mine!

Papa let out a shout. Sweat rained down his face.

Not if I can help it, I thought. "Merrick," I said, putting a hand on his arm. "I'm going to distract Mabel."

His eyes snapped onto mine. "Bianca—"

"Papa won't make it if I don't," I said, pressing a hand to my pounding head.

"What if you die with Mabel?" Merrick asked.

If I die, I die. But Merrick wouldn't stand for that answer. "I won't."

"You don't know that."

Papa continued to struggle, his legs growing weak. Mabel tilted her head back and laughed. It didn't matter if I survived my last foray into Mabel's mind. Without Papa, the Central Network would fall.

"This will give him a chance. Trust me, Merrick. You have to go to him. Tell Papa to kill her. He'll feel her powers lessening as she turns some of her attention to me. She's tiring. It may not seem like it, but she is. As soon as he feels a lessening, he needs to act."

I touched Merrick's face with the tips of my fingers and gave into the overpowering pull of Mabel's mind before he could protest.

Entering Mabel's consciousness felt like dipping into a warm pond. The battle of her own mind pulled back and forth in a tug of war between an irate Mabel and a weary one.

So tired.

I will win! I'm so close. I will prove I'm better than all of them. Then I shall sleep. I shall find the peace I've sought for . . . so long. I'm better than May.

So tired.

Though I thought of Merrick and Camille to keep my own mind fresh, I sank into the pain of Mabel's existence. Maintaining ties to my own personality wasn't as difficult this time. The delineation between us had grown. Either that or Isadora was right, and I had strengths greater than Mabel's.

What comes next, Mabel? I asked, interrupting her internal dialogue. *What will you do when you win?*

The voices stopped, pausing in a long moment of silence.

Why are you here? she hissed. *Do you want to share in my greatness?*

No, I said. *Your time for greatness has passed.*

Then let us sleep, said the weary voice.

No! I shall never rest! I shall conquer the Central Network.

Mabel's frenetic energy drowned out everything else. The voices spoke over each other with surprising intensity. I could barely decipher the words.

You were so lonely, I said. *Just a child who wanted love.*

Yes, weary Mabel said, surprised. *I was lonely.*

But I'm not lonely as the Almorran Master, you fools!

You didn't understand why May didn't love you, did you? I asked, ignoring the irate Mabel and prodding the quiet, vulnerable voice that spoke so softly.

No, she whispered. *I didn't understand.*

Sharing her mind, feeling her vulnerable confusion for a third time made me realize that I'd been trying to categorize Mabel wrongly all along—she was neither merely a bitter witch nor a lost child. She was both. While she'd chosen to kill those I loved, she hadn't chosen a horrible childhood. One side of her personality, I realized, could not negate the other.

I didn't do anything wrong, she whispered.

She was terrible to me, came the soft, childlike voice. *Mother left me. She left me for her other family. And it must have been my fault.*

No, I said. *It wasn't your fault.*

Then why did she leave me?

I will show all of them! said the frantic Mabel. Her words had slowed and lost some of their hysterical edge. *I will . . . I will prove that I'm better than my mother. I . . . deserve May's love! I've worked hard for her approval.*

Leave!

I battled a second wave of pain by picturing Leda and Camille. Mama's gray eyes. Memories spun through Mabel's mind at such a rapid speed I only caught glimpses of them. Crying in the dark. Burning arms. Scars. Mocking laughter. A growling stomach. I thought of Papa, of Merrick, of Letum Wood, of anything to keep me from getting lost in the frightening pull of her agony. She was losing control over her own mind. Her obsession with the magic turned to fear.

Leave my mind! Mabel screamed. *Leave me, Bianca. Leave now! The magic will not tolerate you here!*

Why did she leave me? Mabel's young voice cried, wavering into a final, keening sob. *Why did she leave me?*

The world went dark.

I woke with a gasp.

"B?" Merrick asked, crouching over me. "Are you all right?"

Mabel lay prostrate on the ground a few paces away, her arms flung wide, Papa's sword embedded in her side. I leaped to my feet and scrambled over the rubble separating the two of us, lightheaded but coherent.

Blood trickled from both of Mabel's nostrils and pooled on her upper lip. A cough rattled deep in her chest. Her dying eyes flickered to me. The color had seeped out of her skin, leaving her face translucent. Veins tracked across her cheeks like the lacy fingers of a spiderweb.

"What are you . . . doing?" she hissed with a gasp.

Blood stained her once-perfect teeth, which had begun to decay. Her skin puckered and wrinkled as she stopped maintaining the magic that made her beautiful, revealing the old woman I'd seen in the dungeons of Chatham Castle. She lay like a pathetic raisin, shriveled and alone, surrounded by ash and blood. I fell to my knees at her side.

"No one should die alone," I whispered, placing a shaking hand on top of hers. "Not even you."

Tears filled her wide, bloodshot eyes. She coughed, and flecks of blood appeared on her lips. Her nostrils flared. She gurgled with every breath.

"Oh, Bianca darling," she whispered, her pale lips barely moving. "You know as well . . . as anyone. There will be no peace . . . for my soul."

Tears clouded my vision. She struggled to take in another breath as she stared at the smoky sky. Not even my hatred could overcome my compassion for such a tortured soul.

"I feel nothing," she whispered. "It's much . . . easier that way."

Her chest stopped moving. Her eyes, still the same brilliant blue as the summer sky, stared out at nothing.

A crippling, consuming pity swept over me. Mabel had never really lived or loved, and now she never would. She'd been vile and full of vitriol, but she had once been a little girl who only wanted acceptance. My hand still trembled when I reached out and closed her eyes.

"Merry part, Mabel," I said, a tear flowing down my face. "May you fare better on the other side."

A hand rested on my shoulder. Papa stood behind me, his body shaking. He looked like he was two shades away from death. I glanced around. The Clavas were gone. The oppressive air had lifted, and I felt light. In the distance, I could hear shouting and celebration.

"It's over," Papa whispered in a husky voice, squeezing my shoulder. He fell to his knees next to me. I felt a vast emptiness, a fatigue I couldn't put into words.

"Yes," I said, grabbing his bloody hand. "Yes, it is."

Moving Forward

S unlight streamed down from a pristine blue sky when Papa walked up to me, a book in his hand. The scent of fall hung in the air, making my mouth water for pumpkin pie. Even though the war was over, we were still recovering, and novelties like pie were a long way away. I straightened, setting aside the book I'd been reading. Reeves puttered in the background, muttering under his breath and casting furious glares at the wall above the fireplace.

"Doesn't belong," he mumbled. "Not even spelled right."

I looked slyly up at the embroidered sign I'd hung the night before. The Wits stared down at me, a comforting, fitting reminder of days past. Camille's memento hung on my chest, next to Mama's.

"The Guardians found this not long after Mabel's death," Papa said, setting a book on the table. Mabel's *Book of Contracts*. Or, as we'd discovered, the Almorran *Book of Spells*.

"It makes sense, doesn't it?" Papa asked, lowering himself onto a chair next to mine with a grimace. He moved a little slower these days. "Mabel carried it with her everywhere, protecting it."

"Yes," I said, running my fingertip along the worn leather binding. "I suppose it explains why she was always so careful with it . . . but it says it's the *Book of Contracts*. She even wrote contracts and bindings in it. How do you think she altered such a powerful book of magic?"

"She could have used a special incantation to manipulate it so it wouldn't be recognized. No doubt it allowed itself to be protected."

"But Angelina was the Master until recently, not Mabel. Why wouldn't Angelina have had the book?"

Papa thought for a moment. "The Master wouldn't need the book, would she? Mabel had likely been studying from it, learning the magic. Angelina wanted her to follow in her footsteps and rule at her side."

"If forty years ago, during the Resistance, May had somehow become High Priestess the way she wanted, she would have had the counter magic and the Almorran magic," I mused out loud. "She could have truly ruled the world."

Papa was quiet, then grunted. "Huh," he said. "I hadn't thought of that."

"Do you think they knew?" I asked. "Do you think May, Mabel, and Angelina knew that the counter magic was in the Esmelda Scrolls?"

Papa nodded. "I think that's why they feared Mildred so much and then why they feared me. But I don't think Mildred knew we had the counter magic, or she would have found some way to tell me before giving her life."

Mabel had had many reasons to fear Papa—his natural talent at reading witches, his decades of experience working as a Protector, and an uncanny, powerful ability with magic. But his instinct to protect, to hold sacred important things, was what I imagined had scared Mabel the most.

"I don't think that's the only reason they feared you," I said, but he didn't ask me to expound. The sound of angry shouting came from the hall. Reeves paused mid-stride to listen. Papa and I stared at the door.

"The fairies must go!" Mrs. L cried, her voice shrill. Her shoes tapped in a furious staccato as she strode down the hall past the apartment. "Whoever gave them permission to live in the high turret is going to hear from me! They're tearing apart the castle, the little hellions. Four tapestries . . . gone!"

I bit my bottom lip and choked back a laugh. Papa raised an inquisitive eyebrow.

"B?" he drawled. "Do you know something about that?"

"No," I said, laughing. "Not at all."

"Right," he said, leaning back in his chair. "You know, Letum Wood isn't what it used to be." The lingering timbre in his tone told me he had an agenda.

"I know. The West Guards burned a lot of it."

I'd spent the last two days on the Volare riding over the entirety of the forest, mapping out the destruction, and listening as Letum Wood drew me to the worst places. Merrick and I had started coordinating efforts to clean it up, but it would take time to coax the natural flora and fauna back to vitality.

"It's going to need a little help," he said. "In fact, I'm thinking of appointing a caretaker over Letum Wood to clean things up and help it get back on its feet. Although the forest clearly has magic of its own, I think we can assist it back to life."

Desire grabbed at my heart. Caretaker of Letum Wood? What a wonderful job!

"Oh really?" I said, lifting one eyebrow.

"Someone trustworthy, who isn't afraid of the forest—which is hard enough to find—who can take care of themselves in a sticky situation but who has that special touch with nature. Sound like anyone you know?"

"Out with it, Papa."

He grinned, his chocolate eyes lighting up in a way I hadn't seen since before Mama died. "You want the job?"

My heart beat double time. Take care of Letum Wood? Work in the forest? Run barefoot in the trees?

"Are you serious?"

"Dead serious."

"What about . . . I mean . . . that will only last for so long. Give it a little while, and Letum Wood will be fine on its own."

A conspiratorial gleam lit up his eyes. "It will give you the time you need."

"For what?"

"To train."

I paused, waiting for him to finish, but he didn't. "Train for what?"

"Wolfgang, Farah, and I have had a few interesting conversations lately. Wolfgang has a group of twenty witches called the Masters with the same mission as our Protectors, only . . . they allow women."

Merrick had told me about the Masters when I visited the North. I straightened. "You have my attention."

"I've been thinking about starting a Sisterhood. You've proven you're capable of intense magic, and you seem to be drawn to danger. It's unconventional, but all of Antebellum is starting over these days. Women, I've realized, are their own force worth reckoning with. A Master named Regina has expressed an interest in training you, but you aren't ready for her yet. So while you're learning what you need to know, you can take care of Letum Wood."

"You'd let me?"

Papa's face scrunched a little. "I'd say that the risks are decreased now that we have the *Book of Spells*. There will always be danger, of course, and the Networks still have issues to work out, but I think women can be handy in tight places where men can't be."

"I'm in, Papa," I said. "I'm all in. It's everything I ever wanted."

An affectionate smile broke out across his face. "I know, B. And I'm proud of you. I know your mother is too. You've become a fine young woman, despite kidnappings and war." His gaze softened. "And loss."

I felt a pang of sadness as I thought of Camille. We'd lost others too, I'd later found out. Jackie, Ijet, Stella. Not to mention my loyal friend, Viveet, broken beyond repair. Merrick and I had gathered all Viveet's remnants and planned to go to the Southern Network to seek Andrei, the witch who had forged her.

I wrapped my arms around Papa. "What are you going to do with it?" I asked, motioning back to the *Book of Spells*.

He stood and braced one hand on either side of the old tome. "Destroy it," he said.

"How?"

He gave me a sly smile. "With magic. At the meeting of the Networks tomorrow. An appropriate new beginning, don't you think?"

I grinned. "Definitely."

"Now go get dressed," he said, whacking me in the thigh with the old book. "Your grandfather is coming for dinner in ten minutes."

The baileys teemed with witches the next day.

Weeks had passed since the final battle, but the slightest hint of smoke still lingered in the air when the wind rustled by. The distant sound of hammers rang from the new Chatham City. The gypsies had been given the privilege of picking their own section of town to start building in, and they hadn't wasted any time. Lingering members of the Antebellum Army who didn't want to return to their own Networks had started to help with the construction. Chatham City, it seemed, was already on the rise.

Papa had released the dragons from their responsibility to protect Chatham Castle from Almorran magic. A few of them still circled in the night sky, directly over Sanna and Isadora's graves, but for the most part they'd retreated. The empty sky felt lonely and wide without their flaming breath and shiny scales.

A delegation of witches representing the Southern Network filled the southeast corner of the bailey with stoic silence, their silk shirts flapping in the breeze. Wolfgang and Farah represented the Northern Network in the northeast corner of the bailey. The tattered Western Network, which only existed now in small settlements spread out over the desert sands, had no official representative. Their fate would be decided soon enough.

Leda hovered in the shadow of her new employer, High Priestess Scarlett, whose intense eyes darted around the crowd in shrewd assessment. While Scarlett didn't have the extensive knowledge and experience of a Council Member, Papa had bucked the old traditions yet again and appointed her as High Priestess. Her steady spirit and impeccable organization would help him pull the Network back together. I couldn't have agreed with his decision more.

Niko stood on the Wall with the rest of the Network leaders. Priscilla lingered not far away, her beautiful red hair chopped close to her head after an encounter with Clavas. Still, she looked beautiful.

But where had Michelle gone?

"Well?" Merrick asked, his voice low. "Do you think that's Council Member Quinn's real hair or not? If you're wrong, you owe me an entire pie."

I rolled my eyes. "There's still no sugar."

"I never forget a debt." He nudged me in the arm. "I hear you may have found a new job, by the way."

"Did Papa tell you?" I asked, grabbing his arm. "Isn't it wonderful?"

"No. Your grandfather. And Wolfgang. Regina is quite excited to work with you. She says you have spunk. I told her you have attitude. They're different things."

He dodged a playful jab to the arm.

"And what about you?" I asked with a slight tremor of fear in my stomach. Training with Regina would take me to the North more often, but I'd still live in the Central Network. I didn't want to go either place without Merrick. "What are your plans? Papa said you can leave the Brotherhood in full fellowship and return to the North if you want."

His lips puckered on just one side. "I thought about it."

"And?"

He grabbed my upper arms and pulled me close. His warm breath rolled across my cheek, smelling cool, like mint.

"And I think I have sufficient reason to stay."

A slow smile spread across my lips. "What reason is that?"

He pulled me closer, as if there had been any space between us. The press of his body against mine had never felt so much like a hug in my life. I nearly melted but forced my knees to keep me upright.

"Oh, a few things," he said, his lips so close I could feel them graze mine. I closed my eyes. "Or maybe I just really like you, Bianca Monroe."

The heat of his kiss traveled from my lips to my toes in a hot streak. I wrapped my arms around his shoulders until the rolling sound of a bugle trumpeted across the bailey, calling us to attention.

Papa stood on the Wall near the Gatehouse, his hands spread. "Friends," he said in the common language, using an incantation to project his voice. "Let us begin."

The low buzz of conversation faded.

"In the wake of such disastrous times, some witches have called for a total reformation of Antebellum's political structure." His eyes flickered to the Southern Network witches and their stern expressions. "To destroy the Networks and start over. The gathered delegation of the appointed leaders of the Networks voted on it this morning."

Murmurs spread through the crowd again, but Papa ignored them.

"The Networks are our history and our heritage. They've survived millennia, and though they're not perfect, they've given us safety and security. Witches made the system imperfect, so the repair falls to us. We have decided to maintain the Network structure."

Scarlett leaned over to whisper something to Leda. Leda handed her a rolled-up scroll, and a look of surprise flittered across the new High Priestess's face. I smiled. A more perfect Assistant to the High Priestess would never be found. Leda caught my eye and winked. Although her loss had also been great—like Antebellum's—she'd resolved to start over, to honor Camille and her brother.

"As a symbol of our newfound unity," Papa continued. "Let us destroy the Book of Spells and banish all traces of Almorran magic together."

Marten appeared at Papa's side, holding the *Book of Spells*. The Esmelda Scrolls appeared in Papa's hands. Were we really going to destroy the magic that had been pressing into our lives from the past? The idea was breathtaking. There had been so much destruction and loss that it had never felt like we won anything.

For the first time, the battle against Mabel felt like a victory.

The Esmelda Scrolls unfurled before Papa in a beaming explosion of light. The *Book of Spells* rose in the air and lingered above the scroll for only a moment before bursting into white flames. The pages curled and fell apart. Within minutes, the once-powerful book was nothing more than a trail of ash disappearing into the wind. Once the *Book of Spells* disintegrated, the light from the two Esmelda Scrolls faded. They fell, drifting to the Wall, looking no different for having destroyed one of the most dangerous magics to come to our Network.

"It's done," Merrick said, pulling me into his arms with a laugh. "We really won this time."

The little cottage in the woods waited in a pool of sunlight. I crossed over the bridge spanning the babbling brook. Michelle was standing back, staring at Sanna's old house, when I walked up to her side.

"I thought I'd find you here," I said. "We missed you at the big meeting just now."

Michelle let out a long breath.

"We're just saying goodbye to the old house," she said with a note of finality in her voice. "It seems weird that Sanna isn't here."

"You're leaving?" I asked.

She hesitated before nodding. "We're going deeper into Letum Wood. Nicolas wants to find the place where Sanna and all the other Dragonmasters used to live. There's a written record of the destruction of the Dragonmasters in the sisterwitches' old childhood home, hidden deep in Letum Wood. Isadora returned and left it there ten years after they had to desert their homeland during the formation of the Mansfeld Pact."

"Why didn't they just bring it?" I asked.

"Isadora had foreseen that they'd send someone to find it after she and Sanna were gone. They didn't think it was safe to bring it at the time. Angst against the Watchers and Dragonmasters was still high. Anyway, Nicolas wants to spend more one-on-one time with the dragons. Most of them were raised by Sanna. But as you saw, there are many more scattered throughout Letum Wood that she kept track of. We're going to find them and get to know them. See where else they live and how many there are. Besides," she said, biting her bottom lip. "It'll . . . I need . . ."

She didn't have to say it. I knew she was thinking of Camille and all the memories of her left behind at the castle.

"I know," I said. "I understand. And what about your baby?"

She put a hand on her growing belly, appearing relieved at the change of subject. "Nicolas thinks we'll find their old home before we have the baby. If we don't, we'll transport back."

Nicolas emerged from the forest, the red dragon close behind.

"You'll come back though, won't you? To Chatham, I mean. You aren't going to wander in the forest forever?" I asked.

Michelle smiled. "Of course not. We'll come back to live in Sanna's cottage."

Nicolas walked up to his wife's side, but the red lingered back near the trees, her slitted yellow eyes focused on me with intense suspicion. I sighed. Even after we'd fought a war together, some things never changed. Nicolas put a large but gentle hand on Michelle's elbow.

"It's time to go," he said. I threw my arms around Michelle and the brand new life growing inside her, so grateful that they'd come through unscathed.

"Be safe," I said when I pulled away. "Good luck with the baby. You'll be a wonderful mother."

She beamed. "I don't remember much of my own mother, but I took care of my brothers for so long that I can't wait to have my own family. Isn't it interesting how it's all worked out? Despite all we've lost and all the pain, somehow life really does just keep going?"

"Yes," I said with a contented smile. "It really does."

Michelle and Nicolas entwined their fingers and headed toward the red dragon together. They climbed on her back, sending one last wave my way before the red's massive wings unfolded, and they took to the sky. The two red babies followed close behind their Mama. I watched them go until they faded into the distance on the wings of a brand new adventure.

Home

L etum Wood seemed to stare back at me when I stood at the be-ginning of the trail, studying all the new growth.

Months had passed since the battle for Chatham Castle. The forest had been polluted with bodies, weapons, blood, and even dead Clavas. It had taken months to clear the debris. The magic of Letum Wood had whispered directions to me, telling me where to go next and how to salvage what could be saved. The foliage wasn't the same anymore. Undergrowth was trampled. Trails lost. Saplings hewn down. Soot stained the bottoms of the giant trees. But the high canopy didn't fail. Despite the destructive power of Almorran fire, Letum Wood continued on.

Just like the rest of us.

I stepped on the trail, soothed by the dirt between my toes. A slight chill in the air heralded the beginning of winter. I closed my eyes and pulled in a long, sweet breath of the tangy air.

There was still enough warmth left in the day for one more run.

Come, the magic whispered, stirring up my heart. *For you belong to us.*

I sprinted through Letum Wood, my legs flying with reckless, glorious speed. Leaves whipped past me. Sunlight spilled through the natural awning in patches, illuminating a few spots of ground. The comforting smell of wood and earth filled my nostrils.

Home, I thought with a smile. *I've finally come home.*

THE END.

Made in the USA
Charleston, SC
22 December 2016